Lingering Spi:

A Paranormal An

From WordC

Introduction and Epilogue by Kaye Lynne Booth

Compiled and edited by Kaye Lynne Booth

Cover by *WordCrafter Press*

This anthology bundle contains both American and British spellings.

Whispers of the Past

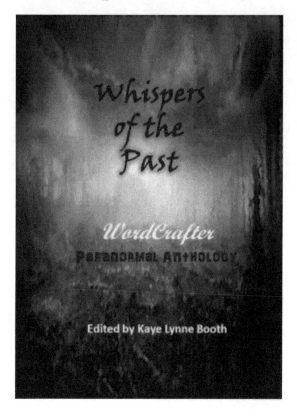

Introduction

What is it about the paranormal, the ethereal realm that draws us humans to it? I think it is because most of relate with it and are fascinated by what they can't explain. Who hasn't had at least one seemingly unexplainable experience that was kind of creepy? Maybe it even sent the chills through you and gave you goosebumps and made your surface hairs stand on end.

I too am drawn to the paranormal, although there is a ton about it that I can't begin to explain. I've had several experiences in my lifetime which I believe were encounters with the spirits of those who have passed to the other side; a whiff of perfume as you walk through a room, a glass that leaks out its content with no reason, an object that flies across an unoccupied room. I believe that my experiences were indeed visitations from beyond the veil. But then again, I have always loved a good ghost story.

The stories included in this anthology are each very different stories, but each have a paranormal element, and each one is well written. But they have something else in common, too, because each of these stories reaches out to touch the past, but in very different ways. I do think you'll enjoy all of them. So, with that said, and without any further ado, let's get started and you can tell me if I'm wrong.

Author Kaye Lynne Booth

https://kayelynnebooth.wordpress.com

Kaye Lynne Booth lives, works and plays in the mountains of Colorado. With a dual emphasis M.F.A. in Creative Writing, writing is more than a passion. It's a way of life. She's a multi-genre author, who finds inspiration from the nature around her, and her love of the old west, and other odd and quirky things which might surprise you. Her western Delilah and her time travel short are both available and you can get a copy of her paranormal mystery novelette by signing up for her newsletter. In her spare time, she keeps up her author's blog, *Writing to be Read*, where she posts reflections on her own writing, author interviews and book reviews, along with writing tips and inspirational posts from fellow writers. She's also the founder of WordCrafter, offering quality author services, such as editing, social media & book promotion, and online writing courses. When not writing or editing, she is bird watching, or hiking, or just soaking up some of that Colorado sunshine.

The Woman In The water

Kaye Lynne Booth

The water is high, flooding over the banks of the river's outlet and into the trail and parking area. It isn't a big lake. I can look all the way across to the other side. The water looks majestic, spilling down over the edges of the dam. I park up above the dam and walk down to a spot below the falls.

From below it looks much bigger because of the amazing volume of water which rushes down from above. The water's roar fills my ears, deafening me as it flows over the top and down over each successive level. It overflows the sides of the dam, creating smaller falls in the canyon walls on either side.

I find a large rock to sit on, observing my natural surroundings. Below me, red-winged black birds commence the activities of their mating season. I catch glimpses of red and yellow, flashing through the air as they flit from here to there, the males raising interest from the females with loud, distinctive calls. For a few seconds, a northern flicker lands on a rock in the cliff to my right. Then, offering a view of his salmon-colored underwings, he once again takes flight.

The green of the grassy meadow at the top of the hill is broken with splashes of reds, oranges and yellows, as well as spots of purple and white from the local wildflowers. The same colors are found on the hill, in the grass between the rocks and boulders. A blue heron glides along the river's course, its long legs stretched straight out behind, its wings gently pushing it along with an appearance of ease and I can feel the stresses of daily life melt away.

I glance down at the washed-out trail below me. From around the corner leading further down the trail, a woman appears. Did I say woman? No, that's not right. She is more of a goddess, with long black hair flowing down over her shoulders in straight, shiny strands that hang well below her buttocks, gleaming in the sunlight.

She walks so gracefully that glide would be a better word. Her motion is comparable to the effortless flight of the heron above. She is wearing blue jeans, a rose-colored tube top that accents the natural dusty rose hue of her cheeks on her dark olive complexion, and gray hiking boots.

It is puzzling to see her there, strolling up the marshy path which I avoided in order to keep my feet dry. Maybe I'm a sissy, although I've never considered myself to be one. Maybe, I'm just not as adventurous in my old age as I used to be. She stops at the river's edge, looking out over the water, unaware of my presence above.

What she does next, leaves me with my mouth gaping open. She grasps the lower edges of her tube top and pulls it up over her head, draping it over a nearby bush. Still gazing out over the water, only her bare back is visible to me, but that's enough. I sit there on top of my boulder, gazing down at the half naked beauty that stands below me and do nothing, unable to pull my eyes away from her.

Then, she unlaces and removes her boots, one at a time, setting them under the bush that holds her top, and eases her jeans down over her perfectly curved hips. She takes out, first one leg, and then the other. Then, the jeans are hanging on the bush with the tube top.

Still, I don't move. It's as if I am glued there. I make no sound, no attempt to alert her to my presence so she can cover herself. It is as if my voice has suddenly decided to go on vacation without me.

She stands there in all her nude glory before stepping into the river and walking upstream toward the rushing falls of the dam. I find my voice and call out to her, warning of how high the river is, telling her to turn back, but the roaring water from the falls drowns out the sound.

She keeps going, one delicate, elegant step at a time. She doesn't seem to fret over where to place her feet on the slippery rocks that lay below the water's surface. As on land, her movements are graceful, flowing, making her appear to glide through the water effortlessly. Her slow, casual strides give the impression that the terrain is familiar. She moves without hesitation, without pausing, straight into the raging falls. I catch glimpses of her through breaks in the water's cascade as she makes her way toward the center of the dam.

Once she reaches the center, I can no longer see her. Still, I sit frozen to the rock beneath me, gazing after her. I do not see her move toward the other edge to emerge on the opposite bank. She must have stopped in the middle of the dam, letting the water flow over her nakedness from above. I imagine her in my mind, standing there letting the roaring falls immerse her bare skin, its cold chill flooding over her body.

The realization that I am sitting here with a hard on brings me back to the here and now. I feel heat rising in my cheeks as guilt steals over me. Sitting here, watching her as she disrobed felt a little like spying, although at the time, I'd had no qualms about it.

The sun beats down on my skin and I can feel heat from sunburn on my bare legs below the hem of my shorts. Have I been sitting here that long? I look at my watch; three forty-five. Although it seems as if only a few short minutes have passed since the woman appeared on the trail, my timepiece tells me that it has been more than two hours. How long since I last saw her through the curtain of water? She has to come out eventually.

Only, she never does. I sit here on this rocky perch until almost eight o'clock, as dusk falls over the surrounding terrain. She never reappears from beneath the torrents of the waterfall. I finally hike back up the hill to my Jeep as daylight fades from the spring sky.

*****

I play the scene from that day over and over again in my mind all summer, and into the fall. I never forget the beautiful woman who disappeared into a wall of water right before my eyes. One brisk autumn day, when I can't stand wondering anymore, I slip on my sweater and head to the lake.

The water is low this time of year, and the path that leads to the base of the dam and parking area are dry. No water flows over the top of the dam now. I park the Cherokee and easily amble up the path, feeling just a hint of chill, even through the scratchy wool of my sweater. The colors of autumn fill the landscape. The oranges and reds of scrub oak blanket the rocky slopes leading to the lake above, and the yellows of aspen quiver in the breeze.

I reach the place that had been the river's edge that day, examining the bush over which she had draped her clothes. I didn't expect to find anything there after all this time, but you never know. I walk along the previously flooded riverbank, now easily maneuvered. The dropping temperatures chill the water. Already, a layer of ice is beginning to form on the lake, but just at the water's edge.

Thinking ahead, I'd worn my old tennis shoes. I knew I couldn't make it to the center of the dam without getting my feet wet. I carefully place my feet with each step as I wade into the water, its iciness chilling my feet through the heavy canvas of my shoes.

By the time I reach the center, my feet feel like popsicles that haven't frozen quite solid. I thought that by coming back to this place, I might discover what had happened to that mysterious woman who I saw last spring, but there are no secret passages leading beneath the dam that the water might have hidden. The dam is as solid here as it is all the way across. I can't fathom where she might have gone.

I notice a tall boulder that rises up from the riverbed, just a little way out from the wall of the dam, almost in the center of the river. It catches my eye because it protrudes from the water and doesn't look natural. It is shaped eerily like the figure of a woman, with curves just where her hips would be, and two smooth round bumps where breasts belonged. As I look closer, I see the top of it is rounded, the back smooth. I can almost make out facial features, with indentations in all the right places to imitate eyes and protrusions where the lips and nose would be.

I stare at that stone, standing there in the middle of the river and in my mind, I can almost see that goddess-like woman, who I'd watched as she walked through the water to this spot last spring. Then my head clears and it is just a rock again.

I can no longer feel my feet, so I decide to head back. On dry ground once more, I pause to look back at that tall stone rising out of the river. Nah, couldn't be.

Author Roberta Eaton Cheadle

https://www.robbiecheadle.co.za/

Robbie, short for Roberta, is an author with six published children's picture books in the *Sir Chocolate* books series for children aged 2 to 9 years old (co-authored with her son, Michael Cheadle), one published middle grade book in the *Silly Willy* series and one published preteen/young adult fictionalised biography about her mother's life as a young girl growing up in an English town in Suffolk during World War II called *While the Bombs Fell* (co-authored with her mother, Elsie Hancy Eaton). All of Robbie's children's book are written under Robbie Cheadle and are published by TSL Publications.

I am an author who has recently branched into adult horror and supernatural writing and, in order to clearly differential my children's books from my young adult and adult writing, these will be published under the name Roberta Eaton Cheadle. My first young adult supernatural novel, *Through the Nethergate*, has recently been published.

I have two short stories in the horror/supernatural genre included in *Dark Visions*, a collection of 34 short stories by 27 different authors and edited by award winning author, Dan Alatorre, as well as three short stories published in *Death Among Us*, a collection of murder mystery short stories by 10 different authors and edited by Stephen Bentley. These short stories are published under Robbie Cheadle.

The Last of the Lavender

Roberta Eaton Cheadle

As June follows the rough path built of railway sleepers towards the back of the house, the strong fragrance from the many lavender bushes overflowing the flower beds, reminds her of Grandmother. Surrounding the purple flowers are long-tongued bumble bees, moving lithely from one flower head to another, foraging the nectar efficiently to take back to their hives.

Watching them, June recalls reading somewhere that while long-tongued bumble bees favour long tubed flowers like lavender, they are less attractive to short-tongued honey bees who have to stick their whole heads inside the tubes in order to extract the nectar. This results in unnecessary delays to their nectar gathering process so they prefer other types of flowers.

Bees have an efficient work structure and amazing survival instincts, there is no doubt about that, she thinks and recalls further that worker bees kick the surviving, unmated drones out of the hive at the end of the mating season, dooming them to certain death.

They are programmed for survival with no emotional baggage to consider. Maybe they're the lucky ones.

Lavender had been Grandmother's favourite flower. June hates lavender nearly as much as she hates bees. Bees are her nemesis and one sting could be fatal.

Opening the two cans of flying insect spray she carries and pointing the nozzles towards the lavender bushes, she activates the sprays by simultaneously depressing the switches. Walking slowly along the edge of the flowerbeds, she makes sure that every bush is enveloped in a cloud of choking poison. When the cans are both finished, June walks back, noting with pleasure the many dead bees on the ground beneath the bushes. There is a certain grim pleasure in seeing so much death.

June recently became the owner of the cottage and now, at last, she can get rid of the hateful lavender bushes which act like bee magnets.

Grandmother had willed the cottage to her. She had died a few months ago, at the incredible age of ninety-six years old. June deserves to own the cottage as she looked after her ailing grandmother for years before her death. Towards the end of her life, Grandmother had become like the old man of the sea.

Her mind likes this analogy. The old man of the sea in the Sinbad tales tricks kind hearted travelers into helping him cross a stream by riding on their shoulders. Once across, the old man will not release his grip and the traveler becomes his slave. The old man makes his victims carry him all over the island, never allowing them to stop and rest. Eventually, the victim dies of this miserable treatment.

June's parents had died in a car accident when she was twelve years old and she had come to live with Grandmother in this cottage. Right from the beginning, Grandmother had made her life miserable. June was forced to go to school wearing a skirt that reached her mid-calf. She wasn't allowed to highlight her hair, shave her legs, grow her nails or attend school social events like the other children her age. In her final year of school, June had been the only student who didn't own a cell phone. This excluded her from all the WhatsApp groups and made her a total social outcast.

During the afternoons, she had helped Grandmother with the washing, cleaning and cooking and also studied hard enough to maintain a straight "A" aggregate despite the fact that, when the time had come for her to choose subjects for senior high school, Grandmother had selected the ones she didn't particularly enjoy.

June obtained a scholarship to study law at a well-known university. Boarding would be necessary as, even travelling by car, the university was a few hours away from her hometown. Grandmother did not support June aspirations to become a lawyer.

"A university education is wasted on a girl," Grandmother had said. "They get married and have babies and never make a meaningful contribution to the corporate world. That place should be given to a man who will need to support a wife and children one day." She arranged for June to attend a secretarial collage and learn short-hand, typing, computer skills and business English. A forceful and intimidating personality, Grandmother got her way and, as the college was only a bus ride away, June had continued to live with her Grandmother and see to the running of the house.

On completion of her two-year secretarial course, Grandmother found June a job at the local lawyer's office. Grandmother was a wealthy woman and she used Mr. Edwards for any legal work she required. Mr. Edward's was happy to oblige Grandmother and give June a job as a legal secretary. The salary he offered was lower than the market norm for such a position, but Grandmother said she shouldn't complain.

"He is doing you a favour giving you a job so close to home. Querying the pay is ungrateful. It is not as if you need to pay for your keep," Grandmother had said.

Working for Mr. Edward's kept June at home with Grandmother and under her thumb. Resentment grew within June as life passed her by and her youth started to fade. She hadn't had the gumption to find herself a job in another town or city and leave Grandmother's house.

The morning June discovered Grandmother, dead in her bed from a stroke, was the first time in twenty-five years that June was free to do as she pleased.

The first thing she did was remove all traces of Grandmother's existence from the house and move into the larger bedroom, with a view of the garden. The second thing she did was go shopping. She came home the Saturday after Grandmother's funeral laden with parcels from upmarket clothing shops. She stuffed all her old clothes into black garbage bags and filled her new, large cupboard with pretty, flowery dresses, full mini-skirts, sheer blouses and pantyhose, as well as a selection of high heeled shoes.

Standing in front of the lavender bushes, June grinds her teeth at the memories.

The lavender has got to go.

In her high heels and short skirt, June leans forward and starts wrenching the lavender out of the ground by its roots. She throws the bushes into a pile on the lawn. She drags more and more bushes out of the reluctant earth. Red welts mark her palms as the lavender bushes resist her vigorous tugs. She doesn't care. Each bush seems to represent some insult or infringement on her personal time and space by the crazy old bat.

Forty-five minutes later, her fine blouse clinging to her sweaty body and her hair lank and dusty, her vengeance inspired spree of destruction ends. She surveys the damage and a small smile plays across her narrow lips. The lavender bushes lie in untidy heaps ready to be dragged to the bonfire pile.

Tomorrow she will get the gardener to chop the bushes up into pieces and ask him to plant something she likes in their place.

Roses, that's what I'll plant.

June loves roses, with their delicate-coloured petals and beautiful smell. She will plant roses in every colour she can find. Grandmother hated roses.

***

Everything is ready. June has invited a few friends from the office over for a relaxed Friday dinner. Mr. Edward's attitude towards her has changed now that she controls Grandmother's wealth. He gave her a pay increase and tells her he hopes to retain her business going forward. June graciously accepts his generous offer. She has her own office agenda.

Her guests include a single man, Peter Richards, whom she has known for a few years. Her new hairdo and wardrobe have attracted some admiring glances from him and she thinks there might be an opportunity for her to get to know him better.

June hears the doorbell ring and, with a final pat of her blonde streaked hair, she strides to the front door.

Her guests enjoy the homemade beef stroganoff, rice and vegetable sides she has cooked and praise her culinary skills. Wine and conversation flows and, at the end of the evening, Peter suggests they meet for coffee the following afternoon at a local bookstore.

"That will be lovely. I'll see you there at 3P.M." she says.

After the last person leaves, she shuts and locks the door, going into the dining room. The table is a mess with the pudding plates still on the table, together with an assortment of coffee cups and wine glasses. Walking through to the kitchen it is an even worse sight, with pots, pans and unwashed dishes stacked everywhere.

Grandmother would turn in her grave if she could see this mess in her kitchen, thought June. *She was always so fussy about everything being left in perfect order before she retired to bed in the evenings.*

June smiles.

Well, this is my house now and I can do things my way. I'm exhausted and I'm going to bed. I'll sort this lot out in the morning.

Upstairs in her bedroom, June undresses, tossing her clothes on a nearby chair. Climbing into bed, she closes her eyes and sinks into a deep sleep.

Smash! Crash!

The sound of glasses and crockery smashing on a hard floor jerk June from sleep.

"What the Hell?"

She jumps out of bed and drags on her dressing gown. Cautiously descending the stairs, she wishes she had something to defend herself with, but there is nothing to hand.

The noisy pandemonium continues as she approaches the kitchen door. Throwing it open, she draws herself up as tall as she can and marches into the room.

A large plate dripping with gravy soars past her head, missing her by a fraction. Pots and pans blast in every direction. Glasses and crockery methodically smash itself, one piece at a time, on the debris strewn floor. June hears Grandmother laughing.

Gasping with horror, June leaps back and slams the door shut. Her limbs shake uncontrollably as she considers what she had seen on the other side of the door.

What's going on? There is no-one in the kitchen. I heard Grandmother laughing. Is she hurling the crockery and cookware about from beyond the grave?

Unexpectedly, her gorge rises and she leans over, vomiting onto the floor.

I am reacting to shock.

The noise stops abruptly. After waiting a few cautious minutes, June opens the door. The kitchen is completely wrecked. Broken crockery and glassware litter the floor, and bent pots and pans lie where they had fallen, but nothing stirs.

June stands staring at the mess, eyes enlarged with fear and uncertainty, before years of regimented self-discipline can kick in. Then, she sets about sweeping up the shards of glass and pottery that cover the floor. By mid-day, the kitchen has been restored to its usual orderliness, although there is nothing she can do about the chips, holes and other damage to the walls, counters and cupboards from the various flying projectiles.

***

June doesn't mention the bizarre events of the morning when she meets up with Peter that afternoon. There is no rational explanation for what had occurred, and she would have brushed off the whole experience as a weird nightmare, if it wasn't for the very real damage to her kitchen.

She did her best to focus on Peter, enjoying the cappuccino and a delicious slice of red velvet cake which they share in the small coffee shop, adjoining the large bookstore. Reading had offered her a much needed escape from her grandmother-dominated life when she was growing up, so Peter's obvious enjoyment of books pleases her. This common pleasure gives them plenty to talk about.

The lovely afternoon culminates into a pleasant meal out at a local restaurant, with June arriving home later than planned. The house stands silent and still, its dark windows gazing sightlessly at June as she fiddles her key into the lock.

Opening the door, she draws back in surprise and displeasure as the strong fragrance of lavender assaults her nostrils. Swamping the garden with lavender bushes had not been enough for Grandmother. She had also dabbed herself daily with a strong lavender essential oil. Before her death, the strong odor had permeated every corner of the house.

Why can I smell this? I threw out all the bottles of lavender oil in the house. I drove them to the dump myself.

Upstairs, June notices that the curtains have been drawn and the master bedroom is dark and gloomy, just the way Grandmother liked it.

She heads over to her wardrobe to change into her pyjamas. Pulling the door open, she gasps in surprise and bewilderment. Her new clothes and shoes are gone, replaced by the old ones she had left in the plastic garbage bags downstairs, ready to take to a local charity. A sudden sensation of being watch causes her to whip around. Grandmother, dressed in a long white nightgown, sits at the dressing table brushing her long, grey hair. During her sixties and seventies, Grandmother had grown her thick hair long. She liked to give it one hundred strokes with her hairbrush every night to keep it healthy.

Heart thumping in her chest, palms slicked with sweat, June watches Grandmother slowly dissipate and disappear.

***

Distress and anxiety keep June awake that night. Eventually she resorts to taking a sleeping tablet which forces her into a drug-induced sleep, plagued by a strange dream.

The bees are swarming. The children watch from behind the safety of the window glass as the vicious creatures sweep through the garden; a threatening cloud of angry insects, attacking any living thing in their path.

A number of the bees hit the glass, smashing into it like kamikaze pilots. The loud buzzing of the swarm can be heard through the glass, a frightening sound to the children who had experienced swarming before. They had watched a similar swarm attack their dog the previous summer, stinging the poor animal over fifty times. George had died later at the veterinary clinic.

June awakens with a start, sitting bolt right up in her bed. There is something crawling on her arm.

Bees, five or six of them; they all sting her simultaneously.

She can hear bees buzzing, not the few that had stung her and now lie dying on her bedspread, but a lot more. Shrieking with terror, she reaches out and hits the switch for her bedside lamp. It comes on immediately, flooding the room with light. Black and yellow stripped creatures swarm in an angry cloud. The smell of lavender is overwhelming and there are bushes everywhere, growing out of the walls, the floor and even her bed.

She grabs a magazine from off her nightstand, knocking over the glass of water, frantically swatting at the insects.

Her body itches as if she had been bathed in itching powder. June races to the bedroom door, avoiding the bushes as best she can, using the magazine like a fan to clear her way through the swarm. She yanks it open and then closed again, before dropping to her knees in the passageway, clutching her cramping stomach. It burns like red-hot fire. Red fluid-filled hives appear all over her body.

Where is my EpiPen? Did I leave it in the lounge?

June can hardly see out of her swollen eyes, the puffing up of her tongue and throat making it difficult to breath. She needs to get help fast.

Lurching up onto her hands and knees, she tries to force herself to stand, but her cramping legs will not hold her. Sweat drips down her body and face as she attempts to pull herself forward on her belly, one inch at a time, using her hands and feet.

She stops. *I can't don't it.* A few minutes later she tries again, and manages to pull herself another few thirty centimeters. Fresh sweat pours from her body and she shivers with a burning fever.

I'm so hot.

She makes a final attempt to reach the staircase, wriggling forward like a snake, but the world starts spinning. June falls over and lies still. She is too tired to try again now.

I'll just lie here and rest for a moment. She closes her eyes and the last sound she hears before her soul drifts away is the sound of Grandmother laughing.

***

Monday afternoon Peter finds June's body when he drives to her house after she hasn't arrived at work or answered his repeated calls.

It's not like her. June has only missed one day's work in her entire career and that was the day of her grandmother's funeral.

Her car is parked in the garage, but she does not come to the door or respond to his insistent ringing of her bell.

In desperation, he calls the police. The pair of officers that respond to his request for help, quickly force the lock and, together, they enter the dark and foreboding house. The curtains are closed and the house has an abandoned smell.

June's body is discovered at the top of the stairs. It displays all the symptoms of death due to a severe allergic reaction to bee venom, but no puncture wounds are evident anywhere. There are no dead bees anywhere in the house either. Other than some damage to the walls and counters in the kitchen, there is no sign of any violence or unusual activity in the house. No-one has any way of knowing that this damage was caused by a poltergeist throwing pots and pans in rage.

***

Ten years later, Peter is driving past the house. No explanation has ever discovered for June's death and he has never forgotten her.

He pulls over and gets out of the car. The house is empty and has the abandoned and decrepit look of a dwelling that has not been lived in for a long time. Sagging curtains are drawn over the windows, giving it an added atmosphere of lonely secretiveness.

While he is gazing at the unkempt garden and peeling paintwork, one of the curtains covering the master bedroom window twitches. A greyish white hand pulls it slightly open. Peter sees a pair of dark eyes peering at him through the dirty windowpane. They glow with the deranged look of a mad woman.

He gasps and steps back, then turns around and walks quickly back to his car. Maybe one day he'll investigate what he thinks he saw more closely, but not today.

Missed Signs

Roberta Eaton Cheadle

The thick, gloomy trees merged into one dark mistiness that concealed everything in the forest, animate and inanimate, sane and insane.

Anxiety compelled Jack and Mary to follow the muddy footpath that wound through the dense trees, despite the poor visibility. Sean could not be left to wander about alone in his current deranged and hallucinatory state.

They had missed the signs completely. By the time Jack had guessed the cause of Sean's increasingly hyperactive, excitable and erratic behavior, it was too late. He had snuck out of the house and completely disappeared into the surrounding wilderness. The thick, swirling mist was not conducive to any sort of search and Mary was worried.

She berated herself for being so foolish. When the squirrel had bitten Sean a few months ago, he had come straight to her for help. His eyes were large and shiny with panic as his numerous fears for his health overwhelmed him. Mary knew that his obsessive-compulsive behaviour-centered on fears of ill health and resulting death.

"Will I get rabies, Mary?"

"Of course not. No-one gets rabies anymore. I'll bath it in some disinfectant and then bandage it up."

"Will it be okay, Mary?" his eyes pleaded with her to co-operate with his ritual which followed a specific question and answer format.

"Yes," she sighed.

"Do you promise?"

"I promise."

One repetition of this affirmation had not been enough. They had gone through this same question and answer pattern repeatedly that day as Sean's anxiety about the bite ebbed and flowed. It was like this most days, regardless of whether there was a real physical cause or not. The rituals could be triggered by a stomach ache or a sore throat or something as innocuous as a scratch or drinking too much water.

The wound had been red and angry looking for a few days. Mary bathed the small wound twice every day, applied an anti-bacterial cream and then bandaged it up.

They were temporarily living in a remote cottage on the edge of the Knysna forest while her husband, Jack, worked on some complicated mathematical problem that required intense focus and concentration. His irritability made it hard for Mary to talk to him about Sean's bite and his concerns.

Jack didn't take Sean's health complaints seriously anymore. He was the boy who had cried wolf once too often.

It's not a real concern anyway, Mary thought. *I have never heard of anyone contracting rabies in my life. Of course, this is South Africa and not the UK but I am sure it is the same here.*

When they first arrived in South Africa, Mary had no idea that remote in this vast country was a different concept altogether too remote by English standards. She had assumed that there would be bus services to and from their temporary home, so she hadn't bothered to get an international driving license.

I'll ask Jack to take us to the doctor to get the bite checked. It is better to be sure that everything is okay.

Jack didn't think Sean needed to see a doctor.

"He's had his tetanus injections," he said, "Just carry on bathing it and keep it covered and it will be fine."

Mary did not argue with him. Jack had been very patient, almost saintly, about taking Sean into their home when Mary's parents died a year ago. She was his only surviving relative and he had nowhere else to go. Living with a teen suffering from chronic mental illness was difficult and Mary didn't want to ask more of Jack than he was willing to give.

The wound healed. Sean continued with his on-line A-levels programmes and Mary and Jack got on with their jobs and lives. Fortunately for Mary, the magazine she worked for back home in Reading had been happy to allow her to work remotely for the nine months they planned to live in the Western Cape in South Africa. Jack had chosen this remote location to work on his new project because he had grown up in the nearby town of George.

"It's tranquil and inspiring," he had said.

He is right about it being tranquil. The forest and mountains are beautiful but I couldn't live here indefinitely. It's so lonely.

Sean was a loner. His condition meant that he didn't socialise well, particularly, with other teens. The idea of another person touching and contaminating his computer, books, phone or other things filled him with an anxiety so intense his face went deathly pale. He would not use another person's stationary, books or electronic devices either. Other people's things were dirty and he didn't want to touch them.

Mary was enjoying not having to deal with the after effects of his having to contain his anxiety all day long at school. In the past, when he arrived home from school, all the accumulated anxiety from his day poured out of him like lava from an erupting volcano. He spent up to an hour in the bathroom washing his hands and doing other rituals. When he was finished, Mary had to clean up the flooded bathroom. She tried to be patient and understanding but it annoyed her and she shouted at him.

Once his uncertainty following the move and the change of environment had settled, Sean's condition was more manageable.

It's better for us all, even if the psychologist does say it enables him to employ avoidance tactics. It's easy to make comments and stand in judgement when you're not the one dealing with all the fall out.

Two days ago, Sean woke up with a fever and complained of feeling tired and weak.

"You must have picked up a virus," Mary said. She treated him with pain medications and administered large doses of vitamin C to boost his immune system. Dark circles under his dull, tired eyes told her that he wasn't sleeping well and he seemed more anxious and aggressive than usual. He could be aggressive when anyone tried to interfere in his rituals and obsessive routines but this time, the cause had to be something else. With his psychologist far away in England, she was being more accommodating of Sean's rituals than she was at home.

Before Sean went to bed the previous night, his muscles had been visibly spasming and he was clearly confused and aggressive. His behaviour and symptoms had penetrated Jack's single-minded focus.

"I'll drive you both to the doctor first thing tomorrow morning," he said.

The morning had dawned cold and misty. Mary checked on Sean first thing and discovered that he was gone.

Dressing hurriedly in warm clothing, they grabbed a few energy bars and set off into the forest to look for Sean. On their way out of the house, Mary had absent-mindedly pushed closed a partially open drawer in the kitchen. Her action was subconscious and she did not think about it.

The mist clung to the ground like a thick carpet. Swirling tendrils wrapped themselves around the trees making them look like they were wearing white nightdresses.

As they ventured further into this dripping wet world, Mary could hear faint rustling sounds, like an animal disturbing wet leaves.

She tensed. "What's that?" she whispered to Jack. The sounds of the forest always unnerved Mary, but today the thick undergrowth seemed to clutch at her feet and legs and the dank mist, which coloured everything grey, was making her feel apprehensive.

"It sounded like a bushbuck," he answered unconcernedly. "The forest is full of them."

Mary was unsure. The mist seemed much denser in this section of the forest, like thick smoke. She felt as if something was watching her from within its murky depths. Something wild and demented. Something that was not human.

"I think we should go back to the house," she said. "We can wait for the mist to lift. It will be much easier to search for Sean if we can see."

"Don't be ridiculous, Jack said, moving purposefully forward. "We can't leave Sean out here for hours. He's sick."

Jack shared that he thought Sean might be suffering from rabies. He had typed Sean's progressively unusual symptoms into the on-line search engine yesterday evening, together with the fact that he had recently been bitten by a wild animal, and rabies had popped out as a suggested diagnosis.

Mary's stomach clenched so tightly she thought she might vomit.

Oh my God, I hope it's not rabies. He was so worried about getting rabies and I promised him.

"Come on," came Jack's voice, sounding some distance away.

She realised that she had been hanging back. She took a deep breath and plunged forward through the whiteness.

"I'm coming," she yelled loudly. "Wait for me."

A terrible scream ripped apart the silence. A fine spray of blood splattered across her face and dress.

She stopped, drawing back in shock. "Run," cried Jack. "Run, Mary." His words turned into wet gurgling sounds. Horror momentarily paralysed Mary. Then, she whirled around and bolted in the general direction of the house.

***

His headache was at low tide due to the complete blackness of the cloudy early morning. It would intensify as the day brightened, like the tide coming in, until it turned into a sickening sledgehammer, crashing into the soft tissue of his brain.

Sean threw off the covers of his bed and scrambled to his bedroom door. The walls of his small bedroom moved forward, surging towards him as if they were going to crush him. He must escape. Within moments, his bare feet were padding noiselessly across the kitchen floor. At he passed the large drawer in the middle of the storage cabinets, he hesitated. The drawer slid silently open on its runners. Mary's array of kitchen knives lay in the drawer, shiny and sharp.

He reached in and selected the largest butcher knife. Shoving the door closed it caught on something and stopped halfway. Sean did not notice. He was focused on escaping from the kitchen before the moving walls closed in on him.

***

A few hours later, Sean woke up feeling cramped and stiff. He was lying on the cold and damp earth, in a glade in the forest. He stretched and contemplated the nearby trees, they whispered words of comfort and support which eased his anxiety and fear. The unpleasant claustrophobia he had suffered in his bedroom felt remote and surreal. The lack of brightness of the overcast day was a welcome relief and helped to keep his headache at manageable levels.

His ears pricked up. He heard the distant sounds of people crashing through the undergrowth. Their calls were sound waves that caused the pain tide to surge across his brain, drowning all rational thought. He stood up, biting down hard on his lip as the movement seemed to wrench his brain loose from his skull. Blood dripped down his chin and splashed onto the ground.

Skulking forward, more animal than man, insanity in firm control of his nervous system and actions, he set out to hunt his tormentors. The people inflicting unbearable pain on him with their loud shouts. From his hiding place behind a thick tree trunk, Sean saw an unfamiliar man walk through a small natural clearing. He was only a few feet away from Sean now. The man stopped and shouted. Senseless words that seared into Sean's mind like a hot poker.

He's looking for me, Sean thought. *He wants to drag me out of the forest and into the light. The sound waves are not enough. He wants the light to explode my brain.*

Fury surged through Sean, filling his muscles with adrenalin. He raised the butcher knife and leapt forward, bringing it down with all his force and driving the blade deeply into his victim's shoulder. As Sean dragged the knife free, bellows of pain and shock issued from the man's throat. More senseless words slashed into the soft meat of his brain. The blood-streaked blade flashed again and the man's screams reduced to a choking gurgle as the knife slashed through his throat and windpipe.

The hunter smiled and cocked his head in the direction of the fading footsteps.

***

Mary's fear was overwhelming.

Should I run? Should I hide? Where can I hide?

She had lost the path and felt herself flipping and sliding on the wet creepers and leaves beneath her feet. A stitch dug into her side; she had not run like this since she had finished high school six years ago. The dank and damp mist embraced her living body with clammy hands. She visualised death himself sharpening his scythe in readiness for her certain death.

Mary s2topped and looked around her.

Where can I hide?

A large tree with an interesting root system caught her eye. She walked softly over to the tree. She was right, there was a small cave-like gap behind the roots. Mary squeezed herself into the uncomfortable space and shut her eyes tightly. Hard roots poked into her back and her legs ached from being curled-up beneath her. She tried to control her breathing, but could do nothing about the loud pounding of her heart.

In the distance she heard some sort of crash, like a small tree falling over. Complete and undisturbed silence returned.

Mary fin2ally emerged from her hidey-hole. For a long period of time, no sounds had marred the silence except for the incessant chirruping of the insects. Covered in mud, cold and frightened, Mary set off in a direction she hoped would lead her back to their house.

Her relief was overwhelming when she stumbled across the path after wandering around lost in the forest for many hours. The mist had cleared and brief patches of bright light made pattern on the forest floor. Another hour of walking brought her to their house.

Everything looked the same as it had that morning. Mary used her cell phone to summon help before collapsing onto the couch. A violent shaking took possession of her limbs and her legs would not hold her up.

***

The light-headedness descended on Sean unexpectedly. He felt as if his mind had detached itself form his body. Moments later his breathing stopped and his body toppled heavily to the ground.

The teams of searchers came across his body the following day. It lay within a 500-metre radius of Jack's dead and bloody remains.

Death due to sudden cardiac arrest as a result of the rabies virus was the official cause of death.

***

Bella toss2ed her bag onto the floor and sank onto the couch. Exhaustion from her long drive mixed with gratitude that the cottage, which she had rented fully furnished, looked clean and tidy. The furniture was in surprisingly good condition.

Closing her eyes, she fell into a weary sleep.

Tap, Tap, Tap

Bella's eyes snapped open at the continuous tapping sound. Darkness had fallen while she slept, and the room was dark except for the faint light of the sickle-shaped moon shining through the window.

What the hell is that noise? It sounds like someone rapping on glass.

She pulled herself to her feet and looked towards the window. Her heart lurched into her throat as she gasped in fear.

A face peered through the window, its deranged eyes blazed in the dim light and its hair bristled like the tail of a frightened cat. More disturbing was the strange optical effect whereby the face did not obstruct the moon; she could see the bright quarter-moon shape right through it.

Author Julie Goodswen

https://storytellingdancer.com/

My name is Julie Goodswen and I have recently entered my second half century - still marvelling at where the years have gone and concerned I might not have time to finish the novels and stories which are residing in my head.

I am married to Clive and, although we have no children together, we have five grown up offspring, a son-in-law and a beautiful granddaughter who has just turned one.

I am an IT Services Manager at a wonderful public school, set in the grounds of Norwich Cathedral - a beautiful, inspiring backdrop to my daily life.

I struggle to find the time to write as, when I am not working or spending time with my family, my husband and I love to dance which we learned and now give back to by demoing and helping, with Ceroc.

My motto is "I must give more time to writing" and my wish is "I wish there were more hours in the day!"

The Kite Flyers' Lighthouse

Julie Goodswen

Keeping a close eye on the Skoda's built-in satnav, Harriet was almost certain she was on the right road, but it looked so deserted she was beginning to doubt the gadget's accuracy. She had chosen this beach, after all, because it was secluded enough to offer her a complete rest from the world around her, for two whole weeks. Not even her closest family knew where she was headed, simply that she had found a remote spot on the East Norfolk coast and didn't want to be disturbed. Her family had been alarmed when she had told them she would be switching off her mobile phone for the duration of her break, so she had reluctantly agreed she would keep it fully charged and with her, in case of emergency. Harriet smiled to herself as she thought the only emergency would be her family discovering her whereabouts.

In the early dawn light, the satnav was encouraging her to the right, onto an unmade track dotted with potholes of varying depths. Harriet guided Octo, the name she had given to her shiny, new midnight blue Skoda Octavia, around as many of the holes as she could but the suspension was being put through its paces. Checking the satnav screen as Octo had stopped talking two minutes before, she realised that her route had completely disappeared.

Pulling over out of habit rather than the expectation of meeting another vehicle along this deserted track, she reached across to her passenger seat, finding an A4 sheet of directions. Skimming the top half, she found where she was supposed to be and where she thought she was. She had gone off-course approximately two miles back. Harriet thumped the steering wheel, doubt creeping in. There was no turning place along this track. Opting to travel a little further along in the hope of finding a place to turn around, she switched off the satnav and selected her media stick for some soothing music. The thumping rapping of Pitbull drowned out the sounds of the car's engine and Harriet smiled. Pitbull would have to do, she didn't need soothing, she needed cheering up. It had been six weeks since...

The coastal mist was starting to clear, and Harriet could make out the faint line of the horizon. Slowing the car to gaze at the sea, she noticed a tall structure at the end of the track through the departing haze. The lighthouse! How had she not seen that before? There must be two tracks leading to the same place. Harriet muttered to herself, "*Trust your instincts, woman!*" and pressed her foot more purposefully on the accelerator, reaching the lighthouse's garden and rickety old gate in seconds.

Parking the car outside the gate she stepped out, forgetting to close her door, so awestruck at the sight of the looming old lighthouse. It was nothing similar to the lighthouse in her imagination and even the brochure had painted a far more modernised version of the building. Still satisfied she had chosen well for her break, she reached into her back seat and pulled out her small suitcase. Slinging her handbag over her shoulder, she walked confidently to the gate and searched around for the tiny metal, combination protected box which should contain the key to her accommodation for the next few days. Finding no box, she consulted her notes again. It should have been right here in front of her. Approaching the lighthouse's battered door, Harriet noticed it was sitting ajar, the key dangling in the lock, stirring a whole new set of emotions. Nervous now, she tapped on the door and called, "Hello? Anybody here?"

She was about to climb the first of the lighthouse's apparent 68 steps where she should expect to find the living area, when she was startled by a movement behind her. Popping his head around the door was a man who appeared to be in his mid-forties. "Good morning, Ma'am. Sorry to startle you. I was watering the garden. I wasn't expecting you this early."

"Sorry, I left early to avoid the traffic. I can come back?" Harriet could not help but notice the man's piercing blue eyes.

"Not at all, Ma'am. I have finished out here and was about to sort the key for you. Please, take this key and I will be around later in the week if you need anything at all. You know how to contact me."

"I do?" Harriet looked up at the stairs, wondering if he would offer to carry her case for her. Turning back to invite him to stay for a cup of tea, she was surprised to find he had already left. Taking the few steps back to the lighthouse's door, Harriet found no trace of the man, the only movement was the billowing reeds leading to a well-trodden path. Assuming he had gone in that direction, she made a note to explore the pathway later. Lifting her case with ease and removing the key from the door, and in turn locking it from the inside, Harriet began the ascent of the steep iron steps.

Each step echoed eerily throughout the structure and she was astounded at how old and beaten down the lighthouse stairwell was. Sighing, she hoped the accommodation at the top was at least a little more inviting.

Having stopped to catch her breath after approximately half of the steps, Harriet continued towards the top floor, coming face to face with an iron door which she was surprised to find was also locked. Hoping the key from the front door would fit this one too, she balanced her suitcase and handbag on the step below, fumbling to find the key which she had stashed in her jeans pocket. Relieved to find she hadn't any need to traipse down to find another key, the door swung open for her easily and she was greeted by a rounded room, beautifully lit by sunlight from the large windows.

The owner had used the top of the old lighthouse and the whole room was bathed in light from the endless window running around the outer edges. "Wouldn't want to be the window cleaner here!" Harriet muttered, surprised to find the windows were spotless, as was the whole room, although the décor was tired and drab. Placing her suitcase onto a cleverly curved sofa, she wandered over to the kitchenette area and filled the kettle with water from a grumbling tap, a coffee was just what she needed after her early start. A small section of the window gave way to a double door next to the sofa and opened onto a balcony area with not quite enough space to accommodate a chair. Harriet flung both doors open wide and secured them with the blocks hanging to the side, preventing them from slamming shut on her. Dragging a recliner chair from the center of the room its legs had to straddle the ledge, she pulled a book from her handbag, placed her freshly brewed coffee by her side and, making herself comfortable, and took in the beautiful scene playing out below her. The waves crashed onto the flawless sandy beach below. Pebbles which were dotted few and far between tapped an intermittent tune as an occasional one hit another, the waves breaking gently over them. She couldn't remember visiting this part of the coast, but knew she had been to seaside towns nearby, preferring the East Norfolk coast to other local areas.

Moments later, it seemed, Harriet opened her eyes, rousing herself from what felt like a deep sleep. Checking her watch, she was surprised she had been asleep for over an hour. Pushing against her growling tummy, she groaned, remembering she needed to buy groceries. She thought the brochure mentioned the kitchen being fully stocked with essentials, but a thorough investigation of the cupboards revealed no more than coffee and sugar. Sighing, she found her purse in the depths of her handbag, along with a folded fabric grocery bag which she always carried with her and set off down the iron staircase to find the local shop which the brochure had also promised her.

Reaching the bottom of the stairs, Harriet locked the door and realised she had forgotten her car keys. Swearing at her mistake, she looked over her shoulder and back up at the lighthouse looming above her. "Sod that! I'll walk!" Harriet said to herself and headed towards the pathway the gardener had disappeared down earlier. The path, while overgrown, seemed to be well-trodden and Harriet felt comfortable following it, surprised to find it led to the beach, not another building in sight. Looking back, she could see the lighthouse towering above, so she knew she hadn't come far. Choosing a direction, she headed off along the soft, damp sands. The beach was deserted, but it was still quite early in the day. Her gaze fell on a solitary figure in the distance who, Harriet decided, must be walking a dog. It seemed sensible to assume the dog walker would know where to find a grocery store, so she headed towards them, the salty sea breeze misting her face, causing her to squint in the low, rising sun.

Drawing nearer to the figure on the beach, Harriet realised they were not walking a dog, but flying a beautiful kite, its fluorescent sails catching the hazy sunlight, giving the kite an ethereal quality. Mesmerised by the kite's gyrating dance, she was unaware that the kite flyer had approached her and was standing only a few steps from her. "Hello, again, Ma'am!" Harriet looked down from her skyward gazing to find herself face to face with the gardener from the lighthouse.

"Oh, hello there! We must stop meeting like this!" Harriet smiled, cringing inwardly at her clichéd response. "I was trying to find a grocery store, but appear to have found you again. You and your beautiful kite. I am not sure I have ever seen a kite so glorious!" Harriet was genuinely in awe of the beautiful dancer breaking up the morning's blue sky.

"Thanks. I love this kite. I have many, all shapes, sizes and colours. I've flown them for years. My son and I used to fly them together. This is my favourite." The man's voice tailed off as he pulled against the breeze to correct the kite's sharp descent towards the soft, white sand.

"Well recovered! Are they difficult to fly?" Harriet couldn't pull her gaze from the kite, heading skywards once more.

"Not when you have done it a few times. Some of them can be difficult to master, but practice is time well spent. I must apologise, Ma'am. I was supposed to stock up your cupboards, but the morning was so beautiful, I couldn't resist a fly before bringing your goods. Its probably a good thing I have seen you, gives you a chance to request anything else, save you going to the shops yourself. It is, after all, a break away from the madding crowd for you Ma'am."

"Please, call me Harriet. Harry if you like. I don't mind at all." Harriet smiled at the man, noticing how the colours of his dancing kite were reflected in his eyes, the blue replaced by silvers, golds and hints of shimmering red.

"Lovely to meet you, Harriet." He didn't remove his hands from controlling his kite, simply nodded her way, smiling. "I'm Gareth. Please, forgive me. I will bring your shopping to you within the hour. Can I get you anything specific?"

Harriet asked for a few items which she could use for a variety of meals during the week, handing him some cash to cover the extras. Thanking him, she wandered back in the direction of the lighthouse. Along the deserted pathway, Harriet noticed a battered, but still solid, bench sitting among the grasses.

Sitting down to bask in the beauty of the beach, she could still see the tip of Gareth's kite swooping from side to side, then disappearing only to reappear and resume its merry dance further along the beach. She assumed he had gone shopping when, a minute or so later, the kite no longer reappeared. The sun burned the last of the mists away and, warmer now, wandering through the grasses, Harriet picked some wild flowers to take back with her. Reaching the lighthouse, she was amazed to find two crates on the doorstep with a note reading, "*Sorry to have missed you. See you soon, Gareth.*"

Harriet wondered at how he could have bought and delivered the groceries so quickly, but remembered she'd spent much time daydreaming among the grasses, sure she had wasted more time than she'd first thought. She discovered the crates had specially made rope handles and she was able to carry both up the stairs, treading carefully, but avoiding the need to climb and descend them twice in quick succession.

Gareth had done a great job of shopping for her. All the essentials were there; pasta, potatoes, fresh vegetables and salad, long-life milk, cereal and a few little extras upon her request including three bottles of red wine and some dark chocolate. She was on holiday after all! The goods put away, she stored the crates next to the door, ready to take back down when she next left the lighthouse. She would have to plan her journeys in and out, up and down, meticulously to avoid those dreaded, steep iron steps, the least planned-for part of this relaxing break.

Harriet fixed herself a ham salad and took her plate, along with a large glass of red wine, to her new favourite spot by the open windows. She picked up her book and immersed herself in the story, stopping occasionally to pick at some food or sip her wine. She hadn't felt this relaxed for a long time. How much her life had changed over the past six weeks. She hadn't realised just how much she had needed a break from everyone and their constant fussing around her. They meant well, but it was difficult to explain to them that she just needed some time alone without offending their generous efforts to keep her company.

The wine, on an empty stomach, was quickly taking effect, making her feel drowsy and, fighting to read the last few pages of the chapter, forcing her eyelids shut. She drifted into a deep sleep. The sound of pages turning broke through her subconscious and she opened her eyes, expecting to see someone standing in front of her. Feeling momentarily spooked, she took a few seconds to wake up fully, and noticed her book had fallen to the floor by her feet, the pages gently flicking in the breeze from the open windows. Retrieving the book which had opened to the inside page of the front cover, her attention was drawn to the inscription. The neatly slanted handwriting read, "*To my darling Harriet. I hope you enjoy this book as much as I enjoyed choosing it for you. Together forever, xxx.*" Harriet remembered opening the book just a few months ago, on her birthday. Her husband had selected it from a local bookstore, knowing she had recently become attracted to a previously undiscovered fiction genre. She loved reading about a possible, future where technology had taken over and gone horribly wrong. She hated technology, fearing that such a dystopian time was just around the corner. She doubted he had known just how ill he was when he had bought the book for her, but the inscription was nothing new. He always wrote a message inside the books he chose for her as gifts. She had loved him for loving her love of books. No, not had, she still did love him, he might no longer be with her, but she still loved him dearly.

Harriet finished off the salad and took the last few sips of her glass of wine before moving the empty plate and glass to the sink. Standing at the worktop, overlooking the sand dunes, she sensed movement in the long grasses. Expecting to see a wild animal or bird roaming around she watched for a while and was surprised to see a young boy of about twelve years, racing around with a beautiful kite, similar to, but smaller than, the one Gareth had been flying on the beach earlier. She watched until the boy disappeared and, having rinsed the items in the sink, went back to her comfortable viewing point at the window overlooking the fresh white sands and the crashing waves. Harriet had always loved being at the beach. From a young age, she had been taught to swim in the shallows and enjoyed many a holiday digging and building sandcastles with her parents and brother, in later years, with her own family. Watching as the tide exfoliated the shore with its strengthening ebb and flow, she felt the need to go walking among the shallow waves. Quickly changing into three-quarter length cotton trousers and tying a lightweight cardigan around her waist to allow for the temperature drop which would inevitably join her as the sun dipped lower during the latter hours of the departing day, she locked the door remembering to carry the crates down the stairs with her.

Taking the now familiar footpath, Harriet took in more of her surroundings. She had yet to see another building, but she was sure that the young boy and the man must live nearby. She wondered if they were related, or whether this beach was a known location for kite flyers, young and old. She had the sudden urge to fly a kite. It had been years since she had done that with her children, flying the diamond shaped kites of primary colours only. Harriet approached the lapping waves, spotting a random pebble which was almost covered by the soft sands.

Searching around her, she couldn't see another pebble in her immediate vicinity, so she picked it up, softly running her finger along its soft curves as she let it drop into her trouser pocket. Stepping out of her flip-flops, she headed to the water's edge. The crashing waves stung her toes and, bravely, she walked further out until the water reached above her knees, soaking her trousers. The sound of the water slapping against her calves was both calming and frightening at once, and she closed her eyes, savouring the peacefulness, alone with her memories.

A dog barking behind her brought back to the present. Surprised that she had not heard its approach, much less an owner, she turned to see the dog race past her and into the water beyond, chasing unseen objects created in the foamy waters. She turned back to the beach to see if its owner was close by and the boy, she was certain it was the one she had spotted in the dunes earlier, was running towards her calling an indecipherable name. As he drew closer, she could hear he was calling, "Pepsi! Pepsi! Come here, now! Pepsi! Here girl!"

He ran past her and she called out to him, "Be careful in the water! Your dog will come back. Don't go in too far!" The words were already lost at sea, so she took a step towards the boy who was swimming now, trying to catch his little dog. More worried now, she turned back to the shore. Nobody seemed to be coming after the boy, so maybe he was used to swimming out here. Harriet tried to remember back to when her brother was that age. Had he been a strong swimmer then? Had her own children swam in the sea at a young age? They wouldn't have been doing so unsupervised, she was certain of that. The dog barked again, breaking into her thoughts, and she turned as it ran past her, splashing the top of her trousers with cold, salty water. A muffled shout came from behind her. The boy. He was struggling. His hand momentarily waving at her from the water, which was pulling him under. Throwing her cardigan onto the sand, next to her flip flops she pulled off her t-shirt and trousers, flinging them absentmindedly in the same direction. Bracing herself for the icy cold shock, she took a deep breath, and plunged into the water towards the now-flailing boy. His eyes belied his years, his appearance that of a terrified toddler, his screams already being swallowed by the water he was taking in with each swell. The undercurrents were strong, and Harriet fought hard to keep her own head above water level. She was freezing cold and the boy was staying under far longer than he was appearing above, each time she paused to keep track of direction. He seemed to be moving further and further from her with each stroke she made, and she, too, was starting to weaken. Her breath was ragged and rasping, her eyes stinging. The current was pulling her into the depths and the struggle to reach the boy was becoming impossible. She couldn't feel her feet and hands, totally numb with cold, but she kept moving, certain she would reach him. A sudden swell took the boy right under and Harriet pushed herself to swim as hard and fast as she had ever done before.

Glancing back, she realised she was a dangerous distance from the shore, unable to make out her clothes or the dog, if indeed it was still there. She could hear nothing now, the pounding in her ears reverberating inside her brain. The boy had disappeared completely, and she sensed he was past her help. Tears burned the insides of her eyelids; each threat being washed away as sea took her further into the darkening depths. Her strength sapped, she had lost all fight. She stopped pushing through the water and allowed it to carry her at its will. Its might too much for her small frame. Just as she felt all hope gone, she felt strong arms surround her and opened her eyes just enough to see Gareth, his hair and face glistening with droplets of the icy cold water, carrying her back to the shore and to safety. She felt as light as a feather as he maneuvered her from the water and set her gently down on the beach. Turning her head to the side, she saw the outline of the dog, closer to her now. She felt the warmth of its tongue as it licked salt from her forehead and she closed her eyes, safe in the knowledge that kite man had saved her from a certain death.

She gasped and sat up. *The boy!* "The boy!" she called out, looking frantically around for the man who had, moments before, saved her life. She scoured the sea, expecting him to be back in the treacherous waters, looking for the boy. The man was gone, how much time had passed? The dog had left with him. She was lying beside her trousers and t-shirt but there was nobody there. Maybe he had gone for help. The sun was disappearing beyond the horizon and the air was turning much cooler. She had to call someone. She had to do something! She scrabbled around in her trouser pocket for the mobile phone which she had promised to keep with her, but it was gone. Had he taken her phone to call for help? Why had he not come back? Harriet felt confused and more than a little disorientated.

Heaving herself up, pushing through the weakness from her ordeal, she crawled clumsily on all fours towards her clothes and tried to fathom out how to get them back onto her cold, damp body. As she lay back down on the sand to fasten her trousers, she allowed her head to rest on a small mound of sand, a makeshift pillow. She needed to regain some energy and fast. Breathing slowly and methodically, she calmed herself and lay with her eyes closed.

"Hello? Hello? Are you alright?" a lady's voice drew near. Harriet looked up and found herself face to face with a lady, dressed from head to toe in crocheted clothes. Soaking wet crocheted clothes, hanging from her body, limply, her hair, trailing down beneath her headwear, dripping onto Harriet's legs as she spoke. Harriet suppressed a smile – the lady looked like one of those old-fashioned covers which hid spare toilet rolls. Her crocheted top, the holes revealing a vest top underneath, and what looked like a crocheted sarong were sodden and, here and there, were draped with seaweed. The whole outfit was topped off with a soaking, crocheted beret. The strangest ensemble one could imagine, thought Harriet, but smiled at the lady.

"Do you think you can walk? Do you hurt anywhere?" the lady held Harriet's elbow, supporting her as she rose to a sitting position. With the knitted lady's assistance, Harriet walked slowly towards the path leading them back to the lighthouse.

"What's your name?" Harriet asked the knitted lady as they stopped to rest on the battered bench.

"Des. It's short for Desdemona. My mum was a huge fan of Shakespeare and particularly loved Othello. When I was born she thought there could be nobody more beautiful and that is how I came to have this name. It's quite a lovely story, don't you think?"

Harriet noticed that Des did have the most beautiful smile and skin as soft as a rose. "A most beautiful story, indeed. Thank you for helping me, Des." Harriet paused to catch her breath.

"What's your name, beach lady?" asked Des.

"Harriet. Harry. There is no story. I guess my mother just liked the name."

"Did you know Harriet is the English form of the French name, Henriette? Both of which were ultimately derived from a Germanic name. Henrik, I think." She looked skywards, trying to remember if she was right. "I just love the origin of names. Makes introductions far more interesting. Your name derives from the words 'home' and 'power', so you are going to be just fine. You have already lived up to them, we just need to get you back to the lighthouse."

Harriet smiled gratefully, allowing this lovely lady to lead her to safety, never once wondering how Des knew where she was staying.

Remembering nothing more of the journey back to the lighthouse, much less the climb up the 68 steps (she had yet to count them to confirm this). Harriet awoke the next morning on the curved sofa in the lounge. She wondered if the room had a pull-out bed and then thought it strange she hadn't thought of it before. Her head pounded, and she tasted salt in her mouth, which made her feel quite sick. Hitching herself up she realised Des had probably shut the windows, she did not recall doing so herself. She tentatively walked over to open them and secure them back, allowing the rising sun to pour in. Her watch had taken on a lot of water and looked to be beyond repair, but the clock on the wall displayed a very early hour.

She wondered if she should call her family, remembering her promise to take the mobile phone with her always, and then remembered she hadn't been able to find it on the beach. She wondered if Des had locked her in and where her keys were. Finding her handbag where she had left it, she stripped out of her underwear and headed for the cubicle which housed, behind a false wall, the shower, toilet and washbasin. She wouldn't want to be staying here with anyone else, no privacy at all. She smiled, this place was so perfect for her, but she needed to freshen up and go to the nearest town to talk to someone in authority. The young boy was out there somewhere, and she was feeling suspicious about Gareth, the kite flyer. He had not returned, to her knowledge, unless it was he who had sent Des to help her.

Turning the tap for the shower, she was pleased to find the water warm. Not hot, but pleasantly warm, which would do just fine. She took a refreshing shower, toweled herself dry and found some clean clothes. She had already ruined one outfit which she had planned to make use of for a few days.

Sighing in realisation that she would have to shop for clothes if she had any more mishaps, she grabbed her purse from the table and put it in her handbag, noticing her mobile phone sitting in its pocket, exactly where it had been before she went to the beach. She was certain she had grabbed it on the way out yesterday evening, and even more certain it had been taken by Gareth.

Shrugging at the possibility she was losing her mind, Harriet grabbed her bag, slipped into some flat pumps and started the descent. Halfway down she realised she had not locked the inner door, but just couldn't be bothered to head back up the stairs when she had found the key. At the door, which was securely locked, she found a note telling her that Des would lock the door and post the key into the crack between the door and the hinges. Looking down, Harriet found the key where it had dropped, unlocked the door, secured it behind her and headed for her car.

She drove along the bumpy track and back out to the main road, where Octo started talking to her again. *Take the next right* it instructed her where she had turned right previously, which was now on her left, the night before. Harriet realised she hadn't programmed the town into the system and it was trying to take her to the lighthouse via another route. She put the postcode into the system and, following instructions from the ever-patient Octo, headed towards the town.

On arrival, the little town looked very small. She spotted a library, a bank and two general stores, one a chemist and the other professing to sell groceries. Further along a sign indicated a Post Office and what looked like a police station. Harriet would investigate further when she had parked her car, an easy task as the village looked to be deserted.

Looking around for a Pay and Display box, and finding none, she headed into the chemist to buy some painkillers for her pounding head. Next, she headed to the Post Office to buy some stamps and postcards which she would send on her penultimate day, lest they find out where she was staying. The building which she had assumed to be a Police Station was only a tourist information center and looked to be smaller inside than the living room of the lighthouse. *I guess they don't get many tourists around here.*

Entering the general store, she noticed a newsstand and purchased both a local newspaper and a Daily Mail, noting that they were both yesterday's date. *Might as well keep up with all the gossip while I am away, even if I am a day behind.* She found another bottle of red wine, some more chocolate – you could never have enough – and a local map, she would find the official routes from the lighthouse and walk those this time. Heading into the tourist information office, she asked if there was a local police presence. She explained that she'd gotten into some trouble in the sea last evening while trying to save a young boy. She went on to say that she thought kite flying Gareth must have saved the boy, but there was no trace of him or the boy when she was helped by Des. Her words were met with a confused look from the lady behind the counter, who took notes, including Harriet's mobile number, and promised to call the hospital, local police and later Harriet, with any news. The lady eyed her suspiciously as she left the building, convincing Harriet that she would call the police and tell them she thought Harriet had killed a young boy. She was in two minds as to whether to return into the building, but decided to go back to the lighthouse and take a walk along an official pathway.

When she arrived at the track where she had turned right the previous evening, her satnav advised her to take a left turn. Wondering why it hadn't taken her this way the previous evening she followed the satnav's course hoping it would take her back to the lighthouse. She thought she would be able to remember the other way, via the dodgy bumpy track, if she needed to. This track was smoother and certainly felt like more of an official route, and was far less stressful on her car than the other one.

Harriet arrived at the lighthouse within minutes, hopping out of the car. Something was amiss, it felt very wrong. From where she sat, the lighthouse looked completely different, a more modern-looking structure, with freshly painted exterior walls and a metal box outside the door as she had expected yesterday. Harriet turned full circle to take in her surroundings and scanned the coastline, searching for another lighthouse, certain she had made a mistake and had the wrong one.

"Mrs. Harvey?" a lady in shorts and t-shirt, covered by a little apron around her waist came hurrying from a cottage next door to the lighthouse, wiping her hands on the apron. "Sorry, I have been making cookies with my Jenny." She indicated a young child standing at her ankles. "Don't worry, we know you are here for peace and quiet and will leave you be once you are settled. We expected you yesterday. No problems, of course. Let's get you inside. Do you have any luggage?"

"I...well...I stayed at the other lighthouse last night. I left my luggage there. There's been a huge mistake." Harriet stammered, confused.

"Sorry, Mrs. Harvey. You ARE Mrs. Harvey, right? There is no other lighthouse for miles. Are you ok?" The lady grabbed hold of Harriet's elbow, fearing the older lady was going to faint on her.

"Well, yes. I'm Mrs. Harvey. I stayed at the other lighthouse last night, a couple of miles in the other direction. I went for a swim. There was a young boy. He drowned, well I think he did. Oh, I am confused. Would you mind if I sit here a moment?"

"Of course. Sit on this wall. You look very pale. Jenny, call daddy please. Ask him for a cup of sweet tea outside. Run along, lovely." She ushered the child back inside the house and sat herself down on the wall beside Harriet.

"The other lighthouse. I need to get my luggage." Harriet started to stand up and faltered as she peered through the window of her car onto the back seat. Her suitcase was where she left it, packed and ready to come here yesterday morning. "But there really was another lighthouse. I am not mad you know."

The lady's husband arrived at that moment with a large mug of sweet tea, which Harriet gulped down thirstily. "Sorry, I feel as if I haven't had a drink for days."

"Don't be silly," replied the lady, rubbing Harriet's spare hand, which was visibly shaking. "I'm Desdemona. My friends all call me Demi. I hate it. It makes me sound like a wannabe pop star, don't you think? I prefer Des. This is my husband Charles and my little girl, Jenny."

"Des? Desdemona? It can't be. She was called Desdemona too!" The cup dropped from Harriet's grip smashing on the stone slabs in front of her feet, sending the remaining tea everywhere. Harriet apologised and tried to retell the events of the previous day, tripping over her words as they flooded from her.

"You had better come inside, Mrs. Harvey. I have something to show you." Desdemona shot her husband a pointed look as she rose from the wall. Harriet noticed the husband supporting his wife by the elbow. They all followed Jenny who skipped gaily ahead of them. Desdemona headed to the oven, bringing out freshly baked cookies to the table when were all seated. Charles reappeared with a small box which he placed on the table in front of Desdemona.

Desdemona looked intently at Harriet and held both of her hands. "I want to be sure you are not playing a sick prank on me, Mrs. Harvey. I am sorry to ask, but I need to know if what you have told me is the truth." She looked imploringly into Harriet's eyes. Harriet shook her head.

"It's the truth. I promise."

Desdemona removed the lid from the box. "This box was my mother's. She gave it to me a few years ago. It holds the story of my family's past. My great-grandmother, Desdemona, lived a few miles down the road where the old lighthouse used to stand. She lived there with my great grandfather, Gareth and their two young children, Sam and Lucy. Lucy was my grandmother. Lucy's father, my great grandfather died trying to save my great Uncle Sam from the sea, when he tried to save the family dog, Pepita. Sam's body was never recovered, and Gareth was washed up on the shore the next day. My great grandmother was never found, the family assumed she had drowned trying the save them both, but to this day her body has never been found. Lucy was discovered at their beach house, the old lighthouse, crying, waiting for her family to return. She became an orphan and this box is her box, passed down through the generations. Desdemona, my great grandmother was pronounced missing, which is so sad for the family. This is a picture of the four of them together outside their home, the old lighthouse."

Harriet gasped as she took the photo from Desdemona's hand, her own hand trembling. Staring out at her from the yellowing image was Gareth, the kite-flying man, Sam, the kite-flying and dog chasing boy, and the lady dressed in crochet-knit, Desdemona. There was a young girl standing in front of the lady, who she assumed to be Lucy.

"But I saw them. I talked to Gareth, more than once. He showed me to the lighthouse. I slept there for heaven's sake! Don't show me any more pictures. Let me draw what I saw for you. I need you to believe me." Harriet was crying openly, now. Jenny hurried off and brought back some drawing paper and some crayons.

"I have been drawing pictures all my life and have even sold some of my artwork. Please, let me take this back to the lighthouse where I am supposed to be staying and leave you in peace."

"May I come with you, show you around? Help you to settle in please, Mrs Harvey?" Desdemona's voice was pleading. She needed to hear this wonderful visitor's story.

"Of course, dear. I don't really feel much like being alone after all this."

Desdemona asked Charles to watch Jenny, but Jenny became tearful and begged to go with her mother.

"This lady knows Sam! I want to know why he never plays in the morning!" cried Jenny.

"Jenny? Who is Sam?" Desdemona asked her daughter.

"Sam! He brings his dog to the beach and we play. He is always there just before tea time." Jenny looks at the photo. "That's Sam. The boy with the dog. That's Pepsi, his dog!"

Desdemona stares open-mouthed at her daughter. Wondering how it could be possible that her own daughter could be on the beach playing with her great-great uncle Sam, and why she had never told her this before.

Harriet, sensing that a whole new part of this story was about to emerge, said Jenny was fine to come with them. They left Charles clearing away the cookie plates and cups while they headed to the lighthouse. Harriet retrieved her suitcase, which Jenny was determined to carry up the stairs for the upset lady, but she had to give in and accept help when it became too heavy for her.

Harriet gasped again when she saw the layout of the lighthouse. "This is a modern replica of the lighthouse I stayed in last night. I realise there are design constraints but its almost identical, just more modern. Please, make yourselves at home. I will draw."

Harriet spent the next hour drawing and shading, Jenny stopping to peer over her shoulder from time to time, berated gently by her mother who pottered about ensuring everything was up to standard for this special guest. Harriet looked up and watched Desdemona closely before saying, "I never saw Lucy, your great grandmother, you know. I only saw her brother and parents. Why did I not see Lucy, do you think?"

Desdemona was quiet, pensive. "Do you know what I think? They were telling you the story of how Gareth tried to save Sam, how their dog swam to safety, and I think my great grandmother must have seen her husband battling to save their son and hurried down to the beach to help. You saw her soaked and dripping with seaweed, you said? My guess is she didn't want to see another life pointlessly lost at sea. Maybe she saw a sadness in you and thought you were trying to end your own life?"

"I have no idea, love. I don't think that's what I planned when I came here, but I recently lost my husband of forty years and I do feel so lost without him. My family want me to go on as normal and make a new life for myself, but it's so hard. It's so hard. I did wonder about never going home." Tears flooded Harriet's face as her eyes gave in to the torrents she had been holding back over the past weeks. Tears she had been afraid to cry, for fear of saddening her family more.

"Maybe my great grandparents saw a need in you and didn't want you to give up on life, leave your family behind as they mistakenly had to. Maybe they came forward to try and help you through this terrible time." Desdemona watched as Harriet pointed and gazed past her and out to the beach beyond the window. Turning, she followed the older woman's gaze and, standing at the shore were a man flying his shimmering kite, a lady dressed from head to toe in crocheted clothes and a little boy holding onto a dog's lead, with no dog at the end of it. As the two of them watched, the three ghostly figures walked a few steps backwards, their eyes never leaving Harriet and Desdemona. Jenny stood up and came to stand between her mother and Harriet at the window. All three figures on the beach were smiling, waving in unison, turning together and with joined hands, walked into the sea, swallowed by the rising mists. The last to disappear was the shimmering multi-coloured kite, flying lone in the sky, its line disappearing towards an unseen hand beneath the waves.

"Bye, Sam," whispered Jenny.

Author Laurel Mc Hargue

http://leadvillelaurel.com/

Award-winning author Laurel McHargue, a 1983 graduate of The United States Military Academy at West Point, was raised in Braintree, Massachusetts, but somehow found her way to the breathtaking elevation of Colorado's Rocky Mountains, where she has taught and currently lives with her husband. She is the founder of Leadville Literary League, a nonprofit organization with a mission to promote local literary endeavors and the arts, and hosts the podcast Alligator Preserves. She has also been known to act.

Orbs

Laurel McHargue

Hear this story narrated by the author:
https://soundcloud.com/user-564361489/short-story-12-orbs

Lolly thought she might be insane.

She'd communicated with her orb since before she could speak her first word, but when she turned five, it told her she needed to pretend it wasn't there. She wasn't to point to it or speak aloud to it or talk about it anymore, and she wasn't to acknowledge other people's orbs either.

They will never understand. They will make fun of you, it had told her. *We can hear the voice inside your head, and you can hear ours. This is how we will talk from now on.*

She was sad. She liked chatting with her orb.

Lolly's parents seemed relieved when she stopped playing with her imaginary friend, as they liked to call her bizarre behavior. They had tried everything to get their little girl to act like other children. They were especially unsettled by the way her eyes always focused on a point somewhere above the people interacting with her, never in their eyes. And she'd say things about other people. Things she shouldn't know.

"She's so precocious," the older ones would say, and then they'd avoid her.

Doctors found nothing unusual about her physical development, nothing concerning about her vision, and suggested more play time with children her age.

Decades passed, and Lolly learned how to look into people's eyes when she spoke with them. She was sixty now, and pretty sure she was insane.

If she weren't a brilliant journalist, others might agree with her, but her reputation as an international reporter had earned her adulation and awards over the decades. She insisted on traveling alone and taking her own photos and videos. No one could get to the bottom of a story like Lolly could. Time and time again, she'd discover an unlikely source, breathe life into a dead lead, and unearth the missing piece of a puzzling story. No one knew how she did it.

And she could never tell them how. They'd never understand, and at her age, they'd do more than make fun of her.

It is time to find them, her orb told her when she awoke on the first day of her sixth decade. *Three fertile couples on each of the seven continents except for Australia, where you will find two. The third you will find in New Zealand. They have not yet found their mates. You must bring them together.*

"But, how will I find them? Can't you just tell them what to do, where to go?" Lolly spoke aloud when she was home alone, which was always, when she wasn't working. She'd suppressed her communication far too long in her youth and decided early on never to bring a partner into her unusual reality.

They have not accepted us as you have. None on your planet has—none but you. You will know them by their orbs. Couples who are to be together will have orbs that glow the same hue.

"They'll think I'm crazy! They'll—"

They will be joyful. You will liberate them from their secret. They will believe you because you understand.

"Six people on each continent—"

Except for Australia—

"Yeah, yeah, I get it. You want New Zealand to be a continent, but still—how the heck—"

There will be stories for you on each continent. You will be sent to cover them. We will guide you to the individuals. They won't be far from each story.

"All right, then. What's my first lead?"

The disappearing continent. Antarctica. You will bring together environmental scientists from different nations working on similar projects. You will be tasked... now.

Lolly's phone rang just as her orb finished speaking.

"On the red-eye tonight. Got it. First class? Wonderful! Thanks, boss!" Lolly hung up and repacked her "to go" bag for a climate harsher than she was used to.

"And what am I supposed to say when I find these people? 'Hey, I see my orb too, and boy do I have a proposition for you'? Something like that?"

Something like that, yes. They will know when they see you. We will talk to them. When they see you, they will finally be ready to listen.

"You know I don't speak all the languages, right?"

We know. It will not be necessary. You will be understood.

"Okay, so what's going to happen after I finish playing matchmaker on all these continents?" She braced for the answer.

There was an uncomfortably long pause before Lolly's orb spoke.

You know what will happen.

Lolly knew what would happen, but she didn't know how it would happen. And she didn't necessarily want to believe it. And she still considered the possibility of insanity.

Her first assignment was to report on the frightening meltwater lakes threatening the ice shelves surrounding Antarctica, a topic about which she knew little. Arriving rested from her first-class accommodations, Lolly was escorted to several University research teams over the course of her three-day project.

Her preeminence in the media was helpful.

Finding her three couples was easy. Getting them together was not as easy as her orb had promised. Despite her reputation, Lolly had a hard time convincing the scientists to speak with her privately—a necessity for the real work she was doing on the continent.

Only two of the six had eyes that flashed when Lolly introduced herself. They knew right away they were chosen for something far greater than their research. The other four feigned incredulity when they finally consented to speak with her.

Their typical response surprised her: "I know what you're saying, and theoretically speaking, I see your orb... and mine, but I'm a scientist, for goodness' sake. We mustn't speak of it. This doesn't fit our world." She thought they'd be more open to exploring their anomalies.

"Just... find a way to be with this person when your orb tells you it's time," Lolly told them. "Trust me. Much like your work here, it's of global importance."

That got their attention.

Lolly delivered her sensational story just in time to receive her new lead about a dramatic shift in gun legislation on the tiniest continent. She found her couple within moments of stepping into a rowdy crowd chanting around the New Zealand Parliament Buildings. The man and woman were in different crowd clusters, and the noise and heightened excitement allowed her to slip up to each of them unobtrusively.

She whispered into the man's ear first. He dropped his sign and stared at her, wide-eyed, before looking up at her orb. He walked with her to the outskirts of the gathering and over to where they could see the glow from the woman's orb.

"I'll speak to her first," Lolly told him, and disappeared back into the crowd. She smiled at the expression of anticipation on the man's face.

Moments later, she reemerged with the young woman behind her. The man smiled meekly, and the woman didn't hesitate in extending her hand to introduce herself to him. They were anxious for answers, but Lolly was not to tell them any more than she had. They were to be a couple. That was all.

Australia was a fluff piece compared to anything she'd previously reported on—the discovery of a deadly new species, a troubling cross between a snake and a spider.

One couple with matching orbs worked as educators in different cities, the other young man and woman had just graduated from their respective high schools.

"No way! Seriously?" The young woman did a little happy dance when Lolly said, "Yes way!"

Finding and matching couples on the continents of Asia, Europe, Africa, and South America presented unique challenges as Lolly continued to crank out in-depth features on scandals and corruption and unpopular legislation. Her orb told her everything she needed to know, so at least the stories weren't difficult to write.

When Lolly returned to the North American continent for her last stories, she felt sad. None of the people she knew had matching orbs.

"But, I know this amazing couple in my town! They're already together, and—"

No, Lolly. Find the ones we have chosen.

Her head felt fuzzy for a few moments.

Three more months passed while she completed stories on civil unrest and viral epidemics and an upsurge in UFO sightings, successfully matching three more couples in the process.

She finally returned, exhausted, to the relative quiet of her apartment. She considered adopting a cat.

You have done well, her orb whispered as she fell asleep. It had been nearly two years since it had sent her to Antarctica. Consider what may come, and prepare.

Weeks passed, allowing Lolly time to consider her life and her options. Bone-weary, she nevertheless forced herself to connect with friends long put on hold till she'd have time for them. Some of her visits were joyful; others, exhausting litanies of loss and illness and wishes unfulfilled.

It is time, her orb told her as the sun rose on the vernal equinox. But the decision is still yours.

Lolly's joints ached after a restless night of fitful dreams. She gave her orb a sideways glance and flipped on the news. Bombings. Riots. Lies.

Outside, rush hour traffic already clogged her street. Buds struggled to open on the fragile maple surrounded by concrete outside her window. She thought of the unlikely couples and wondered how their relationships were progressing.

She wondered how they'd handle life in a brand new world, twenty-one couples alone on a planet wiped clean when the orbs would deliver their final message to their people.

And she would not be spared.

Yes or no, Lolly. Yes? Or no?

I still might be insane, she thought, and if I am, then—

The television hissed static.

Tanked

Laurel McHargue

Hear this story narrated by the author:
https://soundcloud.com/user-564361489/short-story-5-wet-dreams

Gullible, a dreamer, incurable romantic—these personality characterizations have haunted me for years, but I don't care. I don't see anything wrong with who I am. I'm like Popeye, except for the eating spinach part: I am what I am.

And I have the best job ever. As night shift security guard at the New England Aquarium, I get to see what most people never will. They're different at night, my aquatic friends. When all the people leave and lights in the giant ocean tank dim to moonlight, they relax.

It's not like they can close their eyes and totally sleep, but I sense a fading of fear when they see me. They know I'm not going to bang on the barrier between us or startle them with shrieks and flashes of light. After just one year here, they trust me.

Miranda does too.

At first I thought I was dreaming. I mean, come on. What guy hasn't dreamt of getting it on with a wicked pretty mermaid? She's real, though. Night after night she returns, pressing herself against the glass between us and making me crazy.

I pinched myself hard the first time she emerged, and then screamed like a little girl when the black nose shark appeared behind her. She laughed and showed me I had nothing to fear, latching onto the creepy creature and circling the tank with it.

Since then, we've talked about everything. I can't believe I'm the only one she'll materialize for. She made me promise never to tell anyone she's here, and why would I? She's a little bossy, though.

"Kiss me! Release me!" That's how she's been talking to me—in commands. She knows I like strong women. And I can tell she wants to be mine forever. Why else would she want me to kiss her?

But I can't let her out so easily. At least I don't think I can. How would I explain her? I guess I could say we met at work. There'd be history questions. We'd have to make stuff up. Mom might get suspicious, but all my friends would be wicked jealous. They'd never believe I could land a catch like Miranda.

And they'll want to take her away from me. So, yeah. I can't let her out without a plan.

Just last week I explained what would need to happen before our first kiss, the one that would release her from her wet world. I was getting anxious, and I'll admit it; she was starting to dominate my dreams.

"You'll need to wear clothes," I said, and then I started thinking about how I'd dress her. Tight, shimmery things, like Beyoncé wears on stage. Yeah.

"And you'll need to promise to be true to me and only me forever."

She promised.

"And you'll need to get a job 'cuz it's really expensive to live in Boston and my pay won't be enough for the two of us. Hey! Maybe you could get a job as a trainer here at the Aquarium!"

She thought that idea was wicked good.

"And when we have kids, they'll need to stay in school!" I laughed, but she didn't get the joke. There's a lot I'll need to teach her so she won't be awkward in my world. Mom always said I'd be a good teacher 'cuz of how I relate to little kids, so that won't be a big problem.

And now it's finally time to get her out of this tank and into my bed for real. I brought a bottle of champagne for our special moment—seemed like the thing to do—but now I wonder how it'll affect her. I don't want her staggering the first time she walks on land, so maybe I'll just let her have a tiny sip. It's expensive, so I'll drink the rest. Besides, I gotta tell you, I'm wicked nervous and excited all at the same time.

I'll drink some now before she shows up. I hope she likes her new clothes. I got them at the Goodwill, but she won't know that, and besides, the sparkly pants still have a store tag. Mom taught me how to find bargains all over town. I'm sure she'll teach Miranda too.

Boy, this champagne goes down easy. Wonder what's keeping her. I kinda feel like chuckling, but I want to be serious for our first kiss. It's important to make a good first impression. Mom always says that.

Oh! Here she is now!

I wave her over to me at the edge of the tank and she smiles one of her mysterious smiles.

"Are you excited?" I ask, and she nods, but doesn't come over to me. Instead, she waves me over to where she floats near the center of the tank. Can't believe I never thought of swimming with her.

I kick off my shoes, grab what's left in the bottle, and swim to her. Glad I'm a good swimmer.

I hand her the bottle, but she takes my face in her hands instead and kisses me in a way I've never been kissed before. I feel lightheaded, probably 'cuz of too much champagne. I drop the bottle and cling to her as she circles the tank one last dizzying lap.

* * *

"All right, men, let's get him outta there before the doors open. And grab that bottle too. Drinking on the job. Didn't seem like that kind of guy. Hey! Miss! You're not supposed to be in here yet!"

I watch Miranda smile over her shoulder and sashay away from a bunch of cops on the top level of the aquarium and I'm so glad she's mine. They stare at her and I'm ready to chew them out for their crude comments as they elbow one another and leer, but their boss shouts first, snapping them back to their task. They have to remove some dumb schmuck's body from the fish tank.

Hey, wait a minute...

Author Stevie Turner

Stevie Turner is a British author of suspense, paranormal, women's fiction family dramas and darkly humorous novels, and likes to find subjects to write about that are not often covered. Stevie is married and lives in the wilds of East Anglia, England, and enjoys cycling about the countryside when she is not busy writing.

Partners in Time

Stevie Turner

CHAPTER 1 – July 2017

So this is what it's like to be successful ...

John Finbow, an enigmatic smile lifting the corners of his mouth, kicked up the stand and swung a leg over the seat of his Fireblade, walking it back carefully over the gravel for a few more feet in order to admire his new purchase one more time.

The old south-facing Victorian rectory gazed back at him myopically through sixteen sun-drenched sightless windows framed in drooping wisteria. Ornate chimneys which had survived 170 years of coal fires now stood redundant atop a renewed roof of Welsh slate. A couple of blackened boot scrapers stood symmetrically either side of four grand pillars guarding an entrance portal worthy of one of those historical costume dramas that he knew Kay was so fond of.

He could see Max already hard at work re-training stray fronds of peach, apple and pear along the boundary walls. The jungle of grass had been cut to a respectable length, and John, beginning to sweat in his leathers, let his mind dwell on his as yet unborn child as *he*, it would have to be a *he*, pedaled a red tricycle on the front lawn.

He emerged from his reverie, and took a deep sigh of happiness as he turned a key in the ignition, causing the Fireblade's engine to roar into life. He returned Max's farewell wave with one of his own, and rode gingerly over the gravel until he reached the open iron gates leading out onto Church Lane.

***

He spied her amidst a pile of packing crates in the kitchen, one strand of red hair had escaped from her ponytail and flopped over her forehead as she carefully wrapped glassware in yesterday's news. John let a wave of tenderness engulf him as he snuggled up to Kay's back and wrapped his arms about her slim waist. "My helmet's full of flies."

A snort of laughter escaped from her lips. "You can get some cream for that, can't you?"

"Nah, just a bit of a lick and a polish."

"Ugh." Kay reached down and behind, gently squeezing his testicles. "You're gross."

He pressed his nose into the warmth of her neck, loving her more than he could ever say. He owed her everything. It had been Kay, who without his knowledge had taken that rejected screenplay from the outside bin where he had thrown it in disgust. The rest, as they say, was history.

"The deal's complete now; we can move in anytime."

She turned to face him and slid her arms around his neck. "I told you you'd make it in the end. You should've had more faith in yourself."

"What colour shall we paint the nursery?" He kissed the top of her head. "You know what they say - new house, new baby."

Kay shook her head. "Not yet. Give me time to get used to being Mrs. Finbow first; especially the Mrs. Finbow who wears slinky designer dresses and gets invited to film premieres."

He tried to keep his disappointment hidden. "Okay, but let's not leave it too long, eh? We're not getting any younger."

"Speak for yourself!" Kay thumped him on the chest. "I'm only thirty four!"

"And I'm nearly forty" John sighed. "Some people are grandparents by then. I'm already going a bit grey, for Pete's sake."

She disentangled her arms, and without replying turned back rather too quickly to the packing, and John knew he had pushed the issue a little too far. However, his wife's reluctance to give up her PA post to that Timothy Burns-Williams twat and become a mother was somehow unsettling; *didn't all women want babies*?

***

For the first time in his life he did not have to worry about receiving the removal company's invoice, although he mused on whether they had counted up the number of bedrooms and added on another thousand pounds. Money was dripping through his fingers like water, but with every subsequent TV series he wrote, copious amounts of fifty pound notes were appearing on the tree for picking. He was on a roll, and life was good. He knew it would be even better when Kay decided to stop taking that little pill …

His footsteps echoed on bare floorboards that second morning after Kay had left for work in the nearby village of Brackenrye. He knew he should be unpacking boxes or settling down to work in his new study, but he could almost hear the house demanding that he visit each room to introduce himself.

John decided to start on the large open-plan fourth floor level. He assumed part of it had once been a nursery and schoolroom, as there were remnants of a worm-infested gate guarding past generations from tumbling down the main staircase. He'd noticed a succession of Victorian and Edwardian clergymen on the deeds, and imagined them in the bosom of their families, each one with a wife and at least ten children apiece. The nursery was empty, but the bedrooms for a nanny and governess still had some old carpet down and ghastly flock wallpaper, some of it peeling in long strips where perhaps a child from long ago had decided that they didn't like it either.

The children's bathroom next to the nursery looked as though it had not been updated since the 1950s at least, and John couldn't wait to get the decorating team in. His babies' nursery would be state-of-the-art, with enough painted murals and hanging mobiles to hopefully augment their already higher than average IQ. No governess for them, as only Eton or Harrow would do.

He watched a finger of sunshine illuminate some dust motes in his line of vision before descending to the third floor, noticing as he did so some lighter squares and rectangles on the striped wallpaper where perhaps children's paintings had hung. Eight empty bedrooms and three bathrooms led off from a galleried landing. He opened the doors and peeped into each one, hardly able to believe that his own creative talents had led him so far away from the council estate he had grown up on and from where his seventy-five-year-old mother was still determined to spend her last days.

He looked over the balcony towards their own bedroom and bathroom sequestered away on a kind of mezzanine floor below, next to his study. He gave a wry smile, knowing he would be running up and down the stairs every night to check on his eight children whilst Kay slept the sleep of the unconcerned.

Walking around the ground floor level he basked in the sight of four spacious reception rooms, each one with panoramic views of the extensive grounds. He let his eyes travel over the kitchen, dining room, downstairs cloakroom, and finally the large entrance hall complete with original black and white tiles, swiftly coming to the conclusion that the house needed children, many children, to fill it. He took one last glimpse over his shoulder before strolling out of the door.

CHAPTER 2 - February 1867

There's ice on the inside of the windows again. Peggy needs to re-light the fires; it's six thirty and she should have been up by now.

Emily Cuthbertson drew the ribbon of her nightshirt a little tighter around her neck and burrowed underneath the counterpane, sighing with relief when she heard the welcome light tap on the door. "Come in!"

Peggy, more red-faced and flustered than usual, carried a full scuttle of coal and kindling, and headed straight for a mound of white ash in the fireplace, scraping out the grate with practised ease. Kindling in place, she struck a lucifer and turned to Emily. "Sorry I'm a bit late, Miss Emily."

It had been her father, the formidable Reverend Cuthbertson, who had always dealt with recalcitrant servants. But the reverend was no more, and with her mother still prostrate in her room next door with grief, Emily sat up and realised it would probably always now fall to her to keep the staff on their toes. "Don't let it happen again, Peggy."

"No, Miss. I'll just go and get your hot water."

Emily waited until Peggy had left the room, and then sank back on the pillows. Her life was not panning out exactly as she had hoped. She was twenty five, and as far as she was concerned, although the youngest in the family she was already quite the old maid. One by one her seven siblings had married and moved away or abroad, ensuring they were not the last one left at home and thereby duty bound to provide companionship to their ailing parents. Emily felt a frisson of discontent; the chance to marry and have children of her own was passing her by. Her sixty-four-year-old mother could live for another ten or twenty years at least, by which time her own youthful bloom would have all but evaporated in the ravages of time.

A knock on the door signaled the arrival of the hot water jug. It was time to face another day.

***

"How can I eat breakfast, Emily?" Delia Cuthbertson, pale and wan, sat propped up against a mountain of pillows and pushed away her tray. "Your father is dead."

Emily gently nudged it back towards the widow. "It's been three months now. Papa wouldn't have wanted you to stop eating."

"I want to join him." Delia's eyes filled with tears. "There's no point in going on."

With one uncharacteristic angry sweep of Delia's arm, a plate of hot porridge sailed through the air and landed on the floor, accompanied by uncontrollable weeping. Emily sighed as she looked at the glutinous mess on the rug. "I'll go and find Peggy."

The maid was busy sweeping dust from the entrance hall floor out into the garden. Emily enjoyed a brief flashback as she recalled stepping carefully in each diamond-shaped tile as a child to avoid the cracks. When she emerged from her reverie she noticed a man dressed in strange attire, looking over his shoulder at her as he walked out of the front door into the snow.

"Porridge has been spilled onto the rug in Mrs. Delia's room."

"I'll see to it straight away, Miss." Peggy put her broom to one side. "Shall I take the tray away?"

Emily nodded and took a glimpse outside. "Yes, I think so. Peggy...who is that person you've been speaking to? Is he a tradesman?"

She turned back towards the hallway when she received no reply, but Peggy had already disappeared upstairs. Emily, puzzled as to the man's identity, walked out onto the lawn, but the man had seemingly vanished into thin air.

Her mother's sobbing had reached a zenith in front of a captive audience by the time Emily returned. Peggy stoically scrubbed the rag rug, but remained silent while Emily decided to pour some tea into a cup and place it in Delia's shaking hand. "Drink this. It'll make you feel better."

Platitudes she was certain would fall on deaf ears, but she needed to say something to try and lighten the atmosphere. The spinning vortex of misery threatening to devour them all needed to be stopped in its tracks. Delia took a sip and gazed sightlessly at her daughter, her mind in a state of turmoil.

"I'm so alone!"

"Nonsense." Emily plumped up the pillows behind her mother's back. "You have eight grown up children. How can you be alone?"

"But I only see *you*." Emily was tired of the same conversation going around and around but reaching no satisfactory conclusion.

"Because you won't get out of bed and visit them! They all have busy lives. Mama, you read Lionel's letter last week - he'll be moving back soon to take over father's duties, so at least you'll see *him* every day."

There was no reply from her mother. Emily sighed, and for the thousandth time wished her father was still around.

CHAPTER 3

Days followed the same routine in that she would draw and paint as a means of escape, but try to be the good companion that her mother needed her to be. With the arrival of her clergyman brother Lionel bringing an end to the interregnum and with Emily's cajoling and encouragement, Delia had started to raise herself out of bed. With life on a more even keel, Emily decided the time was right to offer a suggestion as she brushed her mother's long silver hair one spring morning in March.

"It would be nice if Beatrice and Alfred could stay for a weekend with the baby. I think I'll write to them. I know you miss Beattie as much as I do."

She took some pins from her mother's hand and twirled a long ringlet around her finger before affixing it next to the others. When the reply came, a small wave of excitement coursed through her body.

"That would be a good idea, I think. Little Amelia must be nearly two years old now."

Emily could hardly wait to get to the task. When Delia was suitably dressed and engrossed in *The Times*, she opened her father's bureau and selected some notepaper and a matching envelope. As she wrote she imagined her eldest sister ensconced in marital bliss in Lamburn, only six miles from Brackenrye as the crow flew, but now a busy mother and wife to Lamburn's only watch and clockmaker.

With the letter written, she buttoned her boots and fastened her cape securely. It was time to enjoy some fresh air and take a walk to post the invitation. Across the green she spied Lionel, who waved to her as he pinned a notice in the entrance to the church. Miss Routledge cycled towards the schoolroom, where several children were already chasing each other in the playground. Emily walked briskly past the school she had attended for five years and came to a halt outside the post office. A bell above the door tinkled softly as she entered. She smiled at the postmistress and inhaled the familiar sweet aroma of her favourite crystalised fruits and aniseed balls.

"Good morning, Mrs. Edgecombe."

Lucy Edgecombe, large and motherly, returned the smile with one of her own. "It's a fine morning, Miss Emily."

Emily placed her addressed envelope on the counter. "Indeed it is. I need a stamp please, if you would be so kind."

She handed over a penny as the postmistress scrutinised the envelope. "I haven't seen Miss Beatrice for some years."

Emily ignored a stab of irritation and decided to be as affable and charming as Lionel. "Mama would like them all to pay a visit."

"I hope she comes to see me if she does." Lucy took the penny and affixed a stamp to the envelope. "I'll pop this in the sack for you."

"Thank you." Emily gave a little nod. "Good day for now."

She wanted her burst of freedom to last a while longer. It had been quite some time since she had been inside a church, and Lionel had always been her favourite brother.

There was a cool essence of musk or suchlike as she opened the church's heavy oak door. A serene stillness had settled over the pews, their ends still draped in cream organza ribbons from a recent wedding. Emily walked slowly up the aisle, wondering whether one day she might undertake the same walk as a radiant bride. Lionel was seated in the vestry, scribbling frantically in a notebook.

"Emily! How good it is to see you here!" He stood up. "I was just finishing Sunday's sermon."

She shrugged. "I don't know why I came in really. Perhaps I'm getting religious after all these years."

"Each in his own time." Lionel smiled. "I've always had hope that you'd turn to God eventually."

Emily shook her head. "Don't bet on it. God doesn't seem to like me much, I think. Perhaps it's because I don't go to church every Sunday?"

She wanted to hug her brother. He was so earnest and sure that somewhere just out of sight his God was beaming down benignly.

"God loves you, Emily. He has a plan for you. You just have to find Him when you're ready."

"Yes, my plan is obviously to listen to Mama complaining for the rest of my life." Emily laughed, but inside she felt like crying. "Like I said, your God doesn't seem to be doing me many favours."

She did not turn away as Lionel took her hand in his. "Your chance will come when you least expect it. You know my friend Wilkie – I've told him about your paintings. He's writing a book that needs some illustrations."

Affecting a shrill laugh, Emily let go of her brother's hand and walked towards the vestry door. "Don't get carried away with your God and be late for dinner. It'll make Mama cross."

"Look for Him." Lionel gave her a small wave. "And you will find Him."

She thought of his words that night as she donned her nightshirt and got into bed. As she closed her eyes, she wondered where Lionel's supposed God of Love was hiding.

CHAPTER 4

John could almost hear the design team rubbing their hands with glee at the expense of the task in front of them... to work with Kay on refurbishing the glut of empty rooms. He was happy to leave it all to them with one exception – his study. He wasn't sure what the 7ft by 8ft room had been used for in the past, but now it was *his* and his alone. He wanted his handiwork spread all over that study like a rash; plain plastered walls painted in duck-egg blue to show off his certificates and trophies to start with. Then would come the matching vertical blinds he could angle to follow the sun, a dark shaggy carpet averse to showing any dirt, a huge Victorian desk with hopefully a secret drawer or two, and a long Chesterfield taking up one wall where he could imitate Wordsworth in vacant mood.

Simon, his agent, was working on his first million and sending ever-increasing emails. However, John knew he could never settle until his writing area was *just so*. This was why he found himself up a ladder painting the high ceiling instead of starting Series Two of *Love's Tangled Web*.

"Percy reckons yellow crushed velvet curtains in our bedroom would set off the grey carpet *beautifully*."

He laughed as Kay stood in the doorway, hand on hip, in perfect imitation of Percival Ye Myint, the unusual-looking interior designer from un-exotic Hackney Wick.

"Is that his real name?" John slapped on a liberal coating of emulsion. "Anyway...I'm leaving it all to you. Just don't send him in here."

"So this is where it's all going to be happening?" Kay walked towards the ladder and ran her hand up one leg of his trousers. "Will Ethan finally give Annie one?"

John shook his leg free and prepared to flick the paintbrush in his wife's direction.

"You'll have to wait and see. Will you stop that? I'll fall off the bloody ladder in a minute."

"I'm out of this man-cave!" Kay retreated backwards, her eyes following the paintbrush. "I'm running off with Percy."

***

He stepped down off the ladder, pleased with the outcome. The plasterer had taken out all the lumps and bumps in the walls, and they were now painted just the shade of pale blue that Percy disapproved of. John folded up a dust sheet covering the Axminster and prized Chesterfield, and lifted up the sash window to open it fully, taking care not to leave his fingerprints in the still-wet paint. Rays of afternoon sun warmed his face and to his great surprise illuminated transparent contours of a young woman wearing a kind of lacy neck to ankle smock lying prone on the Chesterfield when he swung back into the room. John blinked twice to ensure his imagination was not playing tricks. Sure enough the woman, unaware and fading slightly on his prized sofa as he watched incredulously, slumbered gently on.

"Fuck-a-doodle-do!" He whistled softly through his teeth and stuck his head out of the door. "Kay! Come and have a look at this!"

Deciding not to call again on hearing his wife in conversation with Percy on the top floor, he gently pulled the door to and studied the countenance before him in repose. It was a young face, no more than twenty four or twenty five. A dark brown plait of hair contrasted with the pristine white smock, falling over one shoulder. Black lashes fluttered against a pale, somewhat wan and sunless skin. A thin, noble nose and full red lips completed the most bizarre sight that John had ever seen in his life.

Footsteps sounded on the bare boards of the mezzanine corridor, and the door flew open. John turned towards Kay, still with his mouth open in astonishment and with one finger pointing at the Chesterfield. Kay shrugged.

"Did you call?" She followed the direction of his finger. "So? It's a Chesterfield! Fancy a quick one on it then?"

John twisted around in alarm as Kay took a running jump towards the sofa and landed square on top of its three squashy cushions, flipping quickly over to lie seductively with a shapely leg draped up along its back. The woman in white, whoever she was, could no longer be seen.

"Well? What are you waiting for?" Kay laughed and undid another button on her blouse. "I haven't got all day!"

John managed a nearly normal chuckle.

"Steady on, Percy's still prowling about. Do your button up."

"Oh God, I left him in the top bathroom when I heard you call. He has a friend who can get us a good deal on one of those long Victorian gentleman's baths with the claw feet." Kay leapt up from the sofa. "He's probably more likely to be looking at your chest than mine, anyway."

"Who, the friend?" John, bewildered, checked the Chesterfield for any sign of the woman wearing what he supposed must have been a nightdress. "Or Percy?"

"I'll meet you on the sofa later." She gave him a brief kiss. "Tie a knot in it for now."

As his wife ran back upstairs, John sank down onto his office chair and gazed long and hard at where the woman had lain. He had a thumping headache. He rubbed his eyes, wondering whether he had inhaled too many fumes from the gloss paint. He swiveled around in the chair, folded his arms on the desk in front of him, and momentarily laid down his aching head.

A ten minute power nap eased his symptoms somewhat. Coming to with a start, he remembered the vision he had seen and swung around in the chair.

There she was again...as white as her nightshirt but definitely breathing.

John, heart thumping, crept over to the woman and touched a couple of the cool, soft fingers on her left hand with his own. Her lashes fluttered, her body solidified, and he found himself looking into two eyes of a rather unusual cobalt blue. A voice, rather shaky, whispered a question as their owner looked down at her nightshirt in horror. "Where am I?"

John bit the side of his mouth to confirm he wasn't still asleep and dreaming. "You're in my study."

The disbelieving woman was close to tears. "But how did I get here? Did I walk in my sleep? Who are *you*?"

Her form began to fade. John screwed up his eyes and then opened them again in disbelief; she had become translucent. He touched her hand, and her body reassembled as the energy flowed between them. He kept hold of her fingers.

"I'm John Finbow, the owner of this house. What's your name? What year were you born?"

Emily's voice shook as she got to her feet.

"Emily Cuthbertson. I was born January the twenty eighth in the year of our Lord eighteen and forty-two."

Warmth from her hand spread into his own as John recalled a quick perusal of the deeds and several generations of Cuthbertsons.

"And I was born September the fifth nineteen seventy-seven."

He looked at her features for the expression of surprise, which arrived with some alacrity.

"But that cannot be! Queen Victoria is still on the throne! How can she still be queen in nineteen seventy-seven?"

He wanted to wipe away a tear that ran down her cheek. "It's nearly forty years on from that. "John shook his head. "If I remember rightly, Victoria died a hundred and sixteen years' ago."

The woman stared at him open-mouthed, and the door flew open. John instinctively let go of Emily's hand on seeing Kay's eyes darting about the room.

"Who are you speaking to?"

Men in white coats with jackets that fasten at the back were never far from his mind.

"I'm going over a scene I'm writing. It's better if I talk it through."

"Oh." Kay, mollified, shot him a smile. "Do you want me to help?"

"I'm done now." John took a quick glimpse to his right. "Let's go and talk claw baths with Percy."

CHAPTER 5

March winds rattled the sash window, and Emily, lying under the counterpane in a state of sleeplessness, stared at the ceiling. On the ground floor she could hear Peggy scraping out the parlour grate. Before long the birds would start their morning chorus, Lionel's voice would rumble up through the floorboards as he talked pleasantries with Peggy, and it would be time to attend to her mother's wants and needs for the rest of the day. She thought back to what had happened during the night, and knew she had not been asleep when she met the man who had not yet been born.

She liked the way his salt-and-pepper hair was cropped at the back of his head but left longer on the top. She had seen him before, walking out of the front door into the garden. The clothes were the same; trousers of a kind of blue cotton twill, and a crisp white shirt with knife-edge creases in the sleeves that only a wife would be able to iron in.

Was he married? Emily remembered kindly grey eyes and heat from his hand warming her body. She decided to open up her long-abandoned watercolour set during afternoon nap time, and try to capture his likeness.

***

She could tell that Beattie was in that interesting condition again as she stepped down from the carriage holding Amelia. She recalled arranging a vase of flowers in one of the guest bedrooms while being shocked by William Dugdale's literature on display, and tried hard not to think of her sister and Alfred locked in the kind of marital bliss she would never experience. She took her little niece from Beattie and gave her a kiss. The toddler giggled as Emily placed her carefully back down on the ground and ruffled her hair. "It's so lovely to see you all!"

Alfred waved with one hand and held on to the horse's reins with the other. "I'll take Rubin to the livery stable."

Emily embraced her sister, noticing the first tinges of grey in Beattie's dark curls, which were scraped back into a sensible but practical bun. "Mama's so looking forward to seeing you!"

Beattie stepped back and looked at Emily questioningly. "Is she still bedridden?"

"Some of the time." Emily nodded. "Although she does get up quite a lot now."

Beattie smiled. "Good. Life has to go on, with or without Papa."

And it obviously has for you. Emily wondered if she should make reference to her sister's bulging belly, still visible despite voluminous skirts, but decided against it. She held Amelia's hand and linked her other arm through Beattie's as they strolled towards the front door.

"Lionel moved the beds around, so you and Alfred can have your old room. There's a cot in there too, for Amelia."

"We don't mind where we sleep. It's only for the weekend."

Emily felt a sting of disappointment; by Sunday evening they would be gone again. However, she decided not to think about the emptiness their departure would bring. She stepped lightly into the rectory with Beattie, who embraced a smiling Delia in the hallway.

"Mother!" Beattie feigned surprise. "Lovely to see you up and about!"

Delia appeared pleased at the embrace, and afterwards stooped to embrace her granddaughter, also ignoring Beattie's advanced pregnancy.

"Emily told me you would all be coming today. How's little Amelia?"

"Sleeping better at night now. We're not so tired all the time."

"The Lord is merciful."

"No." Beattie shook her head. "Amelia is."

***

Soon after luncheon she was surprised to find Beattie barging into her room just like she always used to do.

"I've put Amelia down for a nap. Mama is resting, and Alfred is talking to Lionel. What are you painting?"

Emily moved her left arm across the picture, but she was not quick enough. Beattie had seen all.

"Who's he?"

"His name is John Finbow." Emily blushed, and her heart beat a little faster. "Don't say anything to Mama."

Beattie lifted up the likeness and made an approving grunt. "Nice hair. Is he your beau? He's dressed a little strangely. No hat!"

Emily shook her head, but was eager to converse about her experience. "He comes to the house sometimes."

"A tradesman?" Beattie looked questioningly at Emily.

"Not exactly..." Emily sighed. "I see him when I'm asleep. But he won't be born for another hundred years or so. His birth year is nineteen seventy-seven."

A perplexed frown crossed Beattie's forehead. "Are you sickening for something?"

"Not at all." Emily smiled at her sister. "He's the man of my dreams."

Amelia gave a cry, causing Beattie to make for the door.

"I'll be back presently to find out more."

She listened to her sister's footsteps ascending to the next floor, and then retrieved her paintbrush. John's grey eyes bored into hers from their two-dimensional state, born into a world she would never be part of. She wiped away a tear and yearned for the caress of night time.

CHAPTER 6

Lying in post-coital bliss with Kay's head on his shoulder and one of her legs draped over his thighs, John gave his wife a contented squeeze and decided to broach the forbidden subject one more time.

"I love you. You'd make a wonderful mother."

He thought he heard the faintest snort of disapproval emanating from the depths of his chest hair.

"I don't think so." Kay lifted herself up on one elbow. "John, you know how I feel about children. I love you too, but I'm not maternal. To be honest, I don't think I really want a baby at all."

His disappointment was overwhelming. To have to go through life with no sons or daughters to nurture was more than he could bear. He closed his eyes lest Kay could see a river of tears forming. His voice sounded shaky when he eventually spoke.

"That's not what you said when we got together."

He felt her head flop back down upon his shoulder.

"I know. It's just that I've had a few years to think about it, and ... I'm happy with the life we have. I'm so sorry."

Anger was threatening to put words in his mouth that he would later regret. He sat up, swung his legs over the side of the bed, and reached for his dressing gown.

"I'm just going to make a cup of tea. Want one?"

"No thanks." Kay yawned. "I'm sleepy."

He padded down to the kitchen, switched on the kettle and punched the wall; the stinging pain in his hand deflated his anger somewhat. Blowing on his knuckles, he took a cold beer out of the fridge and flicked the kettle off before returning upstairs. Light snoring came from the direction of the bedroom. He wandered into his study, took a gulp of beer, sat down at his desk and sighed. The reflection on his monitor picked out a familiar supine figure upon the Chesterfield.

John swung the chair around and sprang up. He reached for Emily's hand, and her transparent form solidified before his eyes.

"Hello Emily." He chuckled and kept hold of her fingers. "My wife thinks I've started talking to myself."

Her cobalt eyes blinked in recognition, and with a whisper of a smile she sat up. "My sister likes your hair."

"Eh?" John looked around. "Where is she?"

"I painted your likeness. She looked at that."

John's anger had been replaced with an altogether more pleasurable sensation. "Can I see it?"

Emily pointed with her free hand. "Your desk is where my bureau stands. Have a look on that thing behind you."

An accurate replica of his features rested on top of his computer keyboard. John attempted to pick up the picture, laughing as it dissolved through his hands. "You're a very talented artist."

"I might have the chance to illustrate an epistolary novel, being written by my brother's friend Wilkie Collins."

John's surprise was genuine. "Really? Is it called *The Moonstone*?"

Emily got to her feet and pointed with her free hand." "I don't know. He hasn't finished it yet. What *is* that contraption?"

John followed her line of direction. "It's a computer – like a typewriter but better. I type my novels on it."

"I've read about the new-fangled typewriters." Emily replied. "Mama won't have one in the house. So you're a writer?"

"I write screenplays for TV and film." John nodded, but then realised why Emily's expression remained blank. "Sorry, I'm a playwright."

"We both create." Emily smiled. "You with words and myself with pictures, but so far my paintings are just a way to pass the time."

John could not help but ask the question that begged an answer. "When did you die?"

Her reply shocked him to the core. "I'm not dead!" Emily's features took on an air of indignation. "It's eighteen and sixty-seven and I'm twenty-five years' old! I'm too young to die! Look around you – you're in my bedchamber *and* wearing only a dressing gown! If Mama knew you were here she would call the police!"

Her fingers felt warm and solid. John gazed past Emily to the Chesterfield, which had changed to a narrow iron bedstead complete with mattress, pristine bedlinen, and topped with an obvious hand-quilted cover. Embers of an earlier fire burned in the grate. Watercolour paints and a sketchbook were laid out on the fold-down lid of a teak bureau. A jug and bowl stood on a washstand next to the bed. A home-made multi-coloured rag rug covered up polished floorboards in the center of the room.

John's head spun, causing him to utter the first words that came into his head.

"W.T.F dot com!"

"Pardon?" Emily looked at him blankly. "I don't understand what you're saying. Sit down on the bed – you're looking a little pale."

He let go of her fingers and sank down onto the quilt. When Kay burst through the door the next morning and ran to sit beside him, he rose up with a start and realised he had spent the entire night asleep on the sofa.

"Sorry about last night." Kay hit her forehead with the palm of her hand. "But there isn't any other way of breaking it to you gently. But I *do* love you – very much. Will you come back to bed tonight? *Please* don't be mad at me."

John rubbed his eyes.

"I made a cup of tea and sat down to drink it, but must have dozed off."

"Forgive me?" Kay slipped her arms around his middle. "I *have* thought long and hard about this."

He sighed and leaned his head against hers.

"I know you have. I have to admit it's a great disappointment."
Kay's arms tightened around him.

"But we'll still stay together, yeah?"

"Of course." John nodded. "We're married, aren't we?"

He wondered if he'd made the biggest mistake of his life

CHAPTER 7

She found herself making excuses during the day to sneak into her room, in order to unlock the bureau's secret drawer and gaze at her new friend's likeness. She knew Beattie was desperate to discover the man's identity, but she could tell her no more than she already knew. In her half-world of dreams, she remained unsure as to whether John Finbow even existed at all.

Her sister's inquisitiveness came to a head on the Sunday afternoon as they sat together in the parlour. Emily, unprepared, was embarrassed and affronted beyond belief at Beattie's indelicacy.

"Emily has a beau. Did you know that, Mother?"

Delia's face assumed an expression of horror, as Emily blushed and shook her head. "It was a dream. Beattie's made a mistake."

Lionel shot Beattie a disapproving look. "If Emily does have a beau, then I'm sure she'll tell us in her own time."

"Who will look after me if Emily marries?" Delia wailed. "I'll be here all alone!"

Emily stood up and pushed her chair back, ignoring Beattie's crestfallen features."

"Lionel is here, and although the other boys are abroad, I'm sure Beattie, Eliza and Catherine will all visit as much as they can. Alfred, it was nice to see you and Amelia, but please can you take Beattie home after tea."

In high dudgeon, Emily sailed past her sister and fled upstairs to her room, but an inevitable tentative knock could be heard after a low rumble of voices had died down. Emily locked the secret drawer, laid down on the bed and closed her eyes.

"Come in."

The door opened slowly.

"So sorry." Beattie's voice whispered. "I've just popped in to say goodbye."

Emily kept her eyes shut.

"Goodbye."

"I didn't mean to pry." Beattie whispered. "Forgive me?"

Emily opened her eyes, stared at her sister, and then propped herself up on one elbow.

"Why did you act so thoughtlessly?"

"I don't know." Beattie shrugged. "My brain is all over the place at the moment. I blame it on my condition."

"I want no word of this to go to the rest of the family." Emily flopped back down again. "You are forgiven. Now go."

***

His computer overshadowed the various hues of her watercolour set and there he was, waiting for her again, just like before. Emily smiled.

"Hello John." She sat up on the sofa and looked down. "At least I'm wearing my day clothes this time."

She took his outstretched hand, warming up as he spoke in the soft timbre she had come to admire.

"Because it's only five o'clock."

"Yes." She nodded. "I was horrible to Beattie though. Oh, how I wish Father was still alive."

She enjoyed the sensation of him caressing the back of her hand. "Who's Beattie?"

"My sister." Emily looked up shyly before continuing. "I was hoping I'd see you again."

"Me too." Both of her hands were now in his, and she gazed unashamedly at his features, as though memorising each curve for future reference.

"Do you know, you're standing here as solid as I am!"

She laughed. "Why wouldn't I be? I'm not a ghost!"

She saw his face take on a more serious expression. "Emily, where is your father buried?"

She tried to follow his line of thinking, but could only wonder at the reason behind his question.

"Why, in the village churchyard of course. He was the reverend here for many years. Follow me and I'll show you."

***

Bracken, nettles, spring crocuses and snowdrops fought each other for pride of place on top of the moss-covered grave. Emily, still holding John's hand, led him to the stone.

"Here's Father's resting place. Why do you want to see it? It looks more overgrown than I remember though."

She was surprised to see him searching nearby.

"Not particularly *that* one." He announced enigmatically. "*This* one!"

She took a closer look and felt slightly dizzy.

Emily Maud Cuthbertson.

Born January 28th, 1842

Died April 12th, 1868

Rest in the arms of the Lord.

"That's my name! It cannot be!" She shook her head emphatically. "I'm going to die *next year?*"

She felt a rising panic that she could not control, and burst into a flood of tears. Straight away his arms enfolded her.

"Hush. I had to show it to you, so that you realise what's happening. This is two thousand and seventeen. You've already died, but somehow the energy between us causes you to stay alive in my world. I'm so glad that you do though."

She felt more alive than she had ever been in her own time. The nearness to his body was causing the most unladylike thoughts to rush through her mind. She stood wrapped in his embrace on top of her grave and lifted her face towards his.

"Never let go of me."

His kiss was soft and gentle, sweeping away her panic in an instant.

***

Kay's voice brought him back from a far-away place where a creased percale sheet had been all that had stood between their nakedness and the early summer morning.

"Why are you still crashing on the settee? Come on, John. This has gone on for far too long now."

He felt a keen sense of guilt for the adultery, but figured he'd get away with it, just as long as he didn't talk in his sleep.

"Sorry." He jumped up, yawning. "I couldn't relax and came down to watch a film. It wasn't anything to do with you."

Indeed, he had found solace in a body long since dead, a body who had willingly opened up like a flower despite the strict moral codes and etiquette of her time; a body very much alive who yearned for his touch.

"Do you still love me?"

Her anguish at the stark question called for only one answer, which to his surprise now seemed impossible to give.

"Don't be silly. Come here." His arms enfolded Kay's petite frame. He rubbed his nose in the top of her hair and enjoyed the familiar scent of apple shampoo. "It won't happen again."

***

He sought her out during the day instead, when he should have been writing and when Kay was out of the house. His screenplay took a back seat to the heights of passion he could achieve with Emily. He would summon his soul mate, the other half of him, and she would arrive, eager and willing.

CHAPTER 8

What if he was correct? Could she really be dead? After much thought Emily admitted to herself that she never felt hungry, and tried without success to remember the last time she had eaten or drank anything. For confirmation of her demise she realised that her monthly curse had disappeared some time ago, and sadly concluded that dead women did not bleed.

However, when autumn leaves crackled and withered, her belly began to swell with his child. The baby kicked and tumbled about, which proved to her undoubtedly that she was a healthy young woman. Distraught at the scandal and possible ostracization by the villagers, and that Lionel might even lose his esteem and livelihood, Emily decided to say nothing of the pregnancy to her mother, not even to Peggy. She wore looser clothing and was grateful for the onset of winter and the chance to don a few more outer layers.

By Christmastime she could not hide her condition anymore when standing naked before the man she adored.

"John, I am with child; *your* child."

The simple look of joy on her lover's face was worth any amount of possible rejection by the good ladies of the church. She welcomed the touch of his hands on her taut abdomen.

"You're having a baby?"

"*Our* baby. So, you see- there's no way I can be dead!"

She could identify with his puzzled expression – she didn't understand it either. Nevertheless, the baby was a gift from the God she thought had abandoned her. She laid her head on his shoulder and sighed.

"I am so happy."

His reply was not what she wanted to hear. "You will have to see a doctor so that he can examine you and aid with the birth."

"No." She shook her head. "*You* can help me bring our child into the world when my time comes. Nobody must know. Keep me here in your world. I don't want to go back."

She felt his arms encircle her, keeping her and their baby from harm. "I wish I could, Emily. I really wish I could."

***

"You're gaining weight."

Despite the inner turbulence at her mother's remark, Emily kept her expression noncommittal as her brain scrambled for a reply.

"I've eaten a lot over the Christmas period."

"Exercise restraint." Lionel looked at her over his horn-rimmed glasses. "The gates of heaven are narrow."

She realised the idea of a pregnant spinster had not even entered their minds. However, whilst wearing her nightshirt she caught Peggy's beady eyes scanning her belly several times. Emily knew that as far as their maid was concerned, the game was up. When Peggy brought a jug of hot water one morning in late January, she steeled herself for the inevitable.

"Are you with child, Miss Emily?"

"Nobody must know." Emily nodded. "Not even Mother."

Peggy sighed. "I've had three children, all grown now. I can help you when your time comes. Just tell me and then go to my cottage when the pains begin – that's day *or* night. A first baby can take many hours to be born."

Emily, relieved, smiled at Peggy. "You're very kind. Thank you. Please don't tell anybody."

"No, Miss Emily, but if I can see, then so can everybody else."

"Only because I'm wearing a thin nightshirt." Emily climbed out of bed. "Mother just thinks I'm fat."

Peggy chuckled. "What will you do about the baby?"

Emily had thought long and hard regarding this conundrum. "The baby's father will look after it, and I will visit when I can."

"Yes, Miss." Peggy looked unconvinced. "I'll carry on now with my duties."

***

By early April it had become unseasonably warm. Emily awoke at midnight on the twelfth day of the month; not on John's settee as she had hoped, but to a soaking wet bed and griping pains across her abdomen. With no thought of her mother's possible reaction to her disappearance, she threw on her boots and outer clothing over her nightshirt and, in some distress, made her way through the darkened village to Peggy's cottage.

"Peggy!" She rapped loudly on the door with her knuckles. "It's Emily!"

After an agonising wait, flickering candlelight could be seen through the window as Peggy made her way to the door.

"Miss Emily!" Peggy's face was a picture of consternation. "Come in!"

Bent over double with another pain, Emily, frightened at a lack of control over her body, stumbled inside and held onto the back of a chair for support.

"The baby's coming!"

"It'll be ages yet." Peggy replied. "I'll stoke up the fire if you're cold. You make yourself as comfortable as you can. The pains are natural. Go with them and don't fight it."

"I'm not cold! I want John!" Emily cried. "I need him here!"

Peggy, curiosity as far under wraps as she could keep it, ventured a few words. "Where does he live, Miss? I could go and ask him to come."

"He's at the rectory with me!" Emily screwed up her eyes in pain. "He lives in the twentieth century! He won't come now because I'm not lying in bed!"

Agitated beyond belief, she laid down on the horsehair sofa and felt the back of Peggy's hand against her forehead and heard a gentle whisper in her ear. "I ought to call the doctor."

Emily shook her head. "I'm not delirious! Truly I'm not."

"Yes, Miss Emily." Peggy whispered. "Let's get those outer things off and then we can see what's going on."

***

From faraway she could hear a familiar voice as she drifted in and out of consciousness.

"The doctor's here, Miss Emily. I had to call him because only the baby's shoulder is out, and you're losing a lot of blood."

She didn't really care. All she wanted was somebody to stop the grinding pains. She smelled the rubber of a mask as it was placed over her nose and mouth. Doctor Heslop, whom she realised would doubtless go straight to her mother, spoke in an authoritative tone.

"Chloroform, Miss Cuthbertson. I'm going to try and get the baby out."

She floated up to the ceiling with her son and gazed dispassionately at the doctor, who after some manipulations of her body shook his head. Peggy let out a shriek. Emily began to run towards John, waiting patiently for her beyond the fog.

***

John started the Fireblade's engine and thought of his son, the little boy that Kay would never know, the son who called him 'Daddy'. Robbie's delightful laugh filled the house every afternoon before Kay returned from work. The wheels of his red tricycle could be heard racing in and out of all the eight spare bedrooms, with his mother close on his heels to ensure he came to no harm. They visited whenever he summoned them, and he could see that the boy was the very image of him. Life was good. As he sat astride the machine that his son would never learn to ride, he concluded that if you wanted something badly enough, then sooner or later you would find a way to obtain it.

You can read more about John, Emily and Kay in the 43,000 word novella, *Finding David*, by Stevie Turner.

Author Jeff Bowles

https://www.goodreads.com/author/show/
3895499.Jeff_Bowles?from_search=true[1]

Jeff Bowles is a science fiction and horror writer from the mountains of Colorado. The best of his outrageous and imaginative short stories are collected in **Godling and Other Paint Stories, Fear and Loathing in Las Cruces,** *and* **Brave New Multiverse.** *He has published work in magazines and anthologies like PodCastle, Tales from the Canyons of the Damned, the Threepenny Review, and Dark Moon Digest. Jeff earned his Master of Fine Arts degree in creative writing at Western State Colorado University. He currently lives in the high-altitude Pikes Peak region, where he dreams strange dreams and spends far too much time under the stars. Jeff's new novel,* **God's Body: Book One – The Fall,** *is available now!*

---

1. https://www.goodreads.com/author/show/

3895499.Jeff_Bowles?from_search=true&fbclid=IwAR2ReeyOIVb7U-eIRICO6teSn99OSoF-

GUIRf8_31wJ5P1FXAcug-GZiYos

A Peaceful life I've never known

Jeff Bowles

A pair of candles rested on the old leather trunk between Ronnie and Douglass. The room was dark, the air thick with the smell of pungent incense. Ronnie watched as the yellow flames flickered and danced in unison, bending toward Douglass as he took a drag off his cigarette, writhing and peeling away as he exhaled. They cast two shadows of him on the wall, bearded, overweight, fingers running through long, tangled hair. Ronnie found himself entranced by the image, listening vacantly to the dull sound of music and laughter coming from the living room of Douglass's private bungalow.

"I'm not a whole man. That's what they say about me. I'm really only half a man, or maybe even a quarter," Douglass said. "They say my soul will never rest 'til I'm worm food."

"Who says that, Mr. James?" asked Ronnie.

"They, man, them. The press, those worthless teeny-bopper magazines. Hell, my fans have been saying it since '66. But you know that. You're one of 'em."

Ronnie didn't know how to respond to this. He thought back to that night in 1966 when he and his family had gathered around the television to watch Douglass's debut. A shot of fingers flying over a fret board, a cut to The Darklings emblazoned on a kick drum. Then came Douglass's close up, and Ronnie had held his breath. Mad, murderous eyes partially concealed behind thick sunglasses. Ruffled collar, leather jacket, cowboy boots and a sneer. Ronnie had never wanted to be a musician before that night, and he never wanted to be anything else after.

And here was the man himself. Douglass hadn't invited the rest of Ronnie's band to his party, hadn't singled out any of them with a nod and a proposition: I want to write a song with you.

"You know why I picked you?" Douglass asked.

Ronnie shook his head

"*Acta non verba*, man. You got some real fire. Got it like I used to have it. You played like a madman on that stage, like that two-bit dive couldn't contain you."

Ronnie smiled and shrugged. "Where's the rest of your band, Mr. James? Wouldn't you rather write something with them?"

"Call me Doug. 'Douglass' is for the newspapers, and 'Mr. James' is only for people who want my money. You don't want my money, do you Ronnie?"

"No, sir."

"And 'sir' is for the undertaker." He took a final drag off his cigarette then stabbed it out in the ashtray. "You remind me of me, man. I couldn't get enough of this shit either, not until reality set in. Fame is dark as night, man. Pay some bills, Ronnie, have some fun with some people. You're only young once, right?"

Ronnie glanced at his guitar case. "I wouldn't even know where to begin," he lied. Douglass laughed a crackling, whisky-drenched laugh. "Good answer. Only answer a young man in your position should give. Well it's your lucky day, rock star, 'cause I know exactly where to begin."

~*~

"The Indian was dead. I was sure of that much. But I wasn't scared, Ronnie. Nervous, curious maybe. But not scared. I guess I was about eight, maybe nine. I'd gotten out of the house 'cause mom and dad were fighting again. It was mid-August, southern Arizona, Fort Huachuca area. Hot as shit, you know? Bike riding on a dusty back road, I spotted a real nasty car wreck off in the ditch. Smoke and dust rose into the air, partially obscuring the old truck's twisted frame. Headlights gleamed in the haze, little dust devils spinning and pirouetting like Indian gals at a pow-wow.

I hopped off my bike, let it fall to the dirt. There was nobody else around, just me, the dead Indian and his pal. They sat against the truck, both of them bloodied up. Damn thing had flipped right over. This sort of shit happens all the time out on those desert roads. People get going too fast, hit a rough patch, and then *wham-o*!

His pal sensed my presence. His whole face was tore up, especially the eyes. They were bloody and swollen and closed tight. But he still knew I was there.

"How are you, son?" he called to me.

I didn't answer. Didn't think I should.

"Do you see my friend here?" he asked, smiling, his teeth all stained and caked with dust and blood. "He's not gone. His spirit remains. Come closer, son. He was never a man at peace. Always, there was war in his heart."

I can't tell you why, but without hesitation, I climbed down into the ditch. Could smell the gasoline dripping from the tailpipe. The old Indian told me to kneel in front of him, and I did that, too.

"Now, I want you to touch his chest," he said.

I reached out and felt his blood-soaked shirt, sticky pools in folds of fabric. My face so close to his, I kept thinking he'd open his eyes. Not like the whole thing had been a joke. Not like pulling my leg. I thought I could feel his spirit rattling away in there, slumbering and snoring, ready to wake up and make that old Indian dance.

"I'm going to sing a *hataal*, now," said his pal, "and I want you to sing it with me. It's his hataal. My friend never valued life. It is right that we sing it for him now."

He opened his mouth, and the most beautiful, mournful sound escaped him. I sang with him, following along as though I knew the song by heart. Pretty soon, I started feeling sick, like I was gonna throw up. My head hurt. It was like my mind had opened right up, like a breeze running through my screen door, filling my house and whipping up a storm right there in my living room. My hands quivered, my bones stung, my fingertips received a kind of electricity from his chest...Let me tell you something, Ronnie. That dead Indian? His spirit left his body and came into mine. He's still here. He's the one who makes me so crazy."

~*~

Ronnie stared at Douglass, spellbound by the intensity in his eyes. No words passed between them. Neither of them moved, and neither blinked. The only sound to fill the silence was the dull throb of music in Douglass's living room. Suddenly, the rock star's eyes widened. His face twisted and his mouth strained in a silent scream. He pointed at Ronnie.

"Boo," he said, then the rock star let out the most raucous, wild peel of laughter Ronnie had ever heard. He doubled over, laughing harder, nearly falling off the couch.

Ronnie watched in disbelief.

"Should've seen your face, man," Douglass gasped. "You get it, man? People believe all sorts of crazy shit about me." He wiped a tear from his cheek. "And the best part is, I let 'em. It's my favorite joke of all."

The rock star's laughing subsided, but Ronnie felt like a fool. He nodded at Douglass, fully realizing he hadn't been in on that joke.

"So come on, man," Douglass said. "Let's write a song now. Something with all that stuff they want to hear. Verse number one, Dougie and the dead Injun."

Ronnie nodded. He reached for his guitar case and undid the latches. Inside rested one of his most prized possessions, a firebrand 1934 Martin R-1 acoustic. He lifted it carefully and set the body on his leg.

Douglass whistled. "She's a beaut, Ron. Check out that flare."

Ronnie smiled politely and set his fingers to the fret board.

"All right, Mr. James," he said, "you tell me what to play, and I'll make it swing. How do you want it to sound?"

"Sound? Hey, man, I'm just the poet. I leave it to those other guys to do all the musical stuff. You tell me what it should sound like, man. I mean, you're the virtuoso."

The door burst open. Loud music, laughter, and harsh light filled the room. A young man and woman stumbled in. The guy was clean-shaven, his hair slicked back, a sloppy grin plastered on his face. The girl hung off his arm, her hand down his pants. She giggled and leered at him with bedroom eyes.

"I'm your girl, right Mickey?" she said.

"Sure, baby. Sure you're my—" The young man came to a dead stop.

Douglass slipped a cigarette into his mouth. "You forget something, Mick?"

"Oh, man. Yeah, man, yeah I did," Mickey said. "Sorry, boss. Using the, umm, using the..." He looked at the girl. "Why didn't you remind me he was using the, umm..."

"The office, Mick," said Douglass. He shook his head at Ronnie.

"Office," the girl intoned, "*offica, officae, officae, officam, offica.*"

Douglass laughed. "What are you guys on?"

"Oh, man," said Mickey. He bit his lip and let out a high-pitched squeal. "I mean, what a question. Like, seriously, what am I on?"

"Ronnie, meet Mickey," Douglass said. "He's my right hand. Watson to my Sherlock. Garfunkel to my Simon. He takes care of things for me, right Mick?"

Mickey nodded. "Watson to your Garfunkel...Watson to your..."

"You need something, Mick?"

"Oh, umm, the cops. The cops will come. They just will. And then ... what do I do about it, boss?"

Douglass laughed. He raised his arm and flexed his bicep. "You shoot 'em all, muscleman! You shoot every last damn one of them."

Mickey let out another high squeal. "Cool, cool, cool. All right, I'll leave you guys to your, um, duties."

He pulled the girl closer and led her from the room.

"Duty," the girl said before the door closed. "*Officium, officii, officio—*"

The music and laughter cut out. Ronnie blinked a few times as his eyes readjusted.

"All right, rock star," said Douglass. "Come on, play me something."

Ronnie ran a hand through his hair. He closed his eyes and took a breath. *I'm not afraid.* No room for fear, not if he wanted to live the dream. His hand dropped to the neck of his guitar, his fingers finding their way to a G chord. He strummed slowly, softly. The G changed to E-minor, then back again to G. He played a few bars and opened his eyes to see Douglass grinning.

"That's it, man. That's it."

Then Douglass sang.

Electric, dead truck and red blood.

Pandemic, dead man, a new drug.

You see him sitting, a soul to share?

Two minds blown out by desert air?

He gave himself, his life, his kind.

He gave and took, one heart, two minds.

Ronnie let the song build, every strum and chord compelling him to play harder. He came to the bridge, the progression mounting upon itself then bursting into a sleek, driving chorus.

"No," said Douglass.

Ronnie pounded the strings. He let the song ride.

"Stop, man. Cut it."

Ronnie paid him no attention.

"Knock that shit off, you useless little fuck," said Douglass.

Ronnie stopped. The star's eyes burned, vicious, homicidal. Ronnie found himself locked into his gaze, a deer in the headlights, a lamb and a buzz saw, an insect about to be crushed.

"You stop when I tell you to stop," said Douglass. "I run the show, get it? I'm top dog."

Ronnie didn't answer. Those eyes of his, the power they held. *Jesus. Saying anything at all could be deadly.*

Douglass' eyes relaxed, his face returning to that calm, slackened, half-drunk expression.

"Sorry, man," he said. "I got problems, you know? Success comes with more problems than you can imagine. No choruses, that's all. I want it clean, just three sets of verses. And then maybe nine or ten other songs just like it, an A and a B side. Like a tone poem or a manifesto. You dig?"

Ronnie cleared his throat, his voice threatening to fail him unless he put some power behind it. "Sounds great, Mr...Doug. Sounds real groovy."

Doug nodded and closed his eyes. "Yeah, that's what I think, too. All right, Ronnie. What do you say? How 'bout some more fodder for the piggies?"

~*~

"I murdered a man, just a couple days ago. Choked him out 'cause I wanted to see blue lips and bulging eyes. Did it in this very room, right where you're sitting now, then I cut off his pinky and put it in my shirt pocket. Sound good? Yeah, thought it might.

He came to our show at the Hollywood Bowl, just one of thousands, but boy did he make an impression. It was a real bad gig, man. We were really off our game. I drank too much, least that's what the papers said. Hell, we weren't even halfway through the third song when shit hit the fan.

Maybe I was slurring my lyrics, maybe I wasn't. But before I know it, these adoring fans of mine, they start hassling me. They cat-call me and boo and all that noise. So I stop singing, and I tell the boys to stop playing, and then when it gets all quiet-like and all those morons out in audience land don't know up from down, I pull the microphone up to my lips and shout, "You're all a bunch of slaves!"

They don't like that, not one bit. They boo even louder.

"Slaves," I say, "peasants, every last miserable one of you. And I am your new master! You won't need no English where you're going. You won't even need no German. I'm talking crucifixion, my friends. I'm talking whips and thorns and nasty-ass Roman centurions dogging you through the streets!"

It wasn't the alcohol, man. I was drunk, but not that drunk. You know who it was? That dead Indian. Most of the time I'm in control, but every so often, I hear them war drums pounding and I do all sorts of crazy shit.

Anyways, this pretty much shuts the show down. They start throwing crap at me, and then a bunch of them rush the stage. The cops come out from the wings and tug on me. Then the kids start tugging me the other way. It's like they all want to rip me to pieces. And then this one guy, this smarmy looking kid with great big telescope eyeglasses, stands right in front of me, sneers at me, and then puts a boot to my gut. I fall to the stage, and he starts kicking the hell out of me.

This goes on forever before the cops realize that, oh yeah, they're supposed to protect me. They wrestle him down and get me offstage, but not before I tell Mickey to get a good clean look at his face.

It was Mickey who paid his bail, and it was Mickey who drove him here to my bungalow. But it was me, yours truly, who choked that SOB and claimed his pinky as a trophy. You dig, Ronnie? So what if the whole thing never happened? You're intrigued. I can tell. They will be, too, those parasitic sycophants who buy my records but think they own me."

~*~

Ronnie hesitated before he played. He watched Douglass fixedly, entranced, suddenly having a hard time remembering what the chords had been. Douglass urged him on. He took a moment to clear his thoughts, then his fingers found their place on the fret board.

He hit the G, slipped to the E-minor, back again to the G. Douglass sang.

Pathetic, rock show, a black hole.

Parasitic, a no-show at the Bowl.

You see me kicked, the pigs just stare.

Kicked to the ground, too much to bear.

But still they work me to the bone.

A peaceful life, I've never known.

Ronnie stopped playing immediately. There was no way he'd allow himself to repeat that chorus. If he'd ever known panic like this, he couldn't remember. Even when he was a kid, and his mom had suffered horribly from her cancer, he'd never seen such malignancy. When Douglass finally spoke, it was like someone had sucked the venom from his veins.

"Yeah, man. I think I like that," he said. "A peaceful life I've never known. It feels right."

He opened his mouth to say more, but instead let it hang open. He focused on a blank spot on the wall, his eyelids seemingly too heavy to keep open. Out the window, down on the freeway, a police siren wailed. Ronnie listened intently, imagining a woman at Douglass's funeral, shrieking, wailing like the siren. Douglass's eyes opened. Ronnie was taken aback to see them full of tears.

"I didn't want it to be this way. I was a good kid. I've done some bad things."

"What do you mean?" Ronnie said.

The door burst open. Mickey didn't stumble through this time. He rushed in, like his legs had found their purpose. The music had stopped in the living room. No one was laughing anymore.

"It's the cops, boss," said Mickey. "They're on their way."

The siren grew louder still. It seemed to Ronnie that two or three more had joined it.

"All right, Mick," said Douglass. His voice remained subdued, his eyes sad.

"Cops?" said Ronnie. "What's going on, Mr. James?"

"Doug, Ronnie. 'Douglass' for the papers, 'Mr. James' for the parasites, 'sir' for the undertaker. And the cops, I guess. They'll call me sir, too."

Ronnie put the guitar down and got to his feet. "Mr. James..."

"Boss, they'll, umm, be here in a couple minutes," said Mickey.

"Sure they will, Mick. Plenty of time. I only have one more verse to write."

~*~

"That old Indian was with me, Ronnie. He was there my first time onstage. I was fifteen years old, way out of my element. I wasn't scared, though. I was a poet back then, a real beat poet, just like Kerouac and Ginsberg and all those other cats. I showed up at the bar that night, and those hicks and desert rats didn't know what to make of me.

There was a band playing, a real buncha' good old boys. I told them I wanted to do some poetry between their sets.

"Poetry?" the drummer said.

"Yes, sir."

He glared at me. "You see these people, son? You think they're interested in the music we make? Hell no. All they're good for is drinking, fighting, and heckling hard-working boys like us."

He snorted and turned to walk away.

I was desperate, Ronnie. I had that fire in me. I really wanted it in those days. This guy was twice my age, twice my size, but before I knew it, my hand was on his shoulder.

"Have you ever been passionate, sir?" I asked.

He sneered. Man, I didn't know if he wanted to kick my ass or just kill me.

"I'm not talking about everyday passion, now. I'm talking about the everlasting kind. Love so rare it comes out of nowhere, a sandstorm, a prairie fire, an act of God Himself. I'm talking about love that only happens once in a lifetime, in two lifetimes, a dozen. A love so rare most people never see it, and if they do, they're numb for the rest of their lives, battered, broken, and spent. More than man and woman, man and creator, man and the universe and all within it.

I'm a poet, sir. I'll be a poet 'til the day I die. That's my passion, sir. What's yours?"

You know who really said those things, don't you? It wasn't me. It couldn't have been. The sneer was frozen on that drummer's face, but I could tell he didn't believe in it anymore. That's what I do, Ronnie. That's what I live for. There is known and there is unknown. I'm somewhere in the middle.

"You got balls, kid," he said.

I got booed off the stage, but so what? I've been booed off so many stages, they all blur together. I'm a wild man, Ronnie. I'm out of control. And I'm sick to my fucking stomach about all of it."

~*~

Ronnie wasn't listening. Douglass sang without him.

Intrinsic, I'm drowning now, my final trip.

Deliberate, won't you join me for a dip?

A desert rat, one heart two souls.

A poet rat, fifteen years old.

Booed off that stage, worked to the bone.

A peaceful life, I've never known.

"And that's it," said Douglass. "Now we just need to sing the whole thing."

Police lights shone through the window. The two candles had burned down completely and were now little more than stiff white pools of wax stuck to the trunk's dark surface.

"What do we do, boss?" said Mickey.

"You know exactly what to do, Mick. Just like we talked about."

Mickey paused. He frowned, raised his shirt, and pulled a large handgun from the waistband of his jeans.

Douglass chuckled. "Mick, Mick, love the enthusiasm, babe. Please don't kill my guests."

Mickey hummed a few bars of some unknown tune then bolted from the office. He screeched at the top of his lungs, something about bullets and cocaine. A single gunshot rang out, followed by screams.

"Not my guests, Mick," Douglass casually called after him, "just the pigs, all right, man?"

Mickey screeched again in response.

Douglass simply shook his head and snorted.

"Mr. James..." Ronnie felt warm all over. "Mr. James..." It was all he could think to say.

"Shut the door, rock star."

Ronnie did so without a thought.

"Have a seat."

He did this, too, with shaking hands.

Douglass pulled out another cigarette. He didn't light it, just held it between two fingers. "It's a Roman thing, you know? Throw a party, invite all your friends, let them watch you off yourself."

"Did you really kill someone?"

Douglass leaned forward. He took a deep breath and scratched his beard. "Well that's a tricky question, Ronnie. To tell you the truth, I'm not sure who did what. A guy lives a life like mine, he deserves a little rest, don't you think? Is it really too much to ask?"

A deep pounding came from the living room. Douglass' guests screamed, but Mickey shrieked for them to stop. Ronnie kept his eyes on the door, waiting for gunfire, more screams, the massacre to come.

"Sing my song with me, Ronnie," said Douglass.

"Now? Mr. James, I don't—"

"It's not a request, rock star."

"Come on, Mr. James. None of this has to happen."

Douglass stood. He crossed to Ronnie, towered over him; he grinned, his eyes bestial and everything malevolent Ronnie had seen before.

"Know what else that old Indian told me?" he said. "A man's hataal forms an eternal bond. Eternal. As in, even after you're fertilizer. 'Cept it ain't eternal, is it? There's always a way out. You always got one more song to sing."

Ronnie lifted his guitar and smashed it into Douglass' side. He leapt to his feet, took two steps toward the door.

Douglass was on top of him. He sunk a fist into his ribs then, with more strength than Ronnie thought him capable of, threw him against a wall. Douglass stood over him, his hand clenched around Ronnie's wrist. He squeezed it 'til Ronnie thought it would break. He bent closer.

"Put your hand on my chest," he said.

"No."

Douglass squeezed until it broke. *Crack*!

Ronnie howled. The star pulled his limp hand to his chest.

"You're gonna' take this Indian off my hands, now, then I'm checking out. You just see if those pigs haul a corpse to jail. C'mon, man, sing with me."

Douglass began the song, and in spite of himself, Ronnie sang with him.

Electric, dead truck and red blood.

Pandemic, dead man, a new drug.

He felt strange, like he might throw up. His head was ready to explode.

He gave himself, his life, his kind.

He gave and took, one heart, two minds.

The pain built, raging, until he was sure it was endless.

You see me kicked, the pigs just stare.

Kicked to the ground, too much to bear.

The pain transformed into a vast, open kind of feeling. Ronnie felt an inflow of energy penetrate his being.

Douglass stopped singing. He chanted, "I'm not afraid, I'm not afraid, I'm not afraid."

Ronnie sang. He could do nothing else. It was electric, a force of nature. Douglass looked faint, his face drained of color. He bent low enough, everything fell from his shirt pocket. A pack of cigarettes, a book of matches, and something else. A white tube, as long as a cigarette but thicker.

Ronnie kept singing, coming now to the final verse.

Booed off that stage, worked to the bone.

A peaceful life I've never—

The LAPD broke down the front door. Swiftly, they swept from the living room into the office. They barked for Ronnie and Douglass to hit the floor. Ronnie stopped singing. Somehow, he could. He fell backwards, a deep knifing pain in his wrist. The police rushed them and placed him in handcuffs. More pain, but Ronnie didn't mind. The officers stood over him. They kept barking; they were doing something with Douglass.

Ronnie let his head roll to the side. He could see into the living room, more police guiding Douglass' party guests from the bungalow. None of them had been hurt, as far as he could tell. And in the far corner, sobbing, his hands wrapped around his knees, sat Mickey. His gun lay uselessly beside him.

Someone jerked Ronnie to his feet.

He stood eye to eye with Douglass.

"Didn't expect to still be here," the rock star said. "I guess that's showbiz, kid."

They led Douglass from the office.

Ronnie watched him go, through the living room, out the bungalow's front door, all the while, belting out a caterwauling rendition of *Thanks for the Memories*.

One of the cops pointed at Ronnie. "I want everyone checked out. You know what we're after, boys."

Ronnie suddenly felt so tired and frayed, like he was only half a man. He swayed, barely staying on his feet. He gave a solemn nod to the nearest officer.

"Can I sit, sir?" he asked.

The guy looked him over and nodded. Ronnie took a step, his foot touching something harder than carpet. He looked down, saw the white tube that had fallen from Douglass' shirt pocket. The police began picking the room clean, kicking over furniture, knocking on walls. Ronnie bent for the tube. *Paper.* Gingerly, handcuffed and with a broken wrist, he managed to unroll it.

A pinky fell out. Severed at the knuckle, perfectly straight, completely grey. Ronnie watched it roll then settle beside the broken shards of his guitar.

"Captain! I found something!" shouted one of the cops. He stood by the trunk, the one that had held the two candles, the lid unlatched and open, its contents visible to everyone in the room.

Ronnie swayed again when he saw what was inside.

Pinkies. At least half a dozen of them. Long ones and short, thick and thin; painted nails, rings, fresh-cut and rotting and some little more than bone. Ronnie heard something elusive, low and soft enough he thought it must have been in his head. He heard the sound of a wailing song, then the beating of a war drum.

He numbly raised the paper to his eyes, read the note scrawled on it:

For you, future rock star, whoever you may be.

For both of you and not one of me.

Best wishes,

Doug

Epilogue

The present is for the living. Death is inevitably tied to the past, but occasionally the living hear whispers from the past. It may be that the veil between realms is thin in spots and easier for those who have crossed over to reach back and touch the present. Or perhaps they are always here, but only make themselves known when they have a purpose. Whatever the explanation, the idea of the two sides intersecting, fascinates us; the idea of the past not being lost to us in the present gives us hope, yet often scares the hell out of us.

I hope you have enjoyed the whispers contained in the stories of this anthology.

Thank You for Reading

Whispers of the Past

If you liked it, please leave a review for the complete anthology, or for any of the individual stories and show your support for the wonderful authors whose stories are featured here.

Spirits of the West

Introduction

In 2019. *WordCrafter Press* ran a paranormal short fiction contest, and *Whispers of the Past* was the resulting anthology, featuring eight stories, from six different authors, including yours truly. That contest was a lot of fun. I got to meet a couple of great authors, who I wasn't previously acquainted with and I got to work with some truly awesome ghost tales.

In fact, it was so much fun that I wanted to do it again, but I didn't want to run the same theme two years in a row, so I decided to change it up a little. As a Colorado history buff, the western genre seems to be my forte, so I decided to combine the two, making the theme for the *2020 WordCrafter Press Short Fiction Contest* western paranormal.

Many of the authors from *Whispers of the Past* also have stories in *Spirits of the West*, because unlike the immediate response for the previous year's paranormal themed contest, response for this contest was hesitant and slow in coming. I had to practically beg authors to write a contest entry. There's something about the western genre that makes many authors shy away. They can create science fiction and fantasy worlds in abounds, but when you ask them to write a story with western flavor, they balk. As a result, we have some very interesting stories in this collection that I'm sure you will find entertaining.

It is interesting to see the different ways a genre is interpreted by different authors, and some of these authors had to think outside the box a little to create entries for this contest. The resulting anthology, *Spirits of the West*, is a diverse collection of tales with western and paranormal connotations. Roberta Eaton Cheadle lives in South Africa and is not very familiar with the history of the American west, so she's given us two South African western paranormal tales to consider, "The Thirstland Journey" and "The Ghost in the Mound". Last year's winning author, Jeff Bowles, provides a story of the spirits of the American Indian, "Wenekia", and Arthur Rosch even provided a science fiction western paranormal tale, "Clouds in the West", which may even tickle your funny bone. Also featured is a western story written by my friend Tom Johnson, who left us in 2018. Western wasn't really his wheelhouse, he was more a pulp and sci-fi guy, but he did have this one short western, "Gunsmoke", and his widow was gracious enough to allow me to include it here. And then there is my story, "Don't Eat the Pickled Eggs", which is... well, you'll see.

I believe in the old adage, "Save the best for last", so I purposely place the winning story entry at the end of the anthology. This year's contest winner is Enid Holden, and she has provided not one, but two western paranormal stories. "Queen of Hearts", a tale with a tough female character and an old west setting, and of course, the winning story, "High Desert Rose".

I hope that you enjoy reading *Spirits of the West* as much as I've enjoyed compiling it. I could tell you about the stories within all day long, but I think it's better if you just read the stories, so without further ado...

Author Kaye Lynne Booth

https://kayelynnebooth.wordpress.com

Kaye Lynne Booth lives, works and plays in the mountains of Colorado. With a dual emphasis M.F.A. in Creative Writing, writing is more than a passion. It's a way of life. She's a multi-genre author, who finds inspiration from the nature around her, and her love of the old west, and other odd and quirky things which might surprise you. She has short stories featured in the following anthologies: *The Collapsar Directive* ("If You're Happy and You Know It"); *Relationship Add Vice* ("The Devil Made Her Do It"); *Nightmareland* ("The Haunting in Carol's Woods"); and *Whispers of the Past* ("The Woman in the Water"). Her western, *Delilah,* and her time travel short, *Last Call,* are both available and you can get a copy of her paranormal mystery novelette, *Hidden Secrets*, by signing up for her newsletter.

In her spare time, she keeps up her author's blog, *Writing to be Read*, where she posts reflections on her own writing, author interviews and book reviews, along with writing tips and inspirational posts from fellow writers. She's also the founder of *WordCrafter*. In addition to creating her own imprint in *WordCrafter Press*, she offers quality author services, such as editing, social media & book promotion, and online writing courses through *WordCrafter Quality Writing & Author Services*. When not writing or editing, she is bird watching, or hiking, or just soaking up some of that Colorado sunshine.

Don't Eat the Pickled Eggs

Kaye Lynne Booth

"Get your filthy paws off me!" Lilly Belle said, pulling her arm back from the grimy grip of the smelly buffalo hunter. The musky animal scent rolling off of him was nauseating. The piano music was loud near the bar and no one seemed to take notice of the exchange. Fortunately, he had caught her here, rather than at the other end of the bar, where it butted up against the wall at the bottom of the stairs. On this end, she could get the bar top between them to keep him at a distance.

"What's a matter, darlin'" he said, with words slurred by drink, lurching forward toward her. "You're a saloon gal ain't ya? I just wantta have me a little fun."

She took a step back, avoiding his clumsy grab for her. "I'm not. But if I was, I wouldn't take up with the likes of you," she said. "You're drunk and you need a bath."

A look of surprise crossed his face, and Lilly Belle noticed he had bits of food entwined in the hairs of his bushy brown beard. He paused, scrunching his brow. "That ain't any way to talk to a payin' customer. Let's you and me take this upstairs," he said, lurching in her direction once more. If he hadn't caught ahold of the bar top, he might very well have landed face first in the sawdust.

Lilly Belle took another step back, working her way around the end of the bar. Once the bar lay between her and the drunken fool, she bent and pulled the derringer from her boot, palming it, just in case. "Mister, you're drunk," she said. "I think you'd better go sleep it off."

"Wench! You can't talk to me like that," he bellowed, lunging across the bar, his arm swiped at empty air, as she stepped back once more and the barrel of her pistol slid into view.

"Back off!" she said, pointing the gun at his chest. The piano music stopped, and the room fell silent. The only one to take no notice was Stinkweed, the teenaged boy whose mother had been one of the girls until she was beaten to death by one of her customers. Hiram had felt some responsibility for the boy, since his mother had worked for him, and because Stinkweed was a little touched in the head, so he let him earn his keep by freshening up the sawdust and emptying the spittoons, like he was doing now. Stinkweed just kept moving from one spittoon to the next, seemingly unaware of the tension in the room.

Behind her, she heard the familiar snick of Hiram's shotgun and the buffalo hunter's gaze moved to a spot somewhere over her shoulder.

"The lady said it was time to leave, fella," Hiram said. "I suggest you heed her warning."

Recognition crossed over the drunken man's eyes as his hands rose to shoulder height and he began backing away from the bar. "She ain't no lady," he said, moving toward the door. "Never seen no saloon gal so high and mighty afore."

"Lilly Belle isn't a saloon girl, she's my bookkeeper," Hiram said, inching the muzzle of gun forward, so half of the barrel was visible to her. "If you're going to patronize my establishment, you'll treat her with respect."

"You ain't heard the last from me. I oughtta kill you for drawing that thing on me." Then he was out the door, leaving the batwings swinging in his absence. Just as if nothing had happened, the piano music started up and the volume of the din of voices rose to what it had been a few moments before.

Lilly Belle expelled the air she'd been holding inside without even being aware of it. "Thanks, Hiram," she said, turning to face him. His pale blue eyes met hers, but she averted her gaze before she could lose herself in them. "You didn't need to do that. I had him."

She held her derringer up for him, shaking it in front of him, before bending down and sliding it back into her boot.

"Man like that, he wasn't backing down from a woman," Hiram replied, sliding the shotgun onto the shelf under the bar top. "Man like that doesn't know the first thing about how to treat a lady."

She placed a hand on her hip, shaking her head. "You know, it wouldn't bring down hellfire to let him believe I'm just one of the girls. I've been called worse. Is being your bookkeeper so much better?"

"But you're not, Lil," he said, grasping her firmly by the shoulders, his blue-eyed stare burning into her. "You are more of a lady than any other woman I know. I'm hoping that you will be more than just my bookkeeper."

"Hiram, don't." She pulled away from him. Lilly Belle had had feelings for Hiram almost since the day she began working for him, not that she would ever act upon them. Although she'd never said anything to him, lately she got the feeling that he knew, and maybe felt the same way toward her. But he was married, no matter how she felt about him. She couldn't let herself indulge such thoughts. It hurt too much.

Turning, she grabbed the gallon jar filled with pickled eggs from the bar top, busying herself with refilling it even though it was still three quarters full. "Have you forgotten that you have a wife?" she said over her shoulder as she moved toward the barrel of eggs that sat in the back corner of the bar, hoping to mask the tremble in her voice with distance.

"Let's leave Cornelia out of this. I'm not asking you to marry me," Hiram said with a chuckle. He laid his hand gently on her shoulder. "I want you to be my partner in the *Silver Leaf*. I want to give you half of all of it."

Lilly Belle stopped stalk still with her right arm halfway into the near empty barrel. The shock of his words hit her like a double-barreled blast of buckshot. She turned, staring at him in disbelief. "Hiram, are you serious? Why would you do that? What about Cornelia?"

"You know how she feels about this place. She'd have it declared the Devil's den and burn it to the ground, if she had her way," he replied, opening his arms to sweep the room. "You've been keeping the books going on three years now. You know the business. You're the only one I can trust not to run it to the ground."

Lilly straightened up, pulling her arm out of the egg barrel, with the gallon jar no fuller than when it had gone in. Cornelia already thought that Hiram's relationship with her was more than just business. How could he even consider this? She knew she should protest further, but all she said was, "Egg barrel's getting low. Better order more."

"Didn't you hear me, Lil?" His eyes pleaded for her to understand. "I had Samuel draw up the papers," he said, grabbing her by the arm. "Come here. They're right here in the cash box." He reached under the bar top and pulled out a box the size cigars come in. "I've already signed them, so you really can't argue the matter."

"Hiram, Cornelia will never stand for this, and you know it," Lilly Belle said, taking a step back and shaking her head. "What are you trying to do? Ruin your marriage?"

He raised his eyes at that, and for an instant their eyes met before he looked away. Lilly Belle saw a gleam in Hiram's eyes that she didn't like in that brief moment. But before she could give further argument, a familiar figure appeared outside the batwings. "Don't look now..." she said so that only Hiram would hear. She cleared her throat as she turned away to set the jar of pickled eggs back on the bar top and replace the cheese cloth over its mouth to keep the flies out.

The batwings swung inward, as the prominent figure of Cornelia stepped into the saloon, skirts sweeping bare spots through the sawdust with each step. She marched right up to the bar, as Hiram slid the cashbox back under the bar top. "Hiram, I want to talk to you," she said with a scowl. "That is if you're not too preoccupied with your little floozy there." She tipped her head in Lilly Belle's direction.

"Cornelia, please!" Hiram said, slamming a hand down on the bar top. "There is no need for you to call her that."

"It's all right, Hiram," Lilly Belle said. "It's no secret how your wife feels about me. I was just finishing up here anyway."

"That's fine, Lilly Belle," Hiram said. "You call it a night. Things are winding down here anyway. We can continue our discussion in the morning."

Lilly Belle forced a smile in their direction before moving past Cornelia to roust the few customers who were past their drinking capacity and their bedtimes, lolling their heads on the tables, leaving only a lone pair of poker players and Stinkweed for Hiram to clear out. She nodded good-night to Claude, the piano man and headed up the stairs to her room.

***

Lilly Belle woke with a start. She couldn't shake the strange feeling that she wasn't alone. In the moonlight coming through the window, her eyes fell on the meager furnishings of the room she'd occupied above the saloon for the past three years. The vanity with the wash bowl and pitcher sitting atop sat off to the left of her bed, undisturbed. The smoky surface of the reflection glass on the wall above revealed nothing out of the ordinary. The red taffeta dress and lace petticoats she'd worn the previous evening lay over the wooden chair at the foot of the bed, just as she had left them before snuggling down under the quilt her grandmother had made so many years ago. Once the colors had been bright, making the patchwork patterns her grandmother had sewed stand out to grab the eye's attention, now faded, her grandmother's stitching fraying in spots.

Yet the feeling that someone was in the room persisted, rousting her bladder from its peaceful slumber. She swung her legs over the right side of the bed, the cold floor chilling her feet instantly, as she rose with the intent of using the chamber pot in the corner behind the door, but suddenly a cold unseen hand fell on her shoulder. Her eyes darted around the room once more, this time catching the image of a wispy man's form in the reflection glass. It was a form that she recognized, one she worked with every evening and had admired from afar for the last three years.

"Hiram?" she said aloud, unsure what to make of what her eyes were telling her. She glanced back to the empty space in front of her, then back to the mirror, but now there was only the reflection of the empty room and its sparse furnishings. Her mind must be playing tricks on her. There couldn't possibly be anyone else in the room with her.

Her full bladder prodded her, reminding her that her own needs required tending. She rose from the bed and crossed to the chamber pot in the corner. She kept a watchful eye as she tended to those needs, the feeling that she wasn't alone persisting. She couldn't shake it.

"What is wrong with you, woman?" She spoke the words aloud to break the silence that lay heavily in the air. "You gave up on that one a long time ago. Forbidden fruit."

That must be it, she thought. Hiram had offered a safe haven from the rowdy streets of Willow Grove. If it hadn't been for him, she would probably be servicing cowboys instead of serving drinks and tending books in a saloon like this one. It seemed like decades ago rather than three short years. She'd known all along that Hiram was married, and marriage was a sacred institution. Even the unhappy ones. All this time, she'd loved her employer, knowing that he felt the same toward her, both of them knowing it could never be.

"Builds on a person, desires you're not able to realize or even express," she said to the clearly empty room, muttering mostly to herself. "Not even a chance of realizing them in the future, neither." She shook her head as she finished her business and slipped back under her grandmother's quilt. "I'll not be called a whore, nor a homewrecker."

But, where she expected to find warmth, she found an icy chill instead, causing her skin to prickle. Then, she heard his voice, whispering next to her ear. "Lil..."

It was faint, but there was no mistaking that voice for anyone but Hiram's. He was the only person in Willow Grove who called her Lil. She had changed her name to Lilly Belle when she came here, hoping it would help her to get on with one of the dance companies that traveled through. Her intent had been to go to San Francisco and make a name for herself, but instead, Hiram had learned of her talents with numbers and convinced her to stay on to manage the books for the *Silver Leaf Saloon* instead. Her given name reminded her of a life she didn't care to go back to, and so she had kept the name Lilly Belle. Hiram said that Lilly Belle sounded cheap, so he called her Lil for short.

Thoughts of her name quickly left her mind, as she felt cold fingers touch her face, brushing lightly down her neck, and stopping just above her heaving bosom. Her breathing came heavy, although she wasn't sure if it was from fear or anticipation of what was to come next. Strangely, the touch on her neck had sent a shiver of excitement through her body. If this was Hiram, her secret longing might finally be realized.

But that was just plain silly. She shook her head to clear it, squeezing her eyes shut in hopes that whatever this was, it would be gone when she opened them. Whatever was happening here, she knew this presence couldn't be Hiram. She'd left him downstairs only a few hours ago, and Cornelia had been there to hurry him in closing up and usher him home.

Lilly Belle blinked her eyes a few times to chase away the cobwebs. But the feel of his light touch roaming over her skin remained, giving rise to goosebumps as she felt gentle fingertips moving lower tracing the outline of her breast, setting the skin beneath them to tingling and causing her to draw in breath. She felt a stirring down below, too, with the promise of finally getting her secret heart's desire.

Except, she knew that only the dead appeared as apparitions. She'd left Hiram in the saloon, alive and well, no more than a few hours ago. Whatever this apparition was, it couldn't possibly be Hiram. Yet somehow, she knew that it was.

Then she felt his weight on top of her, yet it wasn't pressing down on her, but rather pressing through her. A chill ran up her spine as she felt his whole being move through her as if their souls had joined, as one, sending waves of ecstasy coursing through her body, one after another. The experience was both sexual and spiritual, and now she knew beyond a doubt that this apparition or spirit, or whatever it was, was indeed Hiram.

She couldn't explain how she knew this, but she did know. Just as she knew now that Hiram did have affections for her, although he could not have shown it before. It was clear to her that was why he had come now, to let her know his feelings. As his weight lifted from her, feelings of happiness and contentment washed over her, and she soon drifted off to a peaceful slumber where Hiram inhabited her dreams.

She awoke to sunshine peeking beneath the window blinds and spreading across the wooden planks of the floor. The morning sun wasn't strong enough this early to have warmed the planks just yet, and a chill ran through her as her feet touched the floorboards. She rose from the bed with intentions of relieving herself in the chamber pot, but her progress was halted halfway across the room, as her eyes fell on the words scrawled across the blurred surface of her reflecting glass in bright red letters made with the paint from her rouge pot:

Don't eat the pickled eggs.

Suddenly, visions of last night flooded her mind, and she recalled all of the feelings that went with them. Surely, it had been a dream. But, the lettering on the reflecting glass in front of her would certainly suggest that it had been real. If it was, then Hiram was dead. The thought gave her a sinking feeling in the pit of her stomach.

Lilly Belle quickly snatched her robe from the hook on the back of the door, throwing the light linen material over her shoulders and shoving her arms into the sleeves. She tied the thick cord around her waist to keep herself covered and slipped out her door and crept silently down the stairs to look around the empty saloon. The sun light was stronger now, shining in through the saloon windows, reflecting off the dust particles which floated through the air, brightening the floor and tables nearest to the outside wall. She heard no sounds. Nothing stirred.

She was hoping to see Hiram wiping the previous night's dust off the beer steins on the shelf, as was his habit to do each morning. But there was no Hiram behind the bar. It was still early yet. It wasn't unusual for Hiram to stop off at the café and have breakfast before coming in to get the day started. Saturdays were always busy, so it made sense to start off with a full belly. Hell, the saloon didn't even open for business until near noon most days.

Lilly Belle stepped onto the floor of the saloon, feeling the cool soil beneath her bare feet. Stinkweed had been cleaning up the last of the night's sawdust when she'd gone upstairs. Hiram must have told him to wait until morning to spread the fresh sawdust. Stinkweed was a little slow in the head, but he knew enough to have it down before Hiram arrived. She had no doubt that the boy would be here soon to spread that sawdust. She just wanted to take a quick look around before she went back upstairs to get dressed.

She walked around the room, thinking of all the times she'd imagined revealing her feelings to Hiram. Of course, she never could have. How could she even be thinking in that manner about a married man? She was awful. But she never followed through outside of her dreams. Her dream last night made her think that maybe he'd known all along, but of course, that was just wishful thinking.

She stood, looking up and down the bar, the gallon jar of pickled eggs brought the message left on the reflection glass to mind, and she walked over and picked the jar up off the bar. What could his message have meant? It didn't make sense, don't eat the pickled eggs. She recalled trying to refill the jar last night to avoid the conversation with Hiram. She took off the lid and lifted an egg out of the jar, thinking about her surprise at his announcement of making her his partner. She felt silly thinking that he was going to suggest... well, it had just been wishful thinking on her part.

She set the lid back atop the jar as the batwings swung open behind him. Stinkweed entered the saloon with a bag of sawdust from the mill.

"Stinkweed, I have a question for you," she said, walking toward him, egg in hand, using it like a pointer.

Stinkweed stopped mid-stride; eyes wide as she approached him. The expression on his face made Lilly Belle take pause. It wasn't her intention to frighten the boy. "Hey Stinkweed," she said, brushing the dirty hair from his face with her empty hand, "It's all right. You know I wouldn't hurt you, boy. Don't you?"

This town had not been kind to Stinkweed, she knew. Lilly Belle had always been gentle with the lad. His mother had been murdered by one of her 'callers'. Any one of these cowpokes or mill hands could have been his father, but being slow the way he was, no one had laid claim to him. Hiram had given the boy a cot in the shed out back in exchange for his helping to keep the place in order.

Stinkweed raised a grimy face to meet her eyes, only to quickly look away before giving a brief nod of his head, as she noticed the pickled egg, still in her hand and went to pop it into her mouth.

"N...noooo!" Stinkweed cried, slapping the egg from her hand. It landed on the bar with a splat. "No. No. No. No." he muttered, as he turned away and headed toward the broom closet muttering "Bad eggs. Bad."

Lilly Belle reached out and touched the boy's shoulder and he turned back to face her. "Stinkweed, what was that all about?" she asked, searching his face for answers. "Are you hungry? Because you can sure have one. Here." She stepped over to the bar and took the lid off the gallon jar, but before she could pluck one out for him, Stinkweed lunged for the jar, sending it smashing to the floor.

Lilly Belle placed her hands on her hips and let out an exasperated sigh. "Now what the hell was that all about?" she said. "Stinkweed, what has gotten into you?" She shook her head in disbelief. "Now I have to get another jar to put the eggs in. I hope there are enough left in the barrel to fill it. You clean this mess up now, you hear?"

As she made her way around to the backside of the bar, Stinkweed grabbed a broom and began picking up the scattered eggs from the floor and sweeping up the broken glass, but the liquid they'd been preserved in had already seeped into the dirt, leaving the pungent aroma of vinegar and seasonings tinging the air and a large dark stain. "Who-wee that stinks!" she said, reaching for another gallon jar from under the bar top and grabbing a cloth to wipe it clean. "Get some sawdust down to soak that up. I imagine it will be a while before that clears out. I don't imagine the customers will mind though, as long as we keep the drinks coming. Which reminds me, that's what I wanted to ask you. Stinkweed, have you seen Hiram this morning? He should have been in by now."

Stinkweed shook his head furiously, his dirty hair flying in every direction. "No, no no. Mister Hiram g...gone."

On her way to fill the jar with eggs from the big barrel in the corner of the bar, Lilly Belle stopped in mid-stride and braced herself with a hand against the bar, as his words struck her like a blow. She set down the jar and rushed around the bar to Stinkweed. She lifted his chin, so that she could get a good look at him and wiped a tear from his cheek, smearing grime across his face. "What do you mean, Mr. Hiram gone?"

The look on the boy's dirty face made her regret her harshness. Stinkweed didn't understand her concerns. He reacted like a child in trouble for doing something bad, pulling away from her. "Stinkweed's sorry. S..s...sorry," he said, tightening his grip on the broom handle. "Clean up n...now." He busied himself sweeping up the broken glass from the pickled egg jar, avoiding her gaze.

Before she could explain to the boy that he wasn't in trouble, the batwings swung inward and Cornelia entered in a swish of ruffled taffeta skirts. Stinkweed took one look at her and dropped his broom, heading out the back before Lilly Belle could stop him. "Stinkweed, come back," she called after him, but he didn't pause, and was out of sight before she could say tomfoolery. She turned, shaking her head. "Now, I wonder what's gotten into that boy?"

"Look at you, prancing around here in your nightclothes. I might have figured," Cornelia said with a sneer. "Where's Hiram?"

Lilly Belle stopped, staring at Cornelia as her words sunk in. That sinking feeling in her gut was back, and she figured she knew why. "He hasn't come in yet," she replied. "Did you check the coffee house? He might be having himself some breakfast. Saturdays are pretty busy." But in her heart, Lilly Belle knew that Hiram wouldn't be coming in to open at all today.

"You really expect me to believe you haven't seen him?" Cornelia hissed. "When he didn't come home last night, I knew he was with you. The way you two carry on, all friendly-like, but you think I don't know what you're up to?"

Lilly Belle had had enough of this. She didn't have time to play games with a jealous wife. "Cornelia, you are mistaken, as usual," she said. "There is nothing romantic between me and your husband." She turned, heading for the stairs. "I'll go up and get dressed. I'm sure he'll be in to open up soon."

But even as she said it, she felt in her heart that it wasn't true. Hiram had come to her last night to say goodbye. She knew now that it hadn't been a dream. It was up to her to figure out the how and why of it.

"You had better hope so," Cornelia replied as Lilly Belle climbed the stairs. "If anything has happened to my dear sweet Hiram, I'll see that you pay for it."

Lilly Belle paused mid-stair to consider, before continuing on with her train of thought, choosing not to respond. If he wasn't here and he wasn't at home, then he may have met with foul play. Lord knew, this town was rambunctious enough. Anything could have happened to Hiram. The question was, what did?

***

While brushing through her long blonde tresses, Lilly Belle pondered the unusual turn of events set in motion the previous night. She had no doubt now that something unforetold had happened to Hiram. She believed that it was his spirit that came to her last night and that he wanted to tell her something. What did his mysterious cryptic message on her reflecting glass mean? Why don't eat the pickled eggs? He knew she loved pickled eggs. Was that his way of telling her she couldn't have what she wanted? But they were both well aware of that fact. Cornelia was a constant reminder. No.

Hiram had come to her, and it was up to her to solve this mystery and find answers.

A knock at the door interrupted her thoughts. Startled she turned toward the door and said, "Who is it?"

"Sherriff Bolton," said the voice on the other side. "Lilly Belle, I need to talk to you."

"Just a moment, Jed," Lilly Belle said, reaching back to hastily tie up her hair with the ribbon she'd been holding. "Just let me make myself presentable." She smoothed her paisley skirt and took one more look into the looking glass to straighten her bodice to be sure her ample bosom was tucked out of site. The appearance of the law didn't surprise her, but it did raise her anxiety level. She felt like she was sitting on pins and needles, and she wasn't even sitting down. This confirmed her suspicions that something had happened to Hiram. She turned back to the door and took a deep breath to calm her nerves. "Come on in, Jed."

The knob turned and a booted foot stepped in through the opening, then Jed Bolton was standing in her doorway, all six-foot six of him. She knew those baby blue eyes peering from beneath that wind-blown mop of blonde hair when he removed his Stetson, holding it in front of him. Jed was always the gentleman when he came into the *Silver Leaf,* even buying a drink for one of the girls now and again, but he never took advantage or expected anything in return. He was a good man, and looking into his eyes, Lilly Belle relaxed a little of the tension that had her wound so tight.

"I'm afraid this is official business," he said. "I guess you know Hiram didn't show up at home last night?"

"Of course. I know that, Jed," she replied, throwing her nightgown from the back of the chair onto the bed, and pushing it toward him. "Couldn't help but know it. Cornelia was in here first thing this morning, throwing accusations around. She seems to think Hiram was with me last night, but I retired right after she came in to collect him, so I don't see how."

"Cornelia was here last night?" Jed asked, raising his brow as he took the seat she offered, placing his Stetson in his lap. "What time was that?"

"I don't know," Lilly Belle said, probing her memory for the time. She took a seat on the end of the bed. "Maybe about nine-ish? There were still customers in here, but they were thinning down. Why don't you ask her? She should know what time she marched in here just like she does every night. Stomps in and harps on Hiram while he closes up. She usually doesn't leave until she has him firmly under her wing for the walk home."

"She does that every night?" he asked, raising his brow even higher. "Why would she not walk with him last night?"

"I don't know," Lilly Belle said with a shrug of her shoulders. "Maybe he had something to finish up and she got tired of waiting. Obviously, you've spoken with her. What is she saying about all this?"

Jed reached up, scratching his chin thoughtfully. "Well, that's the thing, Lilly Belle," he said. "Cornelia is saying that you done something to Hiram and she says you had good reason."

"Me?" she said bringing her hand up to her chest. "Why on Earth would I want to harm Hiram?"

"This place," he replied. "She claims you convinced Hiram to make you a partner and will you his half should anything happen to him. Any truth to that?"

Lilly Belle paused, thinking of the paper Hiram was trying to show her last night. The one he had his attorney, Sam McGraw, draw up. Cornelia's appearance had been the perfect excuse to put off hearing what Hiram had to say, because she didn't want to have to turn him down. Making her his partner would only fuel Cornelia's suspicions and stir up trouble. Trouble that she didn't need, and neither did Hiram. Lilly Belle would need to tread lightly and choose her words carefully.

"Maybe," she said. "Hiram was trying to show me some sort of documents last night just before Cornelia came in. I think that might be what she's talking about. But her arrival interrupted him and I never really got a good look at them. Whatever it was, it was something Hiram had gone and done on his own. I certainly didn't ask him to."

"Well, it doesn't make you look good in light of Cornelia's claims," he said. "Anybody else see Cornelia here last night?"

"Let me see, I rousted a few drunkards and sent them on their way, but they were all about ready to pass out, so I doubt that they would be much help," Lilly Belle said, thinking back to the previous night. "But there were still the two card players involved in a game when I left, and of course, Stinkweed was poking around, cleaning up sawdust. He usually hangs around until Hiram sends him to his cot in the shed out back. You know the boy has nowhere else to go."

"Stinkweed could have seen if something happened to Hiram while he was here, but trying to get out of him what he saw could prove difficult, I'm afraid," Jed said with a frown that made furrows in his forehead. "Who were the card players? Did you know them?"

"I think they were a couple of the boys from down at the Bar-T, but I don't know their names. They hired on a new bunch not too long ago," she replied. "Do you really think I might have something to worry about, Jed?"

"I'll send Pete out to the Bar-T to see if he can find them boys," he said. "But if Hiram intended to leave this place to you, it moves you up to the head of the list of suspects. I have to follow up every lead I get, Lilly Belle. It's my duty as Sherriff."

"I know, Jed. But you don't think I had anything to do with this really. Do you?"

"It's not up to me, Lilly Belle," Jed turned his gaze to the door, refusing to meet her eyes, as if an unseen guest occupied the doorway. "You said he showed you those papers?"

"He was going to, but Cornelia walked in before he got the chance," she replied. "I didn't actually see what was on them, but he said he wanted to make me partner because he didn't want Cornelia to get her hands on *The Silver Leaf.* Said she'd destroy it because she believes it is a den of immorality."

"What did he do with the papers, when Cornelia came in?" Jed asked.

"I don't know," Lilly Bell said with a shrug of her shoulders. "I was too busy avoiding Cornelia to notice. I imagine he put them back into the cashbox under the bar, where he got them."

"Has anyone looked to see if they're still there?" Jed said, raising his brow.

Lilly Belle shook her head. "I haven't," she said. "I was downstairs earlier, but then Cornelia showed up looking for Hiram and making stupid accusations, so I came up here to get dressed and let her run out of steam."

"Maybe we should go see if they are there," said Jed, rising from his chair. "It wouldn't do much to clear you as a suspect, but it would prove that Cornelia lied about having them. Can you show me where the cashbox is?"

"Sure. I'd be glad to," Lilly Belle said, rising and throwing her lace shawl from the back of the chair around her shoulders. "But Jed, I need you to know something." She reached out and touched his shoulder. "I do think something has happened to Hiram, but I didn't have anything to do with it. I want you to do whatever you can to find out what happened to him, and I'll do anything I can to help."

"Why do you think something has happened to him?" Jed asked.

"I can't explain really," she said. "You'd think I've gone off the deep end, probably. Let's just say I had a... very realistic dream last night. I suspected something when I went downstairs this morning. I was hoping that Hiram would be there opening up to prove me wrong."

"Well, let's go down and see about those papers," Jed said. "I just hope I don't end up having to arrest you before this is all over."

***

Lilly Belle headed back behind the bar as soon as she stepped off the bottom stair. "Hiram had them in the cashbox, right here," she said, pulling the box from the shelf that lay below the bar top and holding it out to Jed.

He took it from her and flipped open the lid, poking through the contents. "All that's in here is money," he said, looking up at her. "So, he wasn't robbed, but there's no legal papers."

"How much cash is there?" Lilly Belle asked with a raised brow.

"I don't know. I didn't count it," Jed said with a hint of irritation in his voice. "What does it matter?"

"Don't you see?" said Lilly Belle, taking the cash box back from him. Glancing inside, she didn't even have to count. There was too much money there. "Hiram only leaves enough money in here to open up each day. He takes the rest out and gets it ready for deposit. Then he makes his deposit on his way in each morning to start the day fresh. Why didn't he take the money when he closed up last night?"

"So, you're saying there is more money here than there should be?" Jed asked, obviously not grasping the significance of her revelation.

"Right. Since he didn't take the money for his deposit to the bank, that means he didn't close up last night," she explained. "Whatever happened to Hiram, it happened right here, because he never left."

"Maybe you got a point there," Jed said, rubbing the brim of his Stetson. "You can help me look around here. See if you see anything else out of place."

"All right, but first, I want you to take count of this money," she said, handing the box back to him. "Cornelia is on the warpath, and I don't want her accusing me of anything, so it's best if you take charge of it for now."

"All right. I'll count it right now," he said, setting the cash box up on the bar top and opening it once more. He took out the paper money and began counting.

Lilly Belle looked around the room, thinking of Hiram. It hurt to think she would never see him again, but she believed that it was true nonetheless. The empty egg jar caught her eye, still sitting where she'd left it on the counter. She'd never gotten the chance to fill it after Stinkweed had broken the old one this morning. She stepped over to the bar, picking it up, but before she could move to fill it, Cornelia burst through the batwings, slamming them loudly against the wall. She was decked out in her usual bustled skirts, but she had changed into a green velvet dress with embroidered flowers on the sleeves and collar.

"Sherriff, I want you to arrest that woman," Cornelia said, waving an accusatory finger in Lilly Belle's direction. "My Hiram is missing, and that little hussy has something to do with it. I just know it."

Jed straightened up, addressing her as he would a small child. "Now Cornelia, you don't know any such thing. All we know right now is that Hiram hasn't been seen since last night. If you'll just go on home and let me do my job, I'll let you know as soon as I discover anything."

Then Cornelia noticed the cash box in front of Jed. "What are you doing with that cash box?" she said moving toward him. "Was Hiram robbed? Is there money missing?"

"No, Ma'am, just the opposite," Jed said, scooping up all the money from the counter and placing it back in the cash box. "It looks like all the money from yesterday's business is still right here. I just took a count of it, and I'm locking it up at the Sherriff's office for safe keeping until we get this whole mess figured out."

Cornelia frowned in disapproval, but she said, "Well, see that you do." She glared at Lilly Belle as she continued, "Everything in this place belongs to me, as Hiram's only heir. See that it doesn't fall into the wrong hands." With a swoosh of her skirts, she turned and exited the way she had come, leaving only the click of her heels in her wake.

"I told you she has it out for me," Lilly Belle said when she had gone. "Jed, all I ever wanted to do was make an honest living, and Hiram gave me the chance to do that, without laying on my back and putting up my legs, for him or anyone else. I'm not after his money, or his saloon. You know that, don't you."

"Miss Lilly Belle, I know you," Jed replied, tucking the cash box under his arm. "If I thought you had done something to Hiram, you'd be over in the jail instead of helping me try and figure all this out. Had everything else been closed down when you came down this morning?"

Lilly Belle set the jar back down on the bar top to think before she answered. "No, I don't think the bar had been placed across the batwings. Both Stinkweed and Cornelia came through them without any problems, and I know I didn't take it down."

"Well, it sure seems like Hiram didn't finish locking up last night," Jed said, scratching his chin. "But that doesn't prove that he met with ill fortune. Then again, you'd think he'd take the cash, if he wanted to disappear and start a new life or something" He paused, shaking his head. "But, with a wife like Cornelia, who would blame him if he did?"

"Jed, that's a horrid thing to say."

Jed cocked his head and raised his brow in her direction.

"It might be true, but it's still horrid," she said, turning up the corners of her mouth just enough to show him she knew he was teasing. She grabbed the empty pickled egg jar once more and head for the barrel in the corner, determined to get at least this one task accomplished. It was up to her to keep *The Silver Leaf* running until Hiram could be found, one way or another. She heard the whistling sound of lead flying, as the jar shattered in her hand, spraying glass shards all over the area behind the bar.

"Get down!" Jed said, dropping down into a crouch himself.

Lilly Belle didn't have to be told twice. Someone was shooting at her. They both stayed there like that, waiting for a second shot, but it never came. Jed rose part way, remaining hunched over, and shambled to the batwings to have a look at the street outside.

"Well, whoever it was, I think they're gone now," he said, straightening up to his full height of six foot three. "Street's empty. Folks tend to clear out when any shooting starts." He turned, walking back toward the bar. "Are you okay? It didn't hit you did it?"

"No, just shattered the jar and made a mess," she said shaking her head as she stood back up. "Darned if it don't seem like something wants to keep me from refilling the damned pickled eggs. Now I'll have to see if I have another jar after I get this mess cleaned up. That's two broken today. Who do you think was doing the shooting?"

"Well, it might be a coincidence that it happened right after Cornelia said her piece and left," he said, scratching his chin whiskers. "That would be my first guess though. Can you think of anyone else who might want to do you harm?"

She shook her head. "No. None of this makes any sense, Jed. I don't think Hiram ran off, but I don't know of anyone that would want to do him harm either."

"Did you see where the bullet went?" Jed asked as he moved behind the bar top to investigate.

"Be careful now, I've got to get all this glass cleaned up, "she said, heading for the open cubby under the stairs where the broom and cleaning rags were kept. "I didn't see it at all. Just heard the whistling and then the jar shattered."

As she reached for the broom, she glanced down at the pile of old linens that Hiram tore up to make cleaning rags to find a wide-eyed boy staring up at her. "Stinkweed!" she said in surprise. She knew the boy snuck into the cubby to sleep during slow times, when he was caught up on his chores, but she hadn't expected to see him here now.

The tow-head was up like a shot, bolting from the cubby. Lilly Belle made a grab for the boy, but his skinny arm slipped right through her fingers. "Stinkweed, come back here. I want to talk to you."

Jed stepped out from behind the bar and caught the welp by the collar, stopping him in mid-flight. The boy struggled to get away, as Lilly Belle rushed over, squatting down to be at eye level with the boy.

"Stinkweed, nobody is mad at you. I just need to ask you something," she said, taking hold of his thin arm with one hand. She nodded to Jed to turn him loose. After a questioning glance, he did. She lifted his chin with her other hand, keeping a firm, but gentle hold on his wrist, and their eyes met. "Tommy, please. This is important."

The boy nodded and she loosened her grasp on his wrist.

"Tommy?" Jed said, with a puzzled expression. "Is that his real name?"

Lilly Belle nodded, holding the boy's gaze as she spoke to Jed. "Yes. Tommy. Folks just call him Stinkweed because he chased a rabbit into a patch of stinkweed once, when he was just a little tike, and came back into town smelling to high heavens. The smell went away, but the name stuck."

Bringing her attention back to the boy, she released his wrist, reaching up to tousle the straw-colored mop of hair. "Now, Tommy, the Sherriff and I have a few questions to ask, and I want you to do your best to answer them, okay?"

The boy's eyes shifted to where Jed was standing and grew big and round. Suspecting he might try to bolt, Lilly Belle reached out and placed a hand on his shoulder. "It's okay, Tommy. You're not in trouble, not this time. But we need your help. Where were you when Hiram was closing up last night?"

The boy's lip quivered, but he didn't speak. She could tell he was still scared. At least Jed knew enough to put an elbow on the bar and let her deal with the boy. Stinkweed wasn't a bad boy, but he got confused about right and wrong and it had gotten him into trouble at times. Jed had had to bring Stinkweed in on a few occasions, enough for the boy to see Jed as an authority figure and be afraid of him.

"It's okay," said Lilly Belle in a soothing voice, urging him on. She loosened her grip on his arm, but rested her hand on his shoulder. "We know you've done nothing wrong. Please tell me where you were."

He lifted a skinny arm and pointed at the supply cubby under the stairs with a small, bony finger.

"You were under the stairs last night?" she asked, moving her hand to take his chin and turn his face up toward her once more. "What were you doing in there?"

"H... hiding," he said, averting his gaze to the floor.

"Hiding from who?" Lilly Belle asked as her suspicions grew. "Who were you hiding from? Who scared you?"

Stinkweed shook his head, clamping his lips shut tight. Her hand moved from his chin to his shoulder, bringing her other up to grasp his shoulder on the other side. "It's okay. You can tell us."

He raised his head up to meet her gaze with questioning eyes, unsure of what he should do. "It's okay, Tommy. You didn't do anything wrong. Tell me who frightened you and I won't let anything bad happen to you. I promise."

"M... m... missus. Hiram."

"Why, Tommy?" Lilly Belle said, thinking of the way the boy had bolted when Cornelia had come in earlier. "Why were you frightened by Mrs. Hiram last night?"

"M...missus Hiram 'us mad at M...mister Hiram," Stinkweed said, scrunching up his face into a sour expression. "She yelled at him. She chased me."

So, Hiram had had a fight with Cornelia last night. That made things a little clearer, maybe. "What was she mad about?" she asked the boy, choosing her words carefully. They needed to learn what happened here last night, and Stinkweed just might be the key. "What did you see?"

"Papers," Stinkweed said. "She w...wanted Mister Hiram's p...p...papers."

"So, Mr. Hiram had papers and Mrs. Hiram was mad about it?" Lilly Belle asked for clarification. Stinkweed nodded.

"That proves Cornelia was here last night, a fact she neglected to mention," Jed said. He'd been so quiet; Lilly Belle had almost forgotten he was there. "We still don't know what happened to Hiram. It's no crime to argue with your husband."

Lilly Belle held up a finger, asking for his patience as she posed her next question to the boy. "She chased you, so you hid in there, right?" she said, pointing to the open cubby where she had so recently found him. He nodded. Sensing that he was on the verge of revealing the one thing they needed to know, she fought back the impatience she was feeling. "This morning you said Mr. Hiram was gone. Where did he go? Did you see him leave last night?"

Stinkweed's eyes got big and round, and she could see the fear in them. She firmed her grasp on his shoulders, not wanting to frighten him, but still afraid that he might try to bolt. "It's okay. I promise," she said in a soft voice. "Please tell me, did you see Mr. Hiram leave?"

Stinkweed shook his head, dropping his gaze to the floor.

"Tommy, look at me," she said. He lifted his eyes once more to meet hers. "Why did you tell me he was gone? Tell me what you saw."

A tear ran from the corner of his eye, streaking his dirt smudged face, and he shook his head.

"Did something happen to Mr. Hiram last night, Tommy?" she asked. He gave a slight nod. "Please tell me what happened, Tommy. Please help us find Mr. Hiram." He shook his head, more vigorously this time.

"Look boy," said Jed, growing impatient. "It's important that we find Hiram. You need to tell us what you know."

The boy pulled back, and Lilly Belle released her grip on his shoulders. Then she turned and shook her head at Jed.

"Wait," Jed said, kneeling down on one knee to put himself on the same level with the boy. "I'm not going to hurt you. I just want to know what happened here last night. You're not in trouble." Jed offered his hand to the boy, palm up, and Stinkweed took it reluctantly. "There. See. Now we can be friends."

Stinkweed gave Jed a slight smile, turning up the corners of his mouth slightly. Jed smiled back.

"I'm surprised at you, Jed," Lilly Belle said with a laugh. "Keep on like that and you might make a good father someday."

Jed looked up at her and scowled. Then, he turned his attention back to the boy. "If you don't want to tell me what happened to Hiram, that's all right," he said. "We'll try an easier one. Was Mrs. Hiram here last night while Hiram was closing up?" The boy nodded once. "All right, they were arguing. Then what?"

For some reason the boy shied away from talking about whatever happened here. They weren't getting what they needed from the boy, and she could tell he was still on pins and needles, even though it appeared he'd relaxed some. She took stock of the glass shards all over the bar and splayed across the dirt floor behind it. "Jed, the boy's not going anywhere now," she said. "Let him go get the broom, so we can get this glass cleaned up before someone gets cut on it."

Jed looked at her and nodded, releasing Stinkweed's hand. "Go on boy," he said. "You best help Miss Lilly Belle out. Go get the broom."

Stinkweed ran to the cubby to get the broom.

"Thanks, Jed," she said, smiling. "I figured maybe the boy could use a break from being grilled by the two of us. Let him relax a little, then we'll try again. I'm going to grab another jar to put the pickled eggs in. Hiram or no Hiram, this place should be in order when the drovers and the miners start trickling in."

She went to the back room and grabbed a gallon jar from the shelf. When she returned to the barback, Cornelia was standing in the middle of the saloon, hands on bustled hips, demanding to know what was being done to find Hiram. Stinkweed was nowhere in sight. He'd probably seen Cornelia and decided to stay in the storage cubby. She had a couple of hours before the *Silver Leaf* would be open for business, and cleaning up the broken glass was just one more thing it seemed she'd have to do herself.

"Actually, Cornelia, I am trying to figure out what happened here last night," Jed said, facing her squarely. "Maybe once I know that, I'll be able to tell you what's happened to Hiram. But I also have a question for you. Where were you about five minutes after you left here earlier?"

"Last night?" she replied. Her hand went to her throat as she straightened her posture. "If you want to know what happened here last night, I suggest you ask that brazen hussy behind the bar." She pointed a finger in Lilly Belle's direction. Lilly Belle ignored her and moved over to the pickled egg barrel in the corner.

"Hello, Cornelia," Lilly Belle said, her words dripping with sarcasm as she moved toward the big wooden barrel in the corner. "Nice to see you, too."

"Cornelia, why didn't you tell me you were here last night?" Jed asked, ignoring her comment about Lilly Belle. "And where were you about five minutes after you left here earlier, when someone took a shot at Lilly Belle?"

"Me?" Cornelia said with indignation. "Why are you questioning me? It's that homewrecker there you should be questioning."

She froze with her hand on the lid of the barrel, staring in disbelief at Cornelia. Normally, she bit her tongue for Hiram's sake, and swallowed all of Cornelia's spiteful words like bitter medicine, but this time, the woman had gone too far. "What did you call me?" she said, glaring at the other woman. "I never wrecked your home, or anyone else's. You made his life miserable, not me." She turned her back to Cornelia and Jed, prying up the clips for the cover on the barrel to hide the fact that she was shaking with anger. The nerve of that woman. Lilly Belle gritted her teeth, chiding herself for letting Cornelia get to her.

"No, no!" Stinkweed said, appearing out of nowhere, knocked the jar off the barrel lid, sending it crashing to the dirt floor, glass shards flying every which way behind the bar. "B...bad eggs! B...b...bad eggs! No!"

A small shard of glass glanced Lilly Belle's left ankle, drawing blood, but Lilly Belle was too angry to pay it any mind. "Stinkweed!" she said with a raised voice, shaking her finger violently at the boy. "That's the second time today! What the hell has gotten into you!"

The look in the boy's eyes softened her in an instant. She couldn't recall ever yelling at the boy before, so he probably didn't know how to respond. "Oh, Tommy, I'm so sorry," she said. "I didn't mean to yell."

"What is that little urchin doing in here?" Cornelia said, blustering through the bat wing doors. As usual, it sounded more like a demand than a question. "I told you not to come back here. You'd better get out right now."

Stinkweed bolted past Cornelia and out the batwing doors. Lilly Belle called after him, but he was so scared, she doubted that he even heard her.

"Cornelia, you just chased off my witness," Jed said, slamming his fist down on the bar top. "I should site you for obstruction of the law."

"That little street scum?" Cornelia replied with a squeak to her voice, that made the indignation she was going for sound more like a whine. "He can't even talk right. How can he be witness to anything?"

"You had no right to chase Stinkweed off," Lilly Belle said, hands on her hips. "He's in Hiram's employ. You can't fire him."

"Well, I assure you that you have nothing what-so-ever to say about it," Cornelia said. "And for that matter, I want you out, too. There's going to be some changes around here, now that I'm running things."

"You know, Cornelia, we haven't determined that anything has happened to Hiram yet," Jed said, jumping between the two women, who both looked as if they might tear one another apart at any moment. Lilly Belle could confirm that he was right in that assumption, at least on her end of things. "For all we know, he might come through those batwings any time."

"He can't come walking in when he's dead, you numbskull," Cornelia said, snapping at the Sherriff.

Whether it was out of anger, or desperation, Lilly Belle didn't know, but Cornelia had given them another piece to the puzzle they'd been trying to solve, and Lilly Belle jumped on it. "How do you know Hiram is dead, Cornelia?"

"That's a good question," Jed said, scratching his chin. "Do you have something you maybe forgot to tell me, Cornelia?"

Lilly Belle leaned one hand on the pickled egg barrel to watch the show with great pleasure. Cornelia looked like a cornered animal. Her upright stance melted into a cower. Her eyes grew large as tea cups and her lip trembled. "Well, I meant if he is dead, of course," she said, groveling for a way out. "I don't know if he is. How could I?"

"You were here last night." Jed said. "Why didn't you tell me that when you came to me reporting Hiram missing this morning?"

"That's right," Cornelia said, looking at him with a glimmer of hope in her eyes. "I came to you to report Hiram missing. Why would I do that, if I knew he was dead?" She straightened her spine, regaining some of her usual indignant posture. Her hand went up with her forefinger extended once more toward Lilly Belle. "It's her that you should be looking at. She was trying to steal this place right out from under Hiram. I saw the papers."

"Just where are those papers, Cornelia?" Jed said. "I think we should see them."

Lilly Belle felt her ire rising once more. "I never asked that man for anything!" Lilly Belle exclaimed, slamming her fist down on the lid to the pickled egg barrel, causing the rim to pop up and the cover to slide off onto the floor. She moved toward Cornelia with full intentions of scratching her eyes out. "Hiram was kind to me, but he would never do anything that could be considered improper!"

Cornelia paled, suddenly not looking so well, as the lid slid to the floor. It was as if she'd forgotten the woman charging at her, standing there gaping with her mouth open.

Lilly Belle saw the change in the other woman's disposition, but not in time to halt her forward momentum. She slammed into the other woman, knocking them both to the floor, resulting in Lilly

Belle's shoulder smashing into a table, sending it crashing to the floor amidst a jumble of chairs that went over with it. She shook her head to clear the fuzziness out, rolling to her knees. Cornelia lay flat on her back, a groan escaping from her lips let Lilly Belle know the other woman hadn't suffered too much damage. She rose to her feet, heading back toward the bar, the image of Cornelia's expression stuck in her mind, along with Stinkweed's strange behavior this morning and the mysterious words scrawled across her looking glass. "What is it with everyone and those damned pickled eggs?"

Before she could lay a hand on the bar, Cornelia let out a battle cry behind her and she hit the dirt hard, fingers grasping her hair and pulling her head back. Lilly Belle rolled to her back, her hand grasping to take purchase on her attacker, but coming up empty as Cornelia's eyes fixed once more on the barrel and her grasp loosened. Cornelia stepped over her, moving toward the barrel with determination. Lilly Belle reached out with her other hand, catching ahold of Cornelia's ankle. Cornelia landed by the barrel in the dirt with a loud thud.

Both women rose to their feet, Cornelia planting her feet, blocking Lilly Belle from reaching the barrel. They stood facing one another exhausted, panting to catch their breath. Cornelia's hair, usually perfectly centered atop her head, was askew, her prim and proper skirt was ripped in two places, her bustle bent and misshapen. She didn't look so high and mighty now, but if the way she felt was any indication, Lilly Belle figured that she didn't look much better.

"Ladies, I'm sure all of this can be settled," Jed said, moving to stand between the two, "but not with the two of you going at it like a couple of hell cats."

Cornelia gave him a scorching glare before fixing her gaze once more on Lilly Belle. "Are you taking the harlot's side now?" she said, planting her feet firmly in the dirt, hands on hips. "You've no claim here anymore, whore. You'll not touch one more thing in my establishment."

"What makes you so sure Hiram is dead, Cornelia?" Lilly Belle asked, returning a glare of daggers. "How do you know he's not coming back?"

"Yeah, what about those papers you were hollering about this morning?" Jed said, focusing his attention on Cornelia. "You show me those papers and I'll believe Lilly Belle may have had a motive for harming Hiram. Right now, it looks like maybe you know what happened to ol' Hiram. So, what about them?"

"I... I...ah...," Cornelia said, stammering as she tried to decide which question to answer. She shifted her eyes in Jed's direction for a moment, perhaps weighing her options. Then she lunged at Lilly Belle, fingers posed like claws, ready to scratch her eyes out. Lilly Belle saw her coming and stepped back out of the way. Her left foot lingered in Cornelia's path, catching the hem of her fancy taffeta dress, causing the woman to stumble forward into one of the tables, toppling it to the floor, along with two chairs.

Cornelia caught herself before going down on top of the pile, wheeling back to face Lilly Belle once more. Her eyes shifted away toward the batwings, and Lilly Belle wasn't the only one to catch it.

"Cornelia, don't try it," Jed said in warning, taking a step toward her.

That was all it took. Cornelia bolted for the doors and Jed sprang to stop her. "Cornelia, I'm placing you under arrest until I can get all this sorted out," he said, grabbing ahold of her arm. He spun her around to face him. "It's about time you start answering some questions."

Cornelia's face paled to an almost greenish hue, as her eyes shifted from Jed to Lilly Belle and back, finding no help in site.

She knew that it was spiteful, but Lilly Belle couldn't help but get in one last jab. "Looks like your eggs are really pickled, Cornelia."

She said with a sarcastic little smile, revealing a glimpse of the devilishness within her. "You can start by telling us what you've done with Hiram."

Cornelia's eyes darted past Lilly Belle, to the barrel, standing open in the corner behind the bar for just a moment before dropping them to the floor, shaking her head.

"What is it about these damned pickled eggs that has everyone all stirred up?" Lilly Belle said, heading back behind the bar to have a look inside that barrel.

Cornelia gave out a little whimper as Lilly Belle approached the open barrel. With her back turned, Lilly Belle didn't see the other woman break away from Jed's grasp. She wasn't expecting the hard impact of Cornelia's body as it slammed into her own, knocking her into the side of the pickled egg barrel, sending it toppling over onto its side. The pungent aroma of vinegar permeated the air as brine soaked into the dirt floor and Lilly Belle found herself atop the smashed remnants of the barrel, staring into the blank eyes of Hiram through the broken planks.

"Ah, Jed. I think you'll want to take a look at this," Lilly Belle said, pushing herself up and stepping back away from the barrel, hands held out in front of her. It was the grisliest thing she had ever seen. His body had been folded up like an accordion to make it fit. His knees were crammed up under his chin, making his head tilt upward, leaving him staring up at the lid to the barrel. A pickled egg bobbed up from below, suspended in brine near his right temple, and another floated near his chin. Seeing Hiram, the kindest man she'd ever known, stuffed in that barrel brought tears to her eyes.

Jed stepped up and grabbed Cornelia's arm, bringing roughly to her feet as he examined the contents of the barrel. "Cornelia, you've got some explaining to do."

"I didn't mean to kill him," she said, her hand moving to cover her quivering mouth. A distant look came over her face and her voice came out just above a whisper. "He showed me the papers giving everything to her. I got so angry. I've given him most of my life. How could he go and give it all to her?"

"What then, Cornelia?" Jed said, grabbing her shoulders, forcing her to look at him. "What happened next?"

"He bent over the barrel to fill the pickled egg jar and I just pushed his head into the barrel. He tried to fight me, but he was so short that he couldn't get any footing while I held him there. When he stopped fighting, I stuffed him into the barrel. I knew he would be found, but it was all I could think of to do," she said, pausing as if letting her mind drift. "Then, I thought about her. I figured I could make it look like she did it." She pointed to Lilly Belle. "It would have served her right, after she ruined my marriage that way. I took the papers from the cashbox and stuck them in the waistband my dress, because I knew they would show motive for her."

Lilly Belle barely heard the others as she stared down into Hiram's blank eyes with tears rolling down her cheeks. Knowing for certain that Hiram was gone and this would be the last time she ever saw him was too much for her to grasp all at once, and she couldn't seem to pull her gaze away.

But Cornelia's last words got through to her and she snapped her head around to glare at the other woman. "I didn't ruin your marriage, you witch," she said through gritted teeth. "You did that all by your judgmental, criticizing, holier-than-thou self. How could you kill such a kind, sweet man? You killed him."

"They were all supposed to think it was you," Cornelia said, her head hanging as she resigned herself to the fact that she'd been caught. It was as if all the fight had gone out of her. "It would have worked if I hadn't lost the papers."

"Are you really that vengeful?" Lilly Belle said in disbelief, wiping the tears from her face. "Hiram loved the *Silver Leaf*. If he wanted to make me a partner, it was because he knew you hated it.

I didn't ask him to draw up those papers, and I didn't sign them because I didn't want to be the cause of more problems between you two. But you only saw what you wanted to see between Hiram and I. You never bothered to see what was really there. Hiram was my friend. We had too much respect for each other to ever let it be more than that."

"All right, that's enough," Jed said, giving a tug on Cornelia's arm. "If you don't have those papers, there's not much more we can do right now. I'll send a couple of the boys over to remove the body."

Cornelia pulled back, resisting Jed. "Wait. I'll go willingly, but I want her out of here," she said in a flat tone, the fire had gone out of her. "She'll get no charity from me. Without those papers, this place is mine and I want her out."

Jed turned and looked back at Lilly Belle. "Maybe you'd best move your things over to the hotel, or Miss Milly's boarding house, at least until we can get this straightened out."

Lilly Belle hesitated, then gave a nod. Jed headed for the doors with Cornelia in tow. She shuffled along beside him with no resistance this time. "Jed, what happens if we don't find those papers?" she asked in a voice so soft it was almost a whisper.

Jed, turned once more and said, "If we don't find those papers, I'm afraid the *Silver Leaf* goes to Cornelia."

She felt all the energy she had left drain from her, and she reached out to steady herself on the bar top.

Stinkweed crept around the end of the bar, peering at her with eyes bulging. She saw fear in those eyes. He held a fist to his chest, clutching yellowish cloth or paper so tight that only a scant corner poked out by his thumb. He must have been hiding in the storage closet this whole time and overheard all that had transpired. Tommy was a little soft in the head, but he probably understood enough of what Jed had said to realize that he was about to lose the only home he'd ever known.

"Tommy, come here," she said, wiping the tears from her face with her sleeve. The boy hesitated, tightening his fist and pulling it up closer to his chin. "It's okay. Come on over here. What have you got there?"

"What is that little ruffian doing here?" Cornelia said in a raised voice. She glared directly at the boy with hatred in her eyes. "I warned you not to come back when I chased you out last night."

Stinkweed stared with wide eyes at Cornelia, as if unable to turn away, as he moved down the length of the bar. He stepped up before Lilly Belle and extended his arm, opening his hand to reveal what he held. "M...mister Hiram s..says give these t..to you," he said, in a trembling voice so soft, she had to lean closer to hear. His eyes met hers briefly, before falling back to the dust at his feet. "M...missus Hiram d...dr...dropped 'em."

Lilly Belle took the papers from the boy's hand and spread out the crumpled ball to examine them. "Last night?" she said as she looked them over. They were the same papers Hiram had tried to show her the previous evening. "Cornelia dropped these last night?"

Stinkweed nodded.

"Jed, you better have a look," she said, holding them out toward him.

"That's them!" Cornelia said. "Those are the papers! Now you'll see. She wanted to steal this place. Those papers prove it."

Jed stepped forward and took them from Lilly Belle. "Let's just have a look, shall we?" he said, reading over the words there. "They have Hiram's signature on them. All this proves, Cornelia, is that you have no stake in this place, one way or the other." He took Cornelia by the arm once more. "You're still coming with me. I'm afraid you're under arrest."

"What? No." Cornelia said, trying to pull away. "What about her? She's the thief who talked him into drawing up those papers."

"Hiram signed them, but Lilly Belle didn't," Jed said, tightening his grip on her arm. "There's nothing to prove your claim. If I were you, I'd quit worrying about Lilly Belle, and start figuring how you're going to justify cold blooded murder." With that he pushed her through the door ahead of him and the two were gone, leaving the batwings swinging in their wake.

Lilly Belle gazed at the doorway, trying to process Jed's words and all that had transpired. Then, she remembered the boy, on his knees next to her, hiding behind her skirts. Taking him by the shoulders, she knelt down to look him in the eye. "Tommy, when did Hiram tell you to give me those papers?" she asked. "Did he tell you last night?"

The boy shook his head. "H...hiding," he said, lifting a finger to point toward the supply closet under the stairs.

"Just now? *When you were hiding?*" *she asked.* "How can that be?"

A cold wind blew through the saloon, stirring dust up from the dirt floor and sending chills down her, and she knew that it was him. "Hiram, wait. What am I supposed to do now?" *she called after it.*

In response, she heard a soft whisper, "Don't eat the pickled eggs."

Author Tom Johnson

Tom Johnson published multiple novels, which are reminiscent of Edgar Rice Burroughs, or the pulp fiction novels of times past. He wrote or contributed to more than eighty books over the course of his life. Sadly, in November of 2019 Tom passed. He was a great author and a dear friend. It is with honor that I include his short western story, "Gunsmoke" in this anthology. He will be deeply missed.

    Let me tell you about Tom Johnson in life. His dad was a cowboy and cook, giving his family an itinerant lifestyle. Tom changed schools often, as his dad's jobs were relocated. His dad wanted him to follow in his footsteps, but a cowboy's life didn't appeal to him. Instead, during his high school years, Tom dreamed about becoming an entomologist. He loved biology and math, but was weak in other subjects. He read every book he could find on insects, reptiles, and arachnids, as well as paleontology.

Years later, he and his wife, Ginger, started the publishing imprint of FADING SHADOWS, and published a hobby magazine for twenty-two years, and several genre titles for nine years. He was a voracious reader from an early age, and has never stopped reading for pleasure, though his interest in genres often switched from science fiction to western, to hardboiled detectives, the classics, and back to science fiction again over the years. In his own writing readers will often find something about his love of zoology, whether insects, reptiles, or saber-tooth cats. Tom is no longer with us, but his words and books live on.

Tom's Books: http://jur1.brinkster.net/index.html

Gunsmoke

Tom Johnson

Texas, 1882

The stranger rode a cold north wind into the border town across from Juarez. His shoulders were slumped forward with his head resting on his chest, his hat low over his face. The heavy coat was pulled up to cover the back of his neck, a thin bandana wrapped tightly around his face. The trail had been long, but the rider was used to hard rides.

Passing a small building on the outskirts of the little settlement, he recognized the steeple sitting atop the structure, but the church appeared empty this evening, families undoubtedly home where they were sheltered from the winter cold.

Dogs barked in the distance, and as he neared the tiny hub, he could now hear laughter coming from a large wooden building on top of a raised foundation. Wooden steps, weathered with age, led to a wooden sidewalk several feet above the ground. It was a simple reminder that the streets sometimes flooded during the rainy season.

Three horses were tied to the hitching post, saddles and saddlebags still mounted, as if the riders expected to ride out soon. Now the stranger paused for a minute staring at them with sharp eyes. He recognized the big roan and two pintos, and knew his trail ended in this border town.

From down the street he heard the sharp clang of metal striking metal and urged his mount forward. Big doors on the building were slightly ajar where the sound issued, and he saw in the dim light within a man with thick waist and deep chest shaping a horseshoe over an open pit of burning coals. The huge man was sweating over the heat from his exertions. But the big mallet continued without pause rising with the muscular arm, and then slamming down to ring with a loud bang as the shoe took shape.

Dismounting, the stranger led his Appaloosa inside the barn where he saw empty stalls and stacks of hay. Several large cats stared at him from a corner of the room. There would be no mice or snakes here. The big man only glanced at him as he entered, then continued his pounding with the metal hammer. Three horses were already in stalls, and the stranger figured they belonged to the blacksmith.

Removing his saddle and blankets he tossed his bedroll against a stack of hay in the corner of an empty stall while the horse found the water trough and quenched its thirst before sauntering into a stall where more hay was thrown about as an enticement.

Dropping the horseshoe into a large bucket of water next to the fire, the blacksmith set his hammer down, watching the stranger as he approached.

Holding out coins, the rider dropped them into his hand. "I'll sleep here tonight."

The big man nodded as the stranger walked out the doors, closing them now as he hastened away. His steps led to the building where the horses were tied. He paused a moment to check the saddlebags on the roan, and then he climbed the wooden steps. He pushed the door open and entered a dimly lit saloon where three men stood at a bar with Mexican senoritas hanging on their arms. At a table against the back wall near a stack of cut wood, an old Mexican strummed on a guitar mumbling some tune only he knew.

The heavyset bartender nodded as he dropped a coin on the bar, "Whiskey," the stranger said. The three men and senoritas turned and stared at the new man for a second and then went back to their merry-making.

A pot-bellied stove in the center of the big room kept it warm, fed likely by the wood stacked against the back wall. Feeling the heat now, the stranger removed his woolen-lined gloves and approached the stove to warm his hands after the long ride.

He returned to the counter a few minutes later, feeling life back in his hands, and drank the whiskey. The brandy's warmth trickled down his throat warming his stomach now.

An audible sigh escaped his lips as he put the glass back on the counter and motioned to the bartender, "Another whiskey."

Oddly, he didn't touch the second glass. Instead, turning he unbuttoned his coat, as he stepped away from the bar.

"Danvers!" he snarled.

Suddenly the saloon became quiet as the three men turned, pushing the girls away from them as they did so. For a moment there was fear in their eyes, then three hands reached for heavy revolvers at their sides, but the big .44 in the stranger's hand blazed leaden death before the three men could clear leather and fire.

Screaming, the Mexican girls ran from the room, disappearing through a back door as the bartender stood frozen behind the counter. The guitar had gone silent now, the old Mexican staring at the bodies on the floor.

As he turned to face the bartender, the badge of a Texas Ranger pinned to his shirt sparkled as it caught the light from an oil lamp behind the counter. His .44 holstered now, the Ranger pulled a Wanted Poster from his coat and placed it on the countertop. He then reached for the second glass of whiskey, as a cold breeze wafted in from the back door.

And gun smoke slowly drifted towards the ceiling ....

Author Jeff Bowles

https://www.goodreads.com/author/show/
3895499.Jeff_Bowles?from_search=true[1]

Jeff Bowles is a science fiction and horror writer from the mountains of Colorado. The best of his outrageous and imaginative work can be found in *God's Body: Book One - The Fall*, Godling and Other Paint Stories, Fear and Loathing in Las Cruces, and Brave New Multiverse. He has published work in magazines and anthologies like *PodCastle*, *Tales from the Canyons of the Damned*, *Threepenny Review*, and *Dark Moon Digest*. Jeff earned his Master of Fine Arts degree in creative

---

1. https://www.goodreads.com/author/show/
3895499.Jeff_Bowles?from_search=true&fbclid=IwAR2ReeyOIVb7U-
eIRICO6teSn99OSoF-GUIRf8_31wJ5P1FXAcug-GZiYos

writing at Western State Colorado University. He currently lives in the high-altitude Pikes Peak region, where he dreams strange dreams and spends far too much time under the stars. Jeff's new novel, *Love/ Madness/Demon*, is available now.

Wenekia

Jeff Bowles

"You are not yet a man, little brother," said Makoće. "You would not understand."

"But what if evil spirits are watching us?"

Makoće spared a glance at the moon, at the blue sheen it cast over the wild Dakota grass, over outcropped rocks and distant craggy buttes. He thought of white frost giants, of thunder beings and the powers of the four winds. A chill settled over him, but he set his jaw and let their father's pony ride on.

"No spirits will harm us," said Makoće. "They will let us -pass. They will let us see the Wenekia and the wonderful things he has shown to men of many nations."

Kakiuká fidgeted behind him on their mount. He clicked his tongue, saying, "Yes, yes, Wenekia, the great savior. He shows wonderful things to men, but you are only two years older than I, and I am a boy."

"Two years is a long time. Have you ever kissed a girl?"

"No."

"Well I have. You are a boy, but I am a man."

Makoće took a route wide of the fort and the soldier-town-store, and then he led their pony across the creek that flowed south out of Pine Ridge Reservation. At last, they came to the edge of an overlook. Makoće took in the landscape below, tracing the roll of hills and the flats of prairie that trailed far off into the wilderness. In the distance, he spotted two tepees standing in a field of grass, glowing softly from fires within.

Makoće glanced back, ignored the worried look on his brother's face, and urged the pony down. The animal was surefooted, but its hooves kicked up dust and loosened rocks. Kakiuká wrapped his arms around Makoće, relaxing them only after they were down and riding across prairie once more.

"Please, brother," said Kakiuká, "we should go back home. What if father catches us? What if Wasichu soldiers catch us?"

"Soldiers? They have empty heads. If they trouble us, I will take my knife to them, defend us both."

"But I am cold and hungry."

Makoće felt the emptiness in his own stomach. It seemed like he'd been hungry ever since the tribe's rations had been reduced to nearly nothing at all. They took, and took, and took, never once giving back anything his people truly needed. He did his best to push it from his mind. "Stop complaining, little kingbird. We are almost there."

They crested a hill, and the tepees came into closer view. Makoće could spot the figures of horses and men standing about.

"We go on foot now," he said. "If we can see them, they can see us."

They dismounted and tethered the pony to a scraggly tree. Makoće lowered himself onto his hands and knees and motioned for Kakiuká to do the same. They crawled through the tall grass, occasionally peeking above to gain their bearings. After a time, they drew close enough to make out details.

Makoće rolled onto his knees, keeping only his eyes above the grass. Kakiuká did the same. They scanned the men's faces.

"Look," whispered Kakiuká, "there is father."

Makoće nodded. "Yes. Do not talk."

"Who are the others?"

"Big Foot and Kicking Bear."

"Big Foot and Kicking Bear? With father? How does he know them?"

"Father is a very important man. He had many horses until the Wasichus took them away. Now, do not talk."

Soon, two men emerged from one of the tepees, taking up position on either side of its flap. They wore rabbit skins, white and blue-colored shirts with feathers at the arms. Paiute, Makoće realized, not Lakota. A third man followed them, taller than the other two. His silver hair swept over his shoulders, swayed against his back as he moved.

"The Wenekia," said Makoće.

The other men gathered around the Paiutes, leaned in to greet them, and slowly made their way to the second tepee. The Wenekia stopped near the entrance. He turned slowly, looked in Makoće's direction, seeming to stare right at him. Makoće ducked. He dared not move until he no longer heard the men's voices.

"Can we go home now?" said Kakiuká.

Makoće silently rubbed his chin. Kakiuká huffed. He leaned forward and pulled a strand of Makoće's hair.

"Ahsh!"

"Can we go?"

Makoće glared at his brother. "No."

"Why?"

"Because I need to know what they say."

Kakiuká smirked. "Brother, you creep like a buffalo, and you are not invisible. How are you to sneak inside?"

"I am not sneaking anywhere."

Makoće stood, not caring if anyone watched. He strode towards the tepee.

"Brother," said Kakiuká. His voice pleaded. "Do not leave me."

Makoće turned, seeing his brother's wide eyes. He sighed, doubled back, and grabbed Kakiuká by the arm. They made their way to the side of the tepee, and as they did, the sound of muffled voices came to them. Makoće looked at Kakiuká, mouthing the words, *Do not talk.* Kakiuká nodded.

Makoće reached for his knife, unsheathed it. He set the tip lightly against the tepee's skin, applying pressure and twisting it slowly. He then put the knife back in its sheath and bent to peep through the hole.

The men sat in a circle around a low fire, the three Paiutes and the three Makoće knew. They passed around a pipe, held it reverently, put it to their lips and drew smoke.

After the last puff was taken, Big Foot spoke. "We have smoked and so we are friends. We have come in secret, without the consent of the blue coats. We have come to hear your words, Wenekia. We would know your heart."

Makoće squinted, seeing a smile on the Wenekia's face. The man spoke slowly. "My heart, great chief, is like yours. I grieve just as your people grieve. I would see the earth and sky and four winds restored. I would see the buffalo return and our ancestors made live again. I would see the Wasichus washed away like loose earth in a storm."

Big Foot hesitated. "And you could make these things happen?"

The Wenekia shook his head. "No, I *will* make them happen."

Makoće was taken aback by the man's words, yet his mind raced, his imagination flew. He saw it all, saw the proud dead alive, saw the buffalo gather in great herds and thunder over the land once more. He saw the white men leave, run, board ships and flee over the water. He smiled to himself.

Kakiuká tugged at his elbow. "Brother, what do they say?"

Makoće drew a hand back to silence him. He angled his head, pressing his eye closer to the hole. His father spoke next. "Your words fill our hearts with hope, Wenekia. But we still doubt."

Kicking Bear nodded. "Wasichu tongues are forked. Treachery and lies are all they know. Our people are starving, Wenekia. We cannot eat lies, just as we cannot eat hope."

The Wenekia's smile broadened. He rolled onto his knees, slowly rose to his feet. "No, you cannot eat hope, but I bring more than hope. I bring an end to your troubles."

He drew his arms close to his chest, splaying his fingers and circling his hands. Makoće watched in wonder.

"You had a wife, Chief Big Foot?" the Wenekia said.

The old man nodded.

"What would you give to see her once more?"

Big Foot shook his head. "She is gone. Such thoughts are foolish."

"Are they? Do you think so?"

Sudden light filled the tepee, white and shimmering blue. The Wenekia's fingers twisted, swirled about, were chased and trailed by streams of blue. The men gasped. Makoće squinted in the light. His heart hammered; he held his breath.

The light brightened, broadened, thickened, as if tangible. It gathered, formed itself into the vague outline of a person. The figure blinked out, and all at once, blinked in and resolved. A woman stood in the tepee, youthful, in the prime of life. She glowed white, luminous; her outline shimmered and sparkled.

Kicking Bear made a warding sign with his fingers. Makoće's father pressed his back against the tepee. Big foot seemed unafraid. His eyes glistened. He leaned forward and stretched out a trembling hand. "She is young."

The Wenekia nodded. "Yes."

"But she is an illusion."

"No, not illusion."

The Wenekia gestured. The woman's light changed, deepened and solidified into cloth and leather, into skin and hair. She was no longer a woman of light, but a woman of flesh and blood. Her gaze darted around the tepee, onto each man, until she finally saw Big Foot.

"Husband?" she said. "What... where am I?"

Big Foot recoiled. He could not speak.

"I was tending to our meal and..." She shook her head and took a closer look at Big Foot. "You are so old."

A tear slid down the old man's cheek. He moaned and sat back.

The Wenekia gestured a final time. The woman's figure returned to light. She brightened, dimmed, and all at once, blinked out. Kicking Bear and Makoće's father were speechless. Big Foot sat staring at the tepee's floor. The Wenekia bent and whispered into the ear of one of his companions. The man nodded and stood.

"What I show you, great chief," said the Wenekia, "I show not to cause pain. She was there then, and she is here now. And there is more. You say you wish the buffalo to return?"

The Wenekia and his companion faced one another. They put their hands on each other's shoulders and lowered their heads. Nothing happened.

Makoće felt another tug on his arm, but he ignored it. The men in the tepee looked confused. Makoće was confused, too. The two Paiutes simply stood with heads bowed.

"Makoće!" his little brother bellowed beside him.

Makoće huffed and jerked around. A buffalo stood inches away. It glowed for an instant, and just as the woman had, resolved into flesh and blood. It was immense, much taller than either of the two brothers. It stamped a hoof, let out a great snort that blew Makoće's hair. He screamed.

There was a commotion inside the tepee. The men rushed outside. Big Foot and Kicking Bear gasped again at the sight of the buffalo.

"Kakiuká?" said the brothers' father. "Makoće?"

Makoće barely heard him. His eyes were fixed on the buffalo.

"Do you see?" said the Wenekia. "I bring more than hope."

The buffalo became light and blinked out of existence. Makoće stared at the spot it had been. His body shook. A hand gripped him by the neck. He jumped, jolted to see his father's face filled with anger. "You disobeyed me."

Makoće felt a simultaneous rush of relief and dread. He turned to see the shock on the other men's faces, the smile the Wenekia wore. He saw one of the Paiute's hands glow softly and flicker. The same man moved close to the Wenekia. He leaned in and whispered in his ear. The Wenekia's eyes widened. He nodded somberly.

"My friends," he said, "my brothers. You see my miracles. If you choose to follow me, come to me and say so. We leave you now. Travel well."

"Now?" said Kicking Bear. "But we..."

"I am sorry. We must go."

The Wenekia motioned and the three moved toward the horses. He passed Makoće, stopped suddenly, turned. He smiled, yet the smile seemed sad. He tussled Makoće's hair.

"And you, little buffalo hunter. Stay out of trouble." He brought a thumb to Makoće's face and drew it across his cheek and over his lips. He chuckled softly and the three men walked away.

#

They rode across the prairie, Makoće and Kakiuká atop their pony, their father atop his. It seemed to Makoće like their father had been shouting the entire ride.

"You did worse than disobey me. You put your lives in danger. What if a blue coat had spotted you? Do you think he would have been kind because you are children?"

Makoće ground his jaw, but he dared not talk back to his father. He looked at Kakiuká and saw that his lip trembled. He felt a twinge of remorse, deep in his stomach.

"Answer me!" said their father.

"No, father," the brothers said.

"And you, Makoće, you disappoint me most of all. Your brother could have been hurt, and it would have been your fault. I thought you were growing into manhood."

The remorse Makoće felt intensified. His stomach churned.

His father continued. "I was wrong. A man would have respected the wishes of his elder. Did you, Makoće?"

"No, father."

"No, you did not. Other fathers may expect disobedience from their children, but I do not."

Makoće felt queasy. His head drooped and he pitched and fell from the pony, his mind a rush of confusing thoughts, his limbs numb. Time seemed to slow, to cushion and soften the fall, as if Makoće weren't falling at all, but drifting like a leaf on the water. He landed, but not on hard ground. He saw daylight, clouds. The Wenekia stood over him. Makoće blinked once. His father kneeled over him and it was night. "Makoće! Are you—"

Makoće blinked. Clouds again, daylight. The Wenekia kneeled over him. Makoće's dizziness faded; his queasiness vanished. He looked around, found himself lying on a bright auburn cloud. Clouds everywhere. There was no sun, yet there was light, no breeze, yet the air felt cool against his skin.

"Is this a vision?" said Makoće.

The Wenekia smiled. He glanced at his Paiute companions, who stood off to the side, scowling, their arms folded.

Makoće sat up slowly. "Are you spirits?"

The Wenekia nodded.

"Then this is the spirit world?"

"This is a space between spaces, a time between times."

"We are out of time," said one of the Paiutes. "They have found us. We must flee."

The Wenekia sighed, and then his smile became sad again, careworn, as if the man had suddenly been overcome by regret.

"Why must you flee?" said Makoće.

"We are hunted by evil spirits. We are permitted only to observe humans, not to interfere with them. I thought I could help you, little buffalo hunter. I thought I could help all of you."

"They are coming," said one of his companions.

The Wenekia sighed one more time. He nodded slowly and patted Makoće on the shoulder.

"I do not understand," said Makoće. "You confuse me, spirit. Am I to come with you? Do you need my help?"

"No. There is not a soul in all the universes who could help us now. You, Makoće, will be my gift to your people."

A loud boom filled the air, a sound as loud as thunder. A deep hiss followed, and a tearing. Makoće saw the outlines of four glowing yellow men fade in. The Wenekia stood. Another pop, more hissing and tearing. The Wenekia and his companions shimmered and seemed to lose all earthly substance. He smiled at Makoće, and as they blinked away, Makoće no longer saw three Paiutes. He saw men of light, brilliant white and blue light. They were gone.

The glowing yellow men blinked in. They rushed forward, searching frantically, completely ignoring Makoće. Their legs stomped and arms thrashed wildly. They pounded their luminous chests. They gathered together, made sounds together, let out a terrible screeching. Makoće cried out and put his hands to his ears.

The screeching stopped. They turned, stared at Makoće. A smell like burnt pine assaulted Makoće's nose. He forced himself to remember it was only a vision, that they would not hurt him. The yellow men bent and cackled. One reached out and touched Makoće's face. Makoće's skin crawled and his hair tingled. His heart hammered, as it had when the buffalo appeared.

Suddenly, the yellow man let out another screech, shrill and piercing, higher and sharper than the last. Terror filed Makoće. The yellow man pointed its fingertips at him. Its hand began to glow, a deep, blood red glow. Makoće thought of someplace else, of home, of his brother and father. And just as he did, he instantly grew queasy, dizzy. They were going to kill him. They were going to take his soul. He wanted to go home.

Makoće pitched and fell through the clouds. Fell to the hard, grassy ground.

#

Makoće saw the tepee's skin shudder slightly. The tip of a blade punched through, withdrew and left a small hole. His father watched also. He met Makoće's eyes and smiled.

It had been almost a week to the day since the Wenekia had shown them his magic. Makoće drew smoke with Big Foot, Kicking Bear, and his father. Big foot was the first to speak.

"We have smoked and so we are friends. Bad times have come. The Wenekia has left us, and so has our hope."

Makoće's father shook his head. "Hope has not left. We have good things to tell."

"But what you tell is hard to believe," said Kicking Bear. "You tell us that the Wenekia and his friends were not men, but spirits. You tell us that this boy had a vision, that he has great medicine."

"No," said Makoće's father, "this is no boy. There was a time when the dead lived, a time when the buffalo roamed proud and strong. Makoće could make those times our time now. He could take the Wasichus to another place far away. He can do everything the Wenekia could do. This was the gift of his vision."

The vision flashed through Makoće's mind, the terrible electric touch of the yellow man, the way it had screeched, the way his ears had ached.

Big Foot cocked an eyebrow. He leaned over and spoke softly with Kicking Bear. He then nodded and considered Makoće carefully. "And you. You will prove this to us?"

Makoće's thoughts lingered on his vision. He was silent, staring at the floor of the tepee. His father nudged him gently. He glanced at Big Foot and cleared his throat. "Yes, elder."

Makoće stood. He twisted his fingers and circled his hands. Blue and white light filled the Tepee, and a young woman appeared to them all.

After he had shown the elders his power, he left them to speak with his father. He walked along the Tepee's edge, coming to a stop as he spotted the hole in its skin. He was not surprised to find no one peering through it.

"I know you are here, little kingbird. Come out."

There was silence for a time, followed by a rustling in the grass.

Kakiuká stood. "Do not tell father."

"I should tell him. You could be hurt out here."

"Please, brother, I have done nothing you have not done."

Makoće sighed and nodded.

Kakiuká smiled and ran to his brother. "What did they say? Will they follow you?"

"Yes."

"And we will make the dead live and bring back the buffalo and wipe the Wasichus from the land and—"

"Perhaps, brother, perhaps."

Kakiuk's smile broadened, but an instant later, it lost some of its eagerness. He suddenly became thoughtful, more serious than Makoće was used to seeing him. "But what if we are being watched, brother? What if...they come back?"

A chill settled over Makoće. He did his best to push it aside. He told himself to be brave, to be like his father, like Big Foot and Kicking Bear and like the Wenekia himself.

He put a hand to Kakiuká's shoulder. "Who can know for certain what the future holds, little kingbird? Only the spirits above, and I am just a man"

"Brother, why do I always have to remind you? You are not yet..." Kakiuká paused. Slowly, the smile returned to his lips. He tilted his head to the side and squinted at Makoće. "You really kissed a girl?"

Makoće nodded.

"Was she very pretty?"

Makoće tussled Kakiuká's hair. "Come, little brother. I think it is finally time for us to go home."

Together they walked through the high prairie grass, towards their pony, toward home.

Author Arthur Rosch

www.artrosch.com[1]

A Midwesterner by birth, Arthur Rosch migrated to the West Coast just in time to be a hippie but discovered that he was more connected to the Beatnik generation. He harkened back to an Old School world of jazz, poetry, painting and photography. In the Eighties he received Playboy Magazine's Best Short Story Award for a comic view of a planet where there are six genders. The timing was not good. His life was falling apart as he struggled with addiction and depression. He experienced the reality of the streets for more than a decade. Putting himself back together was the defining experience of his life. It wasn't easy. It did, however, nurture his literary soul. He has a passion for astronomy, photography, history, psychology and the weird puzzle of human experience. He is currently a certified Seniors Peer Counselor in Sonoma County, California.

Clouds in the West

Arthur Rosch

As a science fiction paranormal western which takes place in a fictional world, some terms will be unfamiliar.

Glossary of terms used in *Clouds in the West* (in order of usage):

Gnurled hydrospore: Material made from the spores from the hydrosepia tree bark.

Greph: A large, four-legged creature that is smarter than an Earth horse, which carries its rider by common consent. They can be stubborn and cantankerous when riled. They communicate telepathically and have exceptional problem-solving abilities.

Plong vapor: A pheromone expelled by male grephs during mating season, which is basically year-round. Grephs are highly sexual creatures.

Faffo: A grain with narcotic-like properties that is particularly appealing to grephs. When eaten by grephs, it causes them to lose control of their faculties, similar to the effects that catnip has on felines on Earth.

Imonium petals: Used to create an addictive narcotic drug, similar to opium on Earth, which is ingested by chewing the thick green leaves of the imonium plant.

Lamista: A small frontier town located twelve klicks north of the Valuvian Volcano.

The Combine: A large conglomerate who deal in Imonium and weapons, and get rich off of terrorizing small frontier towns and forcing the townspeople to pay for their protection, similar to the drug cartels on Earth.

Shlunk: A classic greph move to dismount an unwanted rider.

The High Woodlands: The original home and breeding grounds of grephs.

I woke up and my gun was missing. How the hell, did someone get up to me and steal my gun? Maybe it was Sami. Maybe she had some reason to steal my gun. Maybe she was in danger.

I love that gun. It's a ShotFix 210, a smart weapon that used electrostatic plasma to discharge a grain of sand moving so fast, that if that grain hit something it was all over: finito! The grip is custom made of gnurled hydrospore. The gunsight is adjusted to my messed-up vision. It aims twenty-two degrees right, compensating for my glass eye on the right, and the distorted astigmatism of my left eye. What use was it to anyone? Of course, it was so powerful that it didn't have to be accurate.

My instinct was to grab my stuff and get behind the tree, but what did that mean, "behind the tree"? Where is a tree's behind? From what direction might my enemy try to kill me? Rather than speculate further, I tossed the saddle onto my greph, tightened the straps, jumping onto its back.

"Ott! Ott!" I said to Spooky, and she took off like a bullet, galloping up the wide meadow towards the tree line on the ridge. The acceleration almost threw me out of the saddle. Grephs cover a lot of ground when they're in the mood.

She was giving off a familiar smell, a funk, and I knew that she sensed a male greph, in season, beyond the ridge. No matter that the male might belong to the person or persons who had taken my gun. Spooky had a one-track mind when plong-vapor touched her pheromone receptors. Then there was the fact that grephs are telepathic. I told myself to relax, that Spooky wouldn't carry me towards danger.

A band of six men, riding in a disciplined column approached. They seemed to appear out of the sunrise; I squinted into the light. "What's up, Spooky?" I sent my thought to my mount.

"Six grephs coming this way. Six riders attached. Neither friendly nor unfriendly."

"Are the grephs eating faffo?"

"Yes, they are deeply hooked. The riders have control over the faffo, that is, they have control over the grephs." Faffo is a grain that grephs love beyond reason. Using faffo on a greph is evil. But it's the only way to get a greph to carry a rider that the greph doesn't like.

A column of six, riding in sync, could mean two things: A sheriff's posse or bounty hunters. It was better to ride in the opposite direction. I asked Spooky to gallop south, and she responded so quickly that I had to grab my hat to keep it from blowing away. I buried my hands in the saddle straps and hung on. My feet bounced in and out of the stirrups, and I would have been thrown had my mount and I not been mentally connected. I used to ride horses. Compared to grephs, horses are stupid.

I have to explain something. The crime that I had committed was busting my lady friend, Sami, out of jail. The crime Sami had committed was busting me out of jail. Sami got caught when her greph threw a tendon. She refused to leave her mount. She climbed with her greph, Jult, up a rocky trail and into a cave. She made a splint for Jult out of sticks and bark and spliced them onto the leg with strips of leather. She nursed Jult on Imonium petals for four days and then she ran out of water. When she left the cave, some ragged Apaches surrounded her and took her into Lamista. They turned her over to Mann Kingslake, the private copper that was hired by the Combine. And so, the story goes...rich guys and their cops, always fucking with people who just want to be left alone. Okay, I know why Kingslake wants to fuck with us. We have property that he wants. We won't sell it. We're troublemakers.

I'm going to bust Sami out of jail again. If I can shake these guys and their stoned grephs. They're looking for me. They may not know it yet, but they are looking for me. Spooky and I are riding back to Lamista, but we're going through the woods.

I hate looking over my shoulder. This isn't a metaphor. I literally hate looking over my shoulder. It makes me feel guilty and look guilty. You know, like in the papers, when they draw a copper taking a guy into custody. That guy always looks guilty and he's looking over his shoulder, as if at someone he hoped would save him, but didn't. I'm going to save Sami. Me and Spooky.

Beyond the woods there's a series of rock spires and these are attached to a huge butte.

The spires look like lion's paws as they spread down the butte wall. There are caves between them, and I took refuge in one of these, waiting to observe my pursuers. If they were bounty hunters, they would kill me. Deputies were more interested in taking me alive. I got Spooky to lie down, resting on her haunches. We kept in the shadows made by the rising sun. I reasoned thus: if there are six deputies out here, that means that the jail in Lamista had but a skeleton crew. Sheriff Kingslake would be there, drinking bourbon with beer chasers, boots up on his desk. He might have a single deputy, but I didn't think he wanted company when he drank. He was a solitary drinker, a real alcoholic.

It was indeed the posse of deputies who swept past me on the road. Good. Now I had to hope that Spooky could control herself with regard to the whiff of plong from the horny male greph.

(Spooky): Grephs are promiscuous. I am a sexy female. When the plong hit my palps, I nearly piddled my crotch fur. Oh, turds! I don't need this when I'm on a mission for Wooly Bill. He's the only human I carry, will ever carry. Wooly Bill is a lot funnier than he realizes. I know he needs Sami. Of course he does; we all need someone or something.

It's all about control, you see. None of us are in control of our fates. Grephs are deeply conscious of fate. We tend to bond with our riders, so that we share their fates.

I want Wooly Bill to have his Sami, and for Sami to have her Wooly Bill. I'm going to send a mind-cloud towards the grephs who are carrying the posse. Here we go:

Why are you carrying those bad men who want to capture my Wooly Bill?

Cloud multiples: We have faffo! We love faffo!

Can you be that stupid? Faffo makes you even more stupid! Shlunk your riders and go back to the High Wildland.

One of the grephs stopped so suddenly that its rider up-ended, flew over its ears and landed face first on the ground. A classic greph Shlunk. That greph galloped at a tangent towards the mountains and was soon lost from sight. The others kept coming towards Wooly Bill.

The narrative had changed, Wooly Bill realized. The grephs had taken over the narrative. That was okay. Grephs were more interesting than humans; they are also more adept at managing the problems of life. If they had decided to help him rescue Sami, that was great. Grephs had a way of succeeding where humans failed.

That's what happened. The rest is mere action narrative. The grephs took care of fate the way they thought would make the most people happy. That's what grephs are like. Better than humans, certainly.

Better than humans.

Author Roberta Eaton Cheadle

https://robertawrites235681907.wordpress.com/about/

Roberta Eaton Cheadle is writer of young adult and adult fiction in the supernatural fantasy, historical horror, and historical supernatural genres.

To date, Roberta has published one novel, *Through the Nethergate*, and several short stories in various anthologies including *Whispers of the Past*, edited and compiled by Kaye Lynne Booth, and *Spellbound*, compiled by Dan Alatorre.

Roberta has a historical supernatural novel set during the Second Anglo Boer War in South Africa coming out in early 2021.

When she is not writing, Roberta enjoys working in the garden and creating fondant and cake artworks.

The Thirstyland Journey

Roberta Eaton Cheadle

As a South African paranormal western, some terms may not be familiar to all readers.

Glossary of terms used in *The Thirstyland Journey* (in order of usage):

Hottentot - Now called Khoikhoi, are non-Bantu indigenous nomadic pastoralists of South Africa

Oom - Afrikaans word for uncle.

Betuanaland – Modern Botswana.

South West Africa – Modern Namibia.

Transvaal Republic - The name of the independent Boer Republic at the time of this trek (1877).

Afrikaans - A West Germanic language descended from Dutch and spoken mainly in South Africa and Namibia.

President Thomas Francois Burgers - the elected president of the Transvaal Republic between 1872 and April 1877 when it was annexed by Britain. He was married to a Scottish woman and bought a piano which offended the highly conservative, Calvinistic Afrikaners who believed that music and dancing were instruments of the devil.

Bechuana - A native of Betuanaland (modern day Botswanian).

His cup of tea crashes to the floor as the emancipated figure materialises before his shocked eyes.

The vision's large blue eyes bulge from a skull that is devoid of flesh and covered by dry and peeling skin. "Water," her cracked lips form the word with a tongue that is swollen and blackish. "Help us, Reverend, you're our only hope."

"Where are you?"

"We are in the Kalahari Desert at Tlakane," the spirit says weakly and then she's gone.

***

"Let's *trek*," calls Papa. Two Boys, the African *voorloper*, is in his place at the head of the oxen, ready to lead them, when John, the African driver, cracks his long whip called a *shambok*. The covered wagon trundles forward across sand which is burning hot to the touch, despite the late afternoon sun's low position in the vivid blue sky.

It's too early in the evening to be trekking into the Kalahari Desert, thinks Elsbet, *Sien says its better to travel once the moon rises and Hottentot's know about the desert. I don't know why we can't leave tomorrow with Oom Lourens' party. His group plan is to wait for the moon to rise before they start. Why is Papa in such a rush to leave now with Oom Jan's group.*

Elsbet knows that Papa holds Jan Christoffel Greyling, affectionately known as *Oom* Jan, in high regard. He has hunted in the Kalahari Desert before and has survived. Papa is confident that he can lead the *trekkers* across the Kalahari Desert, which stretches across most of Betuanaland and the eastern part of South West Africa, and into Angola. The primary destination of the *trekkers* is the Humpata highlands of south-western Angola.

Elsbet's mother, Sarie, also has faith in *Oom* Jan. The previous week, Elsbet had overheard Papa talking to her mother about the planned route. "I was concerned, Sarie, when I heard that the native chief, Khama, had withdrawn permission for the *trek* to go through his land after hearing that Jan Greyling was going to lead us. The compromise position is that Lourens du Plessis will be the main leader of this *trek* and that doesn't please me. Lourens wants to break the groups up into small groups and I think we will be safer travelling all together. There is strength in numbers, isn't there?"

"I would also prefer *Oom* Jan to lead us," her mother had replied, "I have a lot of faith in him with his experience of hunting in the desert."

"Well, because of the change in leadership, Reverend Hepburn, who is working at the Ngami Mission, intervened and managed to get Chief Khama to re-instate his permission for the *trek* to pass through his land so, I suppose, it was a necessary decision. I would rather travel with Jan though, so we'll leave with his initial party tomorrow. Lourens plans to leave the following evening after the moon rises."

Elsbet thinks briefly about Reverend Hepburn. She had met him once and found him to be an inspirational messenger of God. *If I ever need help, he is the one I will ask.*

Despite her trepidation about heading into the desert during the heat of the late afternoon, Elsbet's glad to finally be on the move. Her family has spent months camping at the Crocodile River in the Transvaal Republic, patiently waiting for other interested families to gather in advance of this second migration of *Afrikaans* speaking farmers, called *Boers*, and their families to Angola. Many of the people had succumbed to fever during this waiting period and seventy-five of the would-be *trekkers* had died.

When Papa had first suggested they sell their farm in Rustenburg and travel by ox-wagon to Angola, Elsbet had asked him why he wanted to move away from their established farm and *trek* into the unknown.

"I don't want to live under British rule," Papa had declared. "The financial affairs of the Transvaal Republic are not in a good way under the leadership of that heretic, President Burgers, and an invasion by Britain is imminent. I want to live an independent life and so do some of the other Boers. I have decided to join the next *trek* to Angola."

"Why Angola, Papa? Why will it be better for us there?"

"Angola is ruled by the Portuguese, Elsbet. We will have to submit to the laws of Portugal, but we will be free to speak our own language and will not be subjected to the British ideas about imperialism and anglicisation."

Mother added her own views: "I believe that if we make this journey, God will grant us our Promised Land. God will look favourably upon those of his people who flee heresy and vanquish music and other works of the devil."

It is hot and stuffy in the back of the covered wagon but Aletta and Johannes, Elsbet's younger sister and brother, sit quietly next to their mother. They would not dream of complaining and annoying their father. *They are such good children. They know the Bible tells us to honour our mother and father.*

The wagon is packed with barrels of water, Papa's rifle and rounds of ammunition, collapsible furniture, provisions, including sun-dried game meat, called *biltong*, and sacks of crushed mielies, and everything else the family will need to survive on the journey and when they reach their distant destination.

Another barrel of water and cages containing chickens hang beneath the wagon and all of Papa's livestock, including cattle, sheep, oxen and goats travel with them under the care of their Hottentot shepherds.

"Sien recommended a few Hottentots to help us on this trip," says Papa. "The Zulus won't travel into the desert. Jan told me that all the shepherds in his party are Hottentots."

The sixteen oxen snort and humph as they strain to pull the loaded wagon through the heavy sand which retards their forward motion. Later, after the sun disappears and the moon rises, Elsbet enjoys the cool breeze that flows through the opening in the canvas wagon covering as night progresses. There is an unpleasant dryness to the air that makes her nose and throat itch and this, together with the rough jolting, as the wooden wagon wheels pass over scrubby desert bushes, make for uncomforable travelling and prevents sleep.

At 1.30 a.m. the convoy of forty five wagons halts and everyone enjoys some water and food. After a thirty minute respite, the men get eveyone moving again. "We are heading for a waterhole where we will stop and rest for the day," says Papa, as they all clamber back into the wagon.

An hour after the first rosy glow of dawn flushes the sky, the weary group reaches the spot where the first watering hole is marked on *Oom* Jan's map. "It's supposed to be there, under that large overhanging rock," he says.

"It's not there! There's no water here!" The disappointed shouts fill the air as the men examine the smooth carpet of sand beneath the thick slab.

Oom Jan examines the area carefully. "It looks like animals have trampled this area and the watering hole has filled up with sand."

"There is no water for the animals," said Papa as he gives each member of the family some water and *biltong*. Water and food is also provided to Two Boys, John, Sien and the other shepherds. Mother spreads out some blankets under the wagon for the family. After digging a shallow hole in the sand and covering themselves with bits of branches broken from the scrubby bushes, John and Two Boys sank into a deep sleep. The Hottentot shepherds do not seem to be affected by the heat and simply fling themselves down on the sand, falling into deep sleep within moments.

Elsbet wakes up at about 3 p.m. feeling like a loaf of bread in an oven. The dry hot air underneath the wagon seems to be sucking the blood out of her as she lies there. Flies swarm around the sleepers, settling on their noses, mouths and eyes, seemingly undeterred by the intense heat.

"I'm hot," moans little Aletta as she wakes, waving away the buzzing flies. No-one says anything to her, there was nothing to say.

The heat is searing and unrelenting. Elsbet's clothes are itchy and there are damp patches under her arms.

Papa gives everyone more water from his canteen and they all lie sweltering for the next two hours until it is time to get ready to *trek*. The heavy panting of the animals which have received no water at all for twenty-four hours, plagues Elsbet and makes her head ache violently.

When Papa, Two Boys and John *inspan* the animals, they are restless and aggitated. At Papa's request, Mother and Elsbet walk to lighten the load for the oxen who are weaking from lack of food and water. They creep on through the shifting sand, heads bent and feet shuffling, until sunset, when they halt and wait for the moon to rise and provide much needed light. Papa gives them some of the warm and unsatsifying water and Mother cooks them a simple meal of mielies cooked in the coals of the fire. Papa prays: "Dear Lord, please look out for your humble servants travelling through this desert and help us find water at the next marked spot."

The advent of the full moon, sees the convoy on the move again. "The next waterhole is still a full thirty-six hours away," says Papa. "We need to keep moving so that we can get there as soon as possible."

All of the people, except the very young, are walking now, and many *Boers*, including Papa, have left behind some of their precious funiture, in an attempt to further lighten the wagons. Despite these attempts to lighten the weight of the wagons, the convoy has to stop regularly to change the teams. The oxen no longer have the strength to pull the wagons for hours on end due to the sand, thirst and heat.

Exhaustion yaps at Elsbet's heels as she holds Johannes' hand tightly, helping to pull him along through the deep sand. Her thirst and rash from the prickly heat torture her and not a word passes by her swollen and dry throat. The drifting sand fills her shoes and makes lifting her feet hard work.

After a few hours of walking, one of the Hottentot shepherds lifts his nose and says: "I smell water." The others all spread out and presently a cry of "Water, here is water," causes everyone to rush over and see what the Hottentot, Tom, has found. It is water, but only a small amount which had filled a natural rocky depression during the last rainy season and been covered by the drifting sand. Everyone gets to enjoy a few sips of this filtered and cool water. *I need more. Two sips is just not enough.*

There is not enough to share with the animals and they continue to go without. As they continue walking through the arid environment broken only by the odd patch of scrub, the Hottentots discover similar small pools of water. Elsbet, looks all around carefully, doing her best to spot these water filled depressions but she doesn't have the sharp eyes of the Hottentots.

When the convoy finally stops, soon after the devil sun starts its march across the bleached sky, the family suck down their allotment of water and pass out into a heavy and unfulfilling sleep. "We need to be extra careful about water," says Papa.

On the third evening in the desert, Elsbet wakes and rubs her dirty face with dry and flaking hands. Her lips and eyelids are stuck together and she pries them open with her fingers. Aletta and Johannes are in a similar state and she helps them in the same way. Aletta's small face is pinched and her chubby cheeks seem to have melted away, leaving a skin covered skull with the sharp contours of a much older person. Sheer exhausten has allowed the children to sleep longer and the sun is already dropping behind the horizon.

Mother lights a fire and cooks a meal of thick porridge. She is so sparing with water, it congeals into a thick sticky lump which the children try to choke down their parched throats as best they can.

"Eeeeeek!" Mrs Pietersen from the next wagon shrieks in alarm. Elsbet sees a large cow outlined against the light from her flickering fire. It is trying to lick the flames.

"The poor creature thinks the bright flames are some kind of liquid," says Mother. Elsbet shudders with horror as the cow, beserk with pain from its burned tongue, crashes away from the fire and into the darkness.

"Bang!" A shot rings out and the mad bellowing suddenly stops.

Several of the animals are found to have died during the blazing heat of the day having received no water for over forty hours. The men slit open their bellies and share the small amount of fluid they contain among the people. They also hand out containers of their blood.

The thickly viscous texture of the blood makes Elsbet's gorge rise and little Aletta vomits up a small amount of stinking bile. "Dear Lord, please let us find water tonight. If we don't, we are all going to die," Elsbet prays quietly.

Papa moistens everyone's cracked lips with a little warm water and they depart, walking into the dark coolness of the night. Everyone is walking now, even little girls like Aletta.

When they set off again a number of the wagons, together with piles of furniture and provisions, are abandoned to gradually integrate into the vast and virtually lifeless plain.

Eight hours later, Elsbet is walking as if in a dream. Her mind separates from her body and is floating far away in a lovely lush grassland with a fast flowing stream running through it.

"Nooooo," the hoarse croaking cry drags her from her reverie and she turns her head dully to look behind her. Her mother has collapsed in the sand, Aletta clutched in her scrawny arms.

Elsbet trudges back towards the figure stretched out in the sand, the short but endless time it takes her to reach Mother is too long and Aletta is dead. Papa and John dig a shallow grave in the sand and bury her. No-one cries or laments her death, there is not enough fluid in anyone's body to bring forth tears or utterances of distress and misery, but the pain is deep and searing.

In the early hours of the morning, they discover the shallow watering hole at Inkuane.

Papa comes back with dull eyes, shaking his head. "There is hardly any water here."

Mother, Elsbet and the other women gather around the muddy patch, patiently filling canteens, one teaspoon at a time, with the brakish and tepid water. There is not enough for the people, never mind the animals which are in a terrible state.

Two more excrutiating days pass, with the only water being that found by the Hottentots. The convoy no longer stops during the day as the need to arrive at Haakdoorn Pan is too urgent. The death of animals is frequent and their bodies are pilfered for all sources of liquid before being left where they fell in the endless sand. Some of the cows go blind from lack of water and have to be shot. Others rush up and lick the metal rims of the wagon wheels, which shimmer and shine in the strong light, tricking the animals into thinking they were fluid.

Elsbet didn't care, she is past the point of feeling any empathy or emotion for the animals. In a further effort to shed weight and help the steadily weakening oxen, Papa has dumped most of their provisions. The hunger that gnaws at her empty stomach doesn't compare, however, to the raging thirst that possesses her mind.

On the night following the fifth day, they reach the pan. Elsbet watches as the oxen stop and sniff at the air. They smell sweet water. Almost as one, the animals charge in the direction of the life-giving water, some dragging wagons behind them. Storming up to the shallow water, the animals suck up the black and uninviting liquid. Hundreds of animals roll around in the squelshing mud, churning the thin layer of water into a mud bath in which dozens of them sink and drown.

"The water is gone," the cry goes up when the first of the men are able to reach the pool. The thick mud is full of dead and dying animals who have been crushed in the mad stampede.

"We'll have to try and filter the mud," says Susanna, *Oom* Jan's wife. Using the back of spoons, the women push the oozing mud through their clothing and drain tiny quantities of water. It does little to quench the maddening thirst of the people.

The sun rises on the sixth day in a burst of rosy joy. There is not a drop of water left in the barrels or canteens. Johannes is in a bad state, delirious from lack of fluids and food. He hasn't eaten a morsel of food for the past twenty-four hours as the saltiness of the *biltong* exacerbates his thirst. Mother is also in a bad way and seemed to be keeping herself going on shear willpower.

"I'll light the fire, Mother," says Elsbet in an effort to spare her. She manages to produce some porridge for the family. No-one can eat the hard biscuits, called rusks, or biltong.

"The men are going to walk on alone to Tlakane," Papa says. "You must stay here, Sarie, with Elsbet and Johannes, and I will return with water." He gives them the tiny quantity of fluid extracted from the stomachs of animals the men have killed and a cup full of blood.

Mother drinks her share from the utensils he holds out to her and forces some down Johannes' reluctant throat. She then drags herself under the wagon and lies down with Johannes. Elsbet drinks her few mouthfuls and prepares to crawl under the wagon when Papa says to her: "May God be with you. Do your best to help Johannes and your mother. I will return as quickly as possible."

"Good-bye, Papa," says Elsbet, as she disappears into the suffocating space beneath the wagon. She lies on her blanket and prays silently. As she is slipping into a heavy and dreamless sleep, she hears a deep sigh from Johannes. When she wakes up many hours later it is dark. She has slept for over twelve hours and has been awoken from her almost comatose state by her torturous thirst.

She reaches over to see if Johannes is awake and gasps at the whiteness of his face. His chest no longer rises and falls and she realises that he died when he emitted that great sigh many hours ago.

Crawling out from beneath the wagon, Elsbet wraps her arms protectively around her body and sits with her head supported on her knees, overwhelmed with grief, hunger and the all encompassing thirst. "Johannes is dead," she says when her mother emerges a short while later.

Together, they dig a shallow grave and relinquish the body to the desert to keep forever beneath its shifting sands. Elsbet keeps her sorrow to herself as she sets about cutting open the stomachs of the livestock which have died during the day and squeezing out the fluids as she has seen Papa and the other men do. Occassionally, as she goes about these tasks sluggishly, she glances over at her mother who had now lost two of her three children.

Mother sits with her back propped up against a wagon wheel staring vacantly into space. No flicker of emotion shows in her grey eyes; no pain, anger or accusation. She simply sits and gazes at nothing.

In the early hours of the morning, when the desert is at its coldest, the men return carrying utensils filled with dark and evil looking water. The women and children care little for how it looks, they grab the containers and drank it down in a few great gulps. The men will not let them have too much as the remaining *trekkers* and their livestock must get to Tlakane before there will be any more.

After forcing some thick and glutenous porridge into their resistant stomachs, the party struggles on through the vast and glowing desert. They are travelling with only twelve wagons now and leave a significant number of carcasses to rot in the blazing sun.

There is some water at Tlakane. The uninviting look of this blackish water does not hold anyone back and they rush to it, gulping it down and even stripping off their clothes and sitting in it so that it can be absorbed through their dehydrated skins. The remaining animals also have their turn and are partially refreshed. The water source is limited and after every person and animal has drunk, it has largely been reduced to mud.

The group rests at the blessed pool for a few days and the health of the remaining people improves. They are able to eat small portions of dry biscuits and *biltong*, but the animals are starving. Their bones poke through their tattered hides as they attempt to fill their empty bellies with the limited shrubs and grasses available.

"I'm going to trek on with the men to Meer at the Botletle river," says Papa one morning. "We can only take two wagons as there are only enough oxen left for two teams. If we can get there, we can return with water and help to get everyone there."

Papa leaves that evening with those men who are strong enough to travel. They take the strongest of the livestock and once again, Elsbet and her mother are on their own with the remaining women and children and those animals that are too weak to make the streneous trip.

As the days passed in the camp at Tlakane, Elsbet found herself growing weaker from lack of food and water. Her hands, which lay limply on her lap were yellow with parchment-like skin stretched over the delicate bones.

Thoughts of the good Reverend Hepburn who had helped *Oom* Jan and the other *trekkers* to prepare for this trip fill her mind and she reaches out towards the God-loving presence she can sense somewhere beyond this wilderness.

"Water," she thinks. "Help us, Reverend, you're our only hope." Her mind projects this message across the intervening miles and saps her of the last of her resources. She slumps forward and within a short period it is all over.

***

In King Khama, Reverend Hepburn walks to the hut of a Bechuana named Jeremias. He finds him sitting with a Hottentot cutting up tobacco.

"Jeremias," he says, "have you heard anything about the white trekkers who were travelling to Meer?"

"Yes, Baas," he answers, gesturing towards his companion, "Koos told me that only two of the wagons arrived at Meer. His brother, Sien, was one of the shepherds who travelled with Mister Greyling's group."

"What happened to the rest of the wagons, Jeremias?"

"Sien said that they were left at Tlakane with the surviving women and children. He said they had no water, Baas."

"Thank you, Jeremias and Koos. Your information is most helpful."

Over the next week, Reverend Hepburn manages to procure two strong and light wagons with iron axles and two teams of oxen to pull them. These are loaded with barrels of water and sent to Meer under the dedicated care of Jeremias and his friend, Koos.

He watches as the two wagons trundle away along the dusty track in the direction of Meer and offers up a prayer for the souls of the trekkers. He prays that the wagons arrive before it is too late, and the women and children are all dead.

***

The soul of Elsbet van Rooyen slips away from King Khama where Reverend Hepburn has sent water to help her mother, Papa and the other survivors of the thirstyland journey. Little Aletta, Johannes and she are beyond help, but, if her parents survive, her parents can have other children.

The Ghost in the Mound

Roberta Eaton Cheadle

As a South African paranormal western, some terms may not be familiar to all readers.

Glossary of terms used in *The Ghost in the Mound* (in order of usage):

Veld - Open, uncultivated country or grassland in southern Africa;

Laager - An encampment formed by a circle of wagons which was easily defendable against opponents;

Impis - Zulu word for any armed body of men;

Oom - Afrikaans for uncle, or a respectful term of address for an older man;

Outspan - To unyoke or unharness the oxen;

Tannie - Afrikaans for auntie or a respectful term of address for an older woman;

Trekkers - A collective term used to describe the Afrikaans pioneers who travelled by ox wagon into the interior of South Africa to escape British rule;

Trek - The term used to describe a party of *trekkers* travelling together under a common leader;

Shangaan - One of the African tribes in southern Africa;

Aardvark - A medium-sized, burrowing, nocturnal mammal native to Africa. The staple food of the aardvark is termites;

Biltong - A form of dried, cured meat;

Droë wors - Dried traditional, coriander-seed spiced boerewors sausage.

The termite mound is huge. A reddish coloured mass with one thick section rearing up out of the structure, like a giant finger pointed accusingly towards sky. Glimpsed through the opening in the wagon covering, its long late-afternoon shadow makes Sara shudder involuntarily.

Papa halts the heavy vehicle under a giant baobab tree near the river, approximately 15 cape roods away from the impressive mound. Walking around to the other side, he helps his wife, Darlene, down from the wagon box.

Clutching her precious bundle close to her chest, she pulls back the edge of the blanket and scrutinises the sleeping child's peaceful face. Just eight months old, Baby Kobus looks bonny and plump in the dim light.

"Thank you, Petrus," Mama catches twelve-year-old Sara's eye as she peeps out hopefully. "You can get down, Sara."

Sara jumps down and then reaches back into the wagon, gently lifting out, first, six-year-old Susanna, and then, four-year-old Clara. Her sisters stamp their feet, delighted to be free from the cloying confines of the wagon which has been jolting and bumping its way through the *veld* all day.

"Something smells nice," Susanna breathes deeply, savouring the sweet scent of the showy, white flowers that hang pendulously from the tree.

"We need to set up camp quickly, Darlene," says Papa. "We're late stopping for the night, so the men have decided not to make a *laager*."

"Is that a good idea, Petrus. We saw signs of hunting *impis* about earlier today. I would feel safer if we made a *laager*."

"Some of the men have decided to camp on the other side of the river, Darlene. They think it's too late to get five more wagons and all their cattle and sheep across safely before nightfall. We can't make a *laager* tonight. I think we're safe here so don't worry."

Papa walks away to help his brother, Sara's *Oom* Gerdus, and her older cousins *outspan* the oxen. "It won't take us long to see to the livestock. You start making dinner and preparing for the night."

"Of course, Petrus. Maybe Elsbet and I can use the termite mound as an oven to cook our meal. It would make a nice change to have some bread instead of pap."

"Look after Kobus, Sara," Mama's lips, as she handed Sara the baby, are pressed so tightly together they form a bloodless white line. "Susanna and Clara, take the buckets and fetch some water from the river." Sara cuddles her brother.

Kobus is a good baby and hardly ever cries. The Lord has blessed Papa with a fine son.

Sara watches as Mama and *Tannie* Elsbet inspect the mound. It doesn't look so alien now that she can see it properly. Its bulky presence is almost protective, as if it's overseeing her family's preparations for the night.

"It's extinct so we can use it," Mama announces after a brief inspection.

Crumbling red earth falls from the base of the mound as Mama sets about digging a hole large enough to hold a fire. *Tannie* Elsbet leaves her to it and, after retrieving a basket from the wagon, vanishes into a nearby thicket of trees to gather kindling and firewood.

Mama digs vigorously, her irritation and anxiety evident in every spade full of earth. Up until several days ago, their party had been travelling with another larger party of *trekkers*. Sara had witnessed the public altercation between the leaders of the two parties. It had caused a split and each *trek* had headed off in a different direction.

Frans Malherbe, the leader of the larger *trek* had accused their leader of being trigger happy. "You need to slow down on your elephant hunting, Schalk. We have limited ammunition and we need to use it sparingly. We don't know when we'll be able to replenish our supplies."

"We're hunting elephants so that we have ivory for future trade. That way we'll be able to get more ammunition and everything else we need too."

Schalk Breed's face was red with anger at Frans' perceived criticism of his leadership.

"I'm not saying you shouldn't hunt, Schalk. I'm only suggesting you ensure you have a definite kill before you shoot and that you don't chase after every animal that crosses your path. You are putting the survival of your *trek* at risk with your reckless behaviour."

"I am man enough to look after the wellbeing of my people without your advice."

The next morning the nine wagons under the leadership of Schalk Breed had set off in the opposite direction to Frans Malherbe's party.

Mama is unhappy about the separation, believing it's safer to travel in a larger group.

By the time the hole's finished, Mama's good humour is restored, and she sings softly as she mixes the bread and prepares the meat from a buck the men had shot earlier in the day.

An hour later, the sun slips quickly into the distant *veld* and disappears, leaving the family in darkness until the moon rises and shares with them its cold clear light. Red hot coals glow brightly inside the hole in the mound which belches a delicious smell of roasting meat and baking pot bread into the night.

Free from her baby-sitting duties while Mama feeds Kobus, Sara sits near Papa's campfire and listens to the men talking. Their low voices mingle with the sounds and conversational murmurings from the other four families who are camped on this side of the river.

On the other side of the water, Sara can see the flickering light of the fires belonging to the other five families. Dark shadows move about as the women cook while the men relax. The scene is ordinary and comfortably domestic.

Later, her stomach full after a delicious meal and with all her chores complete, Sara crawls into her handmade sleeping bag in the wagon and quickly drifts to sleep.

***

Slowly, without any indications of haste or anxiety, the *Shangaan* warriors creep forward, halting a few yards away from the five wagons on their side of the river. Across the water, the white coverings of the remaining four wagons shine in the moonlight like smooth pebbles on a dark beach.

At a signal from the leader, the attackers split into five groups and assault the travellers who are lying asleep inside and underneath the five wagons.

Shrieks and bellows of pain ring out, ripping apart the still silence of the early morning, as stabbing spears flash, and clubs connect with soft flesh.

***

Sara jerks awake, a loud shriek piercing the veil of sleep. Splashing sounds, followed by the heavy thud of several pairs of booted feet, mingle with the high-pitched screams of terrified women and the shrill cries of hysterical children.

As she lies shivering with horror, several guns crash simultaneously, summoning savage yells from the African *impis*.

"Wake up! Wake up! We're under attack," Already dressed, Mama is dragging on her boots. "Sara, quickly, you need to dress Clara and get her and Susanna to safety under the wagon." Mama calls to Susanna.

"Hurry, Susanna, get dressed and follow Sara."

Sara dresses and puts on her boots, lacing them tightly. Her eyes have adjusted to the near darkness, but it's still difficult finding Clara's clothing and getting her dressed in the thick gloom. Having managed it, somehow, she sighs with relief.

Slipping down from the wagon, she lifts her sisters down, one by one, and sets them on the dusty ground.

"Here, Sara."

Turning in surprise, Sara takes Baby Kobus from Mama's outstretched arms.

"Keep him safe, Sara."

Moments later, the four children are huddled beneath the wagon. Kobus is awake, but despite the cacophony of noise assailing his senses, he does not cry. Lying quietly in Sara's lap, his eyes shine like two deep pools.

Thank goodness the water barrels are in their places under the wagon. At least I can give the children a drink.

All around the sounds of battle ring out. The survivors of the initial attack join the defenders of the remaining four wagons. The men take up positions around the wagons and fire on their spear throwing assailants. Their guns flash fire in the darkness, reflecting off the razor-sharp iron blades that tip the thinly shafted *assegais* as they fly towards them, lodging in the wagon coverings, ground and surrounding trees.

The women stand behind the men, reloading the rifles after each firing as quickly as possible. Every now and then, one of the *Boers* falls and the attacking force scream with joy.

Crouching uncomfortably underneath the wagon, Sara watches as the sky gradually lightens, turning dark grey, then light grey and finally light as the sun creeps higher into the blue sky. The battle noises have blurred to a continuous din as Sara sets the sleeping baby gently down and peers out from behind the wagon wheel.

She can see Papa, Mama, *Oom* Gerdus and *Tannie* Elsbet through the smoke of the gunfire. Their faces are blackened with gunpowder. Their jerky movements and glowing eyes tell her they're chronically exhausted, having slept little and waged battle for hours.

Mama sees her in the shadow of the wheel.

"Sara, pour me water."

She hands Sara a large mug. Taking the cup, Sara crawls over to the water barrel, filling the mug to the brim. Crawling back, she hands it to her mother who drinks gratefully and then passes the mug to Papa.

Mama crouches down and whispers to Sara, "The battle's not going well for us. We're running out of ammunition and the number of *Shongaan* warriors are too many. I need you to be very brave and do something for me."

***

Grasping the baby tightly, Sara clambers out from under the wagon and sits back on her heels next to the wheel. After passing her the baby, Susanna crawls out, followed by Clara. They both kneel beside her.

In front of them, through the smoky haze, the blurred and agitated forms of the adults move frantically; fire, reload, fire, reload. The noise is immense.

Pointing to the huge baobab tree which stands directly in front of them, Sara whispers to the two younger girls.

"You need to run straight past Mama and get behind that tree. Run as fast as you can, I'll be right behind you. Are you ready? One, two, go!"

The three girls lunge forward and begin to run, their faces drawn and tight with stress and their eyes fixed on the prominent tree. Their swiftly moving feet are accompanied by the crashing of the guns and the shrieks and yells of the enemy.

As the tree draws closer, Sara can see the detail of every leaf and the smooth shininess of its bottle-shaped trunk. The threesome circle behind the great trunk, gasping for breath. Sara drops to her knees; Kobus is heavy and her chest throbs.

The tree's heavy, white flowers are already starting to fade, and a few have already turned brown and fallen to the ground. Their sweet fragrance has a cloying smell of decay.

Sara looks around, considering their options.

Where can we hide?

Her eyes settle on the termite mound, standing proud and tall, surrounded by *veld*. The yellowy green grass between their position under the tree and the mound is tall and thick, offering protection from searching eyes.

Kobus is lying quietly in her arms, his blue eyes round and calm.

It's as if he knows our lives depend on his keeping quiet.

Working quickly and efficiently, Sara unwraps the blanket from around the baby and uses it to secure him to her back, tying the ends of the blanket tightly in front of her. She lets out a gusty sigh.

He's heavy, but it will be easier for me to crawl with him on my back than trying to shuffle forward while holding him in my arms.

Slowly and carefully, in single file, the children crawl through the stems. The greenness of the lower part of the tall blades' dazzles Sara. She keeps a careful note of their direction. She can't see anything except the hard ground below and the waving grass above.

The *veld* starts to thin, the clumps of grass becoming more widespread, and the earthen sides of the mound appear. Sara leads the children around the outskirts of the mound, looking for the hole Mama had dug for an oven the evening before.

A dark opening comes into view. It's big. Much bigger than the hole Mama dug. As the black hole draws closer, Sara smells the pungent stench of an animal.

It's an aardvark burrow. I pray it's abandoned.

Stopping, Sara inspects the earth around the entrance to the hole. It's undisturbed and there are no signs of animal tracks or dung.

Signaling for the younger children to wait, she creeps stealthily closer and peers cautiously into the opening.

There's no sign of any animal. The small exterior hole opens into a much bigger cavern, large enough for them all to squeeze inside.

Sara releases the knot holding the blanket to her back and slips Kobus into Susanna's waiting arms.

"We're going to squeeze through this hole and hide in the burrow until it's safe," she whispers to her sisters.

Susanna and Clara nod.

It's dark and close inside the *aardvark* burrow and the smell is thick and heavy. The four children huddle in the blackness, their limbs cramped and uncomfortable.

Inside the thick walls of the mound, the gunfire is muted, but Sara notices when it stops. The sudden quiet is punctured by muffled shouts, shrill wails and screams, mixed with the anxious low of cattle.

What's happening? What if the warriors find us? What can I do if they find us here?

The thoughts whirl around and around in Sara's mind. The children crouch, terrified, inside the hole until worn out from their disturbed night, terror, and lack of fresh air, they drift off to sleep.

***

The baby wakes and starts to cry lustily. Opening her eyes in the cloying dimness, Sara clamps her hand over the baby's mouth, smothering his howls. Weak light filters through the small opening into their hiding place.

It's still day, but I think it's quite late. The baby's hungry and so am I.

Cramped muscles protesting, she hands the crying baby to Susanna and wriggles through the hole out into the late afternoon sunshine. Insects hum in the long grass and a bird cries as it flies overhead, but other than Kobus' cries, diminished by the thick earth walls of the mound, it's deathly quiet. Retrieving a broken rusk from her skirt pocket she reaches into the hole and gives it to Kobus. He grabs it eagerly with his tiny hands.

"I'm going to crawl back to the tree and see what's happened," she whispers. "You two must stay here and take care of Kobus until I call you."

Susanna nods, her eyes wide and glassy in her pale face.

Turning, Sara creeps away through the *veld*.

***

The wagon covering glimmers whitely, as Sara peers out from behind the relative safety of the giant tree. Her feet crush the brown, dying Baobab flowers which cover the ground thickly. They release an overwhelming stench of decomposition, like rotting flesh.

Stepping out from behind the comforting protection of the thick tree trunk, she freezes, shocked by the scene of destruction. Her breath comes in short gasps and pants as she absorbs the details.

What's left of her parents, uncle and aunt lies within a crimson explosion. Their heads and bodies are smashed beyond recognition. Dried blood and clumps of brain matter splatters the ground, the wagon, and circle of stones surrounding the dead fire.

Forcing her legs to move forward, past her family's wagon, she follows a trail of blood and beaten bodies to the next wagon, and the next, and the next. Men, women and children, their bodies punctured by the sharp, stabbing spears of the *Shangaan* and damaged by their heavy clubs, lay in expressions of mutilated horror.

Everyone was dead. The rank smell of blood hung heavily in the air.

For a short while, Sara just stands there. The baby's stifled cries, carried to her on the warm breeze, slowly penetrate her fog of horror. Dragging her mind back from the brink of the bottomless pit of oblivion into which it threatens to fall, she starts to plan.

I need to get water and food. I must also get some blankets for the night. The others mustn't come here and see this.

Encouraged by her plan, her devastation packed away into a secret place deep within her mind, Sara returns to Papa's wagon and retrieves the metal pail to fetch water from the river. She carries the full pail behind the baobab tree and sets it down on the ground.

Returning to the wagon, her eyes determinedly averted from the scattered bodies, she fills two deep baskets with travelling food including rusks and *biltong*. She lays two small piles of muslin napkins on top of the food.

Thank goodness we did the washing a few days ago and there are clean nappies for Kobus. We're lucky they didn't strip the wagon, or burn it, and I can salvage some necessities. I wonder if they're intending to come back to finish the job.

Alarmed by this disturbing thought, she moves even faster, stowing the heavy baskets under the tree, next to the water. One last trip to the wagon to get blankets and she's ready to return to the mound.

Muscles trembling with exertion, she hauls the supplies the short distance to the waiting children. She makes three trips, rejecting Susanna's offer of assistance. *I can't let her find out what's happened to our parents.*

"Mama and Papa have gone to get help," she tells them. "We need to wait here until someone comes for us."

Sara finds the hole Mama dug for their oven the night before. Using Papa's fire steel and flint, she builds a small fire inside the termite mound to cook a meal of porridge. She boils a bit of *biltong* in water and makes a watery broth for Kobus.

"He needs meat to grow strong," she tells her sisters as they chew on their share of the *biltong*.

At sunset, the children prepare for the night. The *aardvark* hole in the mound is large enough for Clara and Kobus to lie down inside to sleep. Susanna and Sara wrap themselves in blankets and sleep stretched out on the hard ground near the entrance.

Lying in the dark, listening to the soft sighs and snores of her siblings, Sara's calm and controlled façade collapses. Tears run silently down her cheeks and she shivers uncontrollably as the pain of loss, coupled with her anguish at her parent's gruesome deaths, overwhelms her.

The moon is full when Sara awakes to the soft tones of Mama's lullaby. Standing up, she looks out over the beautiful expanse of rippling *veld* grass, shimmering like a calm lake in the silvery moonlight.

A flickering shadow catches her eye and she turns towards the mound. In the soft light it looks slightly furtive, as if it is concealing secrets in the soft folds of velvety darkness that ripple across its rough exterior.

She's not alone. One of the shadows separates from the others and comes towards her.

"Mama," Sara whispers, "Is it you, Mama?"

The ethereal shape moves closer until Sara could see her mother's features clearly in the pale light. Her yellow hair hangs down her back in a thick mass and her pale skin shines like polished bone. She's beautiful. The careworn look that characterised her face in life is gone, replaced with an almost holy loveliness.

She's an angel, thinks Sara. *Mama's come back as an angel to guide us.*

"Sara, my dear girl," Mama-Angel says, moving closer and enfolding Sara in a protective layer of love and comfort, "Papa and I are just beyond the veil. We can't move on to our eternal rest until Kobus, your sisters and you are all safe. It is up to you, Sara, to lead them back to Fran Malherbe's party and safety. His group is not too far away and is moving slowly because of the many cattle and sheep they have with them. You must walk with the sun, due West, and you will find them."

Mama-Angel releases her and looks into her eyes.

"I love you, Sara. Do not dwell on Papa and my untimely deaths. You must focus on the future and ensure your survival. As you travel, look out for clusters of trees and shrubbery. They grow near water and you will need to replenish your supplies. Goodbye, Sara."

Mama-Angel fades into mist which blows away in the light early morning breeze.

***

Sara surveys the items they are taking with them on their journey. There are four gourds filled with water, two blankets, packages of *biltong*, *droë wors* and rusks, Papa's fire steel and flint, Papa's hunting knife and the napkins for Kobus. Susanna and Clara will have to carry most of it and the loads will be heavy, but she can't see any way of reducing the weight.

Sighing, she packs the goods into two bundles and helps the small girls tie them to their backs. A few minutes later, with Kobus attached securely to her own back, they are ready to travel.

"And now," she said, "let's *trek*."

Following the sun, as instructed by Mama-Angel, the children tramp in single-file silently through the *veld*. The grass catches at their feet, making walking difficult, and the sandy soil works into their shoes, necessitating frequent stops to empty them out. By late morning, the sun beats down on their bonnet-covered heads and sweat trickles down their faces, burning their eyes. Fuelled by determination and necessity, Sara keeps the children moving forward and they make good progress until the sun is directly overhead.

"It's time to stop and rest," Sara points towards a clump of trees. "Those trees will protect us from the midday sun and, God willing, we will find water."

God smiles on the travellers and they find a small trickle of water from a rock hidden among the trees. They all drink deeply, and Sara refills their water bottles. The girls chew on a small piece of *droë wors*, while Sara softens broken pieces of rusk and *biltong* in a little water for the baby. She rinsed out the soiled napkins and lies them in the hot sun to dry.

Having sated their thirst and hunger, Sara spreads out the blankets in the shade and the children lie down and go to sleep.

"You are doing very well, Sara."

Mama-Angel and Sara are sitting in the shade next to the pool.

"You've done the right thing resting during the worst heat of the day. When you wake up later you must keep going in the same direction. Before sunset, you will find another clump of trees where you must shelter for the night."

Refreshed after their sleep, the children enjoy another long drink from the pool, and set off again. On and on they walk, their backs aching from the unaccustomed weight of their burdens as they press on relentlessly through the lonely and desolate landscape.

A few hours later when the sun hangs low in the sky, Sara spies the group of trees Mama-Angel told her about. "God has provided, girls. We can stop there for the night." Susanna and Clara gaze at her out of eyes ringed with black smudges of exhaustion. They don't have the energy to even nod their agreement.

They drag themselves to the copse of trees and, after eating and drinking, collapse on their blankets and fall into a heavy sleep.

***

By 12 o'clock on the third day, the children are completely exhausted. Their limbs ache, their feet are swollen and blistering, and their food supplies are low.

We can't keep going for much longer, Mama-Angel. Please help us find Frans Malherbe's party soon.

Sara is walking in front of her sisters, eyes downcast as she takes care not to trip. Fatigue has made them all clumsy and susceptible to falling. She's hauled poor little Clara to her feet twice today already.

Looking up, she stops and rubs her eyes. Just ahead, in the shade of the copse of trees they'd been heading for, she sees a wagon.

"Susanna, Clara, I see a wagon. Just ahead of us among the trees."

"It's a wagon," Susanna's shrill voice carries across the still *veld*.

The *veld* ripples around them in response to a playful zephyr. "You've made it, Sara. You've found Frans Malherbe's party. God bless you, my daughter." Mama-Angel's voice rustles with the long grass.

A figure stirs in the shadows and then steps out into the bright sunshine. It's a woman, dressed in a long dark dress and wearing a sunbonnet. She stops and stares at the children; her mouth slightly agape with surprise.

Sara dredges up the last of her strength and begins to run towards their salvation, Baby Kobus bouncing on her back and giggling with delight.

Thank you, Mama-Angel. Thank you!

Author Enid Holden

Enid Holden is a writer who has honed her talents as a singer-songwriter, playwright, newspaper columnist, book reviewer, and opera librettist. She holds an undergraduate degree from Rhodes University in Fine Arts and English Literature. She completed an Honors degree in History of Art from the University of South Africa and earned a BA in Music at Western Colorado University and an MA in Creative Writing in 2017 from Western Colorado University School of Graduate Studies. She has written three short comedies. She also created the book of *Getting it Wright,* a musical comedy on the Wright Brothers and wrote the libretto of *Lottie Silks,* composed by Justus (Jay) Parrotta, work-shopped in Washington, DC and at Writing the Rockies at Western Colorado University. Her second libretto is T*he Teardrop Tiara.* She completed an MFA in Creative Writing at Western Colorado University in 2019 and is writing her debut novel.

Queen of Spades

Enid Holden

Iris picked her way along the snow-spattered streets, lifting her skirts and petticoats so as not to stain them with a rim of mud. She skidded on Silver Street despite her sturdy laced boots, recovered, then crossed onto Bluff Street hoping that tonight she would be lucky. She didn't believe in luck as a rule. Rather she put her faith her own dependable skills and her sixth sense. She traced the outline of the .38 Smith and Wesson in her right coat pocket with a gloved finger as she walked. Stopping outside the Wanderlust Saloon, she strained to see through its windows murky with frost and dust. Welcoming pools of light, the laughter of men, and the clinking of glasses beckoned, but first she surveyed the surroundings with a practiced eye. Would he be here tonight? Her pulse quickened. The night air was brisk.

She thought she heard hoofbeats in the distance, but she couldn't be sure. Snow had come early this year, muffling the sound. A coyote yipped twice, but there was no sign of movement on the ascending canyon walls. Part of the majestic San Juan range, the slopes veered steep and silent now under the stars, dappled with white except where dark rocks protruded. South of where Iris stood, Henson Creek wound down to San Cristobel Lake with its infamous hanging bridge, but it too lay silent under cover of ice. A horse stomped and whinnied from the sheltered railing behind the saloon, but the street appeared empty. She stepped round, her practiced eye running over the horses tethered there. Her heart skipped a beat as she recognized Robby's horse and the unmistakable pinto dun with its splashes of white dazzling against the darkness.

Iris headed into the saloon; the wooden door banging shut behind her. The warm fumes of wood burning, cigar smoke, alcohol, heated oil, and men embraced her as she shook off her coat, spiriting her revolver from her pocket to her purse.

Iris sidled over to the bar, ordering herself a whiskey. Grizzled Ned Anderson sat at the bar nursing a beer. He winked at Iris, gazing off in the direction of the gaming tables and nodded. He drew an imaginary square tabletop on the bar counter, drumming his index finger to the right. Her gaze swept towards the table, to the man sitting in the indicated position on the right, next to Robby. Her breath caught in her chest. She ordered a pitcher of whiskey for Ned. As she paid, the barkeep gave her a tired smile. Something stirred in the pit of her stomach as she stepped toward the gaming table.

*****

Iris was thought to be in her forties, but she was still considered a handsome woman by the townsfolk. Her long dark hair was drawn back, cinched before it cascaded down her shoulders in ringlets, a row of kiss-curls high atop her smooth forehead. She added drama to her rounded features with makeup. A defined peach mouth and dark shadowed eyes gave her a bland inscrutable mystique. Tonight, she wore a lavishly cut, bronze dress with lace trim embellished at the cleavage. It rustled as she walked, so that she fairly dazzled the five men, including the stranger, seated at the table as she strode over.

"Gentlemen," she said, "may I be so bold as to request to join your table?"

"Does anyone at the table hold an objection?" the man closest to her, Pete Brown, asked, looking around. He paused. "Certainly, you may join us, Ma'am," he said. "But be aware that you do so at your own risk."

"I'm happy to take my chances, I'm sure," Iris said, seating herself in the chair which one man had vacated next to Robby. She avoided looking at the unknown man until she sat down, taking a moment to compose herself.

"I don't believe we've met," she said to the stranger. "My name is Iris."

"Sorry, Ma'am," he said in a low, steely voice. "Lester Grant."

"Five card draw," announced the dealer, who shuffled briskly, dealing out cards face-down to each player in a no-nonsense way. Iris lifted and examined the cards she'd been dealt. The card furthest to the right struck her first. It was the ace of spades. Yes, that was him, all right, her beloved Jim. Her spade, her digger, her life's prospector. Alongside it, was the two of hearts. That stood for their mutual love. She felt the shiver of loss run through her again. Beside that was the treacherous jack of clubs. The trickster across from her with a taste for easy money and a heart colder than glass. Another ace, this one diamonds. She glanced across at Lester's icy blue eyes which scrutinized his hand. His mouth cut a cruel line beneath his abundant moustache. He sat across from her at the table with his back to the wall.

The hand told her everything she wanted to know. It was an okay hand by her reckoning, a pair of aces, but what she read was an inventory of the heart. It promised success if she held her nerve. She chewed her lip, made some mental notes, took a quick scan of the discards on the table before folding. Her opponent swapped out three.

*****

Jim had taught Iris to play poker after they moved to the isolated settlement. With the San Juan Wagon Toll Road, the first road into this mountainous region, Lake City was becoming a supply hub and a speculative town. Developers chose the location because the flat terrain of the valley floor offered a park-like setting, and the convergence of Henson Creek and the headwaters of the Lake Fork ensured abundant water.

When rich mineral deposits were discovered, the native Ute population was pushed from their tribal lands, treaty by traitorous treaty. In their wake, poured an influx of hopefuls, a boom crowd of prospectors who'd heard tales of spectacular mineral finds, intent on striking it rich.

The small town offered several entertainments, but they catered to the needs of men. Hell's Acres, the red-light district located on the south end of Bluff Street close to the Creek, had a number of dancehalls, gaming saloons and brothels where the rough men spent their earnings on the things which were in short supply. They could take a bath, find a woman to dance or sleep with, eat cooked food, and let off steam. The town accommodated the punchers, panners, and prospectors who flooded the area, despite their boisterous behavior, but elected a sheriff to maintain some semblance of law and order.

When they first arrived, Iris stayed back at the cabin reading by lamplight when Jim went out of an evening. But, as the months went by and no child was forthcoming, Iris found it lonely and took to going along with Jim for the company. Iris became a fixture at the saloons and the gaming tables. She would stand behind his chair and watch the men play until she began to understand the variations of the games. *Prospectors are essentially gamblers,* she figured. *They go way down on their luck for the dream that they can strike it rich.* She too decided to make herself rich—but by skill and her gift, rather than luck.

Over time Iris joined in. In fact, she had learned to count cards, figure the odds, and weigh up her opponents. More important, Iris realized that the deck could act as Tarot cards. She read them as symbols for the future. Jim loved to play at cards in the evenings, but ironically he wasn't very good at it. Or as Iris always put it, he never had much of a lucky streak. While Iris could anticipate the winning hands, Jim was often at a loss. Iris also had a good memory if she could refrain from drinking too much whiskey. Folks got used to seeing her around. She started making money, which she would shrug off or hide from Jim so as not to shame him about his own luck, but it came in very useful for buying clothing and refinements, so she didn't have to bother Jim.

As Jim rode off with his partner, Buck, on his spotted dun, to process their silver claims and pan for gold in the Gunnison County, Iris began to sit in on more games, honing her skills. She learned a lot about cards and about men. Men were creatures of habit with developed tells. Their judgment became blunted with drink and pride. Men were foolish and easily distracted. She learned to become a diversion to them with her fine dresses and scents which she ordered from the city. She also knew that she could usually sniff out a man who was telling a lie. She started to win at both poker and faro. Although the last time she played a game of poker with Jim, the ace of spades showed up in a broken straight of hearts which foretold of a threat to their love which would come to pass before very long.

*****

The dealer called the next game, but the man to Iris's right called out for five-card stud and the other players acquiesced. Stud poker, like life, Iris thought, is an open game in which most of the cards are displayed on the table but never all. The dealer dealt each player's first card face down, only glimpsed by the owner, but the others were dealt face up with a betting round after each. Iris scrutinized her cards on the table as they were dealt, forming an idea of the strength of each players' hands, observing their traits and bets accordingly. She guessed at the values of the hole cards which remained concealed until the final showdown. But she had an intuitive sense of the outcome.

Her own hole card, facedown, was a king. A quick survey of the cards on the table told her that she held one of the weaker hands. Not being in a hurry, she nevertheless placed a bet, sitting back to observe Lester. She signaled to the bar tender to bring to the table a round of drinks on her tab.

After a run of stud, the table changed back to five-card draw. There was little conversation, each man intent on the game and the pile of chips changing hands. Iris glanced at her cards. She held another inauspicious hand. She swopped out two cards, but their replacements were also duds. She bet a round, but, seeing no improvement, she folded the hand and sipped her drink. She needed to be patient. Nothing could be gained in haste. She had waited a long while. It meant nothing to wait a little more.

*****

Almost five months before, when Jim failed to come home by Saturday night —as his habit was to return every second Friday—Iris knew in her gut that something was wrong. Friday night she had cooked Jim his favorite beef stew with potatoes, baked a cake, and washed her hair. She planned to go out to the Crystal Palace after eating if he wasn't too tired. But it grew late, he did not arrive, and he sent no word. She gave up and went to bed, listening for the sound of hoof-beats. *He must have had something come up. He'll be home sure as a fox to his lair. Be patient.* Outside her bedroom window a great wind rose in the darkness. It sucked and pulled at the wooden frame of her cabin, stalking and slapping around corners, causing the beams to strain. When she stepped out onto the front porch it clutched at her nightdress and threaded her hair. Iris looked up at the sky, pale with moonlight, but along the horizon a bank of dark cloud brooded.

She shivered, returning to bed, but sleep eluded her. As she lay in the dark, the figure of a man appeared at the foot of her bed. "Jim," she called out, but the man did not reply. He reached out and two cards fluttered onto the bed. She reached for them, scanning them.

They were the two black knaves, clubs and spades. When she looked up, the man had vanished.

The next day she rose to cruel sunshine pouring in the windows. She wondered at the cards as she brewed herself a strong cup of tea. She fretted through the morning, listening for horse's hooves, dabbling at her chores. Her heart soared when she heard hoofbeats. She rushed out, but it was Jim's partner, Buck, riding like a maniac up the street, alone. Something was very wrong.

The way Buck told it, Jim had rotten luck right up until the very end. Jim was dead and Buck had barely escaped with his life. Iris and Buck set off as soon as they could in a horse-drawn wagon to recover Jim's body for burial. Numb with shock, Iris kept her eyes peeled to the trail. Beside her, Buck seemed in an agony of grief and guilt as he recounted each detail, while Iris tried to hold back her sobs.

"Early Friday, we packed up our tents, picks, and pans and set off for the assayer in Gunnison to get a payout for our weeks' worth of gold. It was the best week ever for Jim. We left our equipment with the feller who has a cabin on the edge of town and keeps our horses. I was keen to spend some of our proceeds wetting our throats in the local before we started off home.

"But I could tell at a glance Jim was bent heart and soul on making an early start back to Lake City. I took my cue and kept my mouth shut. Within minutes of leaving the assayer we were in our saddles headed out of town. Well before dark, we crossed the river and started for home.

"At the outskirts of the town we slowed up our horses, taking it leisurely for a mile or so. We wanted to be sure, so if any fellows was to follow, we could have it out with them while it was still light enough to shoot straight."

Buck and Iris rounded a hill, as the trail up ahead of the wagon thronged with mule deer. "Should we shoot one?" Buck asked, slowing the horses and reaching for his gun. Iris shook her head.

"There'll be enough death on the wagon when we find Jim." As the deer veered off the road, the buggy resumed to a gallop.

"But Jim and I cleared the crossing and rode up to elevation, an' there were no sign of trouble, behind or ahead. We made good time. When it came to 'bout midnight, we tethered the horses. Then, hanging our belts on the pommels of our saddles, we placed our money and our six-shooters inside the waistbands of our trousers.

"We had ourselves a fire and a drink of whiskey and were as like to turn in when a gun-barrel flashed in the firelight and a man opened fire on us at short range with a six-shooter. Jim, taking the shot to the skull, fell heavy, like a side of beef.

"I ran for cover in the trees, shakin' like a leaf. Our attacker emptied his cartridges in the open-air, shooting at naught. I returned the compliment until my gun was emptied in the dark. I managed to get 'way while he was still throwing lead after me, some of which came much closer than comfort. When there was no longer any shooting at my flanks, I crawled back to get my horse and fled. I cut loose Jim's horse and took off into the night, hoping it would follow me."

After what seemed an eternity, Buck and Iris came to the spot where Jim's swollen body lay crumpled on the ground, his head shot up, the ground around streaked with blood. His revolver was missing, his money gone, and there was no sign of his horse. Iris covered Jim's body with a blanket, laying him out across the back of the buggy. Then Iris excused herself —for a lady's moment to herself as she called it—to prepare for the trip back. Buck turned his back on her and rolled a cigarette. She slid off behind the trees and wandered off, examining both the trunks and the imprints of tracks on the ground. She could find no bullet marks. A pair of parallel horse tracks led from the site. The land and her instincts told her all she needed to know.

Lake City is a town with a tolerance for both violence and vengeance, Iris thought, an iron grip taking hold of her heart on the trip home. She pictured the lynching in which the Sherriff's death had been avenged by an angry mob of men who seized both the killers, carted them out of the jail, and hung them from the Ocean Wave Bridge in their own heady version of justice. *What was done was done but the future was yet to come.*

When she and Buck got back to Lake City early Sunday, they left the body at the Doctor's station which doubled as a morgue as the sheriff had not been replaced yet. The town opened for business as usual the following morning. Taking inventory of her stash of winnings, Iris was disappointed. She took her wedding ring to the pawnshop and hocked it for a sum large enough to pay for a lavish funeral. After a brief service, she and Buck hoisted Jim's casket into the ground in front of a large crowd. Afterwards, Iris choked back her tears and hosted a fine party in the Wanderlust Saloon. When everyone's glass was filled, she got up onto a table, toasting the crowd. "Here's to vengeance on Jim's death. Promise me you'll help me serve justice on his killer. Buck, come forward and tell us who he is and how to find him." The assembled crowd clinked glasses and chorused "Aye. Justice for Jim."

Buck stepped forward. "The man in question attacked us both in the dark. He got the better of Jim, and I crawled out of there barely alive, but shaken to the core, crying to the Lord for mercy," Buck said. "I can't say I saw aught but the barrel of a gun in the dark and bullets flying around my person and my horse."

As the men digested this, Iris spoke again.

"From the scene of the crime, which I examined with my own eyes and compared to Buck's account, I swear Jim had two killers. I believe his partner here turned traitor and is deserving of our wrath. If you cared for Jim, then show it now. Arrest this false-hearted counterfeit so he can be made to answer for his crime."

Into the stunned silence which followed, Iris urged the men, "Seize him now." An answering cry went up from the attendant men who were full of drink. "Yes, by God, we'll teach that murderous fraudster a lesson or two." But when they looked among them, Buck had fled. A group of howling men pursued Buck into the night. The sound of horses' hooves pounded through the town and died.

Iris wiped the tears from her eyes as she sat down at the largest gaming table in the saloon. Luckier at cards than in love, she won enough money at poker that night to buy back the ring Jim had given her the very next morning. But the men straggled back into town, reporting that Buck had escaped and was nowhere to be found. Over the next weeks, Iris earned enough at cards to hire the two trusty, but rough and tumble townsmen, Ned and Robby, to follow Buck's trail and find Jim's horse. They had strict orders to discover the identity of Buck's sidekick and find a way to lure him back to the town and into the poker hall.

*****

Iris sipped her drink. At last, things were beginning to go her way. She had a good hand, heavy with courts. She held the one-eyed royals—the jacks of spades and hearts and the king of diamonds, the man with the axe as she thought of him, and the other red suicide king. *Interesting.* When she drew the jack of diamonds, the laughing boy card to complete a full house, it assured her of success tonight. The last laugh would be hers.

The table was piled high. Lester sniffed as she raked in the pot. Inside, she gloated. The other men at the table paid no heed. They knew of her prowess with the deck and that she played a straight game. They seemed to appreciate her witty and vivacious manner, that she was generous with rounds of liquor when she won, that she always paid up with no whining when she lost, and sometimes regretted it when she took their money off of them.

Skill, patience and a close observation of her opponents almost always paid off for Iris in the course of an evening. She kept her cool whether she was under the gun or on the button. But tonight, the stakes for her were at an all-time high. She sipped her drink, knowing that keeping her mind clear would work to her advantage later on. She noted that Lester's play depended part on skill, part on chance, and part on sleight of hand. Her goal was to bait him. She wasn't one to be tricked easily, or to lose her money to a rigged game, but for now she watched him bet, bluff, and to her delight, she saw him palming cards. Of course, he was a high risk-taking character, a cowardly blackguard, but now she knew he was also a miserable cheat. This observation changed everything. She sat back to review her strategy. Lester won the pot off Robbie, who refrained from looking at her.

Back in the game, she goaded Lester after playing another favorable hand.

"Well sir, you had your doubts about me, but I think I've proved my skill superior to yours,"

"You've had a fortunate run, I'll warrant, but that's not skill, it's luck," he said, gritting his teeth, his voice as mean as a snake's hiss.

"Luck be damned," she said. "I'm made of sterner stuff, unlike some of my opponents." She gestured his way dismissing him along with the others. He grabbed up his drink swallowing hard.

"In fact, sir, I would go as far as to say your play, like yourself, was positively flaccid."

Lester flushed, turning away. "A lucky draw turns anyone into a winner. Three card monte," he declared to the dealer. The table complied and they played a round. Then he requested a game of Chuck-a-luck followed by Brag.

Lester's play did not improve and the table reverted to poker. The dealer announced several wild cards to change up the game. "Deuces, aces, and one-eyed faces," he said.

"Acey, deucey and one-eyed jacks," mumbled Robbie to himself as he examined his cards. An assorted group of liquored up local miners, travelers, and speculators had gradually ringed the table, watching the play with interest.

Iris focused intently on the game. It looked like she had a good shot at a straight flush. Her hand showed all diamonds, bar one, again the death card, the single ornate ace of spades. She watched as Robbie bled out his bankroll, obviously hoping for a flush.

"Show us what you got, Lester," she teased. He folded tersely.

As the evening wore on, Iris made steady progress. She was using her skill at counting to weigh the odds. But her real aim was to get Lester rattled, desperate to prove himself and acting rash. She knew that he played by a quick and violent code. He was capable of swift action on the green cloth and in life. Iris again pulled a great pile of winning chips toward her. She needed an audience for the feat she was about to attempt. She drew her bag towards her side, opened it, and assured herself that her gun was at the ready. "Five-card draw," she requested, hunching over her hand once it was dealt. She held the queen of spades with a scepter, the bedpost queen which she recognized as herself, the black lady, the widow. Beside it was the queen of clubs holding a mournful flower. There was also a deuce and a pair of knaves. She saw Lester deftly retrieve a card from his sleeve. This was her moment to act.

She leaped up, shouting, "Show me your hand. If you have more than five cards, I will take you for a cardsharp and kill you on the spot." Quick as a lash, Robbie grabbed Lester's wrist, twisted it, and six cards fell to the table. Lester gave a howl and jumped to his feet brandishing a pistol, but Iris's gun barked out a bullet first.

Lester staggered back, stunned, shot in the chest, and howling with pain. Then, he rocked forward in slow motion, his torso crashing down onto the table, scattering cards and chips. The assembled group jumped back. Chairs flew backwards. Blood pooled on the back of his coat as his limbs flailed in the air before going slack.

"Self-defense," said Iris. "You all saw him play a cheating game, then jump at me like a rattler."

She stashed her gun, gathering the dispersed chips. "Drinks on me till that shadow of a Sheriff arrives," she said. She leaned over the dead man, pulling another gun from his holster — Jim's gun. "I believe this belongs to me," she said, brandishing it, "and I'm gonna use it to gun down that traitor, Buck, soon as I find him. Ned and Robbie, I might need some company."

"Aye," said the assorted crowd. "You do that, and Jim will rest peaceful. Don't forget to take Jim's horse home. We'll vouch for you with the new Sheriff, we surely will."

High Desert Rose

Enid Holden

A fierce wind battered the warped timbers that made up the buildings of Pitkin, as if trying to rouse the townsfolk, both past and present, from their rest. Blake Adams woke in his cabin as the blasts pounded the walls and rocked the door, invisible hands reaching like tendrils to claw at the latch. Blake shuffled out of his bed and over to the window which rattled in its socket as shadow arms swayed and snatched at the glass. He leaned out to draw in the shutter, taking in the aisles of swaying pine, the galaxy wheeling in the blackness beyond. Blake's hair swept into a wild red tangle; his beard stubble glinted in the dim light.

He stumbled over to the stove, threw a log on the smoldering ashes, and swilled some grinds with water in a metal jug which he set to brew. The smell of coffee rose with the steam, gurgling with the wind.

Outside, the voice of the dead girl scraped through the branches and whispered on the wind. "I'm here," she said. "Never really left. My time's coming. Don't forget about me, Blake."

Blake sat for a while near the fire, leaning his head on his hands, remembering. His shirt was so worn it should have been used for a rag. He lumbered over to a fill a striped mug with the dark brew, added a pinch of sugar, and sipped at it, avoiding the chips in the rim. An image of Mollie rose unbidden in his mind. Not her beautiful face, but the dead Mollie, her face set in a death grimace as he had seen her where she lay, a rose of blood blossoming on her chest where she had been shot at close range. Blake cursed himself out loud now. He should have been around to save her. Mollie knew how to please a man, but she was no pushover. She had grit. He knew now that he'd loved her.

The coffee sobered him. *There are forces in the wild, eerie spirits which play tricks*, he thought. *This is the burden of men living in solitude, the thoughts that steal into their minds in the dark.* He missed the nightly banter of the sporting hall after a long day's work. He missed Mollie's arms around him in her small candlelit room. It had been many months now that she'd been gone. *Damn yourself to hell, you should have married her, you fool. Sheltered her, but you thought you were above her. Well, you don't amount to much if you have to live in a shack with nothing but the memory of a dead whore.*

The next morning Blake awoke to someone knocking furiously on his cabin door. It was Kitty, a girl who had worked with Mollie at the Desert Rose.

"I seen hem. It's hem alright. No-one thought to let him know he ain't welcome in this town after what he dun," she gasped out as soon as Blake opened the door.

"What's this?" Blake asked. He thought about Mollie's voice in the dark.

"The man, Mollie's killer, goes by the name of Jed. I seen him ride into town last night. We can't let him loose in the streets here again, seen as what he dun to our poor ᾽Mollie."

Blake nodded. "Are you sure, Kitty? He's the one?"

"Sure as can be, Blake. He pulled the trigger on her when she flat turned him down."

"Will you walk through the street with me and put your finger out if you spot him?"

"Yes Blake, I c'n do that much for Mollie. And I'm frightened for the other girls."

"You can't make no error now, ya know. A man's life is on the line."

"There's no mistakin' the man. His name's Jed and he's the killer," she said and shivered. "Mollie's been known to take a major licken' with no whimpering. But that un shown no mercy or humanity."

As they walked down the Main Street early at dusk persistent ghosts still hovered. Every building held a memory for Blake. He looked up at the sun hovering behind the buildings casting long strips of shade. *Seems as though the shadow of old lives lays yet on the land.*

"You haven't been out and about much in recent months," Kitty said.

"I haven't been much in the way of livin', but I don't aim to stop if I can still stand. I got a debt to pay."

"We don't know much about him," Kitty said. "Came through a time or two, and then he turned into a ragin' beast. Maybe he found the drink or grew mad lookin' for gold. Either way, Mollie wasn't havin' him."

They entered establishment after establishment, with Kitty peeping in the dusty windows or through the doors to see if she could spot him. Once she saw him sitting at the bar, she shrank back, nodded, and pointed. Blake saw the paleness of her face, her frightened eyes.

"Wait back at my place, Kitty. You'll be safer there till we know how things turn out."

"What you plannin' on doin, Blake? Shouldn't we send for the sheriff?"

"In this short-grass country we gotta do our own regulatin' of the law. In these matters I consult mainly my own self. I'm mostly right and I'm mostly unanimous."

Kitty smiled as she slipped away.

Blake stomped the mud off his boots at the door. "Howdy," he said to Jimmy who was tending bar.

"The day flew by like a week," Jimmy said, his eyes bloodshot, his hands trembling slightly.

Blake raised his eyebrows as he removed his hat. Jimmy's eyes clouded over. He too had looked on terrible wrongs. His once handsome face had grown sullen with bitterness. The balding bartender angled his head slightly towards the stranger, lowering his lids.

Blake gave Jed a quick appraisal. A tall, heavy-set man with dark unruly hair, pale watery eyes. Blake felt his heart pump heavily and the muscles in his stomach tighten. He sat down at the bar next to the man, beckoned for a drink.

"Pass me a double," Blake said. "My throat's got to thinking my mouth is sewn shut." The barkeep slid a glass over to him and Blake sipped in silence.

"Cheerful place, this," Jed said, looking around the sparse, dusty bar.

Blake moved uneasily on his barstool. He swiveled towards the man, anger flushing his cheeks. "I've got a lot of thoughts stored up, but no mind to speak 'em," Blake said.

"This here town is a heller," the bartender said. "Nobody comes through here if they can help it."

"Not sure it's as bad as painted," Jed said. "I've snarled misself some mischief in the past."

"It's those passing through make it ugly," Blake said, slamming his drink down on the counter.

"Now, what would give a man rise to suggest that?" Jed took a slow sip of his beer and looked up in innocence at Jimmy.

Jimmy picked up a glass and polished it.

"Heard some girl around here had been sore mistreated. Ring a bell of any kind, Jed?" Blake said.

"Makes a man feel low in his spirit to hear that," Jed said.

"A thankless task," Blake said with venom. "Asking a murderer to fess up to his crime."

"My pleasure. If you can make it stick." But seeing the look on Blake's face, Jed rose from his seat at the bar and stepped away a pace or two. A silence settled into the room. Two gamblers who had been scuffling quit, waiting to see what the two men would do.

"You can't fight the drop," Jimmy said as Blake rose, gestured to Jed, and walked to the door. Jimmy pointed at Blake's holster. "How good do you think you are with that thing?" he called after him.

"No-one has killed me yet," Blake said, the doors slapping behind him. "He and me gotta do a ghost dance. A grave apiece. It's time to pay the ferryman."

Blake walked out into the street. Turning, he watched the doors flap behind Jed as his broad shape came off the boardwalk and into the street, scuffing up dust in the fading light. The gamblers stumbled out the door to watch. A wind from nowhere lifted, grew wild, and puffed out great tendrils of dust. The gusts intensified, became savage and moaned, whipping up Jake's shirt and tearing at his hair.

More stragglers huddled out onto the deck to witness.

"I guess the cards are dealt," Jed said through the gale.

"Then play your han..."

Blake didn't finish the sentence but shifted to his left. His gun curled up and settled in his grasp as he heard the sharp crack of Jed's revolver. *Damn, the man was fast.* The blow of a bullet slammed into Blake and he veered back. He didn't know where he was hit, but he didn't care. He was still standing and he twisted to fix his gun on the target, taking deliberate aim through the roaring wind as he heard another roar to his right. *Damn.* A second later Jed was cocking his gun for yet another shot but a sharp spurt of wind lifted a fistful of fine gravel and dust and hurled it into his eyes. Jed jerked his head aside, eyes squinting closed, cussing in pain.

The wind stopped as quick as it had blustered up. The dust that settled on it formed the lazy curve of a woman's ample form, which shimmered there for a second or two before dispersing to the ground it came from.

Then Blake fired.

In seconds Jed shuddered back, his body went slack, and he crumpled down with a crash that seemed to shake the town. He got an arm up and fired off another bullet in Blake's direction before collapsing on his side.

Blake had never been good at waiting, but now he was unhurried and unperturbed. The dust tendrils snaked around and down as the wind died, and Mollie's vague form disappeared from his sight as he slumped forward.

"You delivered the goods as per invoice," Jimmy said, running up.

"Even when ya win, you almost lose," Blake choked out. Then he went silent.

Blake lay face down in the dirt. Jimmy came up, nudged him over with the toe of his boot. He took in his peaceful face and the copious blood that leaked from his threadbare shirt. He was dead for sure.

"He and me gonna do our ghost dance," a woman's voice sighed on the wind. "A grave apiece. It's time to pay the ferryman his dues."

Epilogue

As you can see, the spirits of the west can be found in some unexpected places. The western genre has a spirit of its own which can pop up its head in the most curious of settings. And the paranormal genre adds an unusual twist that lends itself to even more surprises. Put the two together, and you never know what you might get, but the stories in this anthology offer some good examples.

I hope you have enjoyed the spirits of the west contained in the stories of this anthology.

Thank You for Reading

Spirits of the West

If you liked it, please leave a review for the complete anthology, or for any of the individual stories and show your support for the wonderful authors whose stories are featured here.

Where Spirits Linger

Introduction

For the 2020 WordCrafter Short Fiction Contest, the theme outlined in the submission guidelines was a paranormal short fiction story in which the setting is central to the story. In many ghost stories, the location or setting is a central element in the story. Certainly, a spooky setting can be a key element in getting buy-in with a paranormal tale.

Did you ever wonder why many ghost hunts take place in hotels, hospitals, battle fields, cemeteries, etc...? Ghost hunter, Connor Randall says that this is because these settings are liminal places, locations of transition which attract more paranormal energy. Randall claims many hauntings are caused by "residual spirits", or building memories, caught "like a broken record", repeating the same actions over and over again, apparently unaware of our presence on this side of the veil.

Although that doesn't explain reports of non-repetitive and unpredictable manifestations, ghosts which don't seem to be attached to a place, but perhaps an object or even a person instead, it does explain why location is central to so many good ghost stories. The spooky setting makes the story all the more believable.

Whether ghosts or some sort of ethereal imprint, places where hauntings are said to occur, liminal locations, seem to provide wonderfully scary settings. Let's face it, a ghost story that takes place in a park on a sunny day wouldn't be nearly as believable as the same story, but in a nearby cemetery at dusk, during an impending thunderstorm with thunder and lightning crackling all around. The scary setting helps to set the right tone in which to believe in the paranormal and is vital to the tale.

The winning story from the above-mentioned contest was "Olde-Tyme Village", by Christa Planko, who found the perfect ending for her story. You find it in the following pages, along with other contest entries and stories by invitation, including one by the author of last year's winning story, Enid Holden. I hope you enjoy each one as much as I have, as we explore the places **Where Spirits Linger**.

Author Kaye Lynne Booth

https://kayelynnebooth.wordpress.com

Kaye Lynne Booth lives, works, and plays in the mountains of Colorado. With a dual emphasis M.F.A. in Creative Writing, writing is more than a passion. It's a way of life. She's a multi-genre author, who finds inspiration from the nature around her, and her love of the old west, and other odd and quirky things which might surprise you. She has short stories featured in the following anthologies: *The Collapsar Directive* ("If You're Happy and You Know It"); *Relationship Add Vice* ("The Devil Made Her Do It"); *Nightmareland* ("The Haunting in Carol's Woods"); *Whispers of the Past* ("The Woman in the Water"); and Spirits of the West ("Don't Eat the Pickled Eggs"). Her western, *Delilah,* her paranormal mystery novella and her short story collection, *Last Call*, are all available in both digital and print editions.

In her spare time, she keeps up her author's blog, *Writing to be Read*, where she posts reflections on her own writing, author interviews and book reviews, along with writing tips and inspirational posts from fellow writers. She's also the founder of *WordCrafter*. In addition to creating her own imprint in *WordCrafter Press*, she offers quality author services, such as editing, social media & book promotion, and online writing courses through *WordCrafter Quality Writing & Author Services*. When not writing or editing, she is bird watching, or hiking, or just soaking up some of that Colorado sunshine.

The People Upstairs

By Kaye Lynne Booth

June 16*th*, 2012

Dear Diary,

Today was about as awful as any eight-year-old girl ever had. I don't think I'll ever understand why folks have to be so mean. And poor Edna. She's just on old woman who thinks a little different. That's what Mom says, and I think she's right. Edna is one of the nicest ladies I know.

I saw Edna outside the supermarket when I was waiting for mom to pick up Gram's grocery order. Michelle Jones and the group of girls she hangs out with just kept taunting her, calling her 'Crazy Edna', trying to yank her shopping cart away from her. As sure as my name's Cassie Cook, somebody had to do something.

I could see in her eyes how scared she was. Edna thinks people are after her anyway. She's been our housekeeper and Mom's friend since before I was born. For as long as I've known her, she's talked about how everyone is after her: the government, her neighbors, the mailman, the church... but mostly the government. Edna thought they were all after her at one time or another, forming conspiracies against her, trying to kill her.

One time she stopped opening mail for two years, because she was convinced that her mailman was poisoning her envelopes with something that would seep into her skin and kill her if she touched it. I know. That does sound crazy, even crazier than the voices she hears in her head or closing off entire sections of her house. Mom says she just *passes through phases, and no one is really after her, but she isn't hurting anyone living like she does, so we should humor her as much as we can.*

I could tell those mean girls really frightened Edna. So, Diary, you can see why I had to step in. Edna may think a little differently, but she's my friend.

Michelle and her bunch are the type who make themselves feel better about who they are by talking down everyone around them. They are a couple of grades ahead of me, in the sixth grade, and I avoid them all as much as possible around school. I knew trouble was coming as soon as I came around the corner of the grocery.

"Well, well. Look what we have here, girls," Michelle said, twirling a lock of golden blonde hair around her finger. "It's Crazy Edna, the bag lady." She sauntered over to block the sidewalk ahead, Tara, Ashley and Sharon all trailing behind her like a line of baby ducklings imprinting on their mother. Michelle reached out and grabbed Edna's cart, jerking it toward her. "What do you have in that cart, Crazy Edna?"

Edna tightened her grip on the shopping cart and pulled back. "Here, now. You stop that," Edna said, her voice rising. "Those are my groceries. I need them. I paid for them."

But Michelle didn't let go of the cart, instead giving it another tug. "Are you sure that you paid for them? Maybe the little green men beamed them down to you."

"Is that what really happened?" Sharon said, stepping up next to Michelle with her fuscia pink hair gathered up in short ponytails that looked like balls of porcupine quills spiking out on either side of her head. A nose ring with a small ball on each end hung from the piercing in her nose, making it look like she has a booger there. "Or maybe you're beaming them up to them as an offering. Do you worship them?"

"You let go of my shopping basket!" Edna said, yanking back hard, ripping the metal wires from Michelle's fingers.

"You are crazy!" Michelle yelled, shoving the shopping cart into Edna's ankles, causing her to cry out in pain. Michelle stepped forward with her fist drawn back.

I thought she was going to punch poor Edna in the face! "Hey Michelle! You can't talk to her like that." I said, stepping in between them.

I wish you could have seen the surprised looks on all their faces, Diary. It was as if they hadn't really seen me standing there before. Of course, that's when Michelle hit me right in the eye. My head started spinning from the blow and I fell to my knees, scrapping my elbow on the sidewalk. But that wasn't the worst part.

My mom came out of the store then, with Gram's groceries and put a stop to the whole thing, chasing those girls off. Mom is a big lady with a loud voice. Those nasty girls didn't have the guts to argue with her. They scattered as soon as they saw her coming out the door of the grocery.

When I told her what had happened, she said, "That's ridiculous. Edna hasn't ever claimed to see an alien. She hears voices. It's a totally different thing."

At home when Gram found out, things got really bad. Mom and Gram got into an argument about Edna while Mom was cleaning my scrapped elbow, putting anti-biotic ointment on it.

"Now, Sherry, how many times have I told you that woman is bad news," Gram said in that lecturing tone that means she's about to lay down the law. "I don't know why you don't fire her and hire someone who has all their wits about them."

Mom dabbed at my wound with a wet washcloth, while I gripped the back of the kitchen chair, gritting my teeth and trying to pretend it didn't hurt.

"Edna is a perfectly good housekeeper," Mom replied, pouring peroxide over my elbow, making me wince. "In all the years she's worked for us, have you ever had complaints about the cleanliness of this house?" She grabbed a clean dish towel from the drawer and patted the wound dry. "She keeps the dust off the furniture well enough to pass your white glove inspection, and that's no easy task, Mother. She keeps the silver polished, waxes the floors, and even keeps the cobwebs cleared from the ceilings. What more could you want?"

"The woman talks to people who aren't there," Gram said, countering Mom's argument with her hands on her hips. It was a stance that said she wasn't prepared to back down. "She's not a good influence to have around the child. Cassie is impressionable."

"So, she talks to herself as she cleans. So what? She's harmless," Mom said. "She's more than just our housekeeper. She's my friend, Mother. And I don't have so many of those that I want to throw her to the wolves just because she imagines things."

"She's my friend, too," I said, but I don't think they heard me.

"Just look at what's happened to this child already because of her," Gram persisted. "A black eye. A black eye, for God's sake!" She placed her hand under my chin and raised it, so Mom could get a good, clear view of my face. "It's neglectful, I tell you, for you to allow such a thing to happen."

"Mother, that was not Edna's fault, nor mine," Mom said, raising her voice to my grandmother, which is something she's never done before, at least not in my lifetime. She pushed down harder than intended, making me wince as she applied anti-biotic ointment with a gauze pad. "Why don't you make yourself useful and go make an ice pack for that eye you're so concerned about."

I don't think anyone has ever talked to Gram like that before, not even Pops. But she did as Mom instructed without saying another word. She was silent even as she placed the ice pack over my eye, which was beginning to swell shut.

After supper, Mom came to my room and told me she was going over to Edna's to see if she was doing okay. She wanted me to stay home and rest and keep ice on my eye, but I begged her to let me go with her. I hated to use it against her, but in the end, I did what I had to do. I threatened to go tell Gram if she didn't take me with her.

I wasn't sure Edna was going to let us in when we got there. She was confused at first, and we had to convince her that it was really us, and not some imposters trying to trick her into opening the door.

It was me who finally convinced her it was us when I mentioned the day trip we took to the mountains, when we happened upon thousands of lady bugs, covering the rocks as we crested the top of one hill that day. All at once, they took flight, filling the air around us until we were standing in a cloud of red and black, and then they were gone. They didn't just thin out, moving all together as one. No one else knew about that day or that amazing sight but she, my mom and me.

So, that did it. She let us in, but she wasn't in a good state of mind. Mom told me to go sit in the living room and watch television, but Edna didn't want the set on. She was very agitated. She said the government agents who were after her were using the airwaves to try and tap into her brain. There was a partially assembled puzzle laid out on the card table, but I remembered Edna saying that sometimes 'the people', who she said lived upstairs, on the second floor of her house, came down and re-arranged the pieces when she wasn't looking. I'm pretty good at puzzles, but Mom says I shouldn't add to Edna's delusions.

So, I was left to my own devices while Mom tried to calm Edna and bring her back down to reality, which was okay for a while, because I brought a book with me, Alice in Wonderland, by Lewis Carroll. It's a hard book to read, because the language is so peculiar, and eventually it made my head hurt trying to make sense of it, so I wandered around the living room, looking at all the unusual trinkets and knick-knacks that occupied the shelves upon Edna's walls.

I was looking at her bowling trophies on a table near the bottom of the stairs, thinking about the times Mom and I had gone bowling with Edna. Heck, Edna taught me all I know about bowling.

A rubber ball came bouncing down the stairs and landed at my feet, and a chill ran down my spine. I bent and picked up the ball, peering up into the utter darkness of the second floor. I know Edna doesn't use the second floor. It is scary up there. I squinted to try and see through the gloom, but it didn't do any good, so I placed my foot on the bottom stair and started to climb.

I only made it to the third stair, when Edna came running out of the kitchen waving her hands at me.

"No, no, no, child," she said with eyes as big as saucers. "You don't want to bother the people upstairs!"

"I was just going to return this ball I found," I said, hoping this explanation would appease Edna and she would calm down once more. In three steps I had managed to undo all the calming my mother had done for the last hour. Worse, I had upset her even more.

"Where did you get that?" she asked, snatching the ball from my hand.

"It just rolled down the stairs," I said. "I was going to put it back."

"No, no, no! You can't go up there," she said with a raised voice. "They've already been disturbed. This ball proves that they're stirring."

I didn't know what to say. Luckily, Mom came from the kitchen and put an arm around Edna, guiding her over to the couch. "Now, Edna, it's alright. No one will go upstairs and disturb anything. Cassie was just bored, but she won't go up there." Mom's look said that I'd better come down off those stairs, so I moved back down to the lower floor. "See, she's down here and there's no harm done."

"But the ball..." Edna said, holding it up for Mom to see.

"I'm sorry, Edna," I said. "It came from up there. I just thought I should put it back where it came from."

"That ball proves they're awake," Edna replied. "Now I can't rest until they settle again. The ball should be put back, but I'll have to do it. Nothing can be disturbed." She started to rise from the couch, but Mom stopped her.

"Now Edna, you don't need to be climbing those stairs in this state. You're liable to fall and break a hip."

"That's just what they want," Edna replied, sinking back down into the sofa. A tear escaped the corner of her eye and ran down her cheek. "They want me join them and take care of them forever. They want me to give in and let it happen."

"No, no. No one is after you," Mom said, sitting on the couch next to her. "Cassie and I are here. We won't let anyone hurt you."

"But the ball..." Edna cried. "It must be put back."

"I could put it back for you, Edna," I said hesitantly, afraid of upsetting her further.

"Cassie," Mom said. There was caution in her voice, but I continued my thought before she could stop me.

"I could go up and set it at the top of the stairs. I won't touch anything else. I promise."

"Could you do that?" Edna asked with a spark of hope in her eyes. "Without disturbing anything?"

I nodded and she held out the ball to me.

With the ball in hand, I climbed the stairs, slowly. I was trembling now and had to force my legs to take each step, a ball of hot glue suddenly sitting in the pit of my stomach. The top of the stairs seemed to get farther and farther away, instead of getting closer.

Eventually, I made it to the top and stepped onto the second floor, giving my eyes a minute to adjust to the gloomy dimness of the darkened sitting area. A thick layer of dust covered the old round tabletop and bookshelves. It was all so different from the shining countertops on the floor below. I heard Edna's voice behind me, telling me to just set it down and come back down, so I set it carefully on the small round table, which sat just to the left of top stair, sending up a plume of dust that watered my eyes and made me sneeze. The ball rolled off the top of the

*table and circled my feet, coming to a stop right in front of me and
sending my heart racing in my chest once more. I turned and ran back
down the stairs, where Mom and Edna sat waiting for me.*

*In the car on the way home, Mom scolded me, telling me it isn't nice
to play on Edna's fears, even though I tried to tell her that wasn't what
happened at all.*

"Where did the ball come from?" she asked as the car engine
roared to life. "Did you bring it with you?"

"No, Mom," I said, begging her to believe me. "It came down
from the top of the stairs. Honest."

"Balls just don't roll around without help, Cassie," Mom said.
"You and I both know there is no one upstairs in Edna's house, no
matter what she thinks. She hasn't even been up those stairs in I don't
know how many years."

"I know. It was really dusty up there," I said. "But Mom,
something weird did happen up there."

"Now that will be enough, young lady," Mom said. "Maybe Gram
is right. Maybe all of Edna's crazy stories aren't a good influence on
you and I shouldn't expose you to them. She's just a confused old
woman, but now you're making up crazy stories. That's not good."

"Mom, I'm not making stuff up. I don't think Edna is either," I
said. "What if what she says is true? What if there is something up
there? That ball really did come down those stairs, and then, when
I put it back on the table, it rolled off and circled my feet. It really
happened."

*Mom didn't believe me. I guess she thinks Edna really is crazy, and
now maybe she thinks I'm crazy, too. But the worst part is, now she's
starting to believe Gram and may not allow me to be friends with Edna
anymore. Edna is one of the only friends I have. That's the worst thing.
What if she fires Edna so I can't see her anymore?*

July 14th, 2018

Dear Diary,

    I feel like my heart is breaking. Edna has had a relapse. Poor dear must have thought the mailman was trying to poison her again. She stopped opening her mail, so her bills didn't get paid, and they shut off her all of her utilities last week. She showed up for work today in dirty clothes, crusted with food, smelling of sweat and urine. Mom took the day off work to help her get into a facility where they can take care of her and make sure her basic needs are met. Mom promised we could go and visit Edna, but I feel like I've lost my best friend.

    I've spent my afternoons with Edna two days a week for as long as I can remember. She always made time to talk with me, even though she was working. Ever since the day I found the ball, there have been few social interactions with Edna because Gram convinced Mom that she's not a good influence on me, so I cherish those afternoons.

    It's true, some of the things Edna says are pretty far off in left field, but she has a unique way of viewing the world, and sometimes she'd open up and share her vision with me. I've learned a lot from her, like how a frog might make a home from a broken flowerpot if it's set in the right location, or how to gather mushrooms in the fall and create mushroom prints with them. She's who told me that it was possible to brush your teeth too much and weaken the enamel, after she waited to clean the upstairs bathroom for a half an hour for me to finish brushing. I know her mailman didn't try to poison her, but just the same, I think some of the things she says are true. Maybe even the people upstairs?

    Forget I said that. Mom said if I talk like that, people will start thinking I'm as crazy as Edna. That's what she said the day I found the ball. Mom forbade me from ever talking about that day with anyone, ever. I guess that's why I can tell you about it, Diary. You're not anyone, so I can tell you anything.

Perhaps I could visit Edna on my own. Maybe she'll get better and be able to come back, but Mom says Edna's getting too old to do the work anyway, so I doubt it. For now, Mom has the key to Edna's house and Edna signed a power of attorney, so Mom could take care of her affairs. The power and water are on again, so maybe she'll at least be able to return to her own home soon.

September 21ˢᵗ, 2020

Dear Diary,

I really have lost my best friend this time. We buried my poor Edna today. No one will ever persecute her again, in her mind or in this world. On my recent visits, I could tell that she was slipping away, her mind increasingly often in a world that only she could see. But, on last week's visits she seemed to be calmer, more at ease with her surroundings, and she knew who I was, so I didn't have to remind her of the lady bugs, but I did anyway because her face lights up when she thinks about them. Unfortunately, later in the visit, she became less lucid once more and started going on about how the facility was trying to kill her, and how they were poisoning her food by order of the government, and the visit had to be cut short because she became so agitated. The facility said she died that night, in her sleep, and I can only hope that that means that she's finally at peace.

It was a small service. Mom and I, and a couple of her former housekeeping clients, a man in a dark brown suit and the town librarian. I don't know why she was there. Probably because Edna was an avid reader and library patron for so many years. Edna had no family, and no real friends to speak of, so although sad, this came as no surprise.

What did come as a surprise was when the man in the brown suit approached my mother and I following the service and asked that we follow him to a reading of the will. I didn't even know Edna had a will. I don't think Mom did either. With no family to leave it to, I guess we assumed the house would go to the city or something. There wasn't really much else. Edna had a lot of stuff, but nothing of any real value. Actually, I don't think I ever really thought about it at all.

I was even more surprised to find that Edna had left the house to me! What the hell am I going to do with that creepy old house? I'm supposed to start college in the Spring, for crying out loud. Mom says if I don't want to live there, I should clean it up and rent it out or sell it. I suppose it would bring enough for a down payment on something more modern, maybe a condo with a pool, but I almost feel as if to sell it would be to turn my back on my friend. She left it to me. She must have wanted me to have it, but why? Did she actually expect me to live there?

And what about the people upstairs? I know I shouldn't talk about them, but with the house being mine now, it's not surprising that they are on my mind. No matter what I decide to do with the house, I will eventually have to clean out that second floor. I don't know if I will ever get all the dust out, and after all the years that Edna let it sit untended, who knows what has taken up residence up there. And what if Edna was right? What if there are spirits up there who don't like to be disturbed? I've been convinced of this since the day the ball landed at my feet.

No matter what I said for the benefit of Mom and Gram, I know what happened that day. That ball rolled out of the second-floor darkness and bounced down those stairs, like someone up there wanted to play. And I've never told anyone but you, Diary, about what happened when I climbed the stairs to put it back. I tried to tell Mom, but she wouldn't hear it, but I know that was real. But then, I guess that's just what I would say if I were crazy, because I would believe it, even if it wasn't real.

It makes me think about how unfair the world is. People were mean to Edna because she was different. No matter how crazy some of the stuff she did was, she was still a kind and gentle woman. That's the side of Edna that I knew. That's the Edna who was my friend. I will miss her so.

October 16, 2020

Dear Diary,
Well, it wasn't easy, but I made myself do it. I went and took a look at the house, which I haven't set foot in since the day I found the ball. When Mom and I did go on an outing with Edna after that, we just picked her up outside her house. We never went in. Or at least, I didn't. I know Mom visited her occasionally, but not as much as she used to, and she didn't take me with her anymore. But actually, that was okay with me. After that day, I didn't want to go inside Edna's house. I still get the creeps just thinking about it, even though I know eighteen is too old to feel that way, and if I told anyone, they would think I was crazy like Edna, but it doesn't change the facts. The house gave me the creeps then, and it still does. But that's our secret.
As I opened the door, a musty odor assailed me. Edna hadn't set foot in this house in two years. To my knowledge, Mom hadn't had any reason to come here either. She handled all Edna's affairs, but that was as far as it went. Edna hadn't owed on the house, and there had been enough in her savings to keep the utilities on, so at least I didn't have to face it in the dark.
There was a layer of dust on everything, even Edna's always immaculate countertops, but everything on the first floor was neat and orderly, just as Edna had always kept it. If there had been a mess of food

or dishes from her having no power, Mom had cleaned it all up long ago and no evidence remained of Edna's last days there.

I opened up the windows and let some air flow through the lower floor despite the chill autumn air, while I took a duster and cleared away the dust from atop everything. I'll have to have the furnace checked before I start it up for the cold months, which will be coming soon. I also mopped the floors in the kitchen and bathroom, and ran the vacuum in the living room.

I tried, Diary, but I just couldn't make myself climb the stairs to the second floor. I just couldn't do it. Looking up those stairs, I got the same feeling that I had back when I was twelve years old, and that damn ball landed at my feet. Like something cold just went right through me. I know I can't live there. I don't like that feeling at all.

Oh, what am I going to do? I can't sell the place, because I owe it to Edna's memory to keep it, but I can't go into the house without feeling like someone is walking over my grave. Maybe I'll rent it out and live off the money from it. I think Edna would like that. Maybe I could have a yard sale and sell off her trinkets and other belongings. I could sell the furniture, too, or I could rent it for more money if it's furnished. There's a lot of work to be done and decisions to make before it would be ready to rent. But first, I will have to face that second floor.

November 2, 2020

Dear Diary,

Well today was the day. I finally worked up the nerve to face the second floor of Edna's house. I know I own it now, but I think it will always be Edna's house to me. I can't put it off forever. I've got to do something with it, and soon. The money Edna had left in savings was enough to cover this year's taxes and maintain the utilities for a while, but eventually I must find a way to make it pay for itself, or it could become more of a burden than it's worth. I don't know how Edna did it on a housekeeper's wages.

In addition to my cleaning supplies, I went in armed with flashlights, in case any bulbs had burned out after all this time, and insect spray, and rat poison, just in case. I felt like a tomb raider, entering a sacred domain where no one has been in thousands of years. Okay, maybe not that long, but at least decades.

I didn't find any mummies or anything, but I did find a collection of paintings, which could be valuable. I plan to have them appraised as soon as possible. They were leaning against the bookshelves to the right, at the top of the stairs, with a drawing of a ladybug sitting on top of them. It seems strange that I didn't see them when I returned the ball that day. Even in the dark, I would have almost tripped over them. The drawing of the ladybug gave me a warm feeling inside, and I'm pretty sure that Edna drew it. What I can't figure out, is how it ended up on top of those paintings. She hadn't been upstairs in several years. It was all too weird, and try as I might, I couldn't make myself venture onto the second floor any further. Maybe next time I'll actually get to see what else is up there, past the landing. For today, I brought two of the paintings down for appraisal, and that will have to be enough for now.

November 12th, 2020

Dear Diary,

You're never going to believe this. I don't believe it. I got the appraisals on the paintings today. They are worth more than I ever imagined. I thought I might get a few hundred dollars from them, but we're talking thousands! And that's just for the two I brought down with me. If the other paintings are worth half as much, I'll be sitting *comfortable for years to come. I went over and brought all the other paintings down this afternoon.*

Yes. You heard right. I went and got them. Just marched right up the stairs and carried the whole pile down with me. I even paused long enough to look around in the gloom, and do you know what I saw? Well of course you don't, so I'll tell you. It's just one more secret that we must share, because it sounds crazy. The same ball that landed at my feet that day was sitting on that little round end table, right where I placed it that day. I saw it roll off the table and circle my feet that day so many years ago, but it was back on top of that table today.

Once I spotted it there, I felt that cold chill again and I turned, hightailing it back down to the first floor as fast as I could. The paintings were cumbersome, making the going a bit slow, but I made it down with them all intact. Tomorrow I'm going to take them and find out what they're worth. Maybe I won't have to rent the house out after all. Maybe I'll give living there some consideration. It might not be so bad. Nothing says that I would have to go upstairs. Edna just lived on the ground floor. Who says I can't do the same?

December 15ᵗʰ, 2020

Dear Diary,

I don't know how to explain what happened today. After selling the paintings and putting the money in the bank, I honestly had no intentions of ever setting foot on the second floor of that damned house again. I've decided to live there after all. It's got to be better than living with Mom and Gram, and with me being away at college, I won't be there very often. I reasoned that it will be pretty easy to just not go upstairs during the limited time I will be there.

This afternoon I was there putting up Christmas decorations. Now that I've decided to live in the house, I want it to look festive for my first Christmas there. I want the house to look lived in. I've cleaned and polished all the furniture and knick-knacks, bringing them back up to Edna standards, so it just needed a bit of a festive touch.

I don't know ' what I was thinking when I bought a garland for the banister. How did I think it would get hung? Did I think it would just fly up there and hang itself? So, I found myself left with this string of purple and gold garland, that would look gorgeous wrapped around that mahogany banister, and the only way to hang it was to climb those stairs again. But I couldn't make myself do it.

I left the garland lying in a heap on the couch and gathered up the trash, preparing to leave to have supper with Mom and Gram. But, when I returned to grab my purse, I felt a familiar chill, and caught a whiff of perfume in the air. My gaze fell to the floor at the foot of the stairs, and there I saw that same faded yellow rubber ball. I stopped mid-stride, staring at the ball, unsure what the best course of action might be. I mean, what does one do in these situations? This is the part in most ghost stories, where the monster shows up to kill everybody, so what was I supposed to do?

Then, I heard a giggle of a small child from the top of the stairs, causing me to look up. What I saw was the garland hung magnificently over the banister in beautiful streams of purple and gold. I knew then that Edna had been right all along. There really are people upstairs and now I know it for sure. I haven't seen them, but I've felt them, and smelled them, and now I've even heard them. Edna wasn't crazy. Not about this. They're real and they are in that house.

I have to say that the whole experience has me rattled. I snatched up my purse and ran out to my car. I ran out so fast that I forgot to lock the door, and I almost drove off without going back to lock it. I knew that this discovery was a turning point that would decide the rest of my life for me. I could feel it. I'm now sure there really are people upstairs, but if I could take control now, it would set precedent for as long as I lived in the house. So, I pulled myself together and went back to lock the door, but I didn't feel that was a big enough show of strength. I went back inside and picked up the ball, marching up the stairs with all of the determination I could muster.

Then I saw a small jewel box, in the same spot where the paintings had been. Since I myself removed the paintings, I know it wasn't there before. I picked it up and set it on the table, so I could open it. Inside, was the most exquisite jewel box, gold plated with gemstones embedded in the cover and sides. It has to be worth a fortune. I picked it up and placed the ball back in its spot on the table. I ordered it to stay. I said it right out loud to show I wasn't afraid, even though I was. I think it worked, because the ball didn't follow me back down the stairs, as I exited the house with the box. This time, I turned the key in the lock firmly, and even took time to double-check it. I left feeling confident that I can live in this house. I can live with the people upstairs, whoever they are.

December 25th, 2020

Dear Diary,

This was the best Christmas. I spent the morning and enjoyed Christmas dinner with Mom and Gram. I sold the jewel box, which was plated with twenty-four carat gold and had genuine sapphires, rubies and emeralds set in the sides and cover, and bought each of them very special presents. Mom has wanted to own a diamond all her life, so I bought her a pair of diamond earrings. And since Gram is getting older, I bought her an electric bed, one that she can adjust the head and feet like a hospital bed, but this one has a built-in message unit, and a heating unit, too.

Despite of their protestations, after we exchanged gifts and finished our meal, I came back to my new home. I know I'm just getting settled in here, but I was looking forward to spending my first holiday here, even though I knew I would be all by myself.

That is, if you don't count the people upstairs. They are there, and now I can't deny that. There is a little girl who is a bit mischievous and just wants someone to play with. I call her Evelyn. Until today, she was the only one I was sure of. When I returned to the house today, I found it all light up with Christmas lights, just as I had left it, but there was a large rectangular box sitting under the tree which hadn't been there before. There was no wrapping or ribbons, no name tag, just a plain brown box.

I was hesitant to approach the tree. The ball was one thing. I was getting used to finding it out of place, but this was something altogether different. This was more like the paintings and the jewel box, but they were all upstairs. This was on the first floor, right under the Christmas tree, just waiting for me.

I opened the box to find a beautiful blue cashmere sweater and a string of pearls inside. I held my breath as I lifted the pearls out of the box and held them up for closer inspection. "These must be worth a fortune," I said aloud. Then my hair moved as if with the breeze and I caught a whiff of that same musky perfume that I smelled the day I was decorating. It smells very much like the perfume that Edna used to wear. A soft female voice in my left ear, "It's for you to keep." It was so soft, it could have been only the breeze, but I knew that it wasn't. So, there's a woman upstairs. I also think there may be a man up there, as I have detected the aroma of pipe smoke, cherry jubilee, like Gramps used to smoke.

Of course, both Edna and Evelyn and any other people upstairs must remain our secrets, Diary. I can't tell anyone, not even Mom. She may have been Edna's friend, but she didn't really believe any of what Edna said. If I tell her I now know Edna was right and the people upstairs are real, she'll have me sent to the same nuthatch where she put Edna. Maybe it's good that I don't have any real friends, as the temptation might be too great to confide in someone. Of course, dear Diary, that's why I have you.

I put on the sweater and the pearls. They looked fabulous if I do say so myself. Then I popped up some popcorn in the new microwave I bought myself for Christmas and watched holiday feel good movies until I fell asleep on the sofa. It was grand! I awoke at quarter till twelve, which is why I dated this entry the 25th, but I suppose that's misleading, because now it's really the 26th. I just couldn't go on without making an entry about this very special Christmas day.

January 5th, 2021

Dear Diary,

I know I haven't written in a while. To tell the truth, I've been a little disheartened. Apparently, the man I sold the jewel box to was required to report the purchases to the authorities. So, I received an envelope in the mail from the IRS. They want me to verify where the items I sold came from. I'm sure they just want to make sure I pay all the required taxes, but I worry. Gram says once the IRS gets your number, they never let go. She says once they get you in their sights, they keep tabs on you for the rest of your life, and if they find something on you, they will hound you to the grave.

And how can I give them an answer? What do I say – The people upstairs gave them to me? It's the truth, but I don't have to tell you what would happen if I dared to reveal the unbelievable truth. So, what **do** I say? Maybe I just won't reply. What can they do? It might have *gotten lost in the mail. How would they know if I got it or not? If I don't answer, they won't think I'm crazy, but they might think I'm a thief.*

On the other hand, if I had some other source of legitimate income, it might confuse the issue enough to dispel all such notions. That might keep them off my trail, at least until I leave for school. I may be able to figure out a way around their questions, at least for now.

For the last couple of days, the people upstairs have been quiet. I almost wish they'd let themselves be known to me, so I could tell them about my latest dilemma with the Feds. I'm starting to realize that the people upstairs want to take care of me. Their presence is comforting. I think they took care of Edna, too. I bet Edna had the same problem and the government really was watching her after all.

January 12th, 2021

Dear Diary,

I got my first housekeeping client today. Mrs. Armentrout hired me to clean her house two days a week at thirty dollars an hour! She is also referring me to Mrs. Daley, who also happens to be looking for a housekeeper. It looks like I will have my legitimate business even sooner than I'd hoped. Let those men in black come. I'll be ready.

I feel much better about the whole situation now that the people upstairs have returned. I don't know if they were really gone, but they certainly were quiet all last week, I also learned that there is a man among them, who I call Chester, who does smoke a pipe. He introduced himself with a gift of a beautiful jade chess set. I think it may have been hand carved. It was sitting on the coffee table when I came home from the grocery, with the aroma of cherry jubilee lingering in the room.

Going to the market was energizing. At first, it was a bit uncomfortable pushing Edna's old shopping cart down the sidewalk, but then I decided I didn't care what anyone else thinks, so I just held my head high and pushed my cart with purpose. Now I know it probably seems strange that I would leave my perfectly good car in the driveway and push that old cart all the way to the grocery, but you don't understand how much we miss while driving cars. Today I saw a mother goose and her goslings going for an early morning swim in the lake, even though there is still ice floating on it. And Mrs. Peabody has marijuana growing in her greenhouse, tucked back in between tomatoes. I bet she thinks no one will notice, and with everyone driving, they probably don't.

But I did, walking along with my shopping cart.

February 15th, 2021

Dear Diary,

My mother has done it this time. She totally ruined my day off. It was a gloomy day and I had just started a puzzle that would be a picture of a small cottage with an English garden when all the pieces were properly arranged. I was just separating out the edge pieces when she showed up here unannounced. To say she was a little upset would be the understatement of the year. I swear, I saw steam coming out of her ears. Okay, maybe it wasn't that bad, but you get the idea. Apparently, the school didn't make my address change, and the confirmation of my withdrawal came to Gram's house, instead of here. So, of course, she opened it.

"Cassie, I don't know what has gotten into you," Mom said almost before she was in the door. "I haven't seen hide nor hair from you since Christmas, and now I find out that you've gone and withdrawn from school. Just what do you think you're doing?"

"Come in, Mom," I said, trying to keep the sarcasm out of my voice. "You might as well have a seat since you're here. I think it's pretty clear what I'm doing. I'm living my own life."

"Why would you ever withdraw from school?" She didn't take my suggestion to have a seat, but instead paced back and forth in front of the card table I had set up in the living room in order to do the puzzle. "You were all set up with your scholarship and everything."

"I turned down the scholarship two weeks ago, Mom," I said, placing the bottom right corner piece into my puzzle. "It's all done already. No turning back."

"But Cassie, why?" she asked, sinking down onto the sofa. "What do you think you're going to do with your life? There's not a lot of opportunities out there for a girl with no college degree, you know?"

"Actually, that's where you're wrong, Mother," I said, looking her straight in the eye. "I've started my own housekeeping business, and I already have a full schedule of clients. I've been working for the last month."

"Housekeeping?" she replied. The look on her face said she was having a hard time grasping this concept. "Why would a smart girl like you want to work as a housekeeper?"

"What's wrong with being a housekeeper?" I asked, rising to my feet as my patience grew thin. "It was good enough for Edna. I guess it's good enough for me."

"Edna?!" She arose from the couch and nearly screamed it at me. At this point, she was red in the face, literally. I don't think I've ever seen her that mad before. "I should have known this had something to do with that crazy old woman!"

"You were supposed to be her friend!" I yelled, the pressure building up inside me until I couldn't contain it any longer. My mother sounded just like those mean girls, that day in front of the grocery. "How can you talk about her like that? Why, you're no better than those snooty gossips in your ladies' club. Always in everybody else's business, jumping to conclusions without having any idea what's really happening."

"You think so?" She stopped, placing her hands palms down on the card table and stood across from me, staring me down. "Edna was a sweet old woman, who got confused and talked to people who weren't there, and thought people were after her, and acted crazy sometimes. She was my friend, but I was capable of knowing what was real and what wasn't. I apologize for letting you be exposed to all her crazy ideas, because as a child, you weren't capable of doing that. I should have listened to Gram." She paused, running her hand over the top of her head, pushing the hair back, away from her forehead, wiping perspiration from her brow. "Now you're running around acting and talking crazy, too. It's all my fault."

"Mother, I am not crazy," I said, gulping down my anger. "And neither was Edna. I'm a big girl. I will live my own life. Now I think you should leave."

There was silence between us for several seconds before she let out the breath she'd been holding, causing her shoulders to visibly slump, then she turned to walk out the door. Before she left, my mother turned to look at me with tears in her eyes and said, "What's happening to my little girl?"

I didn't answer until the door had closed behind her. "She grew up, Mother."

March 25th, 2021

Dear Diary,

Things are getting weird around here. Gifts from the people upstairs keep appearing, but the recent items are not of any value. Most recently, I've found a scrap book full of old photos and documents. Certainly nothing I could sell, but the first gifts have provided enough to keep me afloat for quite some time, so perhaps it's best. The art dealer seemed suspicious when I sold him the paintings, but he was shady enough to know not to ask questions. The man who I sold the jewel box to was full of questions, to which I offered evasive answers concerning how I came to have it in my possession. And I certainly don't need the men in black, (it sounds better than G-men, which is what Edna called them), knocking at my door again. So, yes. Maybe it is for the best.

I was looking through the scrap book. There are several photos of a woman who looks just like Edna at different stages of her life. Could the woman upstairs really be the spirit of my old friend?

Mother hasn't spoken to me since she was last here, a visit which I told you about in my last entry. I know these entries are over a month apart, which is a long time with no word from me, but you must understand that I now have enough clients to keep me busy full time, and between that and keeping my own house clean, I've had little time for anything else.

This house is too big for just me, and now I understand why Edna only used the kitchen, living room and bath, closing the rest of the house off. It's too hard to keep it all clean. I believe it wise to continue with that practice. But I haven't had time to write to you here, or worry about mother's disapproval, or even to work on the puzzle I started.

I thought that I had figured out a way to keep from drawing the attention of the men in black, but it just created more problems. I figured I could hide the money from the jewel box in my mattress, since I'm not sleeping in the bedroom anyway. Sleeping on the couch avoids heating the bedroom. It seemed like a good way to avoid putting it in my bank account and raising more red flags. Only problem is, today when I made a slit near the edge of mattress, on the bottom, where my sewing job would be less noticeable, I found that there was already money stuffed into the mattress. Lots of it. It looks like Edna had the same idea that I did. Probably for the same reasons. She wasn't crazy at all.

Now I have to come up with a new place to hide this money. It's not like I could bury it in the back yard. Not without half a dozen neighbors seeing me. Even if I did it in the dead of night, when passers-by wouldn't be likely, many of my neighbors are night-owls, and Mr. Beasley is a night watchman, so he could be home and awake on any given night. There's always someone watching. I wonder how you go about getting a Swiss bank account.

I certainly can't hide it upstairs, where accessing the money would disturb my silent tenants. When they are awake, they can be very demanding, always wanting to be entertained with puzzles or games of solitaire. Of course, the teen boy whom I've named Elijah, is the most demanding in this aspect as he's been suspended in puberty for eternity. I made the mistake of using my cell phone to play one of those dumb game apps one day when he was awake and bored, and now he's always trying to get me to get out my phone, so he can watch the birds beat each other up. But when he's watching, the cursor doesn't always do what my fingers instruct. Sometimes I swear Elijah is manipulating the app. Maybe he taps into the app's wavelengths or something. I can only imagine.

May 3, 2021

Dear Diary,
I have to do something now, but what? How do I keep the men in black from hounding me? I hid the money from the jeweled box in an empty cookie jar in the pantry, and I haven't sold any of the more recent items that keep appearing. There's a deed to a gold mine, (I'm pretty sure that one came from Chester), the emerald necklace, and the diamond cuff links are all wrapped in the silk shawl, (all of which I believe came from the woman), are neatly tucked under the couch cushion, but the men in black still showed up on the doorstep this afternoon. I guess I made a grave error when I sold the paintings all together for such a large sum.

I didn't answer the door. I sat in my chair and quietly worked on my puzzle, being careful not to make a sound until they finally gave up and went away. I finished the puzzle, but now I have to figure out what to do about my afternoon visitors before I can start another.

Obviously, the house keeping income isn't enough to satisfy their curiosity. I see now that Edna was having similar problems, even though no one else believed her. I didn't just inherit her house. I inherited her life. Since I now know that the men in black really were hounding her, it seems that income from housekeeping didn't work for her either. I have to find another means of income that will make all that money seem reasonable. I need a different job.

May 5, 2021

Dear Diary,

You won't believe this when I tell you. I hardly believe it myself. After my last entry, I called an internet server and signed up for service. They installed it this morning. They woke the people upstairs with all the hammering and banging on the roof, (workmen aren't the quietest lot). I may have to entertain them for a few hours until they settle down again, but I think it will be worth it. Now I can pull out the laptop that I bought for school and use it to find something to bring in more money. There has to be something I can do.

Oh dear, I hear the ball bouncing down the stairs. Elijah must be restless. He'll be unhappy that there is no puzzle out to occupy him. I think he may have actually put a few pieces into the last one himself, although I can't be certain. I'd better go and try to find him another form of entertainment.

October 12ᵗʰ, 2021

Dear Diary,

I am happy beyond belief. I just finished the first draft of my first book!

I'm sorry. I forget that I haven't written here for a while and you don't know what I'm talking about. I apologize for not making regular entries lately. You are my only friend. I should be more attentive and keep you up to date.

I think it was really Elijah's idea. I know that sounds crazy, but a lot of things that I say lately sound that way. But I swear they are true. After my last entry, I set up my laptop on the card table where I had previously been doing puzzles. Elijah was upset that there was no puzzle available, but I showed him how the laptop works and that calmed him. I felt his presence watching over my shoulder for several hours, amazed at all that I could do on the computer.

I thought perhaps there would be something I could do with my writing. After all, that is what I was going to go to school for. It seems like a long time ago, but it was a dream that I once had. It's hard to believe that it has only been a few short months. There are plenty of writing gigs out there, but most of them pay in peanuts. Nothing with potential to produce the kind pf money that I would need to cover my tracks.

Then I came back from the grocery one day to find my laptop on and an ad on the screen for a ghost writer. I started researching and learned that ghost writers make a lot of money. So, I got the job and now I have two more clients waiting, and the money will be run through my bank account, so the occasional large deposit won't draw so much notice. I'm free, and I have Elijah to thank for it. I wish I knew his real name. Of course, maybe it's fitting since no one will know my real name either. How ironic. I got the idea to be a ghostwriter from a ghost!

November 12th, 2021

Dear Diary,

We buried Gram today. It lays heavy on my heart that I hadn't gone to see her more this past year. Of course, mother is never one to let me forget it. She must have mentioned it at least seven times throughout the gathering after the service, which was held at what was Gram's, but is now only Mother's house. Although I grew up there, it just didn't feel right without Gram fussing over all the details of the gathering, making sure each hot dish had a turret under it, making sure the silverware was laid out just so.

Mother attempted to tend the details, but it was a half-hearted attempt. I'm sure other folks believed she was distracted by her grief, and I'm sure she was to some extent, but I think she was overcome by the need to control my life and frustrated by her inability to do so. She acted as if it was my fault that Gram passed on. The woman was 83 years old. Did mother expect her to live forever? I tried several times to change the topic of conversation, but it always came back to that.

"Well, I just don't see why you couldn't come around the house more often, now that you've given up on that silly idea of being a housekeeper," Mother said, taking another pan of finger sandwiches out of the fridge. "Gram would certainly have loved to see more of you. She was terribly bored at the end. Just having someone to talk to beside me would have brightened up her days."

"Mother, just because I'm not cleaning houses doesn't mean I have nothing to do," I replied, placing the stack of napkins I had folded in the center of the tray and spiraling them, like the center of a sun which gives off sandwich rays. "Auto-biographies and memoirs don't write themselves."

"You know Cassie, I swear you walk around with your head in the clouds all day," Mother said, shaking her head as she headed for the dining room with her food tray. "What did I tell you when you wanted to major in English? Writers don't make any money until after they're dead."

"That's where you're wrong, Mother," I said, placing my hands on my hips. I had just about had enough of her criticisms. "The first book I wrote is being published as we speak, and I've already been paid a tidy sum for it. I am making money writing."

"What?" Mother stopped in mid-stride and turned on her heel to face me once more. "You actually have a book being published? Why didn't you tell me?" She set her tray of sandwiches down on the counter, looking at me skeptically. "What is the title?"

"It's not out yet, but even when it is, my name won't be on the cover," I said, running short on patience. "That's what ghost writing is. I get paid to write it, so the client can put their name on it as author."

"So, you get all of the struggle, but none of the glory?" Mother said, sinking into one of the kitchen chairs. I saw the color actually drain from her face at this news. "What kind of a living is that? What will I tell my friends when they ask about you?"

"Tell them your daughter is a pretty good writer, who happens to like what she does." I could feel the sarcasm dripping from my words, but she had pushed me too far and I didn't care if she heard my mocking tone. "It happens to be a living that will sustain me quite nicely. I would think you'd be thrilled that you no longer have to tell them I'm a housekeeper. The money was good and well enough, but I wouldn't want you to have to admit I was performing such lowly duties."

"You think you can support yourself with this writing, but how do you know?" Mother threw her arms up as if this was a major crisis. She's always so melodramatic. "What if you can't? What if you just got lucky with this first book? What if you can't please your clients consistently? You don't even have the degree behind you. I don't know what ever possessed you to drop out of school."

"What do you want me to do, Mother?" I raised my voice in frustration. Why couldn't she ever be happy for me? "Maybe I should just go home where my talents are appreciated."

"By whom?" she asked with a warning look.

She knew what I had been going to say and she was challenging me to say it. I didn't dare let the words pass through my lips now, but what else could I say? I had to find a way to skirt around what I'd almost said in my frustration, or my mother was likely to think I was crazy like she'd thought Edna and have me carried away in a strait jacket.

"Come on, Mom," I said, trying to change the subject. "I know you're worried about me, but I'm a big girl. I can take care of myself. Can't you just trust me to do the right thing?"

"Oh, sure. I trust your judgement," she said with sarcasm. "You'd never choose to spend time on your precious writing while your grandmother lay dying in her bed, would you?"

"I swear, you are never happy!" I said rather loudly. "Whatever career I choose, I will have to spend time working, if I'm to make money at it. There's no way for me to please you!"

And so, the day went. Mother and I ran circles around one another. I admit, I went out of my way to avoid her and left as early as seemed proper. I guess I do care about appearances, because that's the only thing that stopped me from leaving the house right then, instead of just leaving the kitchen. I wanted nothing more than to run home to my house and click away on the keyboard of my laptop. My next writing gig is a novel, and the characters are already beginning to speak to me, but it isn't the same as when I hear the people upstairs. I don't actually hear my characters, but just a sort of mental image of what happens next. Now that I am back home, I guess I'd better get to work if I am going to make my deadline for this memoir.

December 1, 2021

Dear Diary,

It's Mother's birthday, and I know I should go see her, but I don't know if I can make myself do it. We haven't spoken since the dinner after Gram's funeral two weeks ago. She just doesn't understand. The people upstairs are real. I'm not crazy.

I don't try to write when they are awake. They are too demanding when they are up and about. But that means I must write when they are at rest, which leaves little time to get any sleep for me. I am so tired. Since they are quiet now, I think I'll try and catch a nap, even though I have an approaching deadline to meet. I don't think I'll make it without some sleep. I'll work on the novel after a short nap. The client will appreciate it more if the words I turn in actually make sense. Maybe I'll give Mother a call later this afternoon.

December 1, 2021 (con't.)

Dear Diary,

The idea of sleeping is out of the question now. Just as I was starting to doze off, a knock at the door brought me back to a foggy consciousness. It was the men in black. They're back. They pounded on the door and rang the bell repeatedly. Of course, I didn't answer. One of them tried to see in through the living room windows and I had to plaster myself against the wall in the foyer, so he wouldn't see me. They sat out front in their tan sedan for at least thirty minutes. I thought they would never leave. My heart was racing long after they drove away.

I've pulled all the drapes closed now, which makes it very gloomy in here, but at least I can move about without being seen. The kitchen curtains are not as thick as the drapes, however, so I'll have to install some type of blinds in there. I have an advantage which Edna never had. She was forced to go out to make purchases, but I have the internet. I can order just about anything online and have it delivered. I still have to be careful not to spend large amounts, but a couple of blinds won't cost that much.

Since sleep has eluded me, I guess I should finish up the ending chapter for that memoir. After all, I have a deadline to meet. Plus, I am excited in anticipation of the novel which I've been hired to write next. It is a paranormal romance, in which the ghost gets the girl. I'm having fun just thinking about it. I'll write more later.

December 15th, 2021

Dear Diary,

The most amazing thing happened! No one else would believe me if I told them what happened, but you, Diary, will always accept what I tell you with nary a doubt. So, here it is.

I pulled all the Christmas lights and decorations out of the hall closet and I was doing a check on each string of lights to replace any burnt out bulbs, when my attention was drawn to that old scrap book, which has been sitting on the card table, next to my laptop ever since that first day when the people upstairs left it for me. I hadn't really thought about it since that day, but for whatever reason, today it drew my attention. I leafed through it, looking at the photos of Edna at various ages, but there was also a very old photo of a young boy named Elijah Mulcahy, and one of an older gentleman with a small girl on his lap, which is labeled Evelyn Louis and Grandpa Chester. They are older black and white photos with their corners curled, but it seems Edna had discovered who her upstairs guests are, and now I know for sure, too. As odd as that may be, that is not the amazing part.

It had been a long day. I hadn't started on the lights because I needed to write three chapters of the novel first. I've set three chapters as my daily writing quota, and I will have to meet it most days if I expect to have it done on the very tight deadline this new client has handed down. Anyway, I kind of got lost in that old scrapbook with the photos of people upstairs and I must have dozed off in my chair with my head lying on the open scrapbook on the card table in front of me, because that was how I was upon waking the next morning. I had slept clear through the night!

My upstairs tenants must have been very busy while I slept because I was surprised to discover the whole living room decorated and lit up! As I rose and headed for the bathroom, I detected Edna's perfume and caught a whiff of Chester's cherry jubilee burning, as if I wouldn't know it had been them. Who else would it be? But now you see why I said no one else would believe me. If I told someone, they would think I'd done it myself, but I know that's not the case. I didn't not decorate my living room in my sleep, and I am not crazy, But that's what people would think if I dared to tell anyone. That's why you are the only one who I can tell, Diary, and I have, so now I'll get back to working on the paranormal romance, which is turning out to be a lot of fun. I'm already on chapter fifteen. I'll write more later.

December 17*th*, 2021

Dear Diary,

   When last I wrote, I told you of the amazing way my living room got decorated, but today I have something even more amazing to tell you about. Earlier, I was feeling tired, so I lay down on the couch to take a nap. When I awoke, the paranormal story I've been working on was finished, with the words "The End" visible on my screen. I suspected that Elijah had the ability to manipulate electronic devices, and this seems to prove my theory out, but that's not what was really amazing. No, the truly amazing part is that when I scrolled back to chapter twenty where I left off and read what had been typed out as I slept, I found that what had been written was some fine writing. The ending to my story was well-crafted and surprising, probably better than the ending I had planned to write. And it was completed in the time frame of a single afternoon.

   All this time I was thinking the ghost would get the girl, but with this new ending, it was actually the girl who got the ghost. In my mind, the girl was to be trapped for eternity, which I'd been struggling with because it wasn't a very happy ever after. With the new ending, the girl *feels relief in her own death and freedom from the everyday dregs of her life, and she is truly happy to spend eternity with her spectral lover.*

It made me think a lot about my own situation. I've been fearing that the people upstairs have plans for me to care for them for a long time. I feared that I would be trapped, like the girl in my story.

And, like the girl in the story, I'm feeling pulled from every direction. Mother is pressuring me to sell the house. I've been careful not to let anything slip, but she showed up at the house the other day with several real estate brochures and a long speech about how this house is way too much for me. I've seen the men in black sitting outside the house several times. I guess they are waiting for me to come out of the house. They may think they have me, but I can stay in this house for a long time.

Are the people upstairs trying to tell me that dying and spending eternity with them is the only way that I'll ever truly be free?

December 30, 2021 – Daily News

Cassandra Ann Cook, age 19, was found dead in her home yesterday from unknown causes. Ms. Cook was a local author, who made her living ghost writing and has been reclusive over the past year. Local authorities say they are investigating the cause of death, as well as several items of interest found in the home. She is mourned by her mother Sherry Cook. The grieving mother has been sedated and under a doctor's care after falling into hysterics, crying "That damned house killed her! I knew it would," when informed of her daughter's demise.

Author Roberta Eaton Cheadle

November https://robertawrites235681907.wordpress.com/about/

Roberta Eaton Cheadle is writer of young adult and adult fiction in the supernatural fantasy, historical horror, and historical paranormal genres.

To date, Roberta has published two novels, *A Ghost and His Gold* and *Through the Nethergate*, and several short stories in various anthologies including *Whispers of the Past* and *Spirits of the West*, edited and compiled by Kaye Lynne Booth, and four of the five *Box Under the Bed* series, compiled by Dan Alatorre.

When she is not writing, Roberta enjoys working in the garden and creating fondant and cake artworks.

Listen to Instructions

By Roberta Eaton Cheadle

It's the voice that bothers Jake the most, its high-pitched waver and petulant undertone sear through his head and reverberate along his nervous system.

An elderly male face of the yellowish-brown colour and wrinkled texture of a dried pear hosts the irritating and persistent voice. There is a calculating look in his dark, rheumy eyes, and his recessive mouth has a discontented downward twist.

The body to which this face belongs is frail, with bowed legs and a back tipped forwards at a forty-five-degree angle.

He looks like he's carrying a heavy load, Jake thinks. *I wonder what greedy or selfish action led to him being cursed to wander the no-man's land, between this life and the next, with a tremendous burden of sin heaped upon him.*

Since moving into his new home some months ago, Jake had caught several glimpses of the phantom, either lurking in the shadows of the dilapidated linen press or hovering around the large built-in fireplace.

From the first, Jake had decided to ignore him.

The phantom will leave if his presence doesn't illicit any reaction.

Long before he bought the ramshackle, late 19th century house with its splintering wood floors and picture rails, rusting bathrooms, and overly large stone fireplace, Jake had known about the haunting.

People living in the area took great pleasure in sharing creepy stories about the phantom during local social gatherings. Jake even knew his name: Simon Pienaar.

The owner of the local general store had been delighted to fill in the gaps in Jake's knowledge.

"On his thirty second birthday, Simon Pienaar was convicted of theft and assault with a deadly weapon. He was sentenced to twenty years in prison. Following his eventual release, he returned to his childhood home and set about drinking himself to death.

"No-one knows why his spirit remained tied to the old farmhouse, but its reputation for being haunted prevented its sale and, as you know, it's fallen into a state of disrepair.

"I'm glad you've bought it and plan to do it up. It's seems a dreadful waste to just let it rot."

Jake bought the house on auction for a competitive price. The building was sound and had lots of potential. He intended to renovate it over time and had no objections to living there while he did so.

The voice that speaks in his dreams, exhaling the stench of graves and rotting corpses and making him thrash about all night, is unexpected. Waking, slick with sweat, in the early hours of the morning has become a daily occurrence.

The voice is insistent in its message. "Help me," it croaks. "Search for a bag of coins hidden in the chimney breast of this house and return them to their rightful owner. I cannot put down my burden until this is done."

Jake takes no notice. He doesn't believe in messages from beyond the grave. He can accept that there might be some sort of negative energy in the house that manifests itself as the dark shadow he sometimes sees, and which fills the gossiping people of the nearby town with such delight, but he does not believe in visitations. The dreams are merely his childhood terrors, knocking on the door of his subconscious while he sleeps.

The old man hobbles along the dark passage, his wooden walking stick thumping heavily on the threadbare carpet. At the doorway into

Jake's bedroom, he pauses. "Help me," he croaks. Lifting his stick with thin, old-man arms, he bangs it on the bedroom door. Bang! Bang! Bang!

"Help me!"

"What do you want?" *Jake cries.* "How can I help you?"

The spectre holds out a gnarled hand towards Jake, lying in his warm bed. The veins stand out on the plains of his hand like lumpy blue hillocks.

"Come," *he says.*

The stooped shape shuffles down the passageway. Following, Jake sees him pass through the door into the lounge. Stopping in front of the impressive fireplace, the walking stick bangs on the brick chimney breast that runs up the wall and into the ceiling.

"Here," *the ghost's rat-like voice shrills.* "You'll find the treasure here. Get it and return it to its rightful owner."

The distrustful dark eyes of the ghost bore into Jake's. "Don't try to deceive me and keep the money for yourself."

Jake wants to run as the twisted fingers reach out towards him. His feet are heavy and in the strange way of dreams, will not react to his nervous-systems command to move.

The hand touches him, pulling on his sleepshirt's sleeve.

"Don't disobey me, Jake, or you'll be sorry."

Jake runs the gold coins through his hands. There are so many of them. A fortune. The early morning sunlight reflects off their shiny surfaces, throwing bright shards of brilliance onto the lounge walls.

Thank you, dear Simon. You've made me a wealthy man.

On his way to his doctor's appointment, Jake stops at the bank and deposits the coins. Plans for spending his newly found wealth fill his mind and make his heart race.

Later that afternoon, Jake returns home a happy man. His doctor is most sympathetic to his sleeping problems and has prescribed strong pills.

Jerking awake, Jake claps his hand across his mouth to stop the scream. The sheets are saturated, and his chest heaves as he pants, blood racing through his veins.

Taking a quick, fearful look around his bedroom, he satisfies himself that Simon Pienaar is not in attendance.

Getting up, he swallows another sleeping pill and settles back down.

He's just a dream. He can't hurt me.

Forced sleep comes and Jake spirals down into oblivion.

The following day, Jake shops for a new car. He's always wanted a Lexus LS and now he buys one. The satisfaction he feels driving his new possession buoys him, suppressing the fug of exhaustion and anxiety that clouds his waking time.

For several weeks, he drives around in his expensive new car and eats out at top restaurants. He books a December skiing holiday to Aspen, in Colorado. He also drinks too much and pops sleeping pills every night.

His doctor adds anti-anxiety pills to his daily medicine regime. They make him feel slow and sluggish. He drifts off to sleep at inappropriate times and wakes up with a dry mouth and a sandpapered tongue.

He loses weight. His clothes hang on his tall frame and his dull, drugged eyes peer out from hollow, bruised sockets.

"Jake," his mother says, "you are losing too much weight. If you are dieting, I think it's time you stopped."

He didn't reply – what could he say?

His bed has become his nemesis and sleep something he approaches with horror. Simon Pienaar's nightly visits filled with angry recriminations at his theft of the coins is a carbuncle on his conscience. Painful and pus filled, it seeps toxins into his mind, poisoning his life.

Something has to be done.

New doors and window frames, tastefully refurbished bathrooms and a modern kitchen, a couple of coats of paint, and some new carpets prove enough of a facelift for Jake to sell the house quickly. It doesn't hurt that Paarl is famous for its five mountain passes and deciduous fruit orchards and vineyards, making it a desirable area for property investors hoping to benefit from tourist rentals.

The move does cost him some pangs of regret, he likes his house and living in this scenic area, but not enough to give up his windfall. He's done his research and moving far away is bound to solve the problem of his nightly visitations by the disgruntled Simon Pienaar.

"Ghosts are tied to the sites of their deaths, Jake," the medium had said. "They do not have the freedom of movement we have but are destined to haunt a specific place for eternity or until they find a path to redemption."

Moving is the only viable option if he wants to keep his new-found wealth and have a good quality of life. Continuing his current path is impossible, the disturbed nights are destroying his good looks and ruining his life. The assiduous ghost must be dealt with.

The big day arrives, and Jake springs from his cursed bed, eager to start the business of the day.

No movers are necessary as he's donated all of the furniture to charity. The last remaining pieces will be collected the following day.

Pulling underclothing out of the chest of drawers, he shoves socks, underpants, and vests into a waiting suitcase. He then lifts his hanging clothes out of the rickety wardrobe and carries the whole lot out to his new car. This constitutes all his packing.

Within two hours, Jake has dropped the keys to the farmhouse off with the agent and is on the freeway heading towards Cape Town and his new apartment.

The sound of the waves lapping on the beach lures Jake from sleep. He's purchased an apartment with a gorgeous view of Camp's Bay. It's serviced every Thursday, making washing and cleaning a concern of his past.

For the first time in months his sleep has been sweet and dreamless. Clambering out of bed, he opens the glass sliding doors and steps out onto his balcony. The greenish blue sea sparkles in the early morning sun, small waves racing each other to the beach.

This is the life.

The apartment is modern with fashionable leather couches, a glass and chrome dining room table and chairs, and several paintings that seem to his uneducated eye to be composed of swirls of different shades of blue with splashes of silver thrown in for good measure.

"Lovely," he mutters, "The external corridors are all brightly lit and there are no disreputable linen presses or Victorian fireplaces in this building. Simon would be most uncomfortable here."

Jake enjoys a cup of coffee and then dresses quickly, whistling while he ties his shoelaces.

That evening, Jake retires to bed early. He has months of disturbed sleep to catch up on.

Tap! Tap! Tap!

The old man stands at the door to Jake's bedroom. His nightshirt falls to his bony knees and his twisted hand clutches his walking stick.

"What are you doing, Jake?" His voice rasps from the collapsed hole of his mouth.

Tap! Tap! Tap!

The stick clacks loudly on the pristine white tiles as the phantom commences pacing round and round the open plan lounge cum dining room.

"Did you really think you could escape me by moving?" Throwing back his grizzled head, peals of guttural laughter accompany the staccato beat of his stick.

Halting dramatically in the doorway, the spectre glares at Jake with angry eyes.

"Return the money and free my soul, or I'll drive you mad."

The old man returns to his pacing. Tap! Tap! Tap!

The sound echoes in Jake's head, holding him in a state of fitful dozing as he finds himself waiting expectantly for the next tap. The tapping on the bare tiles is worse than the thumping on the carpeted passage of the farmhouse.

Sitting up in bed on Saturday night, he waits for the old man to make his nightly appearance. Hands shaking, he puts his latest book down. Reading isn't an option. Switching on the television, he tries to watch a movie, but the meaningless conversations swirl around his head. He can only lie sweating and considering the various possible outcomes of his planned negotiation with the spirit.

Two thirds of the value of the coins remain. *Will it be enough, or will the ghost demand he find a way to repay the money he's already spent?* Jake hopes not, he can't go on like this. Simon Pienaar had said he would drive him mad, and he is doing just that.

Jake has lost more weight and his over-bright, sleep deprived eyes glitter in his bony white face. He knows he looks a frightful mess. People no longer ask him if he's ill. Instead, they avoid him entirely. He passes his days in a blur of exhaustion, dreading the nights and the relentless tapping of the ghost.

More than once he's removed his father's old service pistol from the safe in his cupboard, gazing at its smooth, shining barrel and considering the release in would offer if he worked up the courage to put himself out of his misery.

Time passes. At 12.30 p.m. a dim shape appears in the doorway of Jake's room.

"Hello Jake. You've let me down, my boy. Are you ready to be entertained?"

The phantom does a shuffling turn and starts walking. Tap! Tap! Tap!

"Stop," shouts Jake. "Who does the money belong to? Where must I send it? Please Simon, give me a name."

The old man stops. Slowly, he turns around to face Jake sitting up in bed with the sheets bunched around his waist.

"Ivan Conradie," Simon says in a croaking voice. "He's living in the Netherlands now, but Mr. McMichael can help you find him. His grandfather was my mother's attorney, and Mr. McMichael obtained Ivan's file and contact details when he inherited the firm.

Jake sits in the office of Mr. McMichael, a partner at McMichael & Robertson Attorneys.

On Saturday night three weeks ago, he'd made a deal with the old devil, but Simon had continued his nightly visitations by way of an insurance policy.

It hadn't been difficult to track Mr. McMichael down. He's the only attorney with this name in Cape Town.

True to Simon Pienaar's word, Mr. McMichael knew both Mrs. Pienaar and the Conradie family.

"Simon Pienaar was a bad lot," the attorney tells Jake. "He broke into the Conradie's home one night, slit old Nick Conradie's neck with a knife, and stole his collection of antique Kruger coins. The police arrested Simon Pienaar and he was charged with murder, but the treasure was never found. The Conradie family immigrated to the Netherlands in 1995, but I can still track them down relatively easily. Thank you for coming forward with the hiding place and the treasure you found."

Sixty minutes later it's all done. Jake has signed all the necessary forms to transfer the remaining money to Ivan Conradie, the only surviving relative of Nick Conradie.

Jake goes to bed late. His sleep is pitted with twisted and interlinking dreams where Simon Pienaar attacks him in his sleep, beating him with his heavy walking stick. This scene dissolves and Jake sees himself placing his father's service pistol into his mouth, ready to fire and end it all.

"He didn't come." Jake wakes to a room flooded with light. The previous evening, he'd neglected to draw the curtains across the glass sliding doors leading to the balcony and the early morning sun is saying hello.

"He didn't come," Jake repeats. His shoulders slump and sudden pain flares in his temples

A week passes. Every night, Jake's guts twist with trepidation as he slides beneath the covers of his bed. Every morning, he awakes feeling more refreshed and like his old self.

The following weekend, he has dinner with his mother at her house.

"Jake," she cries, "I'm so glad to see you looking so well. I've been so worried about you."

"I'm feeling much better now, Mom, and I've been offered a new job. I start next week."

"You can tell me all about it over dinner. I've made your favourite roast beef."

Later, in the downstairs guest toilet, Jake gazes at his reflection in the large mirror hanging over the basin. He's gained five kilograms and his cheeks have filled out, giving his clean-shaven face its trademark boyish look. The dark circles beneath his eyes are receding and the haunted look has changed to something else. He can't quite put his finger on what it is.

A shadow stirs behind his reflection. The dark image of Simon Pienaar fills the space behind him in the tiny room.

The shadow raises its right hand and waves at him.

Jake lifts his own hand and waves back.

Sudden recognition of the emotion that shines in his eyes comes to him: It's relief.

Author Enid Holden

http://www.wrightonkey.com/creators

Enid Holden is a writer who has honed her talents as a singer-songwriter, playwright, newspaper columnist, book reviewer, and opera librettist. She holds an undergraduate degree from Rhodes University in Fine Arts and English Literature. She completed an Honors degree in History of Art from the University of South Africa and earned a BA in Music at Western Colorado University and an MA in Creative Writing in 2017 from Western Colorado University School of Graduate Studies. She has written three short comedies. She also created the book of *Getting it Wright*, a musical comedy on the Wright Brothers and wrote the libretto of *Lottie Silks,* composed by Justus (Jay) Parrotta, work-shopped in Washington, DC and at Writing the Rockies at Western Colorado University. Her second libretto is *The Teardrop Tiara*. She completed an MFA in Creative Writing at Western Colorado University in 2019 and is writing her debut novel.

The Chosen Few

By Enid Holden

Six hundred and nine South Ruby Street is a massive structure for a small Colorado town. The house survives from the short-lived Gunnison gold rush in the 1880's, and although it was built as a dancehall and brothel, it's a family residence now. It has a stately entrance, jutting bay windows and Italianate wood paneling to counter its imposing height.

But underneath the siding lurks the lathe and plaster of the original dancehall, though the slatted saloon doors have long been removed.

A few of us … originals choose to remain here.

Families come and go, but we are here for good. Mr. Martins' signature is on the deed, but the house is ours, far beyond the reach of any law.

You see, we long-term residents are a kind of family as dysfunctional as any of theirs. A body of us are permanent, but there are also strays who come and go, drifters who flit through the house seeking solace. Different generations sharing an abode are apt to have conflicts over customs and issues of rank. We form factions and squabble about seniority and who gets the best room and view in the house.

The dourest of our troupe is Daniel, who is still so depressed about being dead he hangs around the drainpipes all day. He disrupts the plumbing, streams the toilet water, bangs about and snivels in the pipes like a restless babe.

But by far the most conspicuous amongst us is Haywire Harry. He's nothing but an angry, misunderstood teenager except he's been fourteen for an annoyingly long time. He thrills at new-fangled electrical things like doorbells, light bulbs, and appliances and loves to hang upside down flicking electric lights on and off late at night. Recently he's learned to occupy computers and make the TV channels randomly change. He's the one who calls attention to our presence here even though I chide him constantly for his recklessness.

When the Martins, the current family, moved in last year, we watched with trepidation to see what our new roommates would be like. We had rid ourselves of some intolerable former residents using delightful pranks that scared them away. Children wailing, lamps crashing, moving ladders, and flying objects. In a matter of days, the house was up for sale.

After that we had it to ourselves for two blissful years —although in truth, our solitary hauntings got old. Mostly we rest, suspended and transparent, in the harrowing boredom of infinite time. So, it's fun to leaven the days by keeping current with trends and social events, spying on the living, and watching their TV. We also stage activities, eavesdrop, bicker and gossip to counter the loneliness.

But then the new family moved in and we receded into the corners again. At first, the family found their new abode charming, not knowing that the house has a scandalous history and blood spattered beneath the dainty wallpaper. But after a time, the Martins noticed the heavy footsteps on the upper floor when nobody but their teenage daughter, Celia, was home.

To make matters worse, they brought two hangers-on of their own — two of our own kind arrived with them. Barely was the furniture unloaded when Betty, Mr. Martin's late mother, moved in downstairs accompanied by a tall moody ghost called George, who dragged in Betty's large trunk. Betty is in love with beautiful things and couldn't give them up, which is why she's still around. Of course, Betty expected the finest room because much of the furniture, art and stemware that arrived with this lot belonged to her. She liked to stay near it, polishing the glass tables, the crystal, and antiques.

Well, I soon relegated her to the powder room where she now stays, straining toward her reflection in the mirror wearing diamonds, weaving her fingers endlessly through her blonde hair, applying and reapplying mulberry lipstick, all the while draped in an auburn fox fur.

Lugubrious George immediately stationed himself upstairs in the corner of the daughter's room, without applying to our counsel for consent. He was Celia's imaginary childhood friend, and they would talk and play throughout the night. But what started out as a protective role has turned into a romantic crush and he gazes down adoringly at his teenage ward. But she ignores him, even refuses to acknowledge him. His stories have grown old, and she dreams instead of handsome youths. As a child, Celia boasted that she could make him disappear by switching on a lamp, but complained that when he laughed, he had no teeth in his mouth. Poor George. He has false teeth and he never thought to put them back in after he was buried without them.

On the first day of the family's arrival, by way of introduction, Harry got into the laptop belonging to the lady of the house. When she booted up, her empty screen read, "Hi," the H typed and the cursor flashing an insistent "I" in neon green. Mrs. Martin tried to delete the greeting, but it persisted. She said, "It can't be. This is crazy," snapped the computer shut and left. She busied herself in the kitchen taking deep breaths and unpacking her baking ware into the musty closets. But after a while she hummed a tune as she worked and heated the oven to start a casserole and I felt a moment's pang. It would be nice to have cooking smells coming from the kitchen again. When she wasn't looking, I wiped down the pantry shelves so they would be free of dust for her.

Mr. Martin, on the other hand, loves computers almost as much as Harry does. But I've seen him using them for some rather dubious materials, not altogether unfamiliar to me given my former profession. And Harry gets into Mr. Martin's chat rooms from time to time and leads him on in scandalous ways. Then, when the poor man switches off his computer, Harry turns it back on again, no matter what time of night. I've seen the exasperated fellow throw blankets over the malfunctioning unit to stop the sites returning and the flickering lights, but Harry cannot resist.

And then there's the problem of the Colonel. One of our core group, we have no idea how he got here or acquired the name. He is tall and large, of military bearing, with unruly grey hair and piecing blue eyes. It was this same Colonel who helped when mortal disaster fell upon me, and I owe him a debt of gratitude. But he ends up in inconvenient places in the house during the night stomping about and smoking foul cigars that trail smoke through the rooms which is very irritating to all the inhabitants, spirit and human alike. We try to turn a blind eye but his habit of leaving by the front door to sit on the porch and smoke of an evening threatens our safety here. "Who says I should forgo the gentlemanly pleasure of leaving the house by the official exit?" he asks when we complain, for even though the house is our sanctuary we can all pass freely through its walls as we wish. Mr. Martin troubles to bolt the door every night yet every morning, to his irritation, he finds it unlocked.

I should tell you about Bob, a bearded man dressed in Victorian clothing, whose another of our tribe. He's a bit of a lowlife, if you ask me, but I try not to get on his wrong side because he's been in trouble with the law. It's a bit of a mystery as to why he's here but after he arrived, a previous homeowner spread stories that she first saw his ghost and then spotted a hanging shadowy corpse with its throat slit behind him in the hallway. "There's plenty in each of us that's unforgivable," he said, when I confronted him, "It makes sense to hide oneself and keep a low profile."

Mr. Martin has also caught sight of this hanging apparition and it makes him uneasy in the house. Now we know that nothing is ever entirely as it seems. Take the Martins, for example. They seem like a happy couple to the outside world, but in truth, they have the most frightful rows. Mr. Martin dislikes the house. He secretly wants to leave. I've seen him looking at real estate advertisements on the sly. I've also seen him looking at sites to meet other women. But his wife, Gail, loves it here. She works in the garden, bakes, and plays the piano. When they fight, their shouting shakes up the shadows and dislodges the cobwebs. But then it passes, and the dust settles and the house sighs and continues on.

As for us, we watch and we wait, but there is nothing we haven't seen before. Occasionally, acting like voyeurs, we take turns to watch the Martins in the bedroom to see if the moderns have discovered any new tricks. They haven't. It's the same old stuff.

We've come to sympathize with Mrs. Martin now, because we see everything that goes on, but at first our group was all set to resent her as she established herself in our home. Mrs. Martin also seemed to wish her in-law's memory out of the way. I saw her glance around then throw Betty's old recipe book into the trash.

However, Mr. Martin has come to suspect our presence here and even started to try and get the upper hand. He insisted the local priest come to perform a house blessing which put at risk all our comforts here.

The next Sunday the priest arrived to consecrate the house. We all knew how sinister that could be and were on our guard. We didn't want to be banished to God knows where, but we didn't want to attack either. Who would risk their immortal soul for doing in a priest on the Sabbath?

The white-haired pastor rapped loudly at the door, his dark robes flowing over a large belly. We retreated anxiously but he swaggered around the house flinging holy water into each room without so much as an incantation before declaring himself ready for the feast — a lavish dinner which Mrs. Martin had prepared. At the table he pulled up his chair, filled his glass to the brim with fine wine from Mr. Martin's cellar—what used to be the coal cellar— loaded his plate, and proceeded to eat without so much as bothering to say grace. It was our kind, instead, hiding in the shadows realizing we were safe, who uttered the only prayer of thanks to be heard in the house that day.

Having survived the threat of an exorcism we banished Harry to the basement then

drifted back into the routines of everyday life alongside our human family.

Betty's husband never visits us even though he's also deceased. However, the Colonel appears to have replaced him as the apple of Betty's eye. She invites him into the parlor to play cards with her before he exits onto the porch to smoke.

It wasn't long before Mr. Martin called in a second intermediary, a so-called paranormal expert. We were skeptical, but this one was a real psychic who sensed the shadows in the house. We all cowered in the recesses to avoid detection, even going so far as to hide outside on the flimsy balcony where Mr. Morley, the geology teacher, had tossed his wife over the rails to her death.

But poor morose George fared the worst.

The expert soon figured George's pathetic hiding place in Celia's room and expelled him from the realm of his beloved. He refused to go, then begged, and tugged at the tenuous thread that still bound him to Celia. Celia took pity on him and persuaded the psychic to show some lenience. She nevertheless placed a blue protective shield around him and now he's confined to a toybox where he's forced to live with her discarded animals.

And so, our uneasy alliance with the family continues. The house itself isn't as fancy as it once was. Not like in its heyday but many of us love the antiques, the parties, and entertainments hosted by the current family. They remind us of the old days and Mrs. Martin, whose name is Gail, has a wonderful collection of vintage dresses that I love to dress up in. One of our collective, Angelina, spent so much time in front of the dresser trying on hats that she got permanently trapped inside the mirror. Initially Gail Martin used to frown when she found her belongings in strange places, but it doesn't seem to bother her anymore. She smiles indulgently and I think she sometimes sees us out of the corner of her eye and winks.

Mr. Martin, on the other hand, spends most of his time engrossed at his computer pretending to work but really visiting inappropriate sites. All that furtive sexuality makes me feel at home in a way, men haven't really changed, and neither have women, but I feel a bit sorry for Gail and besides, I love her classical taste in music. Some of the humans in the house listened to the most wretched tunes on the radio for hours on end. I enjoy her parties and watch TV shows with her and for the most part she leaves us to our business unimpeded.

So, we hoped it wouldn't come to an outright turf war. But our co-habitation with humans involves a myriad of trials.

Time heals all things and I make light of the past. Although this house was full of sound and bright lights and parties, we were no strangers to violence. I came to this house to work for Madam Clara having experienced a tragedy of my own. Madam Clara turned out to be my best friend in the world, but I didn't know it at the time.

On the night that I expired, a gentleman escorted me up to my room as was the practice of the house after a certain hour. It was my job to gratify my clients and I was never one to shirk my duty. However, this particular man showed no respect for the conventions of the trade. As soon as we got into my quarters, he bolted the door and proceeded to rip off every stitch of the clothing in which I was arrayed.

At the time I mistook this for pent up passion or a long absence from female company and thought little of it, although I was sorry to see my satin dress and camisole ripped into shreds. Before I could react, he used his strength to overpower me and tied both my wrists to the bedpost with a rough piece of rope. Even then, I remained unfazed, bedroom games being part of the service of our sport.

By the time I realized his bad intentions, I was tethered to the bedpost like a goat, but rather than seeking relief or titillation, he struck me about the body and the head like a madman. I insisted he stop, but his blows grew greater and more intense. I was in so much pain and so afeared I squealed like a stuck pig and bellowed for help.

My screams grew louder and louder as the blows rained down. Then blessed footsteps thumped down the corridor and Madam Clara rapped at the door. "Open this door right now, Mister, or I will shoot you." At that, my suitor laughed and, laying off his blows, he reached for his gun, pulled back the hammer and aimed at the door.

"Don't trouble yourself to come in," he said. "We have private business here."

"Open up this door or you're a dead man," Clara said.

"Suit yourself," he said, pulling back the bolt and flinging wide the door.

In that instant, a shot went off, closely followed by another. Clara screamed and then the man cursed as her bullet hit him square in the chest. Staggering back, he cursed again, laughed, then aimed the gun at me, tethered naked as I was, screaming. He flagged slightly, blood gushing out of him, and then he raised the gun and sent his lead straight through my neck.

As I collapsed, a different man's voice cajoled me. It was the Colonel. "Hide," he said, in a low voice, but I heard it clearly as the strength drained from my body. I didn't realize it then, but that was goodbye. I escaped my lifeless body, which hung tethered on the bed. Fear kept me rooted to the spot, curious and unbelieving but the Colonel willed me to stay calm and hide, and I retreated further with him into the shadows to wait. I didn't have anywhere to go. I had no-one who loved me to walk me across. My family abandoned me and later I changed my name. I never had true love from a man and I never got the chance to have a child And as for the love of God, the likes of me was never welcome in a church.

I looked for Clara, but the act of her sacrifice lifted her off into another realm and she was gone from me. My torturer lay dead on the floor. The room was bathed in blood which had spattered all the walls. The Colonel remained to comfort me. As I hid in the dark room holding his hand, I detached ourselves from the fate of living men. As the night deepened, I wondered what my eternal fate would be. Then I realized that I wasn't going anywhere. This place was my home.

With this triple death and other bloodshed in the house, a pall settled over the building. Murder begets murder and it wasn't long before a long list of incidents took place. Over time the local society cleaned itself up and swept away all trace of the dance halls, the gambling dens, the houses of pleasure. They wiped away our history and outlawed the working girls. Everything was swept under the carpet, and the house became the subject of rumor and fell into disrepair. Abandoned places tend to ignite the dark side of the imagination and we attracted a motley group of ghosts. That is, until a school headmistress named Mary took up residence here for a while. When illness took her, she elected to stay on as owner of the house, so reluctant was she to relinquish her power. Her ghost lingered. Folks who stayed in bedroom 210, have woken to find their blankets closely tucked around them in bed or their suitcases neatly unpacked.

I was not happy. Mary would also inspect our nails for cleanliness and nag us to go to church.

"This is my establishment," said I.

"House of ill repute, you mean," said Schoolmarm Mary. "More recently it was mine. A very respectable rooming house for teachers that still bears my name."

"It isn't big enough for both of us, and it's not I who's going to leave," I said. At which we all but came to blows. I couldn't wait to see her ectoplasm splashed about the place. Except Mary was anxious to avoid a showdown as she was very orderly and didn't want her ample form pierced or bent out of shape.

Once again, the inmates of the house had to put aside differences and join forces to get rid of Mary. Just because she was more recent didn't mean she had jurisdiction over us. Our collective agreed to go with her to church at Easter. The Colonel gallantly escorted her, looping her gloved hand over his arm. The rest of us straggled behind. Once inside, the Colonel genuflected and fled. Mary kneeled, her eyes shut as she prayed. We all slipped away unscathed, but she was touched by the light and crossed over.

Something of our internal conflict must have communicated itself to the atmosphere in the house. The Martins were fighting more. Mr. Martin was in a rage for much of the time, his temper triggered by triflings. He seemed aware of us, scared and unsettled. His growing paranoia subjected us to a series of well-meaning visitors, each offering some sort of cleanse. First was a feng shui practitioner who looked like a plump fairy godmother, wearing a disheveled floral sack. Then came two spiritualists with a different kind of cleanse. They danced through the house with rattles and doused the house in smoke from a wad of sage. It was very uncomfortable. We could hardly see. The two women smoked us up into the attic. After they left, we slipped back in from the eaves, coughing and shaken up.

We were fed up. We got together and retaliated.

We called on Harry to emerge from banishment, which he did with enthusiasm. He whipped off all the lights plunging the house into darkness, except for a few lamps left burning to create confusion. Daniel terrified them with bangs from within the pipes, George found a child's toy with a squeaker and stamped it down with his foot emitting an eerie wail that echoed through the dark. The Colonel shook the windows so that they rattled in their panes and the frame of the house creaked and groaned. As he did so, Bob rearranged all the glasses into a pyramid on a table in the living room. The Martins heard clinking sounds and found their glasses stacking themselves. Before their disbelieving eyes, Bob tumbled the glasses down and smashed them. We had to choke back our giggles. Later, when they tried to vacuum the rugs, I pulled out the power chords from the walls.

We stopped when we felt we'd scared them enough to back off, but actually we made things much worse.

A trio of shamans arrived from Salida to do a purge. The man was rotund with one eye, his dusty hair dust stretched over his skull. With him was an old witch-like woman with scraggly grey hair, threads of it emerging from her cheeks. The third was enormous with black curls extruding from her skull. They went round the house with black candles, chortling, and calling out to the archangel Gabriel. The old one hissed and pointed, calling us out.

We were frightened and thoroughly ticked off, now ready for a showdown. We decided to stage an extravaganza, invading their Halloween party on Old Soul's Day. It is our special day, the Day of the Dead, when the deceased pass freely amongst the living. Humans have usurped this celebration, their masked antics mock and trivialize the otherworld. On this eve we are free to materialize and pass freely as humans, enjoy reversals, and invoke spells. We reaffirm death and its place as a part of life in an exhilarating celebration of a holy and magic evening. Everyone rallied to get the preparations underway.

Haywire Harry supervised the pyrotechnics. He created flickering black and orange lights and we agreed to actual flame. Daniel wept and moaned from within the pipes, building up to a midnight flood through the ceiling from upstairs. I helped myself to one of Gail's antique dresses and hats, materialized as a lady of the night, and mingled with the guests targeting the gentlemen and touching them inappropriately. Angelina gazed back out of the mirrors at guests in her hats, providing a ghoulish reflection to scare the humans.

George dressed as a wizard to impress Celia, who went as Cat Woman, with his powers. The Colonel unearthed a fanciful military uniform, complete with peaked cap, insignia and munitions and materialized so he could consume in the flesh copious amounts of food and alcohol. Bob came as a strangled corpse.

Betsy added a cloche hat with a veil and extra diamonds around her neck. Daniel cross-dressed as a silver mermaid. Our costumes were spectacular. While we mainly wanted to alive, we noted that the living aspired to be deceased. Pirates, ghosts, and zombies filled the halls.

A psychic from Paeonia had been hired to read fortune cards for the guests and she noticed us as we infiltrated the party. She pointed us out to Mrs. Martin. But Gail laughed and said, "Don't be silly, my dear. Relax and have some fun."

The party got underway. Scarecrows, superheroes, and Cookie Monsters paraded through the rooms. The bass beat thumped, the lights flickered low. Harry's lights glimmered. Gail had laid out delicious platters of food, and bottles of wine. Mr. Martin had contributed some of his finest spirits. I rendered myself invisible and got to work on unsettling the gentlemen. One young man felt a cold hand running down the skin of his back, while another watched as his belt buckle unfastened and looped inexplicably into the air. Another heard a female voice calling him and became trapped in the bathroom where his reflection in the glass rippled into Angelina's.

The Colonel, dressed in uniform, seated himself in a large armchair with a plate of dainty appetizers and a tall glass of beer.

He poised his fork graciously in the air and spoke to the room at large. "I have to make up for lost time," he said. "Indulge me, because I have seen it all." He paused and smacked his lips together as if he had a great thirst, then called for a cocktail. Betty rushed over as fast as her platforms would allow with a drink for him, which he slurped down in a great hurry. Then he called for another.

In no time he espoused on the vagaries of life like an erudite old drunk. He threw out dismissive opinions on modern manners, the inferiority of modern manufacture, the objectionable taste represented by the furnishings, and the frailties of youth. Celia, as cat woman danced with George who looked very dashing in his wizard's cape. But as he laughed, she noted his toothless gums, recognized him, and gave him a hug, before abandoning him for a tall mouse.

Once again, the Colonel smacked his lips together and tasted the air, before deciding on a drink. "I think I'll have a Bourbon," he said.

No-one responded, so he staggered off to get it himself. "I deserve some respect for all my years," he informed the room when he returned to his chair. No-one took much notice of him But then he spotted Celia and her friend, a tall mouse with an outsized head and long whiskers and engaged them in conversation. Now that he had an audience he fulminated. He criticized the medium of film, the current modes of dress and everything else that drew the attention of his eye.

Tapping his empty glass and he demanded a refill and continued to opine. He discoursed on the nature of the universe and showed himself to be both out of date and a know all. "Time is cyclical, and consciousness is infinite," he declared while sipping from his glass.

He went on to explain his taste for intrinsic rhythm in music, defame the practices of the church, and bemoan the lack of benefits in the afterlife. He took another drink, but his glass was almost empty. He staggered up to get a beer but noticed a bottle of Cognac and poured that instead. By now his words rolled around in his mouth.

Finally, Mr. Martin who was dressed as a ghost pirate with a tricorn buccaneer hat swathed in feathers and a long scabbard with sword attached hanging at his hip, walked up to the Colonel in his makeshift buckled boots and said, "It's time for you to leave."

"Leave?" said the Colonel. "Out of the question, my dear fellow."

"Leave this house right away, or I shall be obliged to enlist help."

"How dare you threaten me? I will do no such thing," said the Colonel, setting down his glass. His red cheeks bulged, and he slurred his words.

"This is my house," said Mr. Martin "I'd thank you to leave."

"This is not your house, you ignoramus," shouted the Colonel.

"Get out of my home."

"Let's face it, we're all eternal spirits here, even though your type ... You are just like me, except you're still a temporary host. You haven't discovered the truth yet, you lazy pervert. I know how you spend your time," the Colonel said.

"Enough insults, I'm warning you, whoever you are," Mr. Martin said.

"Don't threaten me in my household," the Colonel said.

With that Mr. Martin pulled a long sword from its sheath and waved it about. He could not see clearly in the flickering light through his face paint with the eye-patch covering his better eye.

"I won't indulge your childish games," said the Colonel. "I advise you not to mess with visitants." He reached for his pistol and drew back the hammer, hoping the threat would cower his attacker.

At the sound, Mr. Martin lunged at the Colonel with his sword, but the Colonel was too practiced at his craft. He sidestepped nimbly and Mr. Martin tripped and went flying through the empty air. Unfortunately, he had little practice with a sword and as he put out an arm to steady himself, he speared himself in the torso. He screamed and staggered forward, impaling himself further as his weight fell onto the sword. He fell to the ground and lolled in a deepening tide of blood. The Colonel swayed back in shock, holstered his gun trembling, then staggered toward the body and reached out his hand. Mr. Martin's body lay spent on the floor, not moving. The Colonel trudged toward the bathroom, bearing the spirit of the expiring man, ushering him into the shadows, concealing him in the gloom. The excited guests gathered around, whooping and clapping, mistaking the collapsed body of Mr. Martin for a murder mystery stunt, with Bob the corpse in cahoots. But when Gail saw the copious amounts of blood and took his pulse she screamed. Someone called the police.

Bob went into hiding. Daniel took this as a cue and rained down a flood, which splashed from the ceiling and dripped down the chandeliers. Harry infused the light show with outlines of sizzling flame, and it melded with the fanning blue and red patches from without when the authorities arrived.

I slipped off before the officers started asking questions, but they rated it an accident, with so many witnesses and Bob and the drunken Colonel disappeared into thin air. After the death we called a truce, admitting a new member to our circle.

We all did our best to welcome Mr. Martin into the fold. The Colonel even offered him his old quarters, presiding over his wife's bedroom, but he prefers to hang out in the basement with Harry, where he set up his computer system and they play interminable video games. Mr. Martin has learned from Harry to infiltrate dirty sites and explore the dark web.

So, we continue on in the brightly lit house with Gail Martin, the parties, and her piano music where life is gaiety and peace.

As I was saying, many people come and go from this house. But let's get this thing straight. It's never a good idea to tangle with the dead.

We have eternity on our side.

Author S. L. Kretschmer

S. L. Kretschmer is a born and bred South Australian, recently embracing both a tree change and becoming an empty nester in the beautiful wine region of the Barossa Valley. She has a BA in Creative Writing, and Graduate Certificate in Museum Studies. Her stories have been featured in the anthologies *A Flash of Brilliance* and *Tales from the Upper Room*, and have also been published by *Haunted Waters Press, Two Sisters Publishing, 101 Words, Beyond Words Literary Magazine, Bluing the Blade* and in*Scribe Literary Journal*.

The Final Portrait

By S.L. Kretschmer

The bus engine rumbles as the rest of the tour group boards. The red-headed woman sitting next to me sniffs the air.

"Ooh. You smell pretty," she says. "Is that Chanel Mademoiselle?"

I smile, opening my backpack and holding it towards her.

"No," I say, "It's Dove."

She looks in my bag at the deodorant stick.

"Well, to be sure, my deodorant never smelt as good on me. And Dove. Quite contrary to today, isn't it?"

I'm not following her. It must show on my face.

"Dove. Peace?"

I nod slowly and take a deep breath. It's going to be a long ride.

👻 👻 👻

It takes three hours to get from Lille to Thiepval. Our tour guide, Brett, a jovial Brit, stands like a bouncy toy at the front of the bus and regales us with stories of the 1916 battlefields. The roads are full of ruts, and he struggles to maintain his balance.

"Who among you has a family connection to the Somme?" he asks.

The red-head, Joyce, raises her hand. Our initial rocky first contact has mellowed into a mutual respect for solitude and reflection. She looks at me and smiles.

"My great-great-uncle fought with the Irish Guard."

I want to raise mine. For the last three years, my life has revolved around the war artist, William Orpen. He feels like family to me. Two weeks ago, I submitted my thesis on his depictions of the Somme. And now I'm finally here.

My heart pounds as I leave the bus. I try to picture the landscape Orpen saw, but the monument makes it near impossible. The rural scene is dominated by interlocking stone arches, the central one soaring 140 feet above the fields, and the Thiepval Wood which borders it. I hear Brett explain more than 72,000 names are engraved on the memorial, but I'm not really listening. I'm here for the Wood, not the monument.

While the others turn left, I head right, following a narrow gravel path towards the forest. A tremor runs down my back. It is easier to imagine the devastation Orpen had seen here: a land devoid of any living thing, pitted with craters and littered with broken bodies. The woods themselves a cemetery for those who died here, their bodies forever a part of the fertile soil, the trees their headstones, the rough bark their epitaph. I search for remnants of a walkway, a crater. I will myself to find the place, making promises and pacts to whoever can help me. And finally, I do.

Opening my backpack, I take out a print of Orpen's painting, my sketch pad, and pencils. The painting depicts the body of a soldier lying on the broken timber of a makeshift walkway. One arm is thrown above his head - his eyes stare at the sky, unseeing. Dark hair frames his face; blood pools beneath him. He lies beside a flooded shell hole. I want to draw the scene as it is today. To put closure to my years of study. Suddenly an image comes to mind which has an authenticity that scares me. I close my eyes tightly, sensing a change in the wood, a darkness that wasn't there before. I shudder involuntarily and recall that Orpen felt these woods haunted. He'd claimed to have been attacked while painting, although his was the only heart beating.

The temperature drops and a whisper surrounds me.

"Why've ye got me painting?"

Startled, I open my eyes, but I'm alone. The voice comes to me again, but louder, more malevolent.

"I said, why've ye got me painting? Are ye his blood?"

I hesitate, my heart in my throat. I say the words out loud without realizing I'm saying them. "Whose blood?" I whisper.

My stomach convulses as the stench of rotting flesh permeates my nostrils. A blast of cold air whips around me and the picture is wrenched from my hand. I watch as it levitates in mid-air.

"I naw wanna be remembered like this," the voice booms in my ear. "What if Mam or Da saw it? Or my Creena?"

The faintest shadow of a man begins to form in a grey mist that has rolled up from the earth. A soldier, no more than eighteen or nineteen, stands a few feet away, his dark hair slick with blood, khaki uniform ripped and stained. His fingers grip Orpen's painting.

"I tried to stop him, told him to feck off. I naw wanted this! This isn't me! A manky body lying next to putrid water. Me death was only a wee part of me! He should've painted me like the buck I was!"

His anguished wail tore at my heart.

"Please," I say shakily, "He didn't mean any harm. The man who painted this was broken from all he had seen, visions of death clouding his sleep. What can I do to help you? How can I give you peace?"

The apparition points to my sketch pad.

"Will ye draw me as I was?"

Nodding, I pick up my pad and begin to sketch the soldier. I ignore the weeping crater that was his skull. I erase the bloody shrapnel that peppers his body. I work like a woman possessed. Finally, I hold up his portrait. A proud young man, black hair slicked back, uniform pristine.

"Thank ye," he whispers. The Orpen print flutters down to the verdant soil as his shadow dissipates into the woods.

I'm trembling when I reboard the bus, physically and mentally exhausted. I sit down and look at the portrait I've drawn, doubting all that just happened. Joyce eases herself into the seat next to me. I hear her gasp; trembling fingers reach down and touch my drawing. I look up at Joyce, her face devoid of colour.

"My god! Where did you find that? That's my Uncle Jimmy!"

I look at her, confused.

"I'll show you," she whispers shakily.

With fumbling hands, she retrieves a faded photo of her great-great uncle from a worn leather purse. A handsome young man, black hair slicked back, uniform pristine, a look of pride on his face.

We look at each other, our eyes wet with tears. She seems to need no explanation, and I offer her none.

"Here," I say, placing the portrait in her lap. "Take it."

I turn to look out the window of the bus, and as I do, a brush of warm air whispers past my cheek, an orb of light forming in the corner of my eye. I watch as the paper on Joyce's lap rises slightly and eases back, as if taking a breath. I smile.

Jimmy's going home.

Author Stevie Turner

http://www.stevie-turner-author.co.uk

Stevie Turner is a British author of suspense, paranormal, women's fiction family dramas and darkly humorous novels, and likes to find subjects to write about that are not often covered. Stevie is married and lives in the wilds of East Anglia, England, and enjoys cycling about the countryside when she is not busy writing.

David's Revenge

By Stevie Turner

CHAPTER 1 - MICK

Mick paced the confines of his Travelodge room. The day was half over and still no phone call. The maids were itching to open the door and although he needed to check out, he had no idea where to go next. He swore under his breath as he heard a gentle tap at the door.

"Give me five minutes and then I'll be ready to go!"

He swung his bag over one shoulder and tried her number again. To his surprise, it rang.

"What?"

Her voice sounded cold and distant. Mick spoke quickly, heart beating fast and with an urgent need to be heard.

"Can we meet? Where are you? I don't know what I've done! I'm at Exeter Services. Are you near?"

"Rae and I are on our way to Ashburton Police Station."

"Who's Ray?" His anger began to rise again. "Where did you meet him?"

"R-A-E. She's female, and a brilliant psychic medium. For your information, I've got David's leg bone in a plastic bag."

"What the hell...?"

Hearing further knocking he stomped over to the door, threw it open with force, and strode down the corridor past the maids with his phone clamped to one ear.

"Karen... will you tell me what's going on?"

The voice that replied was calm and without emotion.

"I'm going to tell the police how you left my son to die on Dartmoor in the depths of winter."

The conversation ended abruptly. Mick slung his room key at the reception desk and tried without success to redial the number. He gave up on the third attempt and ran to his car. With trembling fingers, he tapped in the station's postcode on his satnav, started up the engine, and screeched out of the car park.

"I want to see my wife."

The desk sergeant looked up from his paperwork.

"And who might *she* be, may I ask?"

Mick's fingers balled into fists by his sides, and he took a deep breath.

"Karen Curtis. She told me she was coming here."

"Oh yes. Mrs. Curtis." The sergeant sighed, slightly irritated. "She's in the interview room with her friend. Follow me and you can see her."

"Hang on a minute, mate. I'd like to see my wife alone, without the friend there."

The sergeant nodded while walking along a corridor behind the counter. Mick found himself ushered into a small room at the end.

"Sit here in here and I'll bring her. You and your wife will need to stay nearby until we get the results of the DNA tests."

Mick looked around for a two-way mirror and then up at the ceiling for a camera. Spotting both, he sat down in a chair and closed his eyes, readying himself for the upcoming meeting.

Suspicious and unsmiling, his wife appeared behind another detective, whom Mick supposed would go straight to the two-way mirror after closing the door.

"Hello Karen."

There was no reply. He smiled at her, but her features remained impassive as she took a seat at a small table opposite him. He cleared his throat in preparation for launching a counterattack.

"So, you think I've murdered David?"

"Yes." She fixed him with an icy stare. "It would appear so."

"What proof have you got?" Animated, he sat forward on his seat. "I told you at the time, he went missing at the Christmas fair. I took my eyes off him for a minute or two to look at something. When I turned around, he was gone."

He watched her, hawk-like, as she shook her head.

"David visited Rae Cordelle on the night we went to see her at the village hall. He told her what really happened—how you drove him out to Dartmoor in mid-December and left him there in thin clothing that was no protection from the ice and snow. David and Rae led me to the spot on the moors where he died, and we found a bone. It's being tested now for DNA, and if it matches mine, that's proof enough."

Mick stood up and began to pace up and down.

"*Somebody* drove him there, sure, but not me. I was at the fair looking everywhere for him! You can ask whichever police were there at the time if you can find them. We searched together for a good three hours."

"You're a bloody liar!" Karen banged her fist on the table. "Rae is a *genuine* medium, one of the few about. She's told me things that proves this. How the hell would she know I gave David chocolate button sandwiches when he had chicken pox, and that there's a photo of him on a shelf above our TV?"

Mick shrugged.

"She's guessing. They all do that—and prey on grieving women who'll believe anything they say."

"Well, I *do* believe her." Karen let out a sigh of exasperation. "She's given me the proof I want."

Mick stopped pacing and sat down.

"And you believe *her* instead of me?" He faced Karen and shook his head. "What kind of wife are you?"

She met his look of undisguised hatred with one of her own.

"An angry one."

CHAPTER 2 – KAREN

The guest house owner rapping on her door at six o'clock in the morning was never a good indication of things to come. Karen yawned, climbed out of bed, and wrapped a robe around her whilst stumbling towards the din. She turned the key and came face to face with a six-foot-four-inch wall of stone.

"Mrs. Karen Curtis?"

Karen saw the landlady hovering in the background, still clad in her nightwear. She nodded.

"Yes, that's me."

"I'm Detective Inspector Richardson. I'm arresting you for the murder of David Michael Nelson on or around the date of December the eighteenth two thousand and four. You do not have to say anything, but it may harm your defence if you do not mention when questioned something which you later rely on in court. Anything you do say may be given in evidence."

For a moment she wasn't sure if she had heard him right. She stared at the officer slightly perplexed and open mouthed.

"You think I murdered my own son?"

"Please get dressed as soon as possible." The policeman's features remained impassive. "I will wait here."

Heart pounding in her chest and with no way out save jumping out the upstairs window, she closed the door and looked wildly around the room at her belongings strewn about on various surfaces. Karen had the quickest wash she had ever had, then grabbed any spare clothes and possessions and stuffed them into her rucksack with a sinking feeling of foreboding.

Stonewall stood solid as a rock blocking her escape.

"Come with me please."

"What about my money?" The landlady hopped from foot to foot down by the front door. "She owes me two hundred and eight pounds fifty!"

Cold and hungry, she found herself back in the same interview room facing DI Richardson, who switched on a recording device.

"This is eight a.m. on the morning of February the fourth, two thousand and nineteen. DI Ken Richardson interviewing Karen Curtis."

Karen's mouth was dry with nerves. She cleared her throat and felt like retching. Her voice, when she spoke, sounded croaky.

"Can I have a cup of tea please?"

"It's on the way." DI Richardson sat forward in his chair, elbows resting on the table. "So... let's begin. Where were you on December the eighteenth two thousand and four—the night your son went missing?"

"At work. You would be able to check with my old employers if you like. I worked a night shift from six p.m. to six a.m."

With some relief she saw a uniformed officer enter carrying a tray. Not caring if the tea was scalding hot, she gulped down a mouthful as soon as a cup was set in front of her.

"Thank you." She sighed.

DI Richardson tapped a pen against the edge of the table.

"So... your husband had charge of your son?"

"Yes." Karen nodded and took another sip of tea. "He took him to a Christmas fair at Okehampton, so that I could sleep during the afternoon. He phoned me at work around ten p. m to say that David had gone missing and that he and some officers from Okehampton had been searching the area. The search had been called off, but would resume the next day. David was never found. I couldn't leave work as I was the only staff member on duty. It was a terrible night."

She shuddered at the memory, while DI Richardson opened up a file and scanned the first page.

"The DNA from the femur you found is a match for the DNA on the swab we took from the inside of your mouth. Therefore, the leg bone *is* David's. Are you going to tell me how you were able to go to the exact spot in the middle of Dartmoor and dig it up if you hadn't put his body there in the first place?"

Karen looked at the officer in horror.

"If you think I murdered my son, you're mistaken! He was alive when I kissed him goodbye around one o'clock that afternoon. I've had help in finding him from Rae Cordell, a very gifted medium who was guided there by David himself."

A faint snort of disbelief reached her ears. Nevertheless, she carried on.

"You need to speak to Mrs. Cordell. She'll be able to convince you of her talents. It's quite amazing what she can do."

"Is that so?" DI Richardson's features reflected complete disinterest. "Unfortunately, I don't usually put much stock by spirits and ghosts. I tend to rely on what I can see with my own eyes."

"All I can tell you is that no way would I ever have murdered David." Karen shook her head to emphasise the point. "Perhaps you need to be a bit more broadminded and interview Mrs. Cordell. Anyway... why would I come to you with David's leg bone if I *had* murdered him? It doesn't make sense to me. Does it to you?"

The detective shrugged.

"When you're in my line of work, nothing surprises you anymore. What we'll do is this; *you* get on to your old employers and ask them to provide us with proof that you were at work on the night your son went missing, and we'll interview Mrs Cordell and also your husband. In the meantime, you can go home and go back to work, but stay close to the phone. We'll release you under investigation. Leave all your contact details at the desk."

Karen stifled a sigh of relief.

"Will do."

CHAPTER 3 – RAE

She hated the self-righteous prig on sight. Rae folded her arms and stared at DI Richardson across the cheap Formica table.

"I knew where to dig because David himself was telling me."

His sigh of annoyance grated on her ears.

"You'll have to do better than that. Did you and Mick Curtis conspire to kill David Nelson?"

She paused momentarily as Medicine Horse appeared in her peripheral vision. In his arms he held a chuckling three-year-old girl with curly blonde hair. The girl pointed in the direction of DI Richardson.

"My daddy."

Rae gave silent thanks to Medicine Horse, who bowed his head in acknowledgement.

"Your daughter is here. She's about three years old and has lovely blonde hair, which is curly and in ringlets. She's standing right behind you."

The effect of her words on the officer was instantaneous. DI Richardson, face suddenly pale with fright, lurched around in his chair as though hit with a bolt of lightning.

"What did you say?"

Rae looked above the officer's head, smiled at the infant, and silently asked her name.

"I *said* ... that your daughter is right behind you. She tells me her name is Carrie."

DI Richardson, open-mouthed, swung slowly back in his seat. Rae wanted to laugh at the incredulous expression on his face.

"How are you doing this? I can't see *anything* behind me! I've never told any of my colleagues here about Carrie. She was the eldest of my four children, and she died of meningitis twenty years' ago."

"I'm a medium." Rae sighed with exasperation. "I see people who have died. They come to me via Medicine Horse, my Red Indian spirit guide. Medicine Horse brought David to me in a demonstration of clairvoyance I did recently. His mother was in the audience, and the love link between them is still strong. David told me his step-father purposely left him for dead on Dartmoor in the depths of winter, and so it's my opinion you should be questioning Karen's husband ... not me. David led me to where a fox had buried his bones."

She sat in silence as the officer tried to regain some composure. Presently he closed his file and cleared his throat.

"Tell me something else about Carrie."

Rae looked up at the child, quite content in Medicine Horse's arms. Carrie lifted her right arm and waved a soft toy.

"She's holding a furry light brown teddy bear that's dressed in blue and white stripy dungarees. She says his name is Thaddy."

DI Richardson wiped his eyes.

"We put Thaddy in her coffin with her. She carried him everywhere."

Rae could not help the small self-satisfied smile that briefly softened her features.

"She's out of suffering and has grown up in Spirit, although she comes back to you as the three-year-old child that you remember. Your mother raised her to adulthood by the way."

The officer, by now barely able to contain his emotions, nodded as he exhaled shakily.

"Mum died quite young. Dad brought me and my brother up."

"Can I go now?" Rae stood up. "I take it I've given you enough proof of my innocence?"

DI Richardson rose to his feet, right arm outstretched.

"Thank you for coming in, and for telling me about Carrie. My wife will be absolutely gobsmacked."

Rae shook the proffered hand.

"Good luck with getting a confession out of Mick Curtis."

"Leave that to us." DI Richardson moved towards the door and opened it. "We may call upon your services again in the near future."

"Any time," Rae said, giving the officer a smile. "Perhaps you and your wife might like to come along to one of my demonstrations of clairvoyance? All my dates for the next year are on my website. Just Google my name."

"Yes. We sure would."

Rae nodded, then sailed victoriously out of the door

CHAPTER 4 - MICK

Mick tried but failed miserably to banish the mental picture of a cold prison cell from his mind as he sat before DI Richardson the following day. All the odds were stacked against him, and he had a sinking feeling his version of events had not impressed the policeman at all.

"So..." DI Richardson sat back in his chair.

Mick folded his arms and met the officer's stare.

"So?"

DI Richardson stood up.

"At the moment there is insufficient evidence to charge you with the murder of your stepson. What I'm going to do is release you under investigation, as per the Policing and Crime Act of twenty seventeen. You can go home but be prepared to be called in for another interview at any time or be formally charged and be remanded in custody until a trial, or even be informed that no further action will be taken. Leave any addresses and telephone numbers where you'll be at the desk, and in the meantime, I suggest you seek out a good criminal defence solicitor as well."

Mick felt like leaping for joy as the voice recorder was turned off. However, he kept a tight control of his emotions as he got to his feet.

"Cheers."

Never had he appreciated sunshine more as he walked out of the interview room and into the fresh air. He grabbed the phone from his pocket and tapped in the number he knew so well.

"What?"

"They've let me go under investigation. Load of bollocks. I'm coming home. We'll talk later."

Without waiting for her reply, he ended the call.

He could see her car on the driveway as he pulled up outside the house. Mick sighed and briefly slumped back against the headrest and closed his eyes. Before he knew it he was woken from a brief doze by a tapping at the window and a shrill voice in his ear.

"You don't think you're staying *here*, do you?"

He opened the driver's door and stepped out, facing a furious face of pure hatred.

"Where else is there to go? If you remember rightly, I'm the one paying the bloody mortgage on this place, so I've every right to be here!"

He grabbed his bag from the back seat, locked the car and made towards the house, taking advantage of her silence. The door slammed behind him, and he turned around to face his wife, glad to be out of view of twitching curtains.

"Once again, just for the record. I did *not* leave Davy in the middle of Dartmoor. I love you, for Christ's sake... I'd never do that! No man in his right mind would kill the child of a woman he loves. You're an intelligent lady... Surely you don't suspect me of murder?"

He walked into the living room and flopped into his armchair, not waiting for her reply. She stormed in and stood in front of him, hands on hips.

"You never liked him! Go on... admit it!"

He shrugged.

"Okay, he got on my tits. That's what kids do...they get on your tits! But I never *ever* laid a hand on him and certainly never left him to die! What do you think I am...? Some kind of monster?"

"I don't know *what* you are anymore!" Karen wailed. "The rug's been pulled out from under my feet!"

He looked up at her.

"Trust me. Listen... I took him to Okehampton Fair. It was getting dark when I queued up to take Davy on the ghost train. He was standing next to me. As you know... as *everybody* knows...I chatted with the guy in the ticket office because he was in my darts team. After I paid, I looked round for Davy, but he'd gone."

Like a burst balloon, her anger deflated. Devoid of emotion, she sat down.

"I know the guy was interviewed by police at the time. He always said he didn't see anything."

Mick sat forward in his seat.

"Yeah, because he was too up high in the ticket booth. He would have had to look out the front window and downwards to see anything. All he could see was my head. I don't suppose he *would've* seen Davy as he wasn't tall enough, but just because he didn't see anything it doesn't mean I'm lying."

"I don't know what to believe." Karen sighed. "All these years and never a cross word between us. *Now* look at us."

Mick, now in a calmer frame of mind, leaned back and rested his head.

"I'll take the spare room for now. Just have a think about what I've said."

CHAPTER 5 – KAREN

Try as she might, sleep eluded her. Karen lay wide awake while the rest of the world slept, wondering whether her husband could have really done something so wicked as to leave a child to die. She knew he had always resented the fact that she had been with another man, and David had been proof of that. However, as far back as she could remember, Mick would usually leave punishing the boy to her and had never laid a finger on him.

Tossing and turning had made her hot and sweaty, and she needed a drink. Karen threw back the duvet, climbed out of bed, and put on her robe and slippers. Outside on the landing there were no sounds from the spare room, and as she padded down the stairs she imagined her husband lying there in a similar state of wretched insomnia.

She blinked as the fluorescent bulb in the kitchen spluttered to life. She filled the kettle and switched it on, then slumped onto one of the breakfast bar stools and put her head in her hands.

"Can I have one as well? If it's any consolation, I can't sleep either."

Startled, she sat up and looked around. Mick, clad only in pyjama bottoms, stood in the doorway with his hair standing on end. She nodded and indicated with one hand in the direction of the fridge.

"You get the milk then, as you're up."

She watched him take a half empty milk bottle from the fridge door and then close it. Such a normal action the last time she had seen him do it, but now so much had happened in a short space of time. Karen took the milk from his hand.

"Did you *ever* hit him?"

Mick shook his head.

"You know the answer to that. He didn't like me much... I could tell, but I tried my best with him. Anyway, he wasn't a naughty kid–just irritating sometimes with his constant questions."

Karen nodded.

"He was intelligent. What do you expect with his dad being a university lecturer? David took after him."

"And I'm only a grubby electrician?" Mick's mouth formed a sneer. "Go on, say it ... you know you want to. Bet the bastard couldn't have wired up your house though."

Karen sighed.

"I was going to say nothing of the sort. Stop putting words into my mouth. Here's your tea." She handed him a steaming mug. "If you've got an inferiority complex, it's not my fault. Andrew went off with one of his colleagues, as you know. It should be *me* who still has the inferiority complex, but hey, I got over it."

Mick took a noisy gulp of tea and perched on an empty stool.

"Perhaps you might feel differently if everyone's accusing you of child neglect or even murder."

"They already have." Karen's eyes glittered with anger. "The police asked me how I knew where he was buried, so you're not the only one under investigation here."

Mick stood up and made for the door.

"Perhaps *you* did him in then?"

She felt like throwing her mug of tea at his retreating back.

The aroma of frying bacon had brought him downstairs, and by the look of him Karen guessed her husband hadn't slept at all.

"Is there any for me, or are you only cooking for yourself now?"

His tone was already belligerent. Karen kept her back to him and held up a large packet of rashers.

"There's plenty for you if you want some."

He gave an audible sigh.

"Cheers."

Her thoughts flew back to the three of them sitting around the breakfast table on Saturday mornings. David would wolf down two bacon rolls, enjoying the wind-up as Mick waited impatiently, the smell of bacon making his mouth water. She knew he would complain at being served after a child, but her brief moment of control was somehow enjoyable.

Karen transferred three sizzling rashers to a plate, added two dry rolls, then slid the plate under Mick's nose.

"Butter's still in the fridge."

She took three more rashers out of the packet and laid them in the frying pan, watching the edges crinkle in the heat. After some moments of silence, she voiced a question that had been on her mind.

"What do we do now then?"

The sound of chewing came from behind. She always hated it when he would speak with his mouth full. As if he knew her very thoughts, he remained silent until every morsel had been eaten.

"God knows. Wait for the police to get in touch, I suppose."

"I didn't kill David." She stabbed at her bacon in the pan. "You must know that."

He shrugged.

"Neither did I, despite what that medium said."

She removed her cooked rashers and put them inside two buttered rolls, then added a generous helping of tomato sauce. She stood by the cooker and ate, keeping her distance.

"David told her himself that you'd left him on the moor."

Mick's chair scraping against the lino jangled her nerves. He stormed towards the cooker, his six-foot frame towering menacingly over her. Karen chewed quietly and stood her ground.

"You believe that woman instead of *me*?"

There was a remnant of bacon at the corner of his mouth. In the past she would have reached up and removed it, but now all she could do was step back against the wall.

"I don't know what to believe."

He snorted in disgust, then turned and walked away. Karen sighed in relief and took another bite of her bacon roll. Rae was a gifted and genuine medium, and Karen knew she wasn't in the habit of making mistakes. David had named his murderer from beyond the grave. How could any mother live with the person who had murdered her child? Karen shook her head and wondered if Autumn Glow's guest room was still empty and available for renting.

EPILOGUE – DAVID

Life had been perfect; he had been the apple of his parents' eyes. However, then his dad had to go and spoil it all by running off with Linda from the Exams Department. He had hated to see his mum so distraught and depressed. Nothing he tried to do could help her until Mick had come along to pick up the pieces. Then it was like he, David, wasn't there either. They'd kissed and cuddled and shut him out.

David transported himself back to that chilly day at Okehampton Fair—the noise of excited kids screaming on the rides, people running to and fro, the smell of hot dogs and candy-floss, and the shouts of the stall holders. As his nine-year-old self walked with his stepfather towards the ghost train, he felt Mick's irritation rising.

"What's making that ghost move backwards and forwards on top of the building?"

"It's probably connected to a motor." Mick sighed and lit a cigarette. "Or it might even be a real one and swoop down and carry you off in a minute."

David coughed as a plume of cigarette smoke blew in his face.

"There's no such thing as ghosts."

"What do you know?" Mick exhaled. "You think you know everything, but you know sod all."

David knew one thing; he knew he hated Mick Curtis. Mick was the reason his dad had not come back. When Mick stopped at the ticket office, David shook his head.

"I don't want to go on the ghost train."

He looked up at Mick, who was chatting to the person inside the booth. David, frightened of the darkness and what might jump out at him on the train, sidled away behind the hook-a-duck stall.

"Your mum's finished work now, David. I can take you to her if you like."

David smiled at Mr Simkins, the teacher from Junior One, as the man began to walk away quickly towards the car park.

"How did you know she was at work?" He ran to keep up with Mr Simkins, pleased to be away from Mick. "Did she tell you?"

"I spoke to her at school yesterday."

David remembered stuffy warmth inside the car, a bag of toffees, and a blanket. Over the years his brain had blocked out the worst of Mr Simkins' depraved actions, but it had taken fifteen years for his mother to pluck up enough courage to visit that medium. If only she'd seen one sooner, then David knew his revenge could have started much earlier. Mick needed to pay for ruining the relationship between his mother and father.

Thanks to his cunning plan, the seeds of suspicion had already been planted in his mother's mind. It wouldn't be long before Mick, the stepfather from hell, would be kicked out the door. With a bit of luck after Mick had gone for good, his father and mother might even get back together.

For the first time in a long while David felt content in his limbo.

Author Christa Planko

https://christascorner.godaddysites.com/about-us

Christa is a professional writer with a passion for creative expression. She has had her poetry and short stories featured in several publications, including *River Poets Journal*, *Wingless Dreamer*, *Tanka* and *Haiku Journals*, *Rune Bear*, *Jitter Press*, and *Every Day Fiction*. When she's not writing, she is likely bicycling, kayaking, or dancing. She currently resides in South Jersey with her 4 feline muses.

Olde Tyme Village

By Christa Planko

Potters Village was a charming resort, established nearly two-hundred years ago. I had seen it in a brochure touted as the perfect remote getaway for the overworked needing to unplug. Steve's world-traveling mother gave me the brochure following an earful of my venting about stress and long hours. It astonished me how she had ever gotten wind of a place like this. With limited access to hotspots, the village was considered out of touch with the present world of the living—but little did we know just how much.

As we drove through its entrance, a sign suspended by chains swung from an ornate iron arch. Evening set in, but we could just make out the words looped in fancy lettering: "*Welcome to Our Olde-Tyme Village.*" Gas lamps lined the road, rendering street signs barely visible. Not to mention, a fog had risen following an earlier rainstorm.

"Now I know why the travel agent insisted we arrive before sundown," I said, noticing the darkness and silence surrounding us. "This place really does turn down the shades and pull in its sidewalks afterhours."

"Well, if you had been paying closer attention to the map, we wouldn't have gotten lost along the way," Steve snapped. After six hours on the road, who could blame him? I felt guilty.

Steve glanced over and saw me sulking.

"You're right, though. Place sure is a ghost town," he smiled. "Does the map indicate how many miles to the B&Bs?"

As I pulled a flashlight out of the glovebox to read the map, Steve spotted a flickering light along the side of the road ahead.

"What'd ya know. A sign of life!"

I strained to read the map while Steve continued to drive. As we neared, we could see a shadowy figure of a man carrying a lantern.

Steve pulled alongside the stranger.

"Excuse me, sir!" Steve shouted. "We were hoping you could direct us to the Grande Maison Inn."

The elder scratched his head, leathered face crinkled in thought.

"We're looking for Adams Lane," I added.

"Odd," the man chuckled. "I am Jonah Adams. While I cannot direct you to an 'Adams Lane' per my recollection, I can inform you that the Grande Maison is further up ahead, atop the hill. 'Tis a rather stately residence, so I suspect you shall have no trouble finding it in the dark "

"Thank you," Steve nodded to the stranger. I watched Jonah Adams wave a hand, then seemingly vanish into thin air, lantern and all. I kept quiet, thinking my hunger had made me delusional.

We continued up the street, veering the bend. Within a few minutes, we could see lights atop the hill.

"Ah," Steve remarked. "Our destination lies ahead."

"But just how soon we'll get there is the question," I said, noticing a downed tree blocking the road.

"Dammit!" Steve pounded his fist against the steering wheel. "The storm earlier...Guess this village is slow to respond to these situations."

A woman in a vintage riding habit appeared beneath the glow of a gas lamp. She wore a top hat, cutaway jacket, and a long, dark skirt. In her right hand, she carried a riding crop.

"There's someone who might know a detour," Steve said, then snickered. "They're sure into period clothing around here."

"Ma'am!" I called through the window.

The woman's skirt hung so low she seemed to glide toward us. Her blank stare raised goosebumps along my arms.

"We're heading to the Grande Maison Inn," I explained. "But we can't get around this tree. Is there another way?"

"There is a path behind the riding stables about a quarter mile from whence you came," she pointed back down the road. "It leads to a parallel path that will get you back onto the road."

I didn't recall passing any stables, but then again, we were swallowed in blackness.

"Thank you," I smiled at the woman. She raised a hand to wave, then disappeared into the fog.

As we headed back down the hill, a row of shops appeared.

"'Ye Olde Stables Vintage Shoppes,'" I read above the buildings. "Think she meant this place?"

Steve cut through the parking lot to a path out back.

"Let's hope this parallel road will get us back on Adams," Steve grumbled.

He laid on the gas, then just as quickly braked. He had nearly overtaken a horse-drawn carriage. The frightened horses reared, jack-knifing the carriage, which now blocked the road. Inside, two men donned tailcoat jackets and ascots. Two women wore satin corseted gowns trimmed in lace.

"Good evening, sir!" one of the men called. "My, but what a hurry!"

"Look, I'm very sorry," Steve apologized. "My wife and I have been on the road for over six hours and just want to get to our destination. The road back there was blocked..."

"Pardon me, sir, but you are travel weary and require immediate food and drink. We are heading to a dinner party where you will find good hospitality. I insist you come along."

Steve and I exchanged glances. We were rather hungry at this point.

The other man exited the carriage and began working on a wheel, which had apparently fallen off.

"It may be some time before we get the carriage out of your way. Come—we will go by foot. The house is not more than an eighth of a mile ahead."

Within minutes, we were strolling up the walkway to an elaborate Victorian mansion. We climbed the stairs onto a wrap-around porch. Cheerful voices and music emerged.

A butler greeted us.

"Welcome to the Wellsley Estate," he said, then announced the arrival of "Mr. Ewing and guests."

Mr. Ewing ushered us into the dining area as he set off to find the hosts. Our eyes widened at the spread—baked hams, roasts, and Cornish hens comprised one table. Platters of vegetables and potatoes comprised another. A third served as a Venetian table loaded with tall cakes, tiered cookie displays, and sweets of all kinds. They all looked too pretty to eat. Our mouths watered.

As we lost ourselves in the indulgences, we didn't notice the other man from the carriage had entered. He whispered to Ewing, who promptly crossed over to Steve.

"My good man," he said. "I've been informed the carriage situation has been handled. You may now continue your journey."

Ewing escorted us back to our SUV. We drove off, finding the connecting road to Adams and to the Inn. We checked in and retired to our room where we passed out for the night.

The next morning, we headed to breakfast. We sat at a table and introduced ourselves to a couple named Ned and Janet.

"How did you sleep?" Janet asked.

"After six-plus hours on the road, I could have slept through the apocalypse!"

"Over six hours of driving!" Ned exclaimed. "You must have been famished. There's not much around here after hours."

"Well, lucky for us, we stumbled onto a party with extremely gracious hosts," I said.

"Yes," Steve added. "At the Wellsley Estate. The spread was unbelievable! And the costumes were so elaborate...you'd think you stepped back in time."

Ned and Janet exchanged confused glances.

"Are you sure it was the Wellsley Estate?" Ned asked.

"Yes, why?" I asked.

Ned pointed out the window to a patch of overgrown land. Several dilapidated structures appeared along the property. The main house, a large boarded-up mansion, stood at the center.

"That's the Wellsley Estate," Ned observed. "It hasn't been occupied for nearly 200 years."

An icy chill overtook me. The only other time we spoke of it, Steve swore he felt it, too. We laughed it off, telling Ned and Janet what jokers we are. But now, the couple was very interested in the Wellsley Estate—but for a reason other than ghosts.

"I actually have great interest in Victorian architecture," Ned said as he continued gazing at the Wellsley property from the window.

"Ned's an architect," Janet smiled, lifting her chin up and glancing lovingly at her husband. "I studied art in college and met Ned in an Architecture and Design course we both had."

"Yes, we both had taken a liking to Victorian architecture—fell in love with the styles," Ned smiled back at his wife.

"And each other," Janet winked.

"I wouldn't mind taking a walk to check out the property," Ned said, wrapping one arm around Janet's shoulders. "I'd like to see what's left of the ornate woodwork and decorative trim."

"I'll bet it's exquisite," Janet added. "Would you two like to check it out with us?"

Steve and I looked at each other reluctantly. While part of us longed to jump in the SUV and head right back where we came from, our curiosities were also peaked. What did happen last night? What did we experience, if not a dinner party?

"Sure," Steve answered for the both of us, and I nodded in consent.

"Don't they have security in this place?" I asked. "Wouldn't we be... trespassing?"

Ned and Janet laughed.

"If you're thinking surveillance cameras and the like, that's a bit too high tech for this place!" Ned explained. "They may have a security building in the village, but by the time any of the guards are notified of anything and able to arrive on scene, it'd probably too late."

"Besides," Janet added. "We're not going to take too long. It looks a little dangerous. I just want to snap a few pictures, maybe sketch a few rough drawings—I could try to recreate later how the place might have looked in its prime."

So, we finished our breakfast and met each other outside the gated entrance of the Wellsley Estate at 10 AM. The iron gates stood tall, although tarnished and crooked on their rusted hinges. The chain that bound them shut bore a sign that read: No Trespassing. Janet giggled while snapping a picture of it.

"Shame on us offenders!"

We stood looking up at the turret, peaked roofs, and eclectic array of mostly shattered windows. The paint on the scalloped shingles appeared chipped and faded, but must have been brilliantly colorful at one time.

Ned marveled at the gable ornaments and trim. He pointed out the details with commentary from Janet while Steve and I drifted in thought. Our minds conjured images of the previous night when this structure—in practical shambles now—appeared so well kept and whole.

"...and check out this marvelous porch!" Ned was saying. "Come on! We just have to get a closer look."

We looked around to ensure no one nearby was watching, then squeezed through the gap formed between the uneven gates. The chain did little to prevent trespassers from entering beyond casting a symbolic warning.

My heart raced with equal parts fear of the supernatural and of wrongdoing. I clutched Steve's hand. He turned to look at me, and I saw the fear in his eyes, too. As we approached the porch, we couldn't fathom how we could have possibly ascended these steps and walked up to the entrance. The uneven incline posed a warped and weathered danger. Part of the porch sank where the floorboards rotted through entirely. If this was truly the place we had entered last night, it was a wonder we survived!

"I wouldn't go any nearer or attempt the stairs!" Janet warned her husband as his exploration drew him closer and closer to the structure. "It looks too dangerous."

But Ned was hunkered over, examining something on the ground.

"Honey, look," he called Janet over. "Guys, this is interesting..."

We all staggered forward slowly, navigating through overgrown grass and weeds. My heart pounded with each step closer. Fear and curiosity both took hold.

When Ned rose to his feet and spun toward us, he held in his hand the only sign of life on the premises. It was a vibrant array of ribbons and a cluster of fresh roses. At his feet, a few lace doilies lay scattered and some more decorative ribbons.

"You said there was a party here last night?" Ned directed his question toward Steve and me. "Were you really kidding, or weren't you?"

Flabbergasted, we were unsure how to answer. We stood there open mouthed for what felt like an eternity.

"Obviously we were joking," Steve finally said, pointing out the lifeless, abandoned mansion. "That stuff must have blown onto the property from somewhere else. You can see there's been no sign of life here for decades."

A breeze swept across the property at that moment. It carried with it the whisper of a male voice.

"Welcome home, my good man..."

I grasped Steve's hand so hard, I could feel his knuckles crack. The color had drained from his face as he gaped at me without words. We both stumbled backward.

"You look rather lifeless yourself, Steve," Ned said. "Maybe we should go now. I think this place is starting to creep us all out."

"You all heard that, right?" I asked Ned and Janet as we started making our way back to the gate.

"Heard what?" Janet asked.

I searched her face and Ned's. If they had heard the voice that Steve and I did, there would be no question.

"Th-the birdsong," I stammered, surprised at my ability to come up with a response so quickly, despite the chill still emanating through my body. "So beautiful. Nightingale, I think."

"Nope, didn't hear any birds," Janet said. She looked at Ned who casually shrugged, indicating he heard nothing either. The calm in their walk informed me that they truly had not heard the voice. We parted ways outside the gate, convinced that Ned and Janet thought we were a pretty strange couple by this point. They continued their walk to explore more history and architecture without us.

Back at the inn, Steve and I vowed we would never mention this to anyone ever again. We weren't sure exactly how it happened that first (and last) night at Potters Village, but we were sure of one thing: we now believed in ghosts.

We packed our bags, checked out, and began our return drive home. Once within range of cell phone towers, I called Steve's mother. I wanted to know where exactly she found this place and what else she knew or heard about it from anyone else.

"I've known about it for some time because of my family's history," she said. "My great-great grandfather, Charles Wellsley, owned an estate there in the 1800s."

I gasped, then listened intensely to the remainder of the story. I put the phone on speaker so that Steve could listen along as his mother continued.

"Charles derived his wealth from the iron business he founded. But generations of Wellsleys lost interest in ironwork. Instead, they squandered the money and left the estate to rot. As far as I know, to this day, the estate lay in shambles. It's not exactly something to be proud of."

"Steve and I saw the Wellsley Estate," I said, keeping my details minimal.

Steve's mother sighed.

"Sadly, nobody in the family has taken interest in the estate or its grounds for decades. I was approached about taking ownership of the property—maybe investing in its renovation and running a B&B.

I took one look at the pictures and said, "No way." Now that you've seen it with your own eyes, you can understand why."

Steve and I looked at each other.

"The estate did appear abandoned and unkempt," I said.

"Certainly, no home to anyone—except maybe for a few ghosts."

She meant nothing by it but humor, yet her words resonated. Steve had no idea until now about having any relations to a Wellsley family. Could the universe have arranged this entire adventure so that Steve could make the cross-dimensional acquaintance of long-lost relatives? Perhaps he was beckoned to consider purchasing the property and reclaiming it for the family. Maybe Steve was chosen to return some dignity to the hard-earned fruits of Charles Wellsley's labor. In any case, Steve nor I wanted anything to do with the property at this point. The memories of our ghostly experience would haunt us for a long time. We would never speak of it, let alone ever set foot in Potter's Village again.

Epilogue

Why do spirits linger here in this world, when they could, and perhaps should, pass over into the next? They may still feel attached to something or someone in this world, or they have things they've left undone, or maybe they are out for revenge. Whatever the reason, spirits often do linger on in this world. In hotels, hospitals, theatres, cemeteries, or as in the cases of the stories you've just read, they may be lingering in houses, estates, brothels, or battlefields.

I do hope that you have enjoyed the stories contained within these pages. I know I've enjoyed putting them all together. I only had a few contest entries, but the stories were so good that I had a difficult time in choosing a winner. In the end, Christa Planko's "Olde Tyme Village" stole my heart, but the others were almost as captivating. A short fiction contest is a great way to discover new and promising authors. This anthology features stories by some authors who may be more familiar to you from previous WordCrafter anthologies, who were invited to contribute, but were not considered for the prize. Overall, I feel we ended up with a great group of stories. After reading them, I hope you agree.

Thank You for Reading

Where Spirits Linger

If you liked it, please leave a review for the complete anthology or for any of the individual stories. Show your support for the wonderful authors whose stories are featured here.

If you like a story, be sure to leave a review.
It's okay to post a review that's only about the stories you read.

Also from
WordCrafter Press

Don't miss out!

Visit the website below and you can sign up to receive emails whenever Kaye Lynne Booth publishes a new book. There's no charge and no obligation.

https://books2read.com/r/B-A-JGKG-TLDTB

BOOKS 2 READ

Connecting independent readers to independent writers.

About the Publisher

WordCrafter Press publishes quality books and anthologies. Learn more about *WordCrafter* and keep updated on current online book events, writing contests, up coming book blog tours and new releases on the *Writing to be Read* authors' blog: https://writingtoberead.com/

CPSIA information can be obtained
at www.ICGtesting.com
Printed in the USA
BVHW030847231121
622333BV00006B/66